D0843891

*P*raise for

SHE WAS A WW II PHOTOGRAPHER
BEHIND ENEMY LINES

This is a wonderful historical novel. Author Jeane Slone is especially good at describing a woman's experiences as she struggles to make her way as a journalist during a time, and in an environment (war), traditionally dominated by men. The novel describes both the professional successes and personal setbacks experienced by an independent woman determined to pursue her art and craft of photography and journalism. As a journalist and photojournalist myself for many years, this story held a special interest for me. The book is well researched and presents detailed and moving descriptions grounded in the realities of World War II, perhaps the greatest flood of death and destruction humankind has ever known.

— WILLIAM HAIGWOOD —
Photojournalist, news reporter, and editor
Author of *Journeying the Sixties: A Counterculture Tarot*

As a photographer, I truly enjoyed not only the technical photographic aspects of the story, but the way the main character turned her love for photography into her life's work. It was inspirational to read.

—JOHN S. NELSON —
Acclaimed commercial, landscape, wildlife, street, and sporting events photographer. Member of the Pacific Coast Air Museum.

Jeane Slone continues to amaze us with her historical novels about women who performed difficult tasks in World War II under the most challenging circumstances including sexism in the workplace, an issue that still pervades our culture. Her four novels have been well researched and offer believable characters that perform courageous acts. In this book, *She Was a WW II Photographer Behind Enemy Lines*, we follow the life of Adeline "Addie" Peterson from a young girl with a budding interest in photography through college to an extraordinary career. We go with her during the Great Depression to Oklahoma and its Dust Bowl days, and then to New York City where she films the soup kitchens, marathon dances, and speakeasies. She's just getting warmed up when she's sent to Czechoslovakia by *Life* magazine. From here it's a constant movement during the war photographing the Nazis' actions in London, Finland, Greece, Moscow, D-Day at Normandy, and Paris. Then she's off to the Pacific Theater as she hits the shores of Iwo Jima, Okinawa, and Japan after it surrenders. The most moving and horrifying parts of the book are the descriptions of the concentration camps in Germany and Japan, and the destruction caused by the atomic bomb dropped on Nagasaki. "Addie" is a wonderful character, and you should read this book and get to know her.

— WAIGHTS TAYLOR JR. —
Author of *Our Southern Home* and the *Joe McGrath and Sam Rucker Detective Novel* trilogy

Once again, Jeane Slone has taken us back in time to live the life of a courageous and strong woman during WWII. It's very easy to travel back in time and walk beside Addie Peterson as she breaks barriers women have never dared to challenge. Historical facts are intertwined with an absorbing story of an up-and-coming war correspondent during WWII. As an amateur photographer, it was fascinating to learn the techniques, efforts, strength, and tenacity of the early photojournalist for *Life* and *Time* magazines. A pleasurable history lesson indeed. Well done, Ms. Slone.

— KATHLEEN TURNER —
Avid reader, amateur photographer

Jeane Slone's latest historical novel, *She Was a WW II Photographer Behind Enemy Lines,* captures the life of a young woman taking on a profession only reserved for males. Much like her previous books, with female characters becoming the first to fly bombers, build ships, or spy for her country, this book provides an inside look at the demands of mastering the skills needed to produce eye-catching photography. Her character travels a serendipitous route that puts her in key assignments at historical moments leading up to and during the Second World War, all the while fighting to be allowed to go where women had previously been excluded.

—CHARLEY TAYLOR —
Navy pilot, Vietnam veteran, member of the Pacific Coast Air Museum, and avid WW II history buff

She Was A
WW II Photographer
Behind Enemy Lines

— A Historical Novel —

"Let us work for Peace"

Jeane Slone

Jeane Slone

SHE WAS A WW II PHOTOGRAPHER BEHIND ENEMY LINES
Copyright © 2018 by Jeane Slone

All rights reserved. This book or any portion thereof may not be reproduced or used in any manner whatsoever without the express written permission of the publisher except for the use of brief quotations in a book review.

ISBN 978-1-7320791-0-1

Printed in the United States of America

First Printing, 2018

This historical novel is based entirely on fact. The characters are fictional and are amalgams of real female war correspondents.

All photographs in this book are public domain.

$\mathcal{D}$edicated to...

The 127 brave World War II female war correspondents, who went above and beyond to capture the events of the war to inform the people on the home front. These women fought against condemnation and hostility from male officers in order to perform their jobs, and proved time and again that they were equal to male reporters.

Dickey Chapelle, a war correspondent who served during World War II. She was quoted as saying, "When I die, I want it to be on patrol with the United States Marines." Dickey Chapelle was wearing combat boots, a bush hat, and her signature pearl earrings when she was hit by shrapnel from a Vietcong landmine near Chu Lai Air Base on Nov. 4, 1965. She was the first female American war correspondent to be killed in action.

Table of Contents

Acknowledgments

It takes a "village" to write a historical novel, plus a library. Thanks to:

My husband, for his helpful critiques from the bathtub.

My brother, Tom Slone, for providing information about NYC and the USSR.

My "hawkeyes" who helped perfect the book during its proof stage:

- Charley Taylor, a great proofreader and a World War II buff with a BS in Political Science. Charley received his Navy Wings in 1969 and flew the Grumman A-6 Intruder during two combat cruises to Vietnam. He is a member of the Pacific Coast Air Museum.
- William Haigwood, newspaper editor and photojournalist. His father taught him photography, and how to develop film and make prints, when William was ten years old.
- John Nelson, award-winning commercial photographer and member of the Pacific Coast Air Museum.
- Kathleen Turner, avid reader and hobby photographer.
- Waights Taylor Jr., perfectionist, publisher, and author.
- Beryl Vedros, my neighbor and a voracious reader.
- Alla Crone-Hayden, award-winning author and meticulous proofreader.
- And most importantly, my patient, perfectionist editor, Cris Wanzer.

Thanks also to my daughter, Rose Kerbein, who invited me to Prague during her last year of college there.

And to Kathleen Riley, who photographed me opening the door to the speakeasy at the Grape Leaf Inn, Healdsburg, CA.

Chapter 1
1942 & 1914

A great photograph is one that fully expresses what one feels, in the deepest sense, about what is being photographed.

— Ansel Adams

In the new year of 1942, I was asked to go to Washington, D.C., to become the first official female World War II correspondent. Mr. Luce, the owner of *Life Magazine*, had arranged an appointment with the US Army Air Forces. I was annoyed that I felt nervous about going to the new Pentagon building for the interview. After all, I was certainly more than qualified for the task, after covering six countries during periods of war.

The two-star general who interviewed me asked a series of absurd questions:

Are you athletic?

Do you like camping?

Are you afraid of firearms?

Can you keep secrets?

He leaned over his enormous desk and asked in a serious tone, "Did you know, Miss Peterson, that in the field there are no bathroom facilities for women? You won't be very comfortable, you know, and anything can happen. Do you think you can take it?"

My patience was wearing thin but I politely answered, "General, I have been covering the war for *Life Magazine* since 1938. I've been in Czechoslovakia, Finland, France, England, Greece, and the Soviet Union. I believe, sir, I have proven myself. Now that the United States has entered into World War II, I am needed to continue this work. In order to succeed, I would like to have a uniform and credentials."

The general gave me a long, hard stare, then stamped my

application, signed it, and handed it to me. "These papers are temporary until the Army checks out your background and patriotism. You are the first woman to apply to become credentialed. I'm glad you're experienced. I would like you to go to the War Department on D Street to help design a uniform for women, if you're interested."

"I'd be honored, sir." My hands twitched as I held the coveted papers. I stood and left without a word before he could change his mind.

On the city bus en route to the War Department, I unfolded my papers and noticed that the general had not checked whether I was a reporter or a photographer. With a pen from my pocketbook, I checked "photographer," happy that there were very few of us at the time. A smile spread across my face as I stared at my credentials. I felt like I was floating in a dream.

My first thought about finally becoming accredited was not being able to share this momentous accomplishment with my father. A lone tear rolled down my cheek. I dabbed it with my white lace hanky and turned toward the window. I wished I could go back in time to my childhood home to hear my father's congratulations. I was thankful that he had imparted his great love of photography to me before he died, and could only hope he was up in Heaven watching my achievements. I thought about the magic of Dad's darkroom, where he had shared his knowledge of developing film and fostered my deep love of the craft. I closed my weary eyes and let my mind drift back to my youth...

I remembered well the day Dad allowed me to help him in his darkroom. I was ten years old. He came home from work and greeted my brother, Jimmy. "Come help me develop this roll of film before dinner's ready."

Dad knew I wanted to assist him, but the hall closet, which was the darkroom, was too small for all of us. Besides, Jimmy was the oldest, a boy, and the obvious choice to help him with his work.

My brother was on the floor trying to feed bits of grass to his hognose snake, which was in a box. I stayed away from the slimy gray, rectangular-patterned creature because of its incessant loud hissing. It would inflate its neck and strike out at me with its four-foot-long body. Jimmy enjoyed taunting me with it.

"James, did you hear me?" my father said.

After my brother failed to pry open the snake's mouth, he followed Dad into the closet.

"Why didn't you bring in a blanket for the door?" Dad crossed his arms on top of his large stomach and a scowl appeared on his face.

Jimmy ran back out and grabbed a blanket for the makeshift darkroom.

I was curled up on the couch reading a schoolbook when the crash happened.

"Damn it, now I only have one beaker left!" Dad said as he opened the closet door. "Get the broom, James. Clean it up, then stay out. I'll develop the film myself."

"I'll help, Dad," I begged, seizing the opportunity.

"I suppose you're old enough now. Do you have any homework?"

"I can get up early to finish it."

"All right then, fetch me a glass to replace the broken beaker."

Jimmy was older than I was but was flighty and had no attention span, except with animals. I smugly hoped Dad had given up trying to teach him photography.

When my father went back into the closet, I followed with a glass and stuck my tongue out at Jimmy. Mother gave me a scolding look.

Dad pinned the blanket over the door and checked to see that the light would be completely sealed off when he took the film out of the camera. He set up a small card table and lit the wick of a kerosene lantern. I squinted my eyes.

"Your eyes will soon become accustomed to it," Dad said.

From the cabinet high overhead, Dad retrieved the developing equipment and placed it on the table. "Graduated cylinder, box of developer, box of fixer, glass rod, and thermometer."

I repeated each one.

"Go get me the water on the stove and be careful—it's warm."

I dashed out of the darkroom and returned with the water.

"Now, watch everything I do carefully, Adeline."

Dad put the thermometer into the water and pointed to the rising mercury. "Good, it's close to sixty-five degrees."

Next, he filled the graduated cylinder with water and measured the developing powder into the beaker, then added the water. "Come here, Addie, and mix this for me."

I scooted around his protruding belly as he handed me the glass rod. I smiled up at him while I stirred. The clinking noise made me feel like an important scientist.

The developer was poured into the first of three trays arranged on a table. Dad opened the last box, explaining, "Acid fixing powder." He poured the proper amount of fixer into a drinking glass, added water, and told me to stir again. He then poured it into the last tray. "Fixing bath," he said.

The horrid smell caused me to hold my nose. I licked my lips, swallowed hard, and could almost taste it. Then I sneezed but tried to hold it in, not wanting to spray into the chemicals and mess up the project. The acrid scent reminded me of when I helped Mom pickle our cucumbers.

A rare chuckle escaped from Dad's mouth. "You'll get used to the smell over time. I'll open the door a bit to air it out until I have to remove the film."

He patted my golden-brown hair, then turned the small handle on the camera to wind up the film.

"I have to turn the lantern off now before I remove the film from the camera. Go help your mother with dinner. The developing process in the dark will take a while. I'll show you how to print a negative on Saturday, in the sun."

When I came out, Jimmy was flipping over his snake, exposing its pale-yellow underbelly. I helped Mother with dinner preparations, and sliced carrots to accompany the chicken.

Mother called into the living room, "James, I told you to set the table since you're not helping your father. What are you doing?"

"I'm trying to get my snake to eat a toad I found."

He put his snake back into the box and dashed into the

kitchen. As he grabbed a stack of flowered china plates, Mother scolded, "Don't touch those until you wash your hands."

As James hastily set the plates back down on the kitchen counter, one fell to the wooden kitchen floor and shattered.

"You're so clumsy, James," Mother said. "After you sweep up the glass, go to your room, then recite to yourself, 'I will be more careful. I will concentrate on the task at hand.'"

Later, after dinner, Jimmy was back in the corner with his snake. "Mom, can I listen to the radio?"

"Reading is better. True joy in life comes from hard work and high standards. Isn't that right, Father?" my mother replied.

On Saturday, Dad took his large, heavy Woodward enlarger up a ladder onto the roof while I followed behind with a box of special paper. Dad took a negative image that he had cut from the developed roll and put it in the enlarger. I handed him a sheet of the paper and he placed it below the lens on the easel board at the bottom of the enlarger. It was held flat with two iron bars.

"This is the condenser part of the enlarger, which focuses light from the sun. I have to keep adjusting the enlarger every few minutes for uniform exposure, carefully focusing because fire is common and the lens could act as a burning glass."

I enjoyed being high up on the roof and occupied myself by trying to identify the birds and their calls while Dad made adjustments to the enlarger.

"Come quickly, Addie, here comes the photograph."

The black-and-white image slowly appeared on the exposed paper. I exclaimed breathlessly, "Oh, it's magic! There's a picture of your printing press, Daddy!"

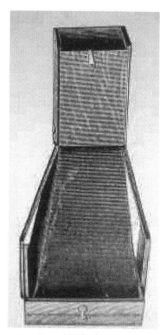

Woodward Solar Enlarger

World War I Vest Pocket Camera

Chapter 2
1917

Leica, schmeica. The camera doesn't make a bit of difference. All of them can record what you are seeing. But you have to see.
— Ernst Haas

Dad came home from work, kissed Mother on the cheek, and went into the darkroom. I put down my math homework as I heard the cabinets open.

"Where's my Leica? Adeline, do you have it?" Dad's voice boomed out from behind the darkroom door.

"It should be in there, Daddy. I haven't touched it."

"Come show me where you saw it last."

I piled all my schoolbooks together, then went into the darkroom and pointed to the open upper cabinet.

Dad's black, deep-set eyes burned into mine as he yelled, "Like I said, it's not here! You'd better find it. The Leica's a prototype, a test model, and I have to return it. You cannot take it without my permission. Find it by the time I develop this roll of film from work."

I stomped over to my brother as he messed with two disgusting snakes. "Jimmy, where's Dad's camera?"

He ignored me, went to his room, and returned with a jar of bugs.

I shook his arm. "I know you have it! Go get it before Dad comes out."

He pushed me away and opened the jar of bugs. A cricket escaped and he pounced on it.

"I'm telling Mother." I pointed my finger at him.

I went to the kitchen, where Mom was putting dinner in the oven. After I told her what was happening, she stormed out into the living room, shaking a wooden spoon. "James, find that camera immediately!"

My brother ran out the door. I scrambled after him, causing some of Dad's framed photographs on the wall to shake as I ran past them.

In the woods, I saw Jimmy slow down and search the ground.

"You took Dad's camera out here?" My breaths came out in short bursts in the fall air.

"I had to photograph my new snake. He was wrapped around that tree, over there."

"You'll be punished in your room for days." I kicked around in the fall leaves, searching for the camera.

Suddenly, Jimmy hollered, "Yahoo!"

I thought he had been looking for the camera, but instead, he triumphantly held up a small snake. I grabbed the hognose puff adder and ran with it into the center of Morley Woods. Jimmy caught up to me and grabbed my wrist, trying to get the baby snake out of the grip of my small hands as it wriggled, hissed, and inflated its neck.

I squeezed it tighter and screamed, "I'll kill it if you don't find Daddy's camera!" I didn't mind Jimmy's turtles, but knew that snakes could be poisonous and didn't like them.

Jimmy kicked my shin and ran the other way. I threw the oily, slimy thing into a hole and rubbed my sore leg.

As the evening sun began to set, I searched the ground once more. A flash of shiny metal caught my eye. "It must be the lens," I said to myself. I cupped my hands and shouted in my brother's direction, "I found it! Now you'll be in trouble forever."

He came toward me yelling, "Just give me the snake! Where is it?"

The leaves crackled and crunched beneath my feet as I burst out laughing and skipped back home, holding the camera safely against my chest.

After handing it to Dad and telling him that Jimmy had taken it and left it outside, I felt like a heroine back from a successful rescue mission.

My brother was sent to his room to repeat, "I will not take items that do not belong to me. I will not take items that do not belong to me..."

When I was almost thirteen years old, my father took me to see his work being produced at the foundry. I felt quite superior, being the only one allowed to go since my older brother had proved his uselessness time and time again. Dad won an argument with Mother to let me miss school by telling her it was an educational trip.

We climbed up clanking metal steps that took us higher and higher above the hot, sooty factory. It was almost dark inside. Nervous, I practiced my steady breathing to calm myself, just like Mother had taught me.

"You're not afraid of heights now, are you, Addie?" my father's voice boomed above the factory noise.

"No, Daddy, not anymore."

My parents let Jimmy and me climb trees and even balance walking on the front picket fence; anything to make sure we got used to heights. My best friend, Mary, wasn't ever allowed to do anything that boyish.

Once on the balcony, I looked down and saw radiant, glittering flashes producing a grand show of light. I was transfixed as I watched giant ladles pour flowing, molten metal into special molds.

Dad removed his hands from the rail and snapped his suspenders. "That's my rotary printing press being made down there and those are the metal machine parts for it being poured. The factory will fit it together to make *my* patented printing press." His big barrel chest thrust out as he emphasized the word "my."

"Oooooh, Dad, look!" Hot, bright-orange and red liquid sparks flew below the balcony. The glow and flashes of iridescent, changing colors left me breathless. Streaks of dazzling gold soared into the darkness.

"That's the iron being turned into liquid to flow in the molds." Dad pointed below.

In one of the factory rooms, I watched Dad supervise the setting up of one of his presses. My stomach rumbled, demanding lunch. At times the factory was boring, but I did enjoy the attention from the workers, who stopped to talk to me. Everyone at the foundry thought my dad was an important man because he had perfected the design of a Braille printing press.

As Dad and I sat down for lunch, I took a bite of a sandwich and asked him, "What's Braille?"

"Louis Braille was a Frenchman who lost his eyesight in an accident when he was young. He designed small, rectangular blocks called cells that create raised dots on paper to make an alphabet that you can read by touching."

"I'd like to see it."

"I'll show you a test sheet of Braille from one of my printing presses after we finish lunch."

Later on, in his office, I got to feel the Braille characters as he explained about the number and arrangement of the dots and how to tell one letter from another.

While Dad laid out plans on his big desk, I shut my eyes, pretended to be blind, and practiced feeling the groups of raised bumps. It was fun to get some of the letters right.

It had been an exciting day for me, and we returned home to a hot meal on the table.

"Where were you all day, Addie? I didn't see you at school." Jimmy crossed his arms in front of his thin, boyish frame.

"I went to Dad's work at the foundry," my voice sing-songed in a nasty tone.

"Speak nicely, young lady," Mother reprimanded.

"I wouldn't want to go to that stupid place anyway." Jimmy shoved a forkful of meat into his mouth.

"Stupid is not a proper word to use." Mother glanced over at Dad to see if he was paying attention, but he was too busy scribbling diagrams on the tablecloth with a pencil.

Dad was in his own world as his mind whirred, its gears turning. He stared out between us all and proceeded to draw his elaborate designs between bites of dinner.

"How was school today, Jimmy?" Mother inquired.

"I learned how to do double-dutch on a jump rope during recess." He took a sip of milk.

Mother repeated, "I meant, how were your academic classes?"

Jimmy recited what he'd done in every class, and ended by saying he'd gotten an A on a biology test. Mother nodded with approval, then questioned me about what I had learned at the foundry.

"I saw liquid metal being poured to make one of Dad's printing presses. It was enchanting." I gave Jimmy a smirk.

"Very good description, Adeline," Mother smiled.

Jimmy snickered again and Mother gave him a scolding look.

He mumbled, "Dumb factory."

After I finished telling my tale of the thrills of being at Dad's work, Mother closed the subject with her usual phrase: "Always do your best, children. Petersons always do their best!"

Dad erased one design, put his pencil down, and patted Mother's hand, then went back to his sketching. After a few bites of roast beef, he put his pencil in his shirt pocket and went into the darkroom. When I heard the cupboard doors opening, I rushed about, hurrying to clear the table so I could join him in our magical world of developing film.

On Sundays, after our chores were done, our family always went on an outing in Morley Woods, right behind our house.

Jimmy asked, "Why don't we go to church like everyone else does on Sundays?"

My dad touched the leaf of a birch tree and smiled. "We don't need to go to church because God is nature. In the woods, our family can renew our souls and give thanks all at the same time."

Mother added, while holding Dad's hand, "Nature teaches more than she preaches. We are very fortunate to have an open-air church right behind our house. Besides, my family was Jewish."

"What's Jewish?" I asked.

"It's another faith to worship God. Jewish people go to temple, not church. There are many faiths that help people to be kind and moral." Mother smiled at Dad as he nodded in approval.

We all walked closer together as a cool breeze brushed past us. A woodpecker drummed on a dry limb.

11

Dad stopped from time to time to examine the light, then reached into his bag for a specific camera. He pulled out what he called a Vest Pocket Autographic Kodak camera. "Addie, we're lucky this compact camera has been invented. And it's made from aluminum instead of cumbersome wood." Dad showed me the small, rectangular-shaped metal box.

"It doesn't look like a camera. Where are all the parts?"

Dad chuckled. "Watch." He pushed a tiny clasp down, which popped open the lid, then he pulled on metal struts and clicked it open. He pushed the fixed lens up and a black leather accordion bellows appeared.

"I see why it's called a Vest Pocket camera, because it can fit in a pocket, but how does it give autographs?" I asked.

"Soldiers in the Great War took photographs to record history. They could write notes or the date right on the negative. Watch." Dad took a tiny iron stylus from the back of the camera, lifted a flap, and wrote the date on the film.

"That's practical."

Dad let me hold the camera. I looked through the viewfinder and clicked the shutter. I took a picture of a wildflower, folded the camera up, then lifted the flap and wrote "zigzag" on the negative. I loved the name of the zigzag goldenrod. I turned the metal loop and advanced the film for the next shot. "That was fun, Dad."

"You'll see the word 'zigzag' appear after the photo is developed."

Mother taught Jimmy and me to walk quietly and use our ears to identify the many birds hiding in the woods. She would imitate one, then had us practice making the calls.

"Jimmy, did you hear that one? What bird do you think it is?"

I interrupted with enthusiasm, "It's a cardinal."

"Very good, Addie, but I did ask Jimmy. You must learn not to interrupt. Jimmy, how do we know that it's a cardinal?"

"Because of its call. He says *what-cheer, what-cheer, what-cheer.*"

"That's correct. Now, children, do you remember the new word I taught you that means a pattern of sounds that helps us remember something?"

"I know!" I said. "It's *mnemonic* and I can spell it because of the school spelling bee."

Dad patted my head with approval and let me take a photo of a wild geranium. I bent over it with the camera and examined it through the viewfinder. My eyes feasted on each showy pink, five-pronged flower on its tall stem, and its six-lobed leaves.

While Mother told Jimmy all about birds, Dad explained cameras to me. He said that artists used a portable type of camera called an *obscura* to help them draw scenes accurately. Light entered through the lens and was reflected by an angled mirror inside the box, and the mirror projected an image on a glass screen at the top. The screen was shielded from the surrounding light by a folding hood. This enabled the artist to place a thin piece of paper on the glass and trace the image. I was fascinated by this information.

All of a sudden, we heard *tea-kettle, tea-kettle, tea-kettle.* Mother glanced over toward Jimmy.

With pride, he announced, "Carolina wren."

The wren was a shy little brown bird that we couldn't spot, but hearing its call, we knew it was there, hiding in the maple tree. We all enjoyed repeating a robin's song, *cheer-up, cheerily, cheerily,* and even Dad joined in. Jimmy and I argued over whether it was a robin or a bluebird's song.

Mother corrected me. "The bluebird's call is close to the robin's: *cheer, cheerful, charmer.* It also has a bell-like sound." She paused to listen to the forest. "There it goes, listen again."

Jimmy was right. We saw the red-breasted bird flit by. Our whole family sang the bluebird's call, then the robin's.

On the way back home, Dad pointed to a low-growing woodland plant with a cluster of small white flowers. "That's wild lily-of-the-valley."

He handed the camera to me. I crouched down low and moved in close, taking my time to get the perfect shot. The smell of the flower was intoxicating—what Mother called "nature's perfume."

Our family had a wonderful Sunday in the woods and I slept well that night, dreaming of birds, flowers, and Vest Pocket cameras.

The Leica camera

Chapter 3
1920, Age 16

Dance is the hidden language of the soul of the body.
— Martha Graham

The only way Mother allowed me to visit my high school friend Mary was if I said I was going to tutor her, since she was not doing well in history. Somehow, I knew in my heart that little white lies were not as harmful as bold-faced, big ones.

I went out the back door, found the family bicycle, and put a schoolbook into the front basket. The ride filled me with exhilaration, giving me energy to pedal the many miles to Mary's house. At last, I got to explore new boundaries besides the woods in my back yard.

One more hill to climb and I would be there. I pumped hard, standing tall on the pedals, and made it to the top with glee, knowing that the ride back would be a joyful sail.

I propped the bike against the side yard fence and tapped timidly on the huge wooden front door, avoiding the large brass knocker. Mary's house was grand; much larger than our bungalow.

My schoolmate greeted me with contagious enthusiasm. "I've been waiting for you, Addie! I want to show you my new dress, then we can act out Little Orphan Annie from the Sunday funnies. I know how to play poker. You know that card game, don't you, Addie?"

Before I could answer, she zoomed into the kitchen and I followed her. It was quiet inside and I knew her parents must not be there.

Thoughts of my mom crept into my head. "Maybe we should study first. I brought a schoolbook. Is your mother home?"

"Nope, she works in town in my dad's office." Noticing my worried frown, she added, "Don't be a stick-in-the-mud, there're many fun things to do besides homework. Let's have some bakery cookies, then I'll show you around."

I'd never had a bakery cookie. Mom always made our cookies, though rarely, and always the same type—oatmeal.

"These peanut butter cookies are yummy, thank you," I mumbled through a mouthful of cookie. They were crisp and made a crunching noise because of the nuts. Mother's oatmeal cookies were not made with expensive ingredients like peanuts.

"Here's some milk to dip the cookies in." Mary poured two big glasses. After she dipped her third cookie, she gave me a quizzical look. "Don't you dip?"

"No, I've never been allowed." I dunked a cookie and relished making a slurping sound as I ate it, just like Mary had.

After she had drenched her fourth cookie and gulped her milk, she announced, "Let's read Little Orphan Annie in the Sunday funnies. You read last week's, didn't you?"

"I'm not permitted to read the funnies." I cracked one of my knuckles but Mary didn't seem to mind.

"You sure have mean parents. What *are* you allowed to do?"

My cheeks reddened. I searched my mind to answer such a forthright question. "Morley Woods are behind my house and I'm allowed to explore as far as I want."

"So. What else?"

"Umm, ummm..." My mouth became dry. I swallowed hard, then blurted out, "My dad's a photographer and we develop film together."

"What's that like?" Mary grabbed the newspaper and searched for the funnies on a beautiful marble table in the large, mahogany-paneled living room.

"It's fun to unwind film from a camera, put it in chemicals, then see an image appear magically on paper." My mouth widened into a confident smile.

"You're lucky to have a camera. That's something I don't have."

"Yes, I am." I failed to mention that it wasn't my *own* camera.

Mary looked me up and down, then felt the hem on my plain, homemade dress. "This dress will do for before Little Orphan Annie moves in with Daddy Warbucks." She dashed into her bedroom and came back with a new, store-bought dress, still in its box.

I saw the price tag, which read $45.95, and almost gasped. Black rhinestones were embroidered all around the waist of the plum dress, which had a high scoop neck.

"It's charming and...uh...smart looking." I fumbled. I had never seen such a glamorous dress.

"Yes, it's silk Charmeuse, New York's latest fashion."

I gingerly touched the rose-flowered bow below the rhinestones. "It's lovely."

"My mom bought it for the school dance. You're going, aren't you, Addie?"

"I don't know yet." I looked down at my worn shoes.

"You can be the before Annie and I'll be the after one." Mary changed the subject.

I sighed. My friend sure could be bossy, but I went along with all her ideas because I was having a wonderful time.

She slipped off her dress right in front of me and put on the new one. I turned my head away. The dress made her plump body look quite feminine.

"Don't worry, I'll give you a chance to wear it in our play."

"Oh, I couldn't. It's too new." I knew that her dress would just hang on my skinny body.

"You must, in order to be the Annie after she moves out of the orphanage."

We read the funnies out loud and switched our dresses off and on. At first, I was self-conscious, but I soon became comfortable in just my slip. Our acting became more and more dramatic as we threw our arms about and changed our voices. I had never laughed that hard or enjoyed being so silly. It was a delightful experience for me, until my mother got inside my head again.

"I'd like to work on our history homework. Let's do it together," I finally said.

"Oh, all right, but after that, we must play cards. I know a new game."

I got out the schoolbook and sat at the kitchen table with two pencils. "This is the answer you got wrong in class. If you had read it carefully, you would've gotten it right." After seeing

Mary's disgusted expression, I realized I sounded just like my mother and decided to speak in a friendlier voice.

We completed the homework assignment and I was happy that I could help Mary with the hard questions. "Mary, what college do you think you'll get into?"

"I want to go to Harvard, like my dad, but they don't allow very many women in. He had me apply to its sister school, Radcliff." She tipped her pencil up and down between her fingers.

"What're you going to major in?"

"Oh, I'll be majoring in 'husband' while I'm trying to get my M-R-S. degree." She chuckled, pleased with her little joke.

"My mother always says the proper place to meet a beau is in college, but I have other interests."

"Where did you apply, Addie?"

"Cornell. I've seen photographs of it and it's very scenic, overlooking Cayuga Lake. It also has many nearby waterfalls."

"It's a good college. You'll find a fine husband there to support you because they have a law school."

"I'm more interested in learning. I want to major in English and take photography classes," I enthused.

Mary suppressed a yawn. "I have an idea. Let's go to the school dance together next month."

I squirmed, shifted, and came up with, "I might be busy."

"You must go! Dancing is good practice to find the perfect husband."

"I...I can't dance." I bit at a fingernail.

"You never took lessons? I bet your parents couldn't afford dancing lessons for you." Mary glanced at my dress.

"My mother doesn't permit dancing or even music. She says it's a wasteful use of time."

"She sounds strict! Your mother seems to have a long list of things you're not allowed to do."

"That's not true," I said, slightly defensive. I reflected on the hours she spent sewing dresses for me and our long walks in the woods together. "Let's go outside." I was not used to being inside for so long, as Mother didn't permit it.

Mary softened. "Oh, Addie, come into the parlor and I'll teach you to dance."

"We have a radio but we only listen to the news to increase our knowledge." I smoothed down the front of my plain brown hair with a moistened finger.

Mary rose from the kitchen table with a burst of energy and signaled for me to come into the parlor. She lifted the finely crafted, golden-oak lid of a four-foot-tall phonograph that stood in the corner.

"A talking machine! It's beautiful." I traced the spiral wooden scrollwork on the front of the cabinet.

Mary opened the double cabinet doors at the bottom. Inside were shelves of records. "This one's my favorite." She removed the paper sleeve and put the record on the pretty purple felt turntable, then got a new needle from an inlaid cup next to it. The old needle went into a second silver cup. The record label had an adorable dog on it with his nose sticking into the horn of a Victrola. Mary turned the thumbscrew to allow the new needle to go in, then tightened it. I watched with complete fascination. The needle looked like the nails Dad used to hammer up the blanket in his darkroom.

Before Mary released the tiny silver brake, she exclaimed, "We sure are different, aren't we, Addie? Stick with me, pal, and I'll loosen you up to have more fun than you've ever had! Besides, you're way too serious."

Mary turned the outside crank once, then noticed how I watched. "Here, you do it. Wind it up twelve times."

She set the brake as I wound up the talking machine.

After putting the tone arm on the record, she released it and the song, "Oh, You Beautiful Doll" broadcast loudly throughout the large room.

Mary grabbed my hands and showed me how to move my feet and before I knew it, I was doing the two-step. She sang along to the record and I joined in. It was quite a lively song. As it scratched to an end, she put the little brake on, tilted up the tone arm, removed the needle and placed it into the used-needle cup, and took a new one.

"Now for the waltz!"

Exhausted after three types of dances, we finally sat down at the kitchen table and drank root beer. It was bubbly and very sweet.

"Addie, you learn fast. Your dance card will fill up fast. Mine always does."

"What's a dance card?"

"It's a small, fancy booklet that you receive when you arrive at the dance. You put it on your wrist like a bracelet. It has a small pencil attached to it. The names of all the dances are listed with the songs. The girls sit on one side of the room and wait for the boys to sign up for a dance. Oh, Addie, we'll have so much fun! I can't wait." Mary slurped the last drop of root beer. "Let's play poker." She dashed into the parlor and came back with a deck of playing cards.

I pouted and looked down at the polished kitchen floor.

"Don't tell me you can't play cards..."

She tried to get me to look at her by staring at me, then gave up and began to mix up the cards. "I'll show you how to play a sample game, then we'll bet."

I pursed my lips, looked down at my hands, and mumbled, "I don't have any money."

Mary mixed up the deck again. "Don't worry, we're not betting with money, you'll see." She displayed a devilish twinkle in her eyes while turning all the cards face up, then selecting certain ones. She pointed to five cards, then fanned them out. "This is a straight flush."

Mary proceeded to demonstrate a royal flush and two-of-a-kind, and explained how many points each hand was worth.

I concentrated on her words, trying to grasp all the new concepts. It was sort of like math. Mother might be pleased that I was learning this new game.

"Do you get it now, Addie? Can we play?"

"I think so. Can I show you examples of some of the hands?"

"Sure, but make it fast so we can get to betting." Her eyes showed that mischievous look again.

After I put out examples of various cards from the deck, Mary scooped them all up and put them all together. "You've got it."

I was fascinated by the noise the cards made. Mary told me it was called "shuffling." I wanted to try but she was in too much of a hurry to get on with betting.

We played a hand and I won. "This is fun!"

Mary took off a shoe and tossed it across the room. I gave her a questioning look.

The next game I lost, and she said with glee, "You must take something off."

"What?" I raised my voice.

"Take something off. We're playing strip poker!"

My heart raced. Mary tapped her foot until I took off my shoe. She lost the next hand, laughed, pulled her dress over her head and sat shuffling the deck in her slip. I concentrated very hard on my cards and drew one from the deck, hoping and praying it would match, but I lost. I took off my other shoe.

When Mary lost the next hand, she stood up and pulled off her slip. Her large bosoms bounced down. She sat back on the chair, giggling, with her breasts exposed.

I suppressed a gasp and, horrified, said I had to go to the bathroom.

"Hurry back. I'll shuffle. Isn't this fun, Addie?"

In the bathroom, I re-evaluated the strange situation I was in, took a deep breath, and came out. "I have to go home now, my mother said not to be late."

As Mary shuffled the deck, her breasts jiggled. She sat there with a Cheshire Cat smile on her face. "Too bad. Just when you were starting to win!" She laughed, stood up right in front of me, and pulled her slip back on.

I got my schoolbook and mumbled, "Thanks for the cookies," then hurried out the door.

Mary came outside after me in her slip. "Would you like a stick of gum for the ride? What flavor do you like the best, Spearmint, Juicy Fruit, or Double Mint?"

I lied, "Oh, I like them all."

Mary handed me one. With a curt thank you, I hurried down the front steps. I put the gum in my bike basket.

Mary called, "Come over next week and we'll play gin rummy!"

I didn't answer and pedaled away from her house as hard as I could. I wondered about the name of the card game, gin rummy. No alcohol ever entered our serious home.

1921 phonograph

Chapter 4
A Dance

Let us read and let us dance — two amusements that will never do any harm to the world.

— Voltaire

As I floated down the hill on the bike, headed back to the safety of my home, a breeze cooled off my hot, red face. My stringy hair flew behind me as the wind brushed against my ears, making a whirring sound. Out of breath, I stopped for a minute, reached into the basket, pulled out the stick of gum and popped it into my mouth. I started pedaling again. As I rounded a corner, I opened my mouth. The air made the gum even tastier. The next street was my house and I made as much noise as I could with the gum, snapping and popping it with my teeth and tongue.

After storing the bicycle in the back yard, I went around to the front door and was met with the delicious aroma of dinner in the oven.

Jimmy heard me come in and stormed toward me. "Where's my bike?"

"It's not *your* bike, you know that. It's the family bike," Dad said.

"What are you chewing?" Jimmy asked.

I headed straight for my bedroom, put the chewed gum on my bedpost, and returned to the living room just before Mother came out of the kitchen.

"Mom, Addie has gum."

"I do not." I grabbed the plates and set the table to avoid Mother's stare.

During dinner, I was able to circumvent all of Mother's questions about Mary and what we had done at her house. I knew I had better avoid the subject of dancing, and of course, strip poker. Thank goodness she was more interested in the house and its furnishings. After I told her about that, I described Mary's dresses and mentioned how much I had helped her with her history.

That night I lay in bed reading and chewing the heavenly gum, then drifted off to sleep.

When I awoke the next morning, I felt something hard and sticky in the front of my hair. It was the gum! Mother called for me to get up for breakfast. In a panic, I found some old, dull scissors in my dresser drawer and cut the gum out of my hair.

She called again, "Addie, hurry, you'll be late for school."

I hurriedly brushed my hair without the use of a mirror, then dashed into the kitchen. When I saw my mother's face, I knew my rushed haircut hadn't been successful.

"What's wrong with your hair?"

"I...I don't know what you mean." I looked down at my oatmeal, grabbed my spoon, and ate quickly, then hurried to get my books.

Jimmy walked by eating a breakfast apple, took one look at me, and began laughing. "You got the gum stuck in your hair, didn't you? Ha! That'll teach ya!"

Mother approached me and felt the bald spot. "This is why I have never allowed chewing gum. Learn this lesson, Addie."

"Good-bye, Mother," Jimmy called as he dashed out the door.

"Addie, come home straight away from school and I'll fix your hair," Mother said.

"But Mom, I have yearbook club."

"Then straight after that. You look horrid."

On the way to school, Jimmy made fun of me until I stomped on his foot and ran to class. School was difficult as my classmates all whispered behind my back.

When I saw Mary after math class, she said, "How can you go to the dance with that hair?"

Tears welled in my eyes.

"I have a fancy barrette you can borrow. Come over later."

The high school dance was just one week away and I had waited until the last minute to ask permission to go. When there was a break in the dinner conversation, I seized the opportunity.

"I want to go to the school dance on Saturday night," I declared boldly. I twisted my napkin.

"You know dancing is a frivolous activity." Mother raised her dark eyebrows. "Besides, how can you go when you don't know how to dance?"

"I learned how at Mary's after we did our homework together." I took a deep breath, getting ready for my mother's dissertation on dancing.

"Petersons don't—"

Mother was interrupted by Dad.

"Marian, I do agree with you about not having a boyfriend until college, but I don't think dancing is all that bad. We must recognize that times do change and there is nothing harmful about dancing. After all, women are allowed to vote now. Surely, they can dance." He took a bite of potato and removed his pencil from his pocket to do some sketching.

"Oh..." Mother was caught off guard by Dad's statement. It was rare for them to disagree, but I did notice that when they did, Dad would get the last word and this is what I hoped for.

Jimmy changed the subject. "Dad, I will need money for books when I go away to college next year. My scholarship does not include books."

My confidence went from excitement to fear after Mary's mother wouldn't allow her to lend me a dress. The bow I fashioned on my bald spot in the front of my hair kept falling off. I clipped on Mary's barrette to help it stay in place but it kept going askew on my thin hair.

"Don't let any boy touch you on top or pull you too close during a slow dance, Addie," Mother lectured.

"Yes, Mother, you told me that already."

"You don't look too good, Sis," Jimmy snickered. "That gum really messed up your hair. You should listen to Mom. She does know best."

"Jimmy, I do know best, but it's not your place to interfere.

25

Dry the dishes for Addie so she can get ready."

It cheered me up a little after Mother defended me and let me use her mirror. After a few long stares, I decided that my hair was hopeless and worked on my dress instead. I fashioned a stylish bow Mom had made just for me around the waist of my plain dress.

Mother made Jimmy walk me to school since it was nighttime. He was exceptionally nice to me. He pointed to the various stars in the sky, then wished me a good time when he departed.

The decoration committee had done a marvelous job transforming our ordinary gym into a soft, romantic atmosphere. Everyone looked different—more elegant and grown-up. The school orchestra was in fine tune and well practiced. I hummed one of the songs I recognized from Mary's house, and sauntered over to the punch bowl where she was sipping from a crystal cup and flirting with Arthur. Her plum taffeta dress with a belted bow was stunning, as were her silver brocade dance shoes and matching mesh purse.

Mary gave me the once-over, then leaned toward my ear and whispered, "I'm so sorry I couldn't lend you my organdy outfit. That sash helps some on your dress, but too bad about your hair." She saw me pout and added, "I'll meet you over there, on the girls' side. Save a seat for me." Mary turned her attention back to Arthur, who looked dashing in his expensive mohair, dark-brown striped suit with cuffed bottom trousers and a smart new bow tie.

When the music stopped, the boys went to one side of the room and the girls to the other. Mary sat down and her excitement spilled over, giving me hope for getting my dance card filled. I felt the intricate paper lace trim on my booklet as the delicate gold tassel tickled my forearm. I wiggled in my seat with anticipation.

Mrs. Butterfield announced that it was time for the boys to sign up for the dances. They came over to our row, looking like handsome men rather than silly schoolboys. Mary was elated that almost every line was signed on her card by a different boy. She glanced over at my blank dance card and sighed. When Edwin went to her to sign up for a waltz, she pulled her card away and said, "No, not unless you sign Adeline's card first."

He saw that Mary had only one dance left and signed mine.

Dancing with Edwin was delightful until he burst the bubble I was floating in by saying, "Thanks for the dance. What happened to your hair?"

I excused myself. "I must go powder my nose," I mumbled and left the gymnasium.

When I got home, Mother was upset that I hadn't waited for my brother to come and get me.

Jimmy saw my sad face, and with a kind heart said, "You look nice in that dress. How was the dance, Sis?"

I held my tears, went to my bedroom, and cried myself to sleep.

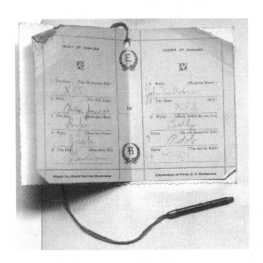

Dance Card

Chapter 5
1921, Age 17

*Graflex, the camera that does the difficult things in photography —
and does them well.*

— Eastman Kodak Company, Rochester, N.Y.

Dad took me out of my little hometown of Long Island for the first time in my isolated life. I missed being able to brag about the trip to Jimmy, but he was away at college studying veterinary medicine — and this time, *I* was jealous of *him*.

We rode a bus to the Washington, D.C. patent office where Dad went frequently to investigate his patent rights. On Dad's lap was a large camera in a leather case. He opened it and I bent over and touched it.

"Be careful, Addie, I just purchased this new camera. It cost $116 and this lens cost more than the camera."

"It sure is a big camera," I marveled.

"Yes, this brand-new Press Graflex is a large-format camera. It weighs eleven and a half pounds. Just like my Vest Pocket camera, it will let you write the date or any information on the negative."

"Can I try it out?"

"Only if you read the manual first, then I'll know you are capable of using it."

He handed me the 64-page booklet titled, "Graflex and Graphic Cameras." I paged through it and learned that the large-format camera had multiple speeds and lenses. I read as much as I could, then escaped into a book I had brought, Edna Ferber's *The Girls*. It was a brand-new novel and there had been a waiting list for it at the library. The story kept me absorbed in the world of strong female protagonists who were not debutants. It was just my kind of story. Dad glanced over at what I was reading, looked disinterested, and went back to his blueprints and papers.

As we approached the capital, the view out the bus window was full of interesting sights. There were still traces of the recent inauguration of the president, with a few stray signs and banners that read, "Elect Warren G. Harding."

At the J Street stop, Dad pointed to the patent office. "It took thirty-one years to build that," he told me.

Once inside the musty, 1836, Greek-style building, he tried to interest me in looking through the towering, dusty shelves filled with documents. When I couldn't stop sneezing, he let me sit out in the hall. I looked into the next room and saw adorable little scale models that inventors were required to submit in order to get a patent. Every once in a while, the clerk showed Dad everything he asked for when he stated a number. The white-haired attendant knew every patent and produced it by memory.

On the bus trip back home, I studied my schoolbook, *History of World War I.*

Dad looked over at it and nodded with approval. He broke the silence, surprising me by saying in his deep, captivating voice, "I'll have you know that, in 1854, Clara Barton was the first female patent commissioner to receive the same pay as men did."

Every hour after that, Dad would tell me something new, like the fact that he had invented and designed one of the portable printing presses that could print maps right on the battlefield during World War I.

The trip with my dad that day widened my little world and left me with a yearning to travel. It also provided the longest conversation my father and I ever had together.

At the end of the year, I was accepted into Cornell University. My parents were so proud. Dad gave me a long, affectionate hug and told me that all of my hard work and studying had paid off. Mother baked me a brand-new recipe called an upside-down cake. It was made from canned pineapple, a fruit from a faraway island called Hawaii. It was fun watching her make it. She arranged the fruit on the bottom of the pan and added expensive, bright-red Maraschino cherries, then poured vanilla cake batter on top. After it had baked and cooled, she was pleased by how surprised I was when she turned it over and a decorative pattern of fruit appeared on top of the cake.

A few days later, I arrived home late after working on our school yearbook. I was in charge of the photographs and enjoyed the responsibility of taking, developing, and printing random photos of all the students doing various activities around the school. Mother was sitting in Dad's comfy chair, staring into space even though it was dinnertime. I didn't smell anything cooking. A sense of alarm stirred within me. I couldn't recall ever seeing her this idle. There was always knitting or sewing in her lap.

"Hi, Mom." I glanced around and felt the stillness.

"Sit down, Adeline."

I sat on the caned chair next to her. "What's the matter? Is something wrong?"

She whispered, "The owner of the foundry came by and said your father had heart failure."

"What are you saying?" I said, a little louder than I intended.

"He's gone..." She gazed out into the room, then closed her eyes, as if trying to shut out a thought. "What are we going to do?"

I yelled, "No!" Shaking my head furiously, I ran out the door to the back yard.

After walking deep into the safety of the woods, I slid my back against my favorite tree, curled into a tight ball, and sobbed into my fists. As darkness crept into the forest, I managed to pull myself together and stumbled home.

Mother was still in the same chair when I returned. I knelt down next to her and placed my head in her lap. Why wasn't she crying?

She spoke in a ranting voice, more to herself than to me. "If he only had been more money-minded we would've been a wealthy family by now. He paid no attention to the budget."

I got up and paced back and forth on the braided wool rug. Mother looked over at the framed photographs that stretched from one end of the wall to the other. I wanted her to comfort me and grieve with me, but I had never seen her cry. This was not acceptable for the Petersons. The single sign of grief I was able to detect was her trembling hand as she touched a brilliant, colorful picture of the foundry.

Now there won't be any more of Dad's photographs... I thought as I stared at them. I held my emotions in until I was in the privacy of my own room, then flopped on my bed and let loose with tears. Neither one of us had dinner that night.

It had been a few months since Dad passed away. *Passed away...* I couldn't bear using the finality of the word *dead*. My grandparents on both sides were gone before I was born. I had only experienced death when seeing an occasional squirrel, bird, or one of Jimmy's stupid snakes lying lifeless in the woods. I locked myself in the safety of the darkroom and developed all of Dad's unfinished negatives into prints. I imagined his deep voice instructing me how to do the entire process. My stomach often made hungry noises as time became elusive in my solitude, but I finished my work. There were many rules in our family, such as if you start it, finish it; don't quit in the middle of anything; and of course, Petersons always do their best.

When I was finally done, and with all the equipment put away in its proper place, I emerged from the darkroom energized, and smelled the delicious aroma of dinner. "Mother, should I set the table?"

"I ate already, dear. I'll reheat your dinner for you. I didn't want to disturb your work."

Astonished that she had let me skip a chore, I recalled that this was something she would say to Dad when he was too busy in the darkroom to come out and join us. A grown-up feeling comforted me as I ate a satisfying meal of chicken and potatoes.

"Mom, have you gotten a letter from Jimmy?"

"Yes. He's working part-time as a veterinary assistant and he's doing well in school. I'm glad he got a job because of our changed money situation." She sat down across from me. The wrinkle line between her eyebrows deepened. "Addie, your father left just enough money for me to live on. I know that you had your heart set on college, but now everything has changed."

"But...but he invented and patented all those printing presses..." I put my forkful of mashed potatoes down.

"He had me pay the bills, but I had no idea that he'd made so many unsound investments."

I gathered my thoughts. "I'm pretty sure he was paid well." I cleared my plate from the table, my dinner only half eaten.

"Yes, he was, but he spent a lot of money on cameras, equipment, and travel. Like I said, he also made some bad investments behind my back."

Mother sounded so mean. I had never heard her say such things about my wonderful father. She washed the dishes and I dried them. I reflected on how proud Dad had been of me when I received the acceptance letter from Cornell.

I was about to go to my room when Mother said, "Addie, I won't sell the cameras. Your father would have wanted you to have them."

I went into the darkroom and stood on a stool so I could go through the upper cabinets. In one cabinet, I found canisters of film along with the Leica and Vest Pocket cameras. In the other was Dad's new Graflex, still in the box, and the manual. I brought them all down carefully. I held the Graflex like an expensive treasure. He never got to use it. It was a true gift of gold, but I would have gladly given it up to have my Dad back. A tear rolled down my cheek as I took the cameras to my desk in my bedroom, crawled into bed, and pulled the covers over my head.

The next morning, I placed all of Dad's cameras on my bed. I held them in my hands and looked through the viewfinder of each one. When I came to the Leica, I froze. The word "prototype" ran through my mind as I recalled my father scolding me when Jimmy had taken the camera without permission. I went to the bathroom and searched through the cabinets. Sure enough, I found a folder containing a letter from the Leica company. The camera was on loan and was overdue. I pinched the letter as tears welled in my eyes. I couldn't return the camera. It represented a piece of my father.

It was during my last month of high school when Mother showed me an ad in the newspaper and asked what I thought about being a camp counselor. Not waiting for an answer, she said, "By working at the camp all summer it would at least pay for some of your college tuition."

I read over the ad. It was for a camp counselor job in the mountains at Camp Catskill. The possibility of a new adventure woke me out of the dull fog that had surrounded me since Dad's passing. Intrigued, I felt a fever deep within me to explore a new world.

Graflex Speed Graphic press camera

Chapter 6
Camp Catskill, 1922, Age 18

With meditation I found a ledge above the waterfall of my thoughts.

— Mary Pipher

The summer of 1922 in the Catskill Mountains was glorious. I enjoyed waking early, before any of the campers stirred and while it was still dark. I would stand just outside my little cabin and let the crisp morning air invigorate my lungs while I stretched my arms up high, reaching for the fading stars. Much to my surprise and delight, I found that I enjoyed teaching the young children about nature. I felt grateful that my parents had taught me how to identify trees, plants, and birds. The campers loved repeating birdcalls, just like Jimmy and had done when we were children.

I was looking forward to a day off so I could learn how to use the large-format camera and try it out in the mountains. The unfamiliar landscape beckoned me to experiment with original shots. Early one morning, I packed my rope bag with some food, a map, a compass, and a lantern. The Graflex didn't fit in my bag and was too heavy to bring, so I had to bring the Leica instead. In the box was a letter I had received from the Leica company. After much thought, I had written to them, explaining that my father had died and telling them about my passion for photography. The company kindly allowed me to keep the camera as long as I filled out their questionnaire about my experience using it. I had done so immediately, and expressed my profuse gratitude for the gift of the magnificent camera.

As I hiked into the woods, I looked at the map of the numerous logging trails in the area. My heart fluttered with anticipation. I was anxious to get to Kaaterskill Falls, the highest waterfall in New York State. There were over thirty-five mountains in the Catskills area for me to explore.

The vertical ascent behind the camp was filled with the intoxicating odor of fir trees. I recalled reading a library book before I left about the very first indoor Christmas tree in this country. It was hauled by a Catskill farmer on an ox sled and brought to New York City to sell. The 1851 custom began so that city people could have a piece of the forest. The scent of the trees was a potent delight and I could imagine why rich people wanted to have a tree right in their own living rooms.

The hike continued to fill my senses with the open-air perfume of the many wildflowers in the woods, until my sour mood surfaced and made me miss not ever being able to take walks with my father again.

The sun began to rise above the dark forest and my heart raced as I reached into my bag for my camera. The spreading rays made the surrounding colors rapidly change as the sky lit up in painted shades of red, orange, yellow, and pink. I smiled. The show reminded me of the streaks of metal being poured to make Dad's rotary printing press at the foundry. My mouth turned into a pout as I realized I would never be able to visit the factory with him again.

For a moment, I closed my eyes and imagined what it would be like to be blind, never to feast my eyes on the glories of nature. I knew reading would still be possible because of Braille, but my passion for photography would be out of the question.

Upon opening my eyes, I searched the sky above the forest as the clouds thinned, making way for more color. At that moment, my anger over Dad's death diminished and was replaced by the pleasant memories that remained within me. Every time I touched a camera, he was there, in my heart, with inspiration and guidance.

Color upon color became more vivid. *Click, click.* I shot away, then slowed down, thinking of the expense of developing the film in the nearby town. I was glad I had taken the smaller camera with roll film, since the Press Graflex only came with a film pack and could only take two exposures at a time. Plus, it required reloading it in the dark, which would be difficult in the woods.

I let the Leica hang by its strap on my neck and looked over at the dark, jagged mountains, savoring the brilliant sunrise through an opening in the trees. Birds flapped their wings and passed through the rays of light. Dawn brought a chorus of birds in full song. I heard a familiar call, *"what-cheer, what-cheer, what-cheer"* and knew it was the northern cardinal; then *"feebee, feebee"* sang the black-capped chickadee. For a fleeting moment, I missed my mom.

I thought I heard something trampling through the leaves nearby and remained still. A mother deer ran out in front of me. I picked up my Leica and got a few shots of her two fawns before they all darted gracefully away.

I reached over to pick some huckleberries from a bush. Then the bushes began to shake and through the early morning haze, I thought I saw a tall man wearing a dark coat picking berries just a bit farther away. He looked at me, then dropped down on all fours. My eyes widened. That wasn't a man, it was a bear!

My body began to tremble. I tried to remain quiet and to maintain my slow breathing. I knew from reading that there were over 2,000 black bears in the Catskills, so a sighting was inevitable. I had the urge to photograph him but couldn't move. He stood and sniffed in the direction of a berry patch farther down the mountain. Once I knew he was moving away from me, I managed to shoot a few pictures as he lumbered off.

On the peak of Plateau Mountain, I sat down to catch my breath as the day unfolded before me. The bear encounter was forgotten. The morning view was breathtaking as the orange-yellow horizon over the outlines of the mountains spread out before me. I looked below at the Hudson River, more than 2,000 feet below. I hung precariously over the side of a sheer drop to get a picture of the valley in the distance, where two grand hotels were situated on opposite sides. With every adjustment and every view in the finder, I felt certain Dad was with me, telling me how to shoot. The picturesque valley stretched out before me, and I captured breathtaking views of the many lakes and streams.

I felt on top of the world, alone, and filled with peace. After putting my camera in my bag, with my eyes closed, I took in a breath and felt the scenery before me. A smooth breeze rippled through my hair and the crisp evergreen scent of the forest filled my nostrils.

"Hi, Dad," I whispered out into the valley. Was it my father? Was he there with me? I felt serene, then confident that he was indeed with me and would always be, guiding me toward adulthood. "I do miss you, Dad..." A lump formed in my throat. A new bird I had never seen before burst into song.

Rays of the sun gilded everything they touched with beauty, color, and life. The earth began to glow in the golden light as the sun climbed higher and higher in the sky. The sunrise was far more spectacular in person than when I had seen Thomas Cole's famous painting of this very spot in a book. I reflected on all the writers, artists, and poets who had been to this wilderness before me. These were the mountains of Rip Van Winkle.

I took out my map. The waterfalls were calling me and I had one more mile to go. Before leaving the peak, I placed my hands in front of the sun and performed "sky-dividing," which Dad had taught me to do to tell time. I knew sunrise would happen at six a.m. and sunset would be six p.m., so if the sun was straight above me, then the halfway mark was noon.

On the way to the waterfall, I recited my favorite part of William Cullen Bryant's poem about Kaaterskill Falls:

'Tis only the torrent tumbling o'er,
In the midst of those glassy walls,
Gushing, and plunging, and beating the floor
Of the rocky basin in which it falls.

A thundering roar in the distance drew me to the captivating waterfall. My stomach rumbled from hunger, but getting to the falls was far more important than a sandwich. Finally, I erupted from the tree line and there before me was the 260-foot, two-tiered natural wonder. Clear, rushing water cascaded over the vibrant moss and jagged rocks. The sound of the powerful water was exhilarating. My heart pounded to the rhythm.

I scaled a dangerous cliff—carefully, as I had read that hundreds of explorers had died in this very spot. As I climbed, my map fell out of my hands and fluttered away. I instinctively reached for it, and my foot slipped on the wet rocks. I grabbed hold of a lifesaving branch as my camera swayed on the strap around my neck. I finally got my footing by wedging myself between two large boulders below a branch. I was able to grab my camera and compose one careful photo. Still balancing between the two boulders, I managed to tuck the camera inside my blouse, then I crawled back to the safety of the ground. I scooped the cool water from the falls and washed away the sweat on my forehead. Out of breath, I reminded myself not to take foolish chances. I rested by lying on the smooth, wet boulders and enjoyed this natural wonder.

The water poured endlessly from the huge granite rocks and cascaded into the valley below. The powerful noise ran excitement through my veins. After a while, the rhythmic noise of the falls put me to sleep. My mind began to formulate new lines of my own poetry.

The majestic waterfall pours music from the harps of stone
The wild tumult of water ate down into the boulders and laid open
the mountain
Rushing falls tumble amid confusion of granite rocks in this
great geological drama...

My rumbling stomach woke me and reminded me to nourish my body after the strenuous hike. I sat by the water's edge and enjoyed a sandwich and an apple. Food always tasted better in the open air of nature.

My blissful moment ended with a jolt. No map! I had lost my map and now had to find my way back without guidance. Would Dad help me? I looked at my pack. By golly, I did have his compass.

I followed the zigzagging trail up the steep side of the waterfall and stopped at a flat spot to measure the sun again. I guessed it was around four o'clock. Without my map, I had to keep better track of the time in order to make it back to camp before darkness held me captive in the forest. With caution, I descended. I found it frustrating to be looking down at my feet to avoid falling, which prevented me from catching good photographs.

At last, I reached level ground and walked toward a meadow. A calm hush filled the air as I walked farther away from the roaring falls. I laid my weary body down on a bed of soft grass, stretched my arms and legs, then closed my eyes, enjoying the ambiance of the gospel of nature.

The sun told me that it was getting late. I didn't want to be caught in the dark or have another possible bear encounter, so I stood up, brushed myself off, grabbed my bag, and headed back into the trees before darkness swallowed me up and I lost my way. I came upon a stream and began to follow it. I thought that the trees surrounding me must be hemlocks, as they always grew near springs. Beetles skittered on the surface of the water, which was clear enough to drink. I knelt and looked closer, and spied a crayfish where delicate ferns grew on the banks. The woodpeckers that had tapped all morning were silent, allowing for the deafening sound of the whippoorwills.

I recalled Mother telling my brother and me to look all around when in the middle of nature, to soak in the beauty of where we were. She told us not to focus on one part only to miss something else. Dad would add that we should use all of our senses, and to be aware of our surroundings for beauty as well as safety.

I entered a part of the woods that began to look familiar. Maybe it was where the bear had been. I held my compass flat in my palm out in front of my chest. The magnetic needle didn't swing off to the side, so I knew I was facing north. I turned the degree dial until the orienting arrow lined up with the magnetic arrow and pointed them both. The travel arrow settled between the N and the E. *Aha, I am northeast, good,* I thought. Even though it was getting late, at least I was headed in the right direction and had a lantern. I stayed on the trail that followed the creek.

A sudden rustle in the bushes caught my attention, followed by an unmistakable buzzing sound. I had disturbed a large coiled snake beside a fallen tree. Yikes! It was definitely a rattler, not a puffer snake. I stood still, staring at its seven rattles and its smooth, pear-shaped button tip shaking in the air. The segmented rattles continued to vibrate together, producing an unnerving sound. The large, venomous snake had light-yellow and rust-colored coils with brown-and-black jagged chevron-patterned bands. It was piled so high it must have been four feet long. I remained frozen in my tracks as I stared at it.

Suddenly, the timber rattler's body swelled up and its vertical, cat-like pupils hypnotized me. The snake's wide, triangular head kept rising higher and higher in the air, ready to strike. I was mesmerized by the terrifying hissing sound as its flicking, forked tongue darted back and forth. The sound screamed at me, *Danger, danger!*

I got my breathing under control and asked myself, *What would Jimmy do?* I reached for a stick and backed away, one cautious step at a time.

The farther I got from the rattling sound the more regretful I became. A photograph of the timber snake lunging out at me would have been fantastic to show to the campers, and I could have taught them that eastern timber rattlesnakes rarely bite humans unless provoked or threatened.

As I made my way back to camp, I began to recognize parts of the forest I had seen that morning: an unusual tree trunk, a wood thrush's nest, even the scat of a skunk near a patch of flowers told me I was walking a familiar path.

I let out a sigh of relief as I took my flashlight out and saw that I was on the path that led to my cabin. In no time, I was trotting up the porch steps and was back inside. I put my camera bag on the small table, spied some stale bread crusts, and stuffed them into my mouth. I read one of John Burroughs's nature essays about his boyhood on a family farm in the Catskills, then fell fast asleep.

On my next day off, I walked into town to get my rolls of film developed and to buy a few more. I set the small tin containers on the counter and watched as the white-haired owner with a big smile waited on a customer.

He looked at the rolls and asked, "Do you have enough money for all these to be developed?"

"How much would it cost?"

After he told me, my face flushed with astonishment. It was more money than I had. "I've always developed my own photographs. Let's just do one roll."

"Do you have a job?"

"I'm a counselor at the camp here."

"Oh, welcome to the Catskills. All the townsfolk enjoy the counselors and campers who come here. I'm Mr. Arnold, by the way."

"I'm Addie Peterson. Pleased to meet you."

"You can leave all the rolls and I'll develop them as you get the money."

I thanked him and left all the film, but did not buy any since I had a few more of Dad's rolls left.

The next week I picked up the developed photos of the falls and shared them with the shop owner.

"I couldn't help noticing when I was developing your roll that these pictures are extremely well taken. Could I print them into postcards and sell them here for you?" Mr. Arnold held up one of my photographs of the falls.

"Do you really think they're that good?" My face lit up.

"They're the best I've seen from all the film I've developed over the years. You were able to obtain brilliant shots of the sunrise and unusual angles of Kaaterskill Falls." He held up another photo. "You must have had a dangerous climb to get this one. How'd you do it?"

A blush came over my face. "I was hanging from a branch and was only able to take that one picture."

"This bear picture you took is a great action shot of it running away."

"Yes, if I hadn't been so scared I would have taken more. Do you get a lot of customers here buying postcards?" My mind ticked away, dreaming of possible ways of making money for college.

"We sure do." He pointed to a rack at the other end of the shop. "Look at all the postcards displayed over there. Your photographs are far superior."

I strolled over to the corner of the shop and studied the postcards, which were good, but I could see that mine were much more original.

On my next day off, inspired by the owner, I took more hikes into the mountains with my Leica. I took pictures at dawn and at near dusk, which made dramatic photographs with the changing light. I stayed up almost all night to get the right shot of Lake North-South.

The picture postcards came out as beautiful as the shop owner said they would. I sold a few to the campers to use to write home. They had arrived with an allowance and were happy to mail them to their parents, who then sent more money and asked for another card.

I had studied how to use the large-format camera, but felt a deep longing for my father, wishing he were still here to teach me how to use it instead of reading the manual over and over again. Nonetheless, I decided to give it a try.

It was painstaking at first to load two sheets of film blindly in the dark of my little cabin. I practiced with ordinary 4 x 5 paper, so as not to ruin expensive film, until I felt comfortable doing it by feel. One box of film contained only five sheets, and I couldn't afford to buy more just yet. I dusted the film holder with a special brush, then turned off the light and took out one sheet. The grooves on it indicated which side was the emulsion side. I opened the latch on the holder and slipped in the film, making sure the emulsion side faced out and was under the black slide of the holder. Then I latched the flap closed, turned the holder over, and repeated the process with another sheet of film. Once everything was secure, I left the dark cabin.

I focused on a young boy in camp who was concentrating on practicing tying rope knots. I adjusted the aperture, then put the film holder into the back of the Press Graflex in front of the 4 x 5 ground glass and removed the black slide, then clicked the shutter. All this effort allowed me to take only two photographs before I had to reload the film back in the cabin again. I wished that I had more than one double-plate film holder, but I didn't have the money to buy extras.

When I wasn't supervising my group of campers, I shot portraits of each individual child doing camp ·activities such as fire building, practicing swimming strokes in the lake, or making crafts.

Mr. Arnold showed me the developed prints from the Graflex. "Your large-format camera took impressive photographs of the campers and the surrounding landscape. As you can see, I enlarged this image of the girl swimming in the lake with the mountains in the background. That is a terrific camera you have there and it enlarges images to a high magnification while still retaining a fine level of detail."

"I can't thank you enough, Mr. Arnold, for developing my film and encouraging me to sell my photographs."

"I think you might have a bright future in photography. Why don't you try a few other stores in town, see if they'll sell the postcards as well?"

Soon, my picture postcards of the Catskills were sold in several of the local stores, just as Mr. Arnold predicted. Most of the campers' parents and grandparents bought photographs. As my adventurous summer came to an end, I had enough money saved to pay for an entire semester at Cornell.

Kaaterskill Falls

Chapter 7
Cornell University, 1923, Age 19

When deeds speak, words are nothing.
— Joseph Proudhon

"Try to find a nice beau at college who will help support you, dear." Mother touched my arm as I packed for my first semester at Cornell University.

"We'll see, Mom. Don't worry about me too much. I'm glad that Jimmy can send you money from his job." I could tell she was adjusting to being a widow because we had shared fond memories of Dad the previous night.

"And don't forget to write."

"Of course I will write." I forced myself to express affection. "I love you..."

She looked away as my sentence dangled in midair, then gave me an awkward hug and hurried to the kitchen.

It was a four-hour bus journey from Long Island to upstate Ithaca, New York. The lush green trees and winding road gave my imagination time to fly away. I had a whole week before the semester started to explore the large campus.

I went straight to my dorm room once I arrived on campus. As I placed my two bags inside, I saw a few fancy flapper dresses strewn on the bed next to mine and wondered what my new roommate would be like. But I didn't linger. I couldn't wait to get outside to explore. I strolled around the campus, gazing at the old ivy-covered buildings and towers. The variety of architecture inspired me to use my camera.

After a few hours of snapping pictures, I returned to my dorm room, where I found a tall, stylish gal with a full bosom.

"Name's Dolly, where do you hail from?" she said.

"I'm Addie, from Long Island. Are you from Boston?" I

admired her sleek haircut, flapper dress, and heels.

"Guess my accent gave me away. Nice camera you have there."

"Thanks. I got it from my dad." I looked down at the bed to cover up the sadness that descended over me as I thought of him.

The next day I searched the job boards. There were cafeteria and waitress jobs, as well as work in the library, but they were all stamped "filled." I tried not to feel discouraged, but I knew I would need money for the next semester. I barely had enough to live on right now. I would have to rely on my skills as a photographer and hoped I could sell my pictures on campus, like I had at camp.

The southern shore of Cayuga Lake was part of the campus and I wasted no time visiting it. I felt the cool water with my fingertips and pushed my worries aside. The sparkling, long Finger Lake with steep-walled valleys gave me hope of creating a unique series of photographs. I could shoot it in a variety of light, from dusk to dawn. I hoped the photography course I had enrolled in would teach me new techniques. With a blissful sigh, I dreamed on while looking out toward the many acres of forest that surrounded the lake.

On my way back to my dormitory, I stopped at a quaint streetlight with a sign at the base. It read that this was the first place in North America with outdoor electric lighting. I snapped a shot of the lamppost, dated 1922 — just last year.

My first class was English. My professor, Mr. Roberts, with his blond hair and fashionable spectacles, was a dream to look at. I was mesmerized by his deep, melodious voice. It was so similar to my dad's that it startled me at first. Later that week, I submitted an essay about the Catskill Mountains and attached one of my photographs of the waterfalls.

Just before the class ended, Mr. Roberts said, "Miss Peterson, please stay after class to discuss your essay."

Shocked and slightly worried, I kept my trembling hands busy reorganizing my books as I waited for everyone to leave. I wondered...was there something wrong with my paper?

Mr. Roberts came over to my desk with my essay. I could smell the scent of soap on his body.

"Miss Peterson, I'm impressed by your writing and this photograph is full of movement. Where did you get it?" He held up the essay and photograph.

"I took it myself."

"You've been to the Catskills?"

"Yes, I was a camp counselor there."

"I own a cabin in the Catskills. This is the Kaaterskill Waterfalls, isn't it?"

"Yes," squeaked out of my mouth.

Mr. Roberts placed my paper in front of me. "As you can see, I gave you an A. Adding this photograph was a nice touch." His eyes locked on mine. "Is this your only copy of the falls?"

"No, I have many postcards of it."

"May I keep this one? My mother would love to have it framed and hung on her living room wall."

I nodded. He took the photo, then returned to his desk to grade papers. I grabbed my books and left. As I walked out the classroom door, I could feel his eyes on me.

From that point on, every English class was exciting. Mr. Roberts called on me for most of the answers to his questions during his lectures. The following month, he asked me to stay after class once again. I stood at his desk, clutching my books tightly to my chest.

"Miss Peterson, I must confess, you're the smartest pupil I've ever taught."

"Oh..." stumbled out of my mouth.

"How are your other classes coming along?"

"Fine. I'm taking Mr. Williams's photography course." I wondered where this conversation was headed.

"Perhaps we could go to the campus play together. There's a comedy that has received excellent reviews."

Little beads of sweat appeared above my lip as I bit it. A warm sensation spread all over my body as he stood up and leaned toward me.

"I...I would like that," I stammered.

"Good. What dormitory are you in? I'll pick you up outside on Saturday night at seven."

After telling him my dorm number, I hurried out the door, full of electric energy.

That night, distractions filled my thoughts and I was unable to focus on my studies. Was this a date? No, it couldn't be a date. Mr. Roberts was much older than I was. I decided it wasn't possible. I must have misinterpreted his offer. Or did I? I didn't know what to think.

Whether it was a date or not, I had very little suitable clothing to wear to the play, so I went into town to buy a new blouse despite my limited funds. The walk down East Hill into town afforded me the opportunity to take a few good photographs. At one point, I stopped to get a shot of the campus from the bottom of the hill, looking up.

The Platt & Colt Pharmacy was the only place where I could buy and develop film. I went inside to delay the difficult decision of spending money on a blouse. While I waited for the clerk, I noticed many college students enjoying bowls of vanilla ice cream with red syrup and a cherry on top. A large sign above the counter read *Cherry Sundae, Our Specialty.*

After the owner took my film, I splurged and ordered the ice cream. A waitress with a bright smile placed the elegant treat in front of me. The smooth vanilla ice cream smothered in bright-red syrup was a joy to look at. At the peak of the ice cream mountain was a cherry. It wasn't an ordinary cherry, but a candied one with its stem attached. I was just about to pluck it off when I realized this would be a delightful photograph. I stood a distance away from it, focused, and shot two pictures, then followed with a few close-ups.

The owner of the pharmacy approached me. "What kind of camera do you have there? I've never seen that type before."

"It's a prototype called a Leica. It was given to my father by the company, to try it out."

The owner looked the camera over. "After you have the film developed of the sundae, I'd like to see the photos. If they're any

47

good, it would enhance my sign and I'll buy one from you. Would you be interested?"

With enthusiasm, I agreed, then sat back and savored my ice cream, happy about my good fortune. Selling a photograph of the sundae would help compensate the cost of my wasteful purchase of an outfit.

In a small shop down the street, I was able to find an inexpensive blouse. It was cheap because it was a girl's blouse, which suited me just fine since I was under-endowed anyway. The saleslady gave me a surprised look when she saw the size as she wrapped it up in a box. I ignored her and couldn't wait to wear the new, fanciful paisley pattern.

I tried on a fashionable bob hat, just like the one Dolly wore, and pushed my wayward, dull-brown hair underneath it. But I knew it was not within my meager budget to purchase it. Besides, I didn't have the latest bob haircut like many of the girls on campus did, including my rich roommate from Boston.

After a quick dinner in the cafeteria, I went back to my room to get ready for the evening ahead. My roommate had left already, leaving the faint smell of her perfume. I looked at her desk and saw that it was Chanel No. 5. I gasped, knowing how expensive it was.

The new blouse gave me the confidence I needed as I waited outside for Mr. Roberts. He arrived on time, complimented me, and held my elbow as he escorted me to the play. His light touch added to my excitement of the evening ahead.

The play was like being placed in another person's private world. We both laughed along with the audience as the story unfolded. *Wedding Bells* was a comedy about a divorced wife who turned up just as her ex-husband was about to marry someone else, then made him fall in love with her all over again.

I caught Mr. Roberts watching me several times during the performance. I shifted in my seat and thought maybe this was a date after all.

On the walk back to my dorm, my teacher guided me by touching my arm once again, which produced sparks of electricity within me. A few classmates stared at us as we strolled past them.

"Adeline, I enjoyed watching your beautiful eyes crinkle when you laughed during the play," Mr. Roberts said quietly.

"Thank you, Mr. Roberts." I felt the color rising in my cheeks.

"Please, call me Martin and I will call you Adeline."

"My friends call me Addie."

"But I want to be more than your friend, Adeline."

My heart fluttered as his romantic words soared within me.

At the dorm, I thanked Martin. He reached out and gave my hand a squeeze.

"See you in class," he smiled.

Dolly came in late, smelling of alcohol. She threw her hat on the bed. "I saw you with that teacher. Did he kiss you?"

"No, I don't even think it was a date."

"Oh, horse feathers! It was a date all right. I noticed the way he looked at you during the play."

That night, I tossed and turned, going in and out of dreams about Mr. Roberts, who repeated over and over, *I want to be more than your friend...*

Chapter 8
The Falls

Work is something you can count on, a trusted, lifelong friend who never deserts you.

— Margaret Bourke-White

The following Sunday was perfect weather for photographing parts of the campus. Tired from waking just before dawn, I settled down by the lakeshore and read a letter from Mother after shooting a series of photographs in the changing light.

Dearest Addie,
I hope this letter finds you working hard on your studies. I have been busy canning some late tomatoes. How is your money holding out? I was happy to read that you sold a photograph to the ice cream shop owner. At least that's a little bit of income. Your brother Jimmy is doing quite well in college and is apprenticing with a well-respected veterinarian. Don't forget to write.
I miss you both,
Love, Mother

The letter made me a bit teary-eyed, but I loved the independence of being away from her constant control over my life and enjoyed my newfound freedom at college.

The rest of the morning I experimented with shots of the rising sun over Lake Cayuga. I tried a few techniques I had learned in class, like shooting out of focus by blurring the camera filter with petroleum jelly. On the hike back to my room, I thought about Mr. Roberts — or rather, Martin. I loved to watch him during class in his crisp, cuffed trousers and his variety of bow ties.

A few days later, I lingered after English class. Martin came up to me with a warm, flirtatious smile. "Let's go to the gorges tomorrow. It's not supposed to rain. I want to show you Triphammer Falls."

"That would be lovely. I've been wanting to photograph the waterfalls."

We started out early the next day. Our hike started at the intersection of University and East Ave., where the trailhead of the north rim was located.

"There are over 100 majestic waterfalls near our campus, but this one's indeed the centerpiece of Cornell and it's my favorite." Martin glowed with enthusiasm.

Even though he didn't vary the tone of his voice much, I enjoyed how he sprinkled delightful adjectives throughout our conversation. I remained quiet while listening to him and took the opportunity to concentrate on my skills as a photographer while we walked.

The view of Triphammer Falls from the East Avenue Bridge was astounding. Small cascades dropped into the thunderous water, which fell hundreds of feet. My hands trembled as I shot a few dramatic pictures.

"See that stone structure within Triphammer Falls?" Martin pointed far below us.

"I was wondering what that was." I leaned over and took a shot of it.

"That's the hydraulics lab. The engineering students use it to study water purification."

"It looks so unusual in this natural beauty."

"Yes, it was specifically crafted in stone to blend into the environment. The total drop of Triphammer Falls is over eighty feet. The freezing and thawing of the shale is how the gorge walls were formed. It's quite a marvel, don't you think?"

I nodded as Martin gazed into my eyes. I stopped shooting for a moment and stared back at him.

We proceeded to hike up the gorge to the upper drop. The foamy white water dressed the smooth rocks. I took a picture, but when Martin frowned, I put my camera away. He held my face in his hands. I closed my eyes, feeling the crescendo of the water as it fell. My first kiss was a dream—more than I had ever imagined it would be. A warm, tingling sensation spread through my body as I melted into Martin's deep brown eyes.

We continued our adventure. As we crossed over the long wooden footbridge, Martin shouted over the thundering of the falls, "Be careful, darling. I wouldn't want to lose you now."

Startled by the word "darling," I smiled as he held my hand. My fingers itched to get out my camera to capture the last of the falls before returning to the campus, but Martin grasped my hand tighter.

"Adeline, the pictures you showed me of the Catskills were extremely professional. My mother loves the one you gave me of Kaaterskill Falls. I hung it on the living room wall for her."

My heart raced and I murmured, "Thank you."

"You're quite a catch." He kissed me again.

My photography class lecture was about a new style called Pictorialism, where the photographer manipulated a typical scene to create an image. It was not just a simple recording of an event. The professor gave us the assignment to change the scene of a subject to make it more artistic. He suggested using a soft-focus lens rather than a sharp one.

"Keep in mind, class, when you are shooting, think like an artist...in brush strokes, not like the simple recording of a portrait photographer. Ask yourself, at a single glance, does your photograph express emotion? I want you all to go beyond ordinary picture taking."

Mr. Williams had a style of lecturing that was filled with infectious passion.

I raised my hand. "Does it have to be on campus?"

"I'm glad you asked that question. For comparison purposes, let's keep the assignment restricted to the college. Go out into our little world here and manipulate the scene, and bring me back emotion. Our campus here is a wonderland for photography."

The bell rang and we all left with a chatter-filled fervor.

After English class, Martin asked me to go to the picture show with him on Saturday. I was anxious to complete my photography assignment and asked him if we could go on Sunday instead. He demanded to see me on Saturday, and even pounded his fist on the desk, which startled me a bit. Annoyed, I became stubborn, insisting that I had a lot of studying to do. He avoided looking at me for a moment, then finally agreed on Sunday.

That weekend, I set out with my camera equipment to look at the campus with a fresh eye. I borrowed a tripod from my photography class and several film holders for my Graflex. I loaded them with film ahead of time, in the campus darkroom. Luckily, I was able to use the darkroom to develop my own film, which saved me money.

I reviewed what my teacher had said: Take a photograph good enough to be put in a museum, like a piece of art. Create an image with a soul rather than just a recording of an event.

A few feet away, a crowd surrounded a student dressed in his Sunday best. He stood behind the pedestal of an ornate fountain with a single sparrow bathing in it. The young man lectured in a loud, deep, emotional voice to the audience.

"It has been four years now since the Volstead Act passed. The saloons have been successfully eliminated, but now we must enforce the closure of the multitude of hidden speakeasies." His hands were full of expression. "The government must provide more police and federal agents."

"What's going on here?" I whispered to a young woman in a burgundy hat.

"Oh, just the usual show of a practicing orator. We call this the philosophy fountain. Sometimes the speech is uplifting and other times it's boring. This one's quite grand. He's in favor of enforcing the abolition of alcohol."

The orator's large, strong stature was captivating as he slapped his fist on the fountain and continued his lecture. "Alcohol ruins families. Fathers are found drunk in the gutter or handle dangerous machinery in factories while intoxicated. It is unpatriotic to drink. Yes, since the passage of the bill, there are fewer men and women dying of alcoholic diseases, but now there are gun-toting gangsters bribing our police. Homemade moonshine is being produced, continuing this evil habit."

A few students were carrying homemade signs. I took a few photographs of them.

The "dries" had signs that read:

ALCOHOL POISONS THE BODY AND THE SOUL!
ALCOHOL IS GOD'S ENEMY!
MONEY SPENT ON BOOZE CANNOT BUY SHOES!

On the opposing side, the "wets," had signs that read:

REPEAL THE VOLSTEAD ACT!
GOVERNMENT: IT'S NONE OF YOUR BUSINESS WHAT I DRINK!

As soon as the orator finished, a huge group of women marched by with a banner identifying them as the Women's Temperance Society. I took a few close-up shots of the speaker. Mr. Williams's assignment went through my thoughts. I wondered, *How can I manipulate this scene to make it more exciting?* The cafeteria was nearby. I ran to it and rummaged through the garbage in the back of the building and found a loaf of stale bread.

The stately man was still revving up, even though the crowd had dissipated somewhat. I broke up the loaf and scattered the crumbs in and around the fountain. Just as I had hoped, more birds arrived on the scene.

The student reached his arms toward the sky, proclaiming, "Enforcement of the law must occur — not a repeal!"

At the same time, sparrows dove down to eat the bread in the fountain. I took one careful shot with my Graflex, which was screwed onto the borrowed tripod. It was a divine shot and I felt satisfied that I had enhanced the scene.

After I had taken a sufficient number of photographs, I went to the class lab and developed the film. *Martin will love seeing these pieces of art tomorrow after our date,* I thought as I processed the film and printed each photograph.

On Sunday, I tucked my best photographs into a book and waited outside the dorm for Martin to take me to the picture show. He never showed up.

In the school hallway the next day, a classmate asked me about a homework assignment. I felt Martin's eyes on us as he walked by and stood outside his room.

After the student left, I swallowed hard and approached him. "Mr. Roberts, uh, Martin...I waited for you yesterday..." I shifted my books in my hands.

"I had to care for my mother." He walked into his classroom and shut the door.

On my way to photography class, I wondered whether he was lying and just didn't want to see me any longer. I shook off my frustration and decided to focus on my schoolwork.

In photography class, Mr. Williams lectured about "chiaroscuro," the use of dramatic lighting and shading to convey an expressive mood in photography. I couldn't wait to try it.

After a quick dinner in the cafeteria, I went back to my room and grabbed my Leica. Dusk was a superb time to take photographs. I noticed the library tower and climbed up inside it to shoot the lake in the distance through the tower's elaborate grillwork.

English class became stressful for me that week. Martin ignored me every time I raised my hand. Frustrated, I lingered after class on Friday.

Martin looked up from his desk as I stood there. "Adeline, I'm glad you waited for me. Let's go to the dance tomorrow night." Before I could answer he said, "I'll pick you up at 7:30. Wear something nice." Without another word, he returned to grading his papers.

I left feeling happy that our relationship was renewed, but at the same time anxious about my dancing abilities.

Graflex Speed Graphic press camera

Triphammer Falls

Chapter 9
Lipstick & Perfume

Work to me is a sacred thing.
— Margaret Bourke-White

My roommate, Dolly, watched me dress for the dance while she stood there in her slip. "I wish I was your petite size, then I could lend you one of my dresses. Yours is quite out of style." As a pout formed on my face, she said, "Here, let me put some of my lipstick on you." She outlined my lips, then stood back to admire her artistry. "Now you're the bee's knees!"

"Thanks," I said. My reflection in her hand-held mirror was one of a woman rather than an awkward girl.

"Here, wrap me tight," Dolly said. "I want to look good in my new flapper dress." She handed me several strips of cloth.

"Where do I wrap you?"

"Around my breasts, silly. It's important to have a flat look in these dresses. You're lucky you're small."

I tied the cloth strips around her large bosom several times. Dolly slipped on the silky dress and it fell loosely to her calves.

"Perfect! Now I'm off to the trolley!" She laughed and put on her new ankle button-strap heels trimmed with sequins.

The decorated Christmas tree in the corner of the gymnasium was grand and its fragrance reminded me of the Catskills. All the students stared as Martin glided me across the floor. I smelled the corsage he pinned on me and felt lucky to be with him.

The band played Charleston music and I slunk down in my seat.

Martin raised his eyebrows. "Don't you do the Charleston?"

"No, I haven't learned it."

"Your roommate sure can," he said, nodding toward the dance floor.

Dolly was dancing in a fury with a dashing, fashionably dressed young man. They were so skilled at the Charleston that everyone moved to the side to let them have more room to show off.

After the dance, Martin and I walked around campus in the chilly December air. I shivered in my thin coat as Martin held me tight. The twinkling stars captivated both of us as he leaned in and kissed me.

Exhilarated from the kiss, I said, "I really like you, Martin." Then I blushed, worried I had been too bold.

"Yes, we make a fine-looking couple. You're just my size." Martin gave my cheek a peck. "Why can't you dance very well?"

I caught my breath and looked down at the path, my cheeks burning with shame. "My mother thinks it's a wasteful use of time. I've only had one lesson, from my friend Mary."

"My mother taught me to dance when I was a young boy. She's wonderful. I can't wait for you to meet her."

When we arrived at the dorm, Martin handed me his handkerchief. "Adeline, you must wipe off that lipstick or I won't kiss you."

I did as I was told and was rewarded with a long, passionate kiss that spun me into a dream state.

As Martin left, I saw him reach into his breast pocket, pull out a bottle of something, and take a drink. Mother always said that alcohol caused an unproductive life. She never allowed Dad to drink. I didn't know what to think as I walked to my room.

Dolly returned from the dance, flopped on her bed, and lifted off her dress. "Your English professor is a nifty dancer and quite a looker, even if he is short!" She took a sip from a flask on her desk.

"He's a dream." I tried to focus on the good parts of our budding relationship instead of his criticism of my dancing ability. I took off my corsage and inhaled its loveliness. "You sure can Charleston, Dolly."

"I noticed you sat out during that dance. I'd love to teach you how to do it. It's all the rage."

"That'd be fun."

As I fell asleep, I thought it would be nice to get to know my roommate more, but my relationship with Martin and my studies took up most of my time.

"Class, your photographs should show emotion at a single glance. Plain, commercial photographs are for newspapers. Yours should affect people; capture fleeting events to share with the world. It's not just a recording of visual facts. Always ask yourself, does this photograph have soul?"

After class, I put on my coat and prepared to leave.

Mr. Williams said, "Miss Peterson, please stay after class."

I looked out through the large classroom windows and thought I saw Martin walk by. Snow began to fall. Mr. Williams approached me and I focused my attention on him.

"You're a very talented young lady, Adeline." He held the orator photograph in his hand. "With your permission, I'd like to submit this one to the alumni magazine."

"Do you think it's that good?"

"It's better than good, and you might receive a handsome check. How did you manipulate this scene?"

"I threw stale bread around the fountain as the student spoke, which made all the birds arrive."

"It's one of the best photos I've seen in a long time."

"Thank you, Mr. Williams. I'd love for you to submit it. I do need the money for tuition for next semester."

"Keep up the good work. I hope you'll take my advanced class in January. You have tremendous potential in this field. I'm curious...how do you know so much about photography?"

I told him all about my father, my last sentence catching in my throat.

"He sounds like a skilled photographer who taught you well. I hope to see many of your photographs in publications in the future."

Before I knew it, the semester was almost over. I juggled getting good grades on my finals while trying to sell enough photographs to save up for tuition. With my photography teacher's help, I was able to get quite a few published in the alumni magazine, which paid well. The cover shots paid the most. I set up a stand in front of the cafeteria and sold postcards of my photographs. Jimmy had opened his veterinary practice and sent me enough money to cover the rest of my tuition. I reflected on our squabbles when we were kids and felt fortunate that my big brother and I now had a close relationship.

Martin and I began to have a whirlwind of Saturday dates throughout the spring. Dolly kept telling me I was head-over-heels in love, but I denied it.

"You've been seeing him every Saturday. Tell me, is he married?"

"No, he doesn't have a ring."

"How old is he, anyway?" she pressed.

"Well, I just found out that he's fifteen years older than me but he always tells me I'm very mature." I fiddled with my hair.

"With your difficult financial situation, you sure could use a sugar daddy." Dolly put the finishing touches on her makeup before I could protest. "Come with me to the speakeasy in town. I know the password. I'll show you how to Charleston there."

"I don't drink. It's illegal, you know."

She giggled. "Oh, Addie, you need to loosen up."

I bit one of my fingernails. "I think Martin drinks."

"You're the only one I know who doesn't. If he's not stumbling around pickled then it's no big deal."

"Aren't you worried about getting arrested?"

"It may be against the law, but it ain't enforced up here in the country, that's fer sure." Dolly laughed, using her fake Southern accent. "In this Podunk town there aren't enough feds to even enforce it. In fact, the one policeman I've seen is always at the speakeasy flirting with me. Most of the arrests happen in New York City, where masses of people just go in and pay the fine on bargain Wednesday." Dolly slapped her leg, laughing. "The way I look at it, Addie, is if *everyone's* breaking the law then it doesn't count."

With that, she left, a trail of Chanel No. 5 wafting behind her. I remained on my bed, deep in thought about what my mother and the orator had said about alcohol.

Don Quixote was at the Saturday matinee, but I wanted to see *The Hunchback of Notre Dame* instead. On our way down East Hill to the theater, Martin stopped.

"I saw the photograph in the alumni magazine of the orator." He reached for my hand. "You're so talented. I'm proud to be with you." He looked around to see if we were alone, then kissed me.

"That means a lot to me." I still felt the glow of his kiss and wanted more.

"We must hurry to make it to the show on time." Martin rushed ahead.

I almost fell asleep because I couldn't follow the storyline. Martin was mesmerized by the entire movie because he had taught the novel for years.

After the matinee, we walked to the pharmacy. I stopped and looked longingly through the window, in hopes that Martin would notice and ask me if I wanted a sundae. My tactic worked. Martin announced that we must get an ice cream.

The shop was busy after the show, and even the pharmacist was serving sundaes. He came up to our table.

"Good afternoon, Professor Roberts, nice to see you. Would you like to order an ice cream sundae?"

"We would indeed. How's business?"

"Excellent since we started serving the special sundaes. Did you see Miss Peterson's photograph?" He pointed with a smile at the photo of a sundae that had my name under it.

"Oh, I didn't notice it the last time I was here. She's a talented young lady, don't you think?" Martin patted my hand.

After dessert, we lingered under the budding crabapple tree in front of the dormitory. I rubbed one of the soft buds that would soon bloom, and looked deep into Martin's eyes as I waited for a good-bye kiss. I leaned in closer to him.

Martin stepped away. "Don't wear perfume. I will not tolerate it."

"But my roommate let me wear hers. It's Chanel No. 5 and is very expensive," I replied.

"Didn't you hear me? No perfume." He stormed away without a good-bye kiss. I saw him reach into his pocket and take a drink from a flask.

My heart sank. I went into my room with tear-filled eyes. Dolly was studying on her bed.

"How was your date?

"It was fun until Martin wouldn't kiss me because of the perfume."

"He sounds like a stick-in-the-mud to me. No perfume or lipstick? He sure is bossy. Tell me, Addie, have you done it yet?"

"It?" I choked out.

"You know, gone all the way. Sex."

"No, he's not that kind of man."

"If he's not, then he must be a nancy boy."

"What?"

"You know, maybe he likes men." She chuckled.

I turned away from her laughter and wondered about something that strange.

On a Sunday, when Martin went to church with his mother, I set up a table in front of the cafeteria to sell my photos. The orator and the many shots of the Triphammer Falls sold well. I felt aglow with the sales as well as the compliments from my peers. While I was packing up, Martin walked by. I greeted him with a big smile, but he just gave me a sharp look and kept on going.

After class the next day, I asked him why he disapproved of me selling photographs on campus.

"Adeline, I'm embarrassed that you have to peddle your photographs in public."

My eyes welled with tears. "I'm proud of my work and Mr. Williams thinks I have the potential to become a professional photographer. Besides, Martin, I have no choice. My father passed away unexpectedly right after I got accepted at this university and I have to pay for tuition somehow."

Martin kissed my cheek. Crushed and humiliated, I left the classroom and walked to my next class in a cloud of deep thought.

Flapper dress

Chapter 10
1923, Age 19

As long as I live, I'll hear waterfalls and birds and winds sing.
— John Muir

"Adeline, I want to take you to Cascadilla Falls next Saturday. Spring is the perfect season to go." Martin stroked my arm, causing a delightful shiver to go up and down my body.

"I'd love to."

"I'll pick you up early and I'll bring a picnic lunch. Dress for climbing." Martin glanced around the classroom before kissing me.

"I've been wanting to go there to…"

I didn't finish the sentence because he was back to grading papers.

"Good-bye, Martin. See you tomorrow."

On Saturday, as I dressed in my old clothes, leggings, and sturdy shoes, Dolly asked, "Another date with your handsome professor?"

"Yes, we're going to the Cascadilla Gorge."

"It's very romantic there. Great spots for some hanky-panky, if you know what I mean." Dolly winked, then handed me her lipstick. I took it with reluctance and put it on.

"Oh, Adeline, you look much better. Makes your lips look more kissable. Be careful not to get pregnant. I have some tricks to prevent that if you need to know."

A blush rose in my cheeks. "Like I said before, he's not that kind of man."

"Well, if he's not then he must be a prude," Dolly said with conviction.

I wanted to bring my large-format camera to the falls. I gathered my camera equipment, took a tripod I had borrowed from Mr. Williams, and rushed toward the door.

"Have fun. Don't do anything I wouldn't do!" Dolly called after me, then busted out laughing.

On the way out, I wiped off the lipstick on the back of my hand. Dolly sometimes reminded me of my friend Mary from high school—brash and bold, yet a good friend.

Martin arrived with a big smile and a large basket of food. Then he noticed my camera bag and tripod.

"You may not bring those." His tone was firm.

"I need to. Mr. Williams gave us an assignment to photograph one of the falls on campus."

"I will not go if you bring all that equipment. Go put it away."

When Martin saw the disappointment on my face, he softened. "How would we hold hands?"

He unlatched my fingers from the camera and held my hand as he kissed me into his spell once more. With reluctance, I returned to my room and hastily put everything away. *I can go back to the falls on Sunday to complete my homework,* I thought.

Dolly was darning one of her stockings as I returned to the room and put the tripod away. I spied my smaller Leica, and impulsively decided to hide it on a strap around my neck tucked inside my blouse.

"Back so soon?"

"Martin doesn't want me to bring my equipment."

"There's that bossiness again. Watch out or he'll start to control your life."

"Well, he did bring a picnic lunch and wants to be able to hold my hand." I hurried out before she could say another word.

As we came close to the falls, the sunlight burst through the trees. I pulled out my camera and couldn't resist taking a photo.

Martin sneered, so I stopped.

It was a strenuous hike but was well worth the climb. We stopped on a quaint stone bridge that looked down over another bridge as the water sprayed in our faces. As we got closer to the bottom, the mighty falls left delightful droplets on our skin. Martin kissed them off of my cheeks, unleashing a passion within me. I kissed him back.

"Adeline, there are more than 150 waterfalls within ten square miles around the university, and I want to explore them all with you." He kissed my hand and saw the smear of lipstick where I had wiped off my lips. "Did you have lipstick on?"

"No, Dolly just put some on the back of my hand to see how the shade would look." I turned away and pointed. "The water is eating away at the stones. It's so powerful." I retrieved my camera again.

"Look over there at the ripple marks on the rock surface," Martin said. "Just think, that used to be the muddy floor of an ancient ocean. Cascadilla Gorge formed as a result of the last Ice Age." Martin leaned over and put an arm around me, tucked the camera back inside my blouse, then pulled me closer.

"I guess we're looking at a piece of history right before us." I nuzzled into his neck.

We watched the falls carving through bedrock made of shale and sandstone. I had to get a photo, but Martin signaled me to put my camera away once again. As he embraced me, we listened to the water talk in its continuous chatter. The rushing noise became a sacred silence between us as we were transported into a dreamlike state. We both closed our eyes, listening to the sound of time going deeper and deeper into the past.

Martin whispered in my ear, "Cascadilla means 'little waterfall'...just like you.'"

We descended down the trail. I slipped on the slick pathway.

Martin grabbed me. "Hold on to my arm as we go down. I certainly don't want to lose you now. Last week a student fell more than seventy-five feet into the gorge, but escaped major injury because he landed on a large raccoon that cushioned his fall."

"Wasn't that an act of fate..." I held on to Martin tighter.

"Indeed it was."

I looked up at the clear sky and pointed, trying to count how many waterfalls there were around us.

Martin read my mind. "Eight."

"Oh Martin, thank you for bringing me to this magical place. It's a photographer's dream."

We headed toward a meadow at the bottom of the falls. I tried to be cheerful, but was upset that Martin wouldn't let me use my camera. I reassured myself that I could come back tomorrow, alone, and concentrate on photographing this paradise. Besides, I rationalized, it was too sunny out today. My teacher had instructed the class to go when it was overcast because the sun could ruin shots of the shadowy falls below.

Martin lectured, spouting fact after fact about the falls. As he held my hand, I gave him all my attention. The high sun shone brightly across the meadow. I tied my sweater around my waist.

Martin found a grassy spot and laid out a blanket, then put out a variety of food from the picnic basket, even grapes.

I popped a luscious grape into my mouth. "This is a wonderful feast. It was nice of you to prepare it all."

Martin handed me a liverwurst sandwich on rye bread. "My mother made it for us."

"I've been wanting to meet your mother."

"You will, real soon."

After a scrumptious lunch, Martin pulled me down next to him. We kissed with a hot intensity. I could tell that he wanted all of me, but he held back like the fine gentleman he was. The waterfalls played a melodious symphony in the distance.

Martin leaped up and wandered around the meadow, then returned to the blanket and presented me with a bouquet of wildflowers. "Adeline, you are very beautiful; your body as well as your mind. I want to be with you forever and watch you blossom." He knelt down on one knee. I gasped as he asked, "Will you marry me?"

Overjoyed, I whispered, "Yes."

He reached into his pocket and pulled out a ring, then slipped in on my finger. We fell to the grass in each other's arms.

After sitting up, I admired the ring, twirling it around on my finger. The sun was higher in the sky now and it was quite hot for early spring. I held the ring out in the sunlight and watched the diamond sparkle.

Martin packed up and we retraced our steps. We stopped on the bridge to listen to the crackles and pops of the small stones falling on the ever-changing shale cliffs.

Later, in front of the dormitory, Martin kissed my ring. Love glimmered in his eyes. "I had a marvelous time, Adeline. We will marry when the semester is over, then be together every day."

"Oh, yes, it will be nice to sleep by your side every night." When I saw him blush, I did too.

I rushed into my room to show Dolly my ring. She held my hand, then wiggled it off my finger to examine it.

"It's quite beautiful but it's a used ring. I can tell by the old style. And the diamond's very tiny. Maybe he was married before."

Her boldness was hard for me to swallow and I was disappointed that she wasn't as excited as I was on this momentous occasion. I grabbed it from her and put it back on my finger.

Dolly hugged me. "Congratulations, Addie. I do wish you the best of luck. When's the wedding? I'd love to be one of your bridesmaids."

My mood changed. "It'll be the weekend after school's over and I can't wait to be with Martin every single day."

"Addie, I really care about you and I know you could use a sugar daddy. Are you sure you're crazy in love with him?"

I hesitated for a moment, then with confidence said, "He's the one."

She squeezed my hand. "He's a good catch for you. I know how hard you work to pay tuition and now you won't have to."

"That's not the reason I want to get married."

"Given your circumstances, it's good enough."

Dolly went back to her studies and I twirled the ring on my finger, thinking I might wind some string on the back so it would fit tighter.

Chapter 11
The Wedding, 1923

Moving in is a bigger step than getting married.
— Joel Kinnaman

Dolly questioned me every day about the wedding plans. How many bridesmaids were there going to be? Where would I get the cake? What about the honeymoon? Every Saturday, I talked it over with Martin.

Two weeks before the wedding, Martin gave me some money to purchase a simple white dress with a high collar and buttons down the front. I had enough left over to buy a matching hat and shoes. Dolly loaned me her white silk stockings. They were embellished in the front with tiny gold-lace flowers. I ran my fingers over the elegant pattern and admired their delicate beauty.

The wedding became more stressful the closer the date came, and Martin and I constantly argued. Martin insisted on getting married in his mother's church. I wanted a simple courthouse affair, like my parents had had. The only thing we both agreed on was the honeymoon. I was overjoyed that Martin owned a cabin near the camp where I used to work. Our entire summer would be spent together in the Catskills until the new semester began.

We had a meeting with the minister, a crotchety old man who smelled of liquor. Martin explained that we had only an engagement ring, which I would wear during the ceremony. The minister nodded, but I could tell he was hard of hearing.

The big day finally arrived. Mother arrived at the church with Jimmy and his fiancée, who looked prettier than I did, even though I was the one in a wedding dress. It was a wonderful touch that Martin had decorated a few areas in the church with wildflowers he had picked. His mother wore a dark widow's dress and had a tiny white French poodle on her lap. My mother sat across the aisle, next to Jimmy's fiancée and Dolly. I could hear the girls both talking about their stylish dresses while I stood in the back.

My brother looked so handsome and mature. I felt proud as he walked me down the aisle, kissed my cheek, and gave me away to Martin. I pushed a tiny tear from my eye and thought of my father.

Martin was in a smashing, brand-new suit and bow tie. His face glowed as he looked at me.

The minister said a few wedding prayers, then looked up from his bible. "You may now present the ring."

Martin answered in a firm low voice, "We don't have one, skip that part."

The minister ignored him and repeated it, only louder this time. Mother got up, took off her wedding band, and handed it to Martin. With a red face, he slipped it on my finger above my engagement ring.

The minister smiled. "You may kiss the bride."

Martin gave me a quick kiss and rushed me out of the church into the hallway. "That damn minister," he grumbled. When he noticed my shocked look, he added, "Darling, you make a beautiful bride. I'm honored to be your husband."

"Thank you, darling," I said, trying out the word for the first time.

We had a small party in the church hall, where Martin introduced me to his mother. "Thank you for preparing these nice snacks, Mrs. Roberts." I took a bite of a heart-shaped liverwurst and rye-bread sandwich.

"Of course, my dear." She carried around her poodle, curling its fur, kissing and cooing to it.

Dolly came up to me and squeezed me tight, whispering, "Your Martin's the cat's meow. Lucky you!" She twisted her dangling pearl necklace, then adjusted her fox stole so that the tiny fox head was positioned just right on her fanciest flapper dress.

Mother gave my cheek a peck. "I'm relieved that you found a beau who will support you. Your dad would have been pleased that he's a professor." Her eyes watered as she went to get a cup of tea.

While Martin doted over his mother, Jimmy came to chat with me.

"You look beautiful, Sis. I'm sorry Dad's missing this big event in your life. How much older is Martin than you, anyway?"

I was startled at his embarrassing public statement. His fiancée giggled.

"I'm happy you came, Jimmy. Congratulations on your new practice and your pretty fiancée." I stood with a smile and went to find my husband, leaving his question unanswered.

I waited for Martin to finish pouring his mother's tea, then introduced him to everyone. I adored watching him chat and shake hands with everyone.

In no time we were on our way to our honeymoon. I felt the warm summer air rush through my fingers as I held my hand out the bus window. Martin stroked my hair. He told me how pretty I looked as I laid my head on his shoulder. Peacefulness fell on my eyelids as I fell asleep on my handsome husband's lap.

I woke up with a start when the bus driver announced, "Catskills!"

The three hours to get to the mountains had flown by.

With my white veiled hat on, I walked with Martin to a row of cabins. Martin put down our bags, unlocked the door to a cabin, swept me off my feet, and carried me inside. I felt like a princess.

He took me to the bed and slowly began to undress me, murmuring gentle adorations as he explored my body for the first time. He searched deep into my face. As he unfastened each button on my dress, he kissed my nose. I played with the waves in his blond hair. I was a bit nervous at first, trying to recall what Dolly had told me, but Martin was so gentle, I fell into a dreamlike trance. He stroked my cheek, my hair, then tenderly felt my breasts. His feather-like fingers caressed every nook of my body, sending a delightful quivering sensation through me that flitted about.

My husband carefully removed my dress and slip but threw off his clothes in a fury. I kept my eyes closed, wanting to feel and not see. Then, kissing each earlobe, he whispered, "my darling" and "my wife" over and over. When Martin stroked my thigh, I stiffened until he kissed my mouth. As he drank me in, his strong, lean, handsome body rose above mine. "Don't worry, my love, I will be gentle."

We became one.

He rolled off of me, falling like a puddle into his pillow. As he embraced me from behind, we cuddled like two spoons together, drifting into each other's dreams.

The early morning light woke me from a deep sleep. I heard a tapping on the front door. I closed my eyes, wondering if perhaps I was imagining it. Martin put on his bathrobe and shut the bedroom door behind him as he went to the door.

I put on my new lacey wedding nightgown, which Martin had surprised me with, and pulled the blankets up over me. My hand went over my mouth with surprise as I heard Mrs. Roberts's voice, then a sharp, high-pitched bark.

Martin came back into our room. He tried to kiss me as he felt the lace of my bodice.

I turned away. "Martin, why is your mother here?"

"You look ravishing this morning," he whispered in my ear.

I asked him the question again.

"She's making breakfast for us. Isn't that grand?"

"But...this is our honeymoon."

"Which is why I rented a separate cabin for her." He slid my nightgown up and nuzzled into my face.

I pulled away and curled into a tight ball, "Don't." I pretended to go back to sleep.

A short while later, Mrs. Roberts opened the bedroom door. "Breakfast is ready. The biscuits are hot out of the oven."

I pulled the sheet over my head as Martin said, "We'll be there in a minute, Mother." He turned to me as his mother closed the door. "Come on, Adeline, you'll love her cooking." He got out of bed and went to the kitchen.

I stayed in bed, deep in thought about this unexpected situation.

"I'm waiting for you, darling! The breakfast is delicious," Martin called.

I ventured out fully dressed. Mrs. Roberts set a hot plate of eggs, bacon, biscuits, and homemade jam in front of me.

"Thank you, Mrs. Roberts," I said politely.

"You're quite welcome, dear."

Martin and his mother chatted away. I kept my head down and took a few bites, but didn't have much of an appetite. The poodle kept brushing against my legs and I tried to push it away with my foot.

After breakfast, Mrs. Roberts announced, "I'll be back to make you both dinner tonight."

"No, Mother, you promised you would only come over for breakfast," Martin admonished.

She snatched up her poodle and left without a word.

I threw most of my breakfast in the trash and did the dishes, banging the pots and pans as loud as I could.

Martin stroked my arm. "Mother has agreed to leave us alone all day and night, except for breakfast." He went over to the Victrola, wound it up, and put the needle on the record. "Come dance with me."

My bad mood dissipated as Martin embraced me in a waltz.

"Adeline, your waltz has really improved." He stopped and gave me a long, sweet kiss.

Lost in our honeymoon world, we spent the rest of the day in bed, making love interspersed with food and reading Shakespeare to each other.

The next morning, we woke up the same way, with Martin's mother and her awful dog interrupting our alone time. When Mrs. Roberts opened our bedroom door and announced breakfast, I turned over and hid in my pillow.

Martin answered, "We'll be there in a moment." He tried to rub my back. After I moved away, he got up. With his robe on, he went to the kitchen and left the bedroom door wide open.

"Good morning, Mother, did you get enough sleep?" I heard

him say.

"Fair, but I do sleep better in our own cabin."

"Darling, breakfast is getting cold," Martin called.

I squeezed my eyes shut and tried to remain still, relieved when I heard Martin say to his mother, "She's not feeling well this morning."

After his mother left, I shut the bedroom door, dressed, then came to the kitchen and ate the cold meal left for me on the table. We had a heated argument. I was distraught that Martin had paid for his mother to be in the cabin right next to us. He explained to me that his mother had been very lonely since his father had passed away. Martin went into the bathroom and I heard a bottle being opened. He came back out and kissed each of my fingertips. When he reached my lips, I tasted alcohol, gagged, and turned away. Martin proceeded to kiss me up and down my neck, then scattered kisses all over my body. I became so aroused that I pulled him on top of me. It was then that I climaxed for the first time. The rest of the day, Martin spoiled me and attended to my every desire with books, dancing, food, and romance. It was heaven.

Chapter 12
Medicine and the Other Woman

Prohibition didn't work in the Garden of Eden. Adam ate the apple.

— Vicente Fox

As the weeks went by, Mrs. Roberts began staying longer and longer after she made breakfast. Martin seemed oblivious and happy to have two women giving him attention. When my mother-in-law managed to stay for lunch one day, I was furious. I grabbed a sandwich and my camera, and stormed out the door.

The mountain air cooled my hot temper as I walked to town. When I reached the pharmacy, I decided to see if my postcards were still there. I spied Mr. Arnold bustling around the store.

"Hello, Mr. Arnold, do you remember me?"

"Of course, Addie," he replied. "Your postcards are still selling. How've you been?"

"I'm well, thank you. I just got married and I'm here on my honeymoon."

"Congratulations! Are you still going to Cornell?"

"Yes. I'll be a sophomore this year and I'm taking advanced photography classes."

He reached into the cash register and gave me money for the postcards he had sold while I was away. I was elated to have my own money. I had very little left after buying things for the wedding.

"Will you be staying in the Catskills long?"

"Yes, one more month until school starts. I'd like to buy two rolls of film, please.'"

Mr. Arnold put the rolls on the counter. "Addie, make sure you take more of your fine photographs while you're here. I'll make them into postcards for you to sell. The customers love them."

After promising to do just that, I left feeling uplifted at having my own money once again, and grateful that Martin was paying my tuition. I returned to the cabin to patch up our fight.

When I walked through the door, Martin looked at me with tears in his eyes. I was overcome with desire.

"You were gone so long I was worried you had left me." He scooped me up and we consumed each other on the bed.

After dinner, Martin read me Shakespeare. His Romeo voice was perfect. He begged me to read Juliet's part. We both read with zeal, and found ourselves aroused once more.

I awoke the next morning and stretched my arms up high. I never knew my body could produce such delights. I reached over to my husband and rubbed his back. Then I heard that dreadful, dirty old dog yapping and stopped. As Martin reached over to touch me, I rose, threw on my clothes, and retreated to the corner of the room to read a book. The aroma of pancakes wafted into the room.

Mrs. Roberts opened the bedroom door without knocking and announced breakfast. I nodded and went back to reading while I bit the inside of my cheek.

Martin stretched, stood up, and put his clothes on. "Pancakes! My favorite. Come on, Adeline, let's go eat."

"I need to finish this chapter," I replied stoically.

"Well, come in soon before they get cold."

I shook my head. He just didn't get it. I gathered my thoughts as I listened to my husband and his mother chatting over breakfast. The Leica was on the bedside table. I put it around my neck, placed a roll of film in my skirt pocket, and went out to the kitchen to eat.

Mrs. Roberts was as overly polite to me as I was cool toward her. Martin volleyed the conversation between us both. The poodle kept nipping at my ankles and I continually tried to kick it away. Mrs. Roberts scooped it up and held it under her arm while serving us more pancakes.

Unable to stand it any longer, I stood up and left the table. "Good-bye and have a good day," I said in a cold tone, then slipped out as fast as I could.

The glorious hike to Kaaterskill Falls renewed my discontented spirit. I pushed all my worries away and welcomed the sights and smells of the forest I had missed during my previous trek. Hearing the melodious falls calmed and mesmerized me into tranquility. I closed my eyes to listen.

After a peaceful period of time had floated by, I was ready to experiment with my camera. My class lecture about in-focus and out-of-focus photography gave me inspiration. I tried a crisp, clear, in-focus shot of the cascading falls, then contrasted it with a series of blurry shots. I turned the focus ring to various numbers on the camera and carefully documented them on a notepad.

Hunger pains in my stomach sent me back to the cabin early. When I arrived, I was stunned to see Martin and his mother eating lunch.

Martin greeted me with a peck on my cheek. I turned away from him. After I grabbed a piece of bread from the table, I went to the bedroom, shut the door, and tried to finish my book.

A short while later, I heard Mrs. Roberts leave, then the sound of music from the Victrola. Martin danced into the bedroom and pulled me into his arms. I wanted to resist but couldn't. We waltzed around the living room. My husband was a wonderful dancer. That night was filled with lovemaking once more and my troubles were forgotten.

As the first month passed by, I tried giving Martin the silent treatment, and even withheld my body from him in a futile attempt to make him understand my frustration over his mother's presence on our honeymoon. I was concerned about getting pregnant, anyway. But no matter what I did or said, our arguments about his mother always ended the same: Martin would win me back with adoration and kisses I couldn't resist.

One night, as we snuggled in bed after our lovemaking, I found the nerve to express my concerns. "Martin, I'm worried about getting pregnant. I do need to get my degree."

"But...we're married and I expect you to have children," he replied. "I certainly can provide for a large family."

"I'm not sure I want a baby. I want to focus on my education and have a career. My teacher—"

"Darling," Martin interrupted, "we need to start a family as soon as possible. I am not getting any younger and have waited a long time to find a good wife. I don't mind paying for your college until you do get pregnant." He turned over and the subject was closed.

I found a routine to help stabilize my moodiness. I left every day after breakfast and didn't return until dinnertime. At least when I got back there was a meal made, Martin's mother was gone, and we were able to eat alone.

There were many mountains in the Catskills and I challenged myself by trying to reach the highest peak of one that was over 4,000 feet high. With my trusty camera, I tried to fabricate a few creative shots. The next day, after my breakfast obligation, I went on a short hike to finish up my last roll, then went to the pharmacy to get it developed.

Upon opening the store door, there was Martin.

"Hello, darling. How was your hike?" He had his hand on two big bottles labeled "for medicinal use only."

Mr. Arnold put the bottles in a bag. "Hello, Mrs. Roberts. I was just telling your husband what a fine photographer you are. I didn't realize you were both married to each other. What a fine match!"

Martin handed him a large amount of money for the bottles, then turned to me. "Your postcard display is wonderful," he said. "I'm very proud of you."

I tightened my lips, placed my roll of film on the counter, said good-bye to Mr. Arnold, and made a hasty exit.

Martin ran after me. "Wait up, Adeline! Tell me which mountain you went to today."

I stopped. "Martin, why do you drink? It's against the law."

"This is my medicine. It says so, right on the label."

I frowned, annoyed, but didn't know what else to say. I wondered if this was why he knew the pharmacist in the college town where my sundae photo was displayed.

Knowing that in a few short weeks the semester would begin,

I spent as much time as possible in the mountains. Mr. Arnold's encouragement led me to be daring enough to get close-ups of a few bears and a rattlesnake. The postcards continued to sell and I hid the money in a special place in my dresser.

After dinner each night, Martin and I would recite Shakespeare to each other and had fun performing our individual roles. Our delicious dessert of lovemaking followed. I looked forward to being alone with my husband back at our house in Ithaca.

When it came time to leave, we all boarded the bus together, Mrs. Roberts kissing and stroking her dog the entire time.

A thought occurred to me as we settled into a seat. I whispered to Martin, "Does your mother live near you?"

"Yes. Shhh...she's sleeping now."

We arrived in Ithaca and Martin helped his mother off the bus. He carried her bags and I was left with ours. I followed behind the dog, who sniffed everything in sight, including up my skirt. We stopped in front of a grand old house and Martin searched his pocket for the keys. The house was much larger than my childhood home. The black shutters contrasted with the bright-white wood and tall columns.

Mrs. Roberts announced, "Isn't it nice to be back in our own home again?"

Our? I suppressed a gasp as we stepped inside. How naïve of me! Of course, they lived together in the same house! And there on the living room wall was my photograph of the orator.

That night Martin and I had a loud argument about our living arrangements.

I kept saying, "You never told me we would be living with your mother!"

And Martin said, "Mother has never recovered from the death of my father and I promised I would take care of her." He touched my shoulder.

I turned away from his affection, anger steaming out of my pores.

The next day, after Martin left to set up his classroom, I was left alone with his mother. I could tell by the look on her face that she had heard our entire fight the night before.

"As you know, Adeline, Martin's father passed away a short time ago. I got Poochy to soothe my loneliness, but I still depend on my son for comfort. Martin is all I have now and I will not give him up." She placed her hands on her hips and glared at me.

I left the kitchen, stomped into the bedroom, and locked the door.

That night in bed, I asked my husband, "When did your father pass away?"

"A few years ago. Pneumonia."

Years? I thought, stunned.

Martin saw my shocked face and added, "Like I said before, Mother has never fully recovered from her loss."

I could barely contain my anger. "The way your mother talks about him, I thought he had died recently!" I shouted.

"Lower your voice, Adeline. I don't want her to hear."

I curled up tight and pretended to sleep.

Martin got up went into the bathroom. I heard a bottle open and liquid being poured into a glass. A short time later, I was relieved to hear him snoring and knew he wouldn't bother me.

To cope with living with my mother-in-law, I left early every day and stayed at college until right before dinner. The developing lab at school became my safe haven.

On Sunday, when Martin and his mother went to church, I met up with my old roommate, Dolly, at the pharmacy.

"How's married life with that handsome professor of yours?" Dolly asked as she sipped her tea.

We ordered a piece of pie to share.

"It has its ups and downs." I examined the trim on the tablecloth.

"What's the matter? You can tell me." Dolly reached over and touched my hand.

"I didn't know we would be living with his mother."

"Oh my, that doesn't give you much alone time." She raised an eyebrow.

"That's the problem. I do love him. He's very affectionate and we read Shakespeare to each other in bed. I just wish we lived by ourselves."

"What's his mother like?"

"She dotes over Martin and her nasty dog. I'm sure she doesn't like me." I looked over at my photograph of the sundae to cheer myself up.

"Well, Addie, she's a widow and I think you're stuck with her." Dolly leaned in and whispered, "Tell me, how's he in bed?"

I blushed. "I wanted to ask you about something."

"Ask away. You know me. I'm not shy about anything."

"I'm worried about getting pregnant. I want to get my college degree," I said in a low voice.

"What does your husband want?"

"I think he wants me to have babies, and a lot of them, as soon as possible...because of his age."

"Do you want children?"

"I'm not sure. I know I want to graduate and have a photography career. My teacher told me I was the best student he's ever had."

"I see the pickle you're in. Well, I have some condoms."

"Some what?"

"You know, rubber condoms. Let's go back to my room and I'll give you some. They will do the trick to prevent babies from coming."

We strolled back to the dorm room. Dolly opened a drawer and showed me a small rectangular tin with a risqué-looking lady on the front. She explained how the condoms were used, which made my cheeks turn color. But I took them nonetheless.

I put them in my pocketbook and closed the clasp. "Thank you, Dolly. I sure appreciate having a friend like you." I kissed her cheek.

"Anytime, Addie. I'm glad to help. Let's get together again soon."

On the walk back to the house, I wondered if Martin would agree to use the condoms. I doubted he would.

Whiskey prescription cards

Chapter 13
A New Career
Summer/Fall of 1926

*One of the most courageous things you can do is identify yourself,
know who you are, and what you believe in and where you want to
go.*

— Sheila Murray Bethel

Month after month, I continued my routine of leaving early
and coming home late during the week. On Sundays, I spent
time with Dolly while Martin and his mother were at church.

In the spring of my senior year, Mr. Williams arranged an
interview with a Cornell alumnus who worked for the firm
Dowler, Gilman and Associates, an architectural firm. I was able
to sneak away to New York City by telling Martin that my mother
was ailing.

After my husband left for class, I reorganized the portfolio that
my teacher had helped me prepare. When Mrs. Roberts went to
walk her dog, I went to the back yard and dug up my secret can of
money. On the way to the bus stop, I bought blue gloves, and a
matching pocketbook and hat to compensate for the plainness of
my dress. The long bus ride gave me time to rehearse possible
answers to any questions I might be asked during the interview.

The skyscrapers in the compact city drew my eyes upward to
find a piece of the sky. I had only been to the huge city once, as a
young child with my family, to visit the Museum of Natural
History.

Outside the firm's building, I had trouble navigating the
revolving door. Once inside, I couldn't figure out which elevator
to take, as there was an entire row of them. One stopped and
everyone rushed in while I stood there like a statue. I managed to
get on the next one, which was less crowded.

I found the waiting room of the architectural firm and sat pulling one glove off and on, off and on, as I looked around nervously.

A well-dressed secretary announced, "Mr. Dowler will see you now, Mrs. Roberts."

Mr. Dowler's office had tall ceilings with polished, dark wood walls. The view of the city from his expansive window was magnificent. Ornately framed photographs adorned the room. Mr. Dowler's diploma from Cornell took center stage. Next to it was a framed cover of the alumni magazine with my photograph of the Cayuga River on the cover.

"Excellent photograph, Mrs. Roberts, and very artistic. Tell me how you created this." Mr. Dowler tapped the picture of the river and straightened his expensive-looking tie.

"Thank you." I relaxed my tight grip on my portfolio and explained that picture of the lake was a view through the campus library's tower grille.

His eyes lit up. "Please...show me your portfolio."

With great pride, I handed it to him. Mr. Dowler savored each page, lingering on the orator and the bridge at Triphammer Falls.

"Our firm has been needing to hire a photographer for some time now, but I always envisioned it would be a man. There are very few architectural photographers, male or female. Your work is exceptional and it touches my heart to hire someone from my alma mater. With this booming economy, we've had many new buildings erected and we need publicity to rent them. When can you begin working?"

"I guess right after graduation."

"Congratulations, Mrs. Roberts. We'll start you off with a low salary until you are able to prove your worth, but with your talent, it shouldn't take too long for you to get a proper raise." He reached across the desk and gently shook my hand.

After graduation, while Martin was in his classroom closing it up for the summer, I dug up my mason jar, packed up my meager belongings, and moved out. Mrs. Roberts was out walking the dog, as usual. I wrote a short letter and put it under Martin's pillow so his mother wouldn't find it. I twisted off my rings and included them in the envelope.

Dear Martin,
I got a job as a professional photographer with an architectural firm. I am leaving you. Thank you for all you have done for me, but I need to be on my own now and begin my career.
Adeline

The four-hour bus ride to New York City was just what I needed to calm my jitters. The warm summer air and country roads soothed my apprehension over ending my marriage. I felt inspired to begin a new life...alone.

After spending all day trying to find an apartment in the huge city, I noticed in the newspaper that rents were far cheaper and apartments more available in Brooklyn. I found a suitable, tiny place across the East River in Brooklyn Heights. It was called a studio, and had no living room. I was lucky it was furnished with a bed in the middle of the room and a desk with a lamp on it. The bathroom had a tub and would work perfectly for a darkroom.

I tossed and turned all night long on the small, single bed. I was used to Martin's rhythmic snoring to lull me asleep. Early the next morning, tired but excited, I left my studio to catch the trolley to the subway, then commuted into Manhattan.

With my camera slung over my shoulder by a leather strap inside my coat, I got off at Sixth Avenue, looked up at a large clock on one of the old buildings, and decided I had time to eat breakfast before going to the office.

A corner building displayed the sign that read *Horn & Hardart* and underneath it was written *Automat*. I looked through the huge windows and saw people eating inside, so I decided to investigate. I sat at a small table and waited for a waitress. When none showed up, I decided to discreetly watch how everyone got their food.

A businessman walked past me and went to the far right corner of the room, where a lady sat in a glass booth. He pushed a dollar bill under her window and she gave him change, all in nickels. The man then went to the side of the restaurant where there was an entire wall of tiny glass doors, row upon row of them, surrounded by marble. He proceeded to get a tray and slid it along metal rails in front of the glass doors, pausing frequently to look into the window compartments. I watched him put a nickel in a slot next to one of the windows, turn a tiny porcelain knob, then lift the window. He pulled out a plate of steaming scrambled eggs. I was mesmerized and decided to try it myself.

The choices were overwhelming. There were many different types of food within the compartments. I found a nickel in my pocketbook and chose a fancy-looking muffin. As soon as I put it on my tray, a worker behind the wall refilled the empty chamber.

A high-fashioned lady next to me put a nickel in a slot and got out an empty coffee cup. She took it to a table where there was a large silver urn. I copied her, got a cup, and poured coffee into it by turning a silver dolphin spigot on the urn.

After sitting down again and enjoying my hot coffee and muffin, I looked at the huge clock with the restaurant's name on it and knew I had better scramble. I was on Sixth Avenue and had to walk the long city blocks all the way to Thirteenth. Would I be late on my first day? I gulped down the rest of my coffee, then walked as fast as I could in my heels through crowds of people. I felt like a country mouse as I looked at what everyone else was wearing. I would need more money before I could buy similar fashionable clothes and shoes, like all the women around me wore.

The revolving doors to the old gargoyle-laden office building were hard for me to negotiate during morning rush hour. All four doors revolved at the same time, rotating in a counter-clockwise direction. I checked to make sure my camera was securely inside my blouse so it wouldn't get damaged if it knocked into anything. Filled with apprehension, I waited on the crowded sidewalk and watched to see how people entered the doors together.

An older gentleman in the crowd came up to me. "Can I help you in, miss?" he asked kindly.

"Thank you. I did this once before, but not with this many people."

We stood together and watched, then he shouted, "Go now!

Don't forget, push hard!"

We slid into the cylindrical enclosure. He held my elbow from behind. Relief washed over my face as I skidded out on the other side and waited in front of the many elevators for one to open.

The nice man, still behind me, asked, "What floor?"

"Sixteen, thank you."

"That's my floor. Are you the new photographer?"

"Yes."

"Glad to meet you. I'm one of the partners, Mr. Gilman."

"Adeline Roberts."

We shook hands, then got on the elevator together.

Mr. Gilman turned to the operator and said, "Sixteenth," then whispered to me, "I was surprised the firm hired a girl, but Jim said you were extremely well qualified."

"Thanks for helping me get into the building. I think I know how to negotiate the doors now," I said, trying to sound professional.

When we got out on the sixteenth floor, Mr. Gilman said, "Revolving doors are an amazing invention. They prevent drafts and allow large numbers of people to pass in and out. You must be from the country."

"Yes, Ithaca. But I do find the doors architecturally fascinating."

"They do the job well and I read in the news that in all the years revolving doors have been around, there's only been one fatality."

"Oh my," I said a little too loud, not sure whether he was kidding or not.

Chapter 14
1926-1927 — A New Life and a New Look

When one door of happiness closes, another opens, but often we look so long at the closed door that we do not see the one which has been opened for us.

— Helen Keller

My first assignment was to photograph a new office building the firm had just built. The work site was a mess. The building was bright and new, but the grounds were wet and muddy, and littered with unused lumber, gravel, and leftover trash from the workmen. My heels sank into the mud as I walked around the site. I struggled to pull them out as I moved to drier ground.

I took a shot with my Graflex, then paused as a lecture by Mr. Williams floated into my head. "Manipulate or change the environment," he had said. As I reflected on the picture I had taken of the orator, I was struck with an idea. I removed my gloves and tucked them into my coat pocket, then took a few more photographs and left. During the commute home, I began to formulate a plan. Exhausted from my first day at my new job, I slept a little better that night in my tiny bed.

The next morning, I bought a newspaper and went to the automat for breakfast. Following the same routine as the day before seemed to comfort me as I adjusted to this large city. On my way to the work site, I found a florist shop and purchased a few bouquets of flowers. At the new building, I placed the bouquets here and there to hide the rubble and to create an attractive flowerbed at the entrance.

I hiked up to the rooftop in my skirt and hoped no one would notice. I tried a long-focus effect, then experimented with blurred and in-focus photographs. The flowers made the building look much more inviting and added just the right amount of color. I had to climb to an adjacent building's roof to get a better shot, but it was worth it.

The following day, I woke early and took the subway, in the dark, back to the building. When I arrived, the shadows from the overcast sky had disappeared and the sun illuminated the site. It was the perfect, majestic lighting—just what I had hoped for. I clicked shot after shot, anxious to see how the photographs would turn out.

On my way home, I ran across a photography shop as I wandered around Brooklyn. The owner was a good-looking, knowledgeable man who introduced himself as Mr. Smith. He happily took my film to develop it. I bought a few film packs and two film plate holders. I asked to see the developing supplies and equipment, but my funds were limited and I didn't have enough money to purchase anything. The owner asked me if I wanted to buy it now and pay for it later since I had a job. After a surprised look came over my face, Mr. Smith pointed to a sign that read:

BUY NOW! PAY LATER!
BUY ON CREDIT
CONSUMERS, HAVE IT ALL! WHY WAIT?
ASK ABOUT OUR INSTALLMENT PLAN TODAY!

Mr. Smith explained the installment plan to me; how, with only a few low payments each week, I could take the developing equipment home today. His enthusiasm almost encouraged me to do it, but I heard my mother's voice in my head: *"Never buy more than you need and never buy anything on credit."* I remembered her sorrow after Dad's poor investments, leaving Jimmy to support her. So, I thanked the shop owner for his time and left.

The next week, Mr. Dowler beamed at me after I showed him the photographs from my first assignment.

"Very clever, putting flowers out," he said, nodding his approval. He looked at my simple dress and handed me a check. "This includes an advance, Mrs. Roberts. Please buy yourself some new clothes."

My cheeks flushed with embarrassment, but at the same time, I was happy to receive the bonus. He handed me the addresses of more buildings to photograph.

On the weekend, I wrote a brief letter to my mother about my job in New York City and my failed marriage. My hands quivered as I applied the stamp and mailed it. I wondered what she would think of me, being a single woman with a job, supporting myself without the help of a man.

With my first check, I bought developing equipment and several film holders. Developing my own film would really save me money. I found a nice suit with a matching hat and gloves, then went to a men's store to get trousers made for boys and had them tailored. After purchasing a pair of sturdy Oxfords, I felt confident that I now had the proper attire to climb buildings.

On my way home amid the crowds of city people, I thought I saw Martin coming toward me. Not knowing what else to do, I hid behind a mailbox and watched him go by...but the man was too short. It was his spectacles that made me think he was my husband. That night in my small, hard bed, I had a nightmare about Martin and his mother screaming at me. After a glass of warm milk calmed me down, I wondered whether I had made a mistake. *Maybe I should go back to my marriage and try to be a good wife,* I thought. I did miss him at night when I was alone. I cried myself back to sleep as I thought about his passionate reading voice and the way he held me when we danced.

In the morning on the trolley, I shook those thoughts away, remembering the reasons why I had left Martin; his drinking, his mother, and most of all, the fact that I was not ready to have his children. Keeping busy was the key to my anxiety over being alone. I slept better when I put in long hours shooting photos and developing them in my bathroom darkroom.

On Saturday, I splurged and bought the August copy of *The Evening Post* at a newsstand. I read a short story by F. Scott Fitzgerald, "Bernice Bobs Her Hair," while enjoying the lunch special at a small restaurant. The tale depicted a sweet but dull young lady who submitted to the barber's shears and was transformed into a smooth-talking, high-society girl. The story gave me an idea and the courage to take the plunge. My hair took a long time to grow long enough in order to fashion it into a bun. I liked the idea of having a short haircut because of all the climbing I had to do to shoot photos of all the tall city buildings. The wind constantly whipped stray pieces of hair into my eyes, and it always seemed to be a mess. This sounded like the perfect solution. The best thing was, there was no one to stop me from making this radical change to my appearance.

After lunch, I strolled around the neighborhood and looked at all the factories, which produced everything from clocks, pencils, and glue to cakes and cigars. The beauty parlors I went to refused to cut the short bob haircut I wanted. Down a side street I spied a pole with the name "Antonio's Barbershop" on it. I practiced my steady breathing, trying to get my nervousness under control, and opened the heavy door.

"Hello, young lady. I'll bet you'd like a bob," greeted a man who I assumed was Antonio. He finished sweeping the floor, then pointed to a chair.

"Yes, I would," I said, somewhat relieved. I took off my old hat, pulled my long, stringy hair out from its bun, and continued to calm myself.

Antonio put a sheet around my neck and his friendly manner distracted me from losing my long hair. "Many actresses have shortened their hair and they look stunning." His shears clipped away and I felt my hair falling onto my shoulders.

While I watched my locks hit the floor, I thought about all the news articles I had read at the automat. A teacher with a bob in Jersey City had been ordered by the Board of Education to let her hair grow. They claimed the style caused too much fuss and distracted from her job. The medical profession found that women were getting shingle headaches from the sudden removal of hair from the nape of their necks, exposing it to blustery winds. Preachers warned parishioners that a bobbed woman was a disgraced woman. Then there was the article that claimed men were divorcing their wives over their bobbed hair. Fathers complained that they couldn't tell their girls from their boys from the back.

After all those negative thoughts, I said to Antonio, "I've seen the before-and-after picture of Coco Chanel and that's what inspired me to do it." I squeezed the cold metal arms of the barber's chair as the last of my hair dropped to the floor. My new hairdo tickled the bottom of my ears.

The barber showed me my new style in his hand-held mirror. I felt the V-shape at the nape of my neck and gasped.

"You'll get used to it," Antonio said. "You are a beautiful young lady."

I tried to smile as I twisted the uneven hair in the front. The barber had left the sides a little longer than the rest. With a fake smile in the mirror, I worried that I looked too boyish with this haircut because of my flat figure.

Antonio reassured me. "Girls put metal pins in at night to make the ends curl. They're called bobby pins."

"Thank you," I mumbled as I put on my hat to hide the haircut, then left. Martin would certainly not approve, nor would my mother.

I went into a five and dime and inquired about bobby pins. The young girl at the counter had a bob and showed me how the pins were used by clipping them in an X shape. She saw me looking at the lipstick and helped me pick out the right shade for my complexion. I bought the lipstick, a mirror, and the bobby pins, and went straight home to fuss with my new hairdo. I also picked up my mail and found the letter I had been dreading.

Dear Adeline,

I am quite shocked by the events you described. You did enter into a legal covenant of marriage. The only factor that sways me to take your side is that your husband hid the fact of having to live with his mother. And then there's his alcohol consumption. But he did financially provide for you. How can you possibly support and take care of yourself? It is a shame that you did not get pregnant. Pregnancy makes a marriage more cohesive. I urge you to reconcile.

Love, Mother

That night I tossed and turned as I dreamed about my husband.

Martin yelled, "You are an embarrassment, peddling your photographs all over the campus! And you look like a boy with that short haircut. I will divorce you!" Then he drank two bottles of his "medicine."

I woke with a cry, then spent hours trying to get back to sleep.

In the morning, I turned on my lamp, ripped the bobby pins out of my hair, and looked in the mirror. As I turned my head from side to side, I grinned. I loved the two curls that had formed in the front. I applied the luscious red lipstick, enjoying the freedom to do as I wanted and feeling free from the confines of my marriage.

At work, Mr. Gillman's eyes sparkled. "Why, Mrs. Roberts, you look very stylish and professional with your new outfit and haircut."

With my face turned to the floor to hide a blush, I said, "Thank you."

My appearance was quite different now and I was beginning to feel confident that if Martin passed me on the street, he wouldn't even know who I was.

Bob haircut

Chapter 15
Gargoyles, 1927-1928

Don't limit yourself. Many people limit themselves to what they think they can do. You can go as far as your mind lets you. What you believe, remember, you can achieve.

— Mary Kay Ash

The economy continued to boom and I was becoming quite an asset to the firm after being there for more than a year. Their newly constructed buildings were filling up with tenants. I tried to write to my mother but was too tired from work, and kept putting it off. I had adjusted to my new life alone and thought about Martin on occasion, but kept as busy as possible.

One day, Mr. Dowler called me into his office. "How was your weekend, Mrs. Roberts?"

"Fine, thank you," I replied. Every time he called me "Mrs. Roberts" I was afraid he would ask about my husband, but he never did.

"I received a call from the magazine *Architectural Digest*. Mr. Jennings saw the fine photographs you took of our buildings. He was in my graduating class at Cornell and has also seen your work in the alumni magazine. He asked my permission for you to do an assignment for him."

"What is it?" I twisted my curls.

"He mentioned something about gargoyles. I told him it would be fine as long as the work was confined to the weekends."

"I'd like that," I smiled.

After accepting the assignment from Mr. Jennings, I stopped at the photography shop to get more film.

"How's work coming along?" Mr. Smith moved his hand closer to mine on the counter.

"I have two jobs now. I just got a weekend job with a

magazine. I'll be photographing gargoyles all over the city."

"You don't say! Well, I must show you the latest in cameras. This one is the Ansco miniature camera. It's the only camera that takes fifty pictures with one roll of film. The roll costs only fifty cents. It's great for private detectives because photos can be taken quickly, one after the other, and the camera can be hidden easily." Mr. Smith presented it to me as if it were made of gold.

I held the 1½ x 4-inch camera. I couldn't believe how small it was compared to my Graflex, and how much lighter it was than my Leica. I was about to ask some questions when the shop owner said in a singing-type voice as he pointed to the credit sign, "It's $20 but you could buy it now and pay later!"

"Maybe. I'll come back on my next payday." I forced myself to push it away and remembered Mr. Williams telling the class that expensive equipment could only get you so far without talent.

Mr. Smith continued to talk to me about the camera while touching my hand, until I put it down by my side. I felt a tingling sensation that I hadn't felt in quite a while.

With my next paycheck, right before my weekend job would begin, I went back to the photography shop and bought a tripod for my Graflex.

After Mr. Smith rang up the sale, he asked me out to dinner. I thanked him but told him I was too busy working.

Before setting out on my new weekend assignment for *Architectural Digest*, I went to the New York City Public Library to study about gargoyles. I learned that these fanciful creatures had a practical purpose. They were artistic waterspouts to drain water away from the buildings to prevent flooding and the erosion of the mortar in the masonry walls. Architects often used multiple gargoyles to divide the flow of rainwater off the rooftops. A channel was cut in the back of the gargoyle and rainwater exited through its open mouth.

I wandered around the city with my Leica and Graflex, but left the tripod at home so I could be free to roam. The tall skyscrapers caused me to crane my neck to look for gargoyles, and I almost ran into an errand boy because I wasn't watching where I was going. Many of the old gothic churches were decorated with gargoyles. I had read that the Catholic Church had these spouts made into images of fearsome, destructive beasts to remind people of the need for the Church's protection. They were designed to frighten off evil spirits.

I came upon the Trinity Lutheran Church and stretched my neck to look at the griffin-like gargoyles occupying each corner of the bell tower. The time of day and lighting were perfect for me, but I needed to get closer. I got up the nerve to ring the bell of the minister's house so that I could ask permission to climb to the tower to get close-up shots. The old minister was happy to accommodate me and I promised him some copies of the photos.

On Broadway, I saw the heads of goat-horned demons lining the windows of a building, and took a shot of each one. In the Garment District, there was a strange character examining beaver pelts. This one sure looked like it would scare off evil spirits! I noticed that most of the gargoyles were in the form of elongated animals. One library book I had read said that the length of the gargoyle determined how far water was thrown from the building.

I enjoyed shooting the lion-mouth gargoyles lining the entire length of an apartment building. A few blocks later, I looked up at a terrifying griffin-human gargoyle holding a cooked chicken in his lap. He sat atop an apartment building that had 1909 carved onto the front entrance. I went into the building, took the elevator to the roof, and got a few terrific close-ups of the griffin. I also composed a shot of a twelve-story apartment building plastered with winged beasts and hunched grotesques sitting low on the façade.

All the climbing was cumbersome with two cameras. I was exhausted but exhilarated by my new assignment. I was glad I had worn my new tailored trousers. I reflected on when I used to balance on uneven wooden fences on my way to school with my brother. We were always allowed to climb trees and dared each other to new heights in the woods behind our house.

I took a subway to 14th Street on Union Square to the Bank of Metropolis. This bank had twelve lion heads on its sixteen-story Renaissance-style building. Afterward, totally spent after so much walking, I headed for home. There I had a bowl of soup, then went into the bathroom to develop the film. I could hardly wait to see what I had captured.

While I worked on my film, an unexpected knock came at my door. Wondering who it might be, I meekly called, "Who's there?"

"Telegram," came the muffled reply.

I threw open the door and signed for it. Telegrams were always bad news. Had Martin found out where I was?

I tore open the envelope with shaking hands, then read the note. "No, no, no!" I shouted.

It was from Jimmy, informing me of our mother's death. I was just as shocked as when Dad had died. Mother was always so opinionated and full of life. She had just written that she was attending the local community college, which was amazing at her age of fifty years old.

I dashed out and called my brother from a pay phone. He told me that her heart had failed and a neighbor had found her the next day.

I made arrangements to go home. A few days later, Jimmy met me at the bus and held me tight as I let loose the tears I had been holding back for days.

"We were lucky, Addie to have had parents who cared for us and loved us as much as they did."

There was a small memorial service held at a nearby funeral home. I wiped my face with my hanky and my chin trembled as I whispered to Jimmy, "I meant to write back to her, but I got too busy with work and never did."

Jimmy kept his arm around my shoulder. "And I should have moved her in with my family. She died all alone." A tear dribbled down his cheek.

We both stood there wallowing in our regrets. A few acquaintances came up to us with sad faces.

After the service, Jimmy suggested that we walk over to the house to sort through a few things. I walked a step behind him, not wanting to face an empty house.

It was quiet inside...almost too quiet. My eyes were drawn to Dad's framed photos on the walls. Jimmy looked over each piece of furniture to see what was worth keeping. He noticed my damp cheeks and held me as I sobbed. He handed me his handkerchief. I blew my nose and asked if I could take some of the pictures.

"Addie, please take them all. They mean more to you than me." He paused and gave me a funny look. "By the way, I love your new hairdo. You look so modern!"

"Oh, Jimmy, I'm lucky to have you," I sniffed as I began taking down the photos. Each one was filled with sweet memories for me, like the one I had taken of my family walking in the woods so long ago.

Later that day, my brother saw me off on the bus and we promised to spend holidays together.

Now that both my parents were gone, I felt the need to work as much as possible to fill the loss within me. The new business magazine *Fortune* saw my photographs in *Architectural Digest* and called me in for an assignment.

I wore a new tan, tailored tweed suit with an attached pocket and silk kerchief. On the broad collar was a white silk gardenia. My swanky hat with its dipped brim, and gloves matching the wool outfit, gave me the confidence I needed to get through the meeting.

A silver-haired editor puffed on his pipe behind his sizable desk. "Mrs. Roberts, our magazine records the importance of industry for our nation. I've seen your photographs in the *Digest* and I'm impressed with how you seem to paint with your camera."

"Thank you. I received a good education in photography at Cornell University." I stared straight ahead with self-assurance.

"The meatpacking industry is the heart of the American economy and must be brought to the public eye. I need a photographer to make it an eye-stopper. No one would dream of artfully done photographs in a place like that. Do you have the nerve to go there? It can be a frightening experience for a girl. Please answer truthfully. If not, I'm sure we can find a male photographer."

"I'm very interested," I answered with conviction. "And I have been in many factories." I embellished the truth a little, thinking of Dad's factory.

He stood up and handed me the address. I rose and adjusted my skirt and hat.

Mr. Goldstein sized me up in my expensive suit. "I hope you

have some work clothes. It's a meatpacking plant."

"Yes, I do."

"They are expecting you on Saturday. Keep in mind, hog-butchering is a billion-dollar industry."

That Saturday I dressed in my trousers, Oxfords, and an old blouse. I took a cab and went to the packing plant with all my photographic equipment, ready to enter the male world of meatpacking.

The owner of the Swift Meat Company looked at me with suspicion while chewing on his cigar. He said nothing and pointed to two battered, red-stained doors.

There were thousands of pigs in procession, and two hard-looking men kept them in an assembly line using poles. These animals were off to be disassembled. As I looked at the thousands of hogs in their pens, I visualized them as repeating shapes, like I was taught in class. I concentrated on shooting rows of their curving tails, then their graceful backs. I took numerous photos of the giant hog shapes before they were led to slaughter.

Next, I came to the succession of hogs strung up by their rear hooves. Their sharp squeals became so loud I almost didn't hear the men say to each other, "What the hell's a broad doing here?"

I ignored them, along with the horrific smell, as best I could.

The stench became so pungent that I fashioned my hanky around my nose and pinned it to my hair. Before each pig was divided and subdivided, I took pictures of the singeing flames and flashing knives. The flames reminded me of the glow of the melted metal in my father's factory. So long ago...

The ugly flamethrower guy stopped and asked me, "What're ya doin' here, lady? This is man's territory."

His boss told him to shut up; that the plant needed the publicity.

All the workers in their white, bloody aprons were distracted as I went fearlessly throughout the entire factory, dragging my equipment with me. During the process, I caught snippets of their snide comments.

"She looks like a boy in them clothes!"

"Look at her boy hair!"

"What's a goddamn dame doin' in this dangerous place?"

Despite the odor of the mounds of pig manure I had to slog through, I embraced the challenge of photographing the plant. The last photos I took were of piles and piles of sliced meat.

At the end of the long day, I left the cloth that covered my camera and my hanky in a pile to be burned because they had absorbed the disgusting smell of the pig manure.

Gargoyles

101

Chapter 16
Chip and a New Name
1928-1929

A wife should no more take her husband's name than he should hers. My name is my identity and must not be lost.

— Lucy Stone

Mr. Dowler saw me struggling with my heavy Press Graflex and assorted photography equipment. I now had to take a cab everywhere so that I could carry several cameras, flashbulbs, film, lenses, and my twenty-pound tripod.

"Mrs. Roberts, I'm happy to see that you have bought new equipment. I have an idea. Maybe the firm could hire an intern to be your assistant. Our buildings are filling up because of your photography. Here." He pointed to a closet. "You can use this closet to store some things."

"Thank you, Mr. Dowler, I would like that."

"Mr. Gilman's son, Charles, is a senior night-school student at Hofstra University. He's looking for a job. I'll see if he's found one yet. We'll pay an assistant for you for our work, but with your freelance jobs you're on your own."

I had been a photographer for the firm for over two years now. Mr. Dowler was able to hire Charles Gillman as my assistant, who was a journalism major at a local college. When we were introduced, I felt sparks of electricity shoot between us. Later that night, I wondered what had caused the sensation...and how did I know it was mutual? He was a man of medium height with neatly trimmed black hair. It was his open, broad smile that attracted me the most. His bright-blue eyes stayed glued to mine every time we interacted. I tried to dismiss the attraction, reminding myself that, technically, I was still married. Charles was younger than I was and I was used to being with an older man.

I received a call for a weekend assignment from *Fortune Magazine* to photograph the construction of the tallest building in the world. It was going to be 1,042 feet tall. The magazine wanted photographs of all phases while it was being built. I would need assistance for this important job, and I would receive the large sum of $5 per photograph.

After a few shoots with Charles for the architectural firm, I asked him, "Would you be available to help me on the weekend? I have a very important assignment."

"Sure, I'd love to. Please, call me Chip. All my friends do." He flashed me an adorable, boyish grin.

"I'm glad you can help," I blushed. "And call me Addie. Where should we meet?"

"Well, most of your equipment is at your place, isn't it? Let's meet there." His gaze locked on mine.

"I live all the way in Brooklyn. Where would you be coming from?"

"The city, but I'm happy to travel to Brooklyn to help you."

I wrote down my address and we parted.

That night, while heating some soup, I was deep in fantasy. I was quite captivated by Chip. *He must know that I'm married since everyone at the office calls me Mrs. Roberts,* I thought.

The early morning light seeped through the curtains as I awoke. I took out my bobby pins and made sure my curls were going in the right direction. Chip was right on time. He seemed a bit nervous as he entered my apartment. I couldn't stop fidgeting with my new hat and angled it one way, then the other.

We maintained simple chitchat on the subway. The skyscraper we were headed to was going to have over forty floors. Once we arrived at the site, Chip and I put all the equipment down and stretched our necks to marvel in awe. Wearing my work clothes, I climbed up the steel framework, looked around, then went up even higher.

"This is perfect," I called down to Chip. "Bring me the Graphic."

Chip stuttered, "Uh...uh...sure..."

He must be afraid of heights, I thought. I scurried back down the frame as he looked at his shoes, then up at the sky again.

"The best antidote for being afraid of heights is deep, calm breathing," I said casually, not wanting to embarrass him. "That's what I do."

He gave me a sheepish look.

"Don't worry, we'll start from the bottom first. You can practice each time we go higher."

He gave me a winning smile. "Sure thing, Addie."

A few hours later, we had lunch at a small restaurant that Chip frequented. Our conversation was stimulating and there was never a pause or awkward silence between us.

Chip took a bite of his sandwich. "You know, the tallest building right now in New York is the Woolworth building. It's 792 feet. Before that, it was the Metropolitan Life tower at 700 feet."

"How do you know all this? I'm impressed."

"I went to my college library last night. Thought I'd better be prepared. You know, Addie, I'm impressed by your work as a photographer. I always thought it was such a simple job, but after today, I realized that in order to be a professional photographer, like you are, a person has to know the mechanics of cameras, the science of light...even the chemistry of developing."

"Thanks. I couldn't have done such a good job without the photography classes I had at college."

Martin crossed my mind. Even though I had left him, I was thankful he had paid my tuition.

The rest of the day went well and it saved quite a bit of time having Chip move my equipment up and down for me.

On the trolley back to Brooklyn, Chip said, "Thanks for helping me with my fear of heights. I was worried I couldn't take the job but I at least wanted to try."

"I'm grateful for your help. We got a lot accomplished."

Chip leaned in and whispered in my ear, "I had a grand time helping you, Addie."

All I could think of to say was a weak, "Thanks..."

After we got all the equipment stored in the apartment, Chip kissed my cheek, then left. I sat on my bed with mixed feelings spinning in my head. *I'm married. But Chip must know I'm no longer with my husband after seeing the single bed in my apartment.*

Early spring of 1929 was wonderful in New York. Once in a while, I strolled around Central Park to catch a bit of nature, which I sorely missed after my country upbringing.

One morning, I left for work early to enjoy a leisurely breakfast at the automat. While reading the *New York Times* and enjoying a fine dish of eggs Benedict, I noticed an announcement in the newspaper.

LADIES!

JOIN THE LUCY STONE LEAGUE!

PRESERVE YOUR MAIDEN NAME!

I tore out the article and decided to attend the meeting, which was to be held the next week. Maybe this group would tell me how I could obtain a divorce. *It's time,* I thought. *I've been away from Martin for almost three years now.* I didn't like being referred to as "Mrs. Roberts"; it always reminded me of my mother-in-law. Actually, I didn't like being referred to as *Mrs.* anyone.

The Lucy Stone League meeting was held in Ruth Hale's living room on Manhattan's Upper West Side. The brownstone was large and full of elegant furniture. Ruth was a tall woman who wore expensive men's trousers and a feminine blouse. I felt secure when I saw that the entire living room was crowded exclusively with women. A butler made sure that everyone had tea.

Ruth called the meeting to order and began telling Lucy Stone's story.

"Lucy founded the League in 1921 with the motto, 'A wife should no more take her husband's name than he should hers.'"

The enthusiastic group clapped.

She paused, then went on to say, "Lucy Stone was the first woman in the United States to carry her birth name through life, despite her marriage in 1855. Because of her, I too have kept my original family name, even though I am married. This way my identity will not be lost."

The women applauded again and I joined in.

Ruth Hale continued, "I am a journalist, critic, and the wife of a *New York World* columnist. I am proud that my passport says Ruth Hale and not Mrs. Walter Farrell. This feat did not occur without a battle. At first, the federal court issued me a passport that read 'Ruth Hale, also known as Mrs. Walter Farrell.' I refused to accept the passport and canceled my trip to France—and so did my supportive husband until the federal court accepted just 'Ruth Hale' on the documents. I also have a real estate deed in my birth name for an apartment house I recently bought."

More applause erupted.

Ruth smiled. "Ladies, we have obtained the right to vote and now we can preserve our birth names. I have successfully challenged the federal court so that a woman can keep her maiden name. I urge you all to follow my lead. My husband is a progressive man. The only person called *Mrs.* in our house is our parakeet!"

All the ladies exploded with laughter.

The meeting gave me the courage I had been seeking. I lingered afterward to introduce myself to Ruth and explain my marital situation. She told me that to obtain a divorce in New York, a woman had to have seven years of desertion. When I told her I had left almost three years ago, Ruth asked, "Have either of you committed adultery?"

"No."

I blushed, thinking of Chip and his kiss. Then I thought about Martin, and how he was probably too busy occupying his spare time entertaining his mother to even consider another woman.

"After seven years, you can file for a separation if you've had no contact with your husband. Do not request any alimony. If your spouse remarries, you could be declared legally dead. Does your husband know where you live?"

"No," I said in a meek voice, worried that Jimmy might find letters I had written to my mother. *He wouldn't tell Martin where I lived, would he?*

I was overwhelmed and stared at a lovely painting on the wall as I tried to absorb all the information.

"What's your maiden name?"

The butler poured more tea into Ruth's cup as I snapped out of my fog.

"Peterson. My first name's Adeline."

"Well, Adeline Peterson, to claim back your maiden name, a good first step is to get a library card. It's easy and there is no proof of identification required. Then open a bank account. Most banks don't require identification either. They're just happy to get your money. After that, keep signing everything in your maiden name. In seven years, you can obtain a passport. And don't forget to register to vote!"

"Thank you so much, Ruth," I said gratefully.

"Well, Adeline Peterson, good luck to you and remember, never respond to your married name again."

That evening, I went to the library and obtained a card in my new name. I was reluctant to go to a bank. I kept my money in a can underneath my bed because of my mother's distrust of banks.

The next day at the firm, Mr. Dowler greeted me. "Good morning, Mrs. Roberts."

"I...um...changed my name to Adeline Peterson." My face flushed.

"Oh, you must have joined the maiden-namers I read about in *The Times*, Miss Peterson." Mr. Dowler's eyes twinkled.

I looked out the office window and said, "Yes," with as much confidence as I could muster.

I left work early that day to go to a bank in the city, where I opened an account in my new name with $5. That night, I lay in bed with a grin on my face, happy to be gaining control of my new life and shedding my old identity. It was empowering.

Chapter 17
Dizzying Heights and the Model A

A customer can have a car painted any color that he wants so long as it is black.

— Henry Ford

The weekends were filled with photographing the new skyscraper. I looked at the lines of the telegraph wires and poles below it, absorbed in the preciseness of all the geometric shapes I could capture in order to make the photographs more dramatic. I became quite adept at conquering the dizzying heights, balancing on the scaffolding and beams. Chip, on the other hand, had to practice calm breathing to master his fears. It was great to have his help retrieving various cameras and lenses, and bringing up what I needed while I balanced on the ledges.

Our relationship began to escalate when Chip kissed me on the lips after work one day in my apartment. I couldn't resist and kissed him back, one thing led to another, and we ended up on the small bed. Chip was awkward. He wasn't as sure of himself as Martin had been. There was a lot of fumbling and his tongue became tangled as he tried to think of sweet things to say to me. Surely, it must have been his first time.

I stopped him as soon as he stood up to take off his trousers. "Do you have a rubber condom?" My cheeks flushed.

Chip mumbled, "Uh, well, uh..."

"I do want you but I don't want to get pregnant," I forced myself to say.

He left without a word. I tossed and turned that night, hoping I had said the right thing.

After the skyscraper was completed, I wanted the last photographs to be an aerial view, like a cherry to top off a sundae. This would impress *Fortune Magazine*.

The weather was cooperating. On Saturday, we went to Brooklyn's Barren Island Airport and I paid for a flight for both Chip and myself on a small airplane.

The rough-faced pilot ignored Chip and gave me the once-over. "Ever been on a plane before?"

With self-assurance, I said, "No, but I'm looking forward to it."

He swaggered toward the small plane. "Get ready for a thrill."

I was over-the-top excited at the thought of experiencing Manhattan from the sky. Chip remained silent and focused on carrying several cameras for me.

The gregarious pilot smacked the fuselage of the Travel Air 4000, bragging, "This honey can fly top speed up to 130 miles per hour, so buckle up and hold on tight." He opened the tiny door to and helped me in.

Chip climbed into the seat next to mine and we put on leather helmets. Chip grabbed one of the cameras and playfully snapped a photo of me before we took off.

The pilot spun the radial engine, revved it up, and we cruised down the dirt runway. My heart pounded so loud I was afraid someone might hear it.

It was a beautiful day with an expansive blue sky and a few wispy clouds scattered about. I took a camera from Chip as we ascended into the air. I could only afford a fifteen-minute ride, and knew I had to make the most of it. As soon as we hovered over the skyscraper in the open-cockpit plane, I started snapping pictures.

After a full five minutes of leaning over the side shooting photos, we headed back. The pilot made a rough decent onto the dirt runway and the plane lurched to a stop. Chip hung his head over the side and threw up.

The pilot pulled off his helmet, laughing. "Told ya it would be a fast flight!"

Later, back at my apartment, I was exhilarated from our flight and kissed Chip with passion. We fell onto the bed. Just as I was about to ask, he pulled out a little package of condoms from his pocket. Now I *really* wanted him. I missed the intimacy I used to have with my husband but didn't want the worry of a pregnancy.

We kissed a while longer. I felt naughty, in a cheating sort of way, until Chip murmured in my ear, "I want you."

A fierce desire rose within me as we stripped off each other's clothes. We fell onto one another with an exploding fire. After we both climaxed, Chip fell fast asleep and I stared out into the darkness. My hunger was satisfied. I shook him awake, determined to not *ever* let a man stay overnight. He looked disappointed, but got dressed, leaned over and kissed me, then left.

"See you tomorrow..." I called after him.

Fortune Magazine was impressed by the aerial shots of the skyscraper and continued to give me further assignments.

The full-time job with the firm, along with my freelance work, allowed me to accumulate quite a nice sum in my coffee cans and I was inspired to buy a car.

"Chip, come with me to buy an automobile. I've been saving up. This will make carrying all the equipment easier."

"A car! That'd be swell! I love your new hat, by the way." He gave me a cute, puppy-dog look.

We went to a car lot and I settled on a 1929 Model A station wagon. The salesman told us that they only came in black because that color dried the fastest in production. He bragged that the car we were looking at was Ford's two-millionth automobile built, and that soon everyone would have a car. The salesman asked Chip how much he wanted to put down for the monthly installment plan.

Chip pursed his lips as his cheeks changed color.

"I'm the one buying the car and I have cash," I answered, and adjusted my fashionable hat smugly.

The salesman's voice rose. "You mean you have $750?"

"Yes, I do, and I earned every cent of it myself." I crossed my arms and smiled.

Chip beamed at me, then stuck his head under the hood. I gave the salesman the cash, and after signing the papers with my maiden name, he gave me the keys. I felt quite content with my purchase. And I still had money hidden away, though I had been meaning to put more of it in the bank.

My brand-new car went a whopping forty-five miles an hour,

not the usual thirty-five. Chip drove us out into the country to teach me how to drive, since he had learned in his father's car.

"Let's go out to the end of the island. There're fewer people and there's more space."

I worried about seeing my brother and what he would think of Chip, since I was still legally married. Mother's voice popped into my head. *"Automobiles are lazy machines and don't exercise your muscles like bicycles do..."*

As we passed by my hometown, I felt a mixture of sad feelings. I missed my brother, but I was such a different person now—a person he might not like to see. We sped down the narrow, winding road that stretched the entire length of Long Island. My new car sure was fast. Every time we passed another automobile we honked, then waved and cheered when they honked back. Chip parked behind a sand dune right near the Long Island Sound.

"Turn it around for me so I can practice," I said.

"Not yet." He gave me that longing look, then gently tickled my hand—a sign that he wanted me.

I scooted away from him. "Do you have..."

Chip finished my sentence by holding up a little package. With a mischievous grin, he said, "There's plenty of room in the back for some hanky-panky."

I agreed. "Yes, let's christen the Model A!"

Off went our clothes. We ravished each other, our bodies twisting together in the back seat. Indeed, it was a fine way to celebrate owning a brand-new car.

When we heard rustling among the golden cattails in the sand, we threw our clothes back on, then burst out laughing when we saw a family of red foxes dash out of the bushes and run past my car.

The Model A

Lunchtime above New York City on a steel beam

Chapter 18
October 29, 1929
A Bull In the Lobby

One of the funny things about the stock market is that every time one person buys, another sells, and both think they are astute.
— William Feather

Chip and I arrived at Metropolitan Bank to cover a special shoot for the firm.

"This is my bank. I have all my savings in this fine establishment," Chip said as he helped me haul all the equipment.

"I've only put $5 in my bank in Brooklyn. My mother struggled for years because my dad made bad investments. It's made me leery of banks."

"The interest is why I opened an account. I like to see my money accumulate whether I work or not."

"Maybe I should open an account here," I mused as I glanced around. "Look, there's the bull!"

We were assigned to photograph a live bull in the lobby of this grand bank the firm had designed many years ago. Boys from a school club in the country had raised this magnificent animal. It was tethered on each side to two of the bank's columns. It was a huge publicity stunt. Many people came in to look at the bull and to have a photograph taken of themselves next to it.

Chip had graduated and was a budding journalist. The firm had paid him to write an advertisement to get people into the bank to see the bull. The bank, of course, hoped it would bring new customers their way.

Chip helped me set up the large-format camera and a string of flashbulbs. I draped one of my curtains over the camera, which I had sewn out of material that matched my outfit. We had perfect lighting and we worked together like a fine clock. All I had to do was nod or point and Chip knew what I needed.

The advertisement worked and a crowd lined up outside the bank entrance to have their photos taken. The manager went from clerk to clerk, making sure they were working fast enough setting up new accounts.

Toward the end of the day, before the bank closed, we heard shouting outside. The bull began to spook. His tether swung back and forth as he tossed his head and moved from side to side. We overheard something about the stock market selling millions of shares on Wall Street that day.

A clerk on the telephone screamed, "The Dow just dropped twelve percent!"

Customers pushed each other aside while waiting in line to close their accounts. The bull snorted, but thank God the tethers were strong. I froze and put my camera down. Chip dropped everything and ran over to the line to get his money out. I looked out through the long bank windows and saw mounted police trying to control the chaos outside.

Chip shook his fist while waiting in line, yelling, "I want my hard-earned money!"

The tellers' windows closed. The panicked bank customers started to leave, and I could hear people moaning and women crying. Chip came over to me, anger ablaze in his eyes, and helped me pack up as fast as possible. After loading all the equipment into my station wagon, we heard people ranting and raving in the streets.

"This is a catastrophe!"

"How could the entire stock market collapse?"

"Our life savings is gone!"

"Those goddamned greedy investors, investing money they didn't even have!"

After all the equipment was packed, Chip mumbled, "Now I'll have to move back in with my parents...if they still have a house."

Before I could reply that perhaps he could stay with me for a little while, he took off, muttering something about beer and a speakeasy.

On the drive down the avenue, I saw that Trinity Church was overflowing with grieving New Yorkers seeking comfort.

When I got back home in Brooklyn, I immediately looked under my bed. Yes, my coffee cans were still full. In my mind, I heard my mother say, *"Hold on to your money and never trust anyone."* Jimmy would chime in and quote Thomas Jefferson: *"The best way to double your money is to fold it in half and put it away."*

I sat at my little table and turned on the radio. It blared with continuous bad news:

"The New York Stock Exchange closed at 5:32 p.m. with a record amount of 16 million shares traded in just one day. The market has now lost $14 billion. Ladies and gentlemen, you should see the wastebaskets all over the United States, overflowing with white ribbons of paper. For every million shares traded, five hundred miles of ticker tape has run through the machines."

I tossed and turned all night, worrying about Chip.

The next morning, I heard President Hoover's voice on the radio: "The business in our country is on a sound and prosperous basis. Any lack of confidence in the economic future or the basic strength of business in the United States is foolish."

I felt better hearing our president's speech and got ready for work while listening for Chip's knock on the door. It was getting late and I couldn't wait much longer. Where was he?

It was easy to get into the revolving doors of the Dowler, Gilman and Associates building because no one seemed to be around. There wasn't even an operator on the elevator. When I got to Mr. Dowler's door, it was locked with a sign on it that read: CLOSED.

I was numb. In a panic, I ran to the storage room where most of my equipment was. Thank God it was all still there. I made two trips, hauling everything down to my car, and kept looking for Chip.

On the drive back home to Brooklyn, I saw lots of automobiles with signs on them. One read:

$100 WILL BUY THIS CAR
MUST HAVE CASH
LOST ALL IN STOCK MARKET

The entire month felt like a long ride on a spiraling roller coaster. I was glued to the radio and bought many newspapers, trying to understand what was going on. *Variety's* banner headline read: WALL STREET LAYS AN EGG. The article stated that it was the end of the good times. Too many people had bought stocks with borrowed money. Another news source reported, *"Brokers believe worst is over, time to buy real bargain stock."*

I counted my blessings that I had never invested nor put much money in the bank. Nostalgia for my mother welled up inside me. She had taught me well.

I hoped a knock would come on the door, and that I would see Chip with his handsome, eager smile. When I compared Martin's lovemaking with Chip's, it was certainly not the same. I did miss having relations with Martin but I came to understand that our relationship was unequal and hindered my personal growth.

When the phone rang, I had a small hope that maybe Chip was calling. We had developed a good working relationship and friendship.

Alas, the phone call was from Mr. Dowler, who told me that, sadly, the firm had lost a great deal of money in the stock market and he had to let me go. Mr. Dowler said he would give me a good reference and urged me to contact newspapers and magazines that might be looking for photographers who had not yet pawned their cameras. I thanked him and almost asked for Chip's parents' phone number, but thought better of it.

Car for sale

Angry crowds gathered outside American Union Bank after the Stock
Market crash

Chapter 19
Freelancing

If you dig deep and keep peeling the onion, artists and freelance writers are the leaders in society — the people who start to get new ideas out.

— Allan Savory

Many houses, as well as apartments, stood dark and empty as I drove around New York City for the first time in weeks. There were lines of men as many as ten deep winding around the city blocks. Everywhere I went, I thought I saw Chip. I missed his deep, sweet-sounding voice and his cheerful laugh, but in all honesty, I knew our relationship wouldn't have lasted.

Construction had virtually halted in New York. I didn't bother going to *Architectural Digest* to look for work. *Fortune Magazine* had very little to offer me. I applied to a few places and brought my large portfolio. Magazines were still in business despite the falling economy. They had laid off many of their salaried staff and only took on freelancers. When I got home, I felt grateful that I had an apartment to live in, a car, and money hidden away.

In the morning, I received a phone call from *People's Home Journal*. This magazine wanted me to photograph what they called "The Depression." The editor asked me if I had an iron stomach for photographing every aspect of present-day life in the city. I decided to take the assignment, even though they would only pay a little per photograph.

First, I investigated the lines of sorrowful-looking men snaking all over the city. The nasty December weather made it necessary to use my flash to enhance photographs of the huge vats of soup being ladled into cups. After setting up my camera on a tripod, a few men sneered at me. I felt like I was being intrusive, and apologized.

"Mind your own business, lady," one said gruffly.

"This ain't no party. Throw that picture-taker out!" yelled another.

Embarrassed, I packed everything up, then drove from one end of the line to the other, which spanned many city blocks. I was astonished at how many unemployed, hungry people there were. A number of men carried buckets to fill with stew to bring home to feed their families.

After taking a few discreet photographs of the soup lines from behind mailboxes and telephone poles, I started to feel like a private detective. I sorely wanted to buy that miniature camera that Mr. Smith had shown me a few years ago, but in this economic climate, I knew I had better save as much money as I could.

At the magazine's office, I displayed the pictures to the editor. The room was filled with only male reporters.

Mr. Solesky took time out to examine them all. He tapped his finger on the ones he wanted. "Miss Peterson, these are fine photos. They capture the expressions of the downtrodden. I have never met or hired a girl photographer before." He sized me up. "Can you type? We could use stories as well as photographs, and we do pay for short articles."

"I'll bring you an article next week." I stood up a bit taller and looked him directly in the eye. I didn't type, but had learned writing skills in English class at Cornell.

"Your photographic talent is exceptional and I look forward to reading your journalism abilities," he said, then went back to studying the pictures.

On the way to my car, I thought about Chip and how clever he had been at fashioning words together to enhance the photographs I took. I hoped I could do the same. There was a pawnshop nearby that I hoped might have a typewriter for sale, so I decided to walk there to check it out. I saw numerous unemployed people sitting against buildings, attempting to sell their possessions on the sidewalk. I spied a man with a typewriter. I knew brand-new typewriters went for over $100.

The sad-looking man stared at me as I asked him how much he wanted for his typewriter. He said, "Twenty-five dollars."

It appeared to be new, and had a manual and a case. After looking it over, I gave him fifty dollars. The joyous look on his face made my day.

The Royal typewriter was quite heavy to carry. I put the case in my station wagon and drove back home to figure out how to type. At my kitchen table, I tried typing with two fingers and didn't get very far, then studied the manual. I got my fingers in the correct positions on the home keys and practiced the silly phrase they suggested — *The quick brown fox jumps over the lazy dog* – which used most of the letters of the alphabet.

Every day, I ventured out with a small pad and pencil, with a camera hidden in my blouse. I discreetly observed the poverty from a distance and used my telephoto lens to capture the faces of the downhearted men in the soup line. I didn't want to humiliate them by sticking my camera lens directly in their faces.

In one of the alleyways, a man was selling piles of books. I looked through them and bought a dictionary and thesaurus. That night, after developing my film, I practiced typing once again. The tapping noise and ringing of the bell when I returned the carriage gave me a feeling of accomplishment, and the more I practiced, the better I became at navigating the keys.

The next morning, I dressed in a worn coat, didn't put any lipstick on, and drove to the city. I parked far from the soup kitchen and stood at the end of the line. Most of the men were embarrassed to talk to me, turning their heads downward, avoiding eye contact, and shuffling their feet. I memorized snippets of conversations I overheard.

"I hope I get some soup with meat in it today to bring home. It would cheer up the missus a little," one man in a tattered hat said.

"I know what you mean. Yesterday it was pretty watery. That's why they call it soup and not stew. Not that I'm complainin'," the man next to him replied.

"The mission on Third Street serves coffee, toast, and oatmeal for breakfast," another man shared.

"Thanks for the tip," a fellow with taped-up shoes answered.

I heard men discussing when they'd gotten laid off and how long the unemployment situation might go on.

One man said, "I heard President Hoover say on the radio that the worst has passed."

The man in a shabby coat next to him answered, "He's full of baloney. He's just sayin' that to get re-elected."

There were no women or children in line. One kind man said to me, "Hey, don't cha know you can go to the front of the line? They always let women in ahead."

I walked a few city blocks to the beginning of the soup line. It led into a church, where everyone sat on long wooden benches to eat a meal of tasteless soup and bread. I saw only an occasional woman. Unable to find work, many husbands stood in line like it was their job, holding their pails tight. It was the only way they could provide for their families.

When I got home, I wasn't full from the gruel, but felt too guilty to eat any dinner. After developing the photos, I looked at them on the clothesline in the bathroom and noticed that most of the men looked ashamed and humiliated; ashamed for having to ask for a handout and humiliated because they were unable to support their families.

My hand shook as I held a photograph of a man crouched beside his shoeshine kit, hugging himself with his head down. My eyes welled up with tears. I let the picture go and cried. Maybe I didn't have the iron stomach for this type of work. My previous work had been joyous—even in the pig factory, where I had found interesting lines and shapes to photograph. Tired from weeping, I crawled into my warm bed and counted my blessings as I fell asleep.

In the morning, I developed the rest of my photographs, then gathered my thoughts and typed up an article. *Who knows...maybe I can make a difference somehow...* I thought as I tapped at the keys.

The army of ragged, threadbare, starving men assemble three times a day beside storefronts, in churches, or outdoors in the chilling rain of January to provide soup for their families...

Mr. Solesky finished reading my article, "Sold! I was hoping that your writing ability would be as good as your photographs." He pointed to the photos he wanted to include with the article. Mr. Solesky chose my photo of men gathering on the cold, windy city street at 5:00 a.m. in front of the Beacon Light Mission, the dejected man next to his shoeshine box, and one of a woman sitting inside a church sipping a spoonful of soup, staring into space.

As the months went by, I occasionally felt lonesome. I missed the fun I'd had working with Chip. After being paid for my freelancing work, I felt that maybe I was making a difference in the world. I was slowly becoming accustomed to being alone.

Time, the weekly news magazine, saw my article in *People's Home Journal* and asked me to write a story about where the homeless lived. I was honored that my writing ability was appreciated, since *Time* had very few photographs and more news articles. They only wanted one photograph to go with the article, and I would have to choose carefully. It was a challenge to rely solely on my writing ability. I turned to my dictionary and thesaurus to perfect everything I wrote. At the library, I read as many back issues of *Time* to enhance my style to suit their taste. I discovered that the power of words did give a photograph more of a sharp focus.

In my Brooklyn neighborhood, I watched a policeman knock on the door of a house to announce, "You're evicted." The family grabbed as many of their belongings as possible and sat out on the sidewalk. The officer padlocked the door, then walked away leaving the children crying and the parents stone silent. I snapped photos of the sad event from far away, so as not to intrude.

Where will these people live? I wondered sadly.

In the city, I wandered around wearing my old coat. My hair had grown long again and I fashioned it into a bun under an outdated hat. It seemed wasteful to keep up with my fancy bob hairdo. I was blending in and observed in all the pockets of the city. There were makeshift homes of cardboard and pieces of wood. Only the lucky families had tents.

Without a camera, I kept a pad in my pocket and practiced the art of eavesdropping. I heard that some people slept on other people's couches or in garages. Upon further exploration, I saw homeless people, mostly men, sleeping under bridges or camped out in public parks. Even derelict boats along the riverfront were being inhabited. One lady told me there was a boxcar village of families living in old trains. I even heard about families living in caves in Central Park, mostly Negroes.

After spending a week writing and rewriting the article, and thanks to my array of tools (my dictionary, thesaurus, and typewriter), my article on the homeless was accepted. The editor liked it so much he gave me an assignment to write an article about how people obtained money and jobs during these hard times.

In a way, interviewing people, which meant invading their privacy, was hard to do. The subject of how people who had lost everything tried to survive was like an escalator that only went down. I tried to keep my spirits up while doing this heartbreaking reporting. This period of time was now being called the "Great Depression." I flinched every time I heard the phrase and couldn't help thinking, what the heck was so great about it? I continued to dress inconspicuously and to memorize conversations as I milled about, collecting information for the article. I wrote down what I could in secret and carried my dad's small Vest Pocket camera so I could take the occasional discreet photograph.

There was a surplus of apples and a company decided to sell crates for only $1.75. A person could sell sixty apples on the street corner for a nickel apiece, reaping a profit of almost $2. Many people were happy to purchase an apple for just a nickel, myself included. A businessman who saw me sneak a photo told me there were over 5,000 apple peddlers in the city. I heard the voices singing, "Apples, apples, get yer apples!" over and over again. Boys as young as five years old sold newspapers to help support their families.

At a shantytown on 12th and 40th, an old woman pushed a heavy wooden cart around for almost fourteen hours a day selling pickles that cost between a penny and five cents each. On other corners, men were shining shoes for the people who still had jobs. On one block alone there were nineteen shoeshine stands. Only one was operated by a Negro.

I noticed men sneaking on freight trains, looking for odd jobs across the country, giving up on New York City altogether. It was a dangerous act to jump on moving trains and I had read about the deaths reported.

Chain letters were becoming a popular way to try to make money. A person sent a dime to the name and address on the top of the list. The recipient then sent out the chain letter to five more people, with the hope that the chain would remain unbroken and they would be the recipient of hundreds of dimes. It was a get-rich-quick type of scheme, and I wasn't certain it was all that effective. But people had no choice but to be resourceful, and often were desperate for a solution.

Royal typewriter

Apples for sale

The soup lines

Train hobos

Chapter 20
Dance Marathons

The greatest generation was formed first by the Great Depression.
They shared everything — meals, jobs, clothing.

— Tom Brokaw

I photographed a dance marathon — another "job" for the unemployed, held at local halls. Couples had to be able to dance for twenty-four hours straight! They would dance for forty-five minutes, then there was a ten-minute rest. That's when a table came out with a magnificent spread of food to feast on. Prize money went to the couple who could spend the most hours moving sleepily about the floor. The contests offered prizes of $500, $300, and $100 for first, second, and third place. Spectators paid twenty-five cents each to watch. There was a variety of performers while the dance was going on and I got to photograph the comedian Red Skelton.

While setting up an array of flashbulbs, a handsome man in a brand-new, blue wool serge suit smiled at me. I flashed my eyes back at him and he struck up a conversation. He introduced himself as John, followed me around, and talked nonstop while I moved around the outside of the dance floor shooting pictures.

"Great equipment you've got there. What newspaper are you working for? How much do they pay you?"

If he hadn't been so good looking, I don't think I would have answered. I'd never been asked so many questions all at once.

"Listen, John, I'm really busy. I've got over a hundred couples to photograph."

He started helping me move my tripod around.

It was important for the dance couples to keep moving because if they stopped, they would be disqualified from the contest. I noticed that many of the women would sleep and their partners would hold them up and drag them around.

"When are you done?" John continued to pester. "Come with me for dinner at the Waldorf Astoria. I'll help you pack up. You have to eat dinner, don't you?"

I did my best to ignore him, but he was helpful and I definitely was happy for his assistance.

George Burns and Gracie Allen performed next. It was a pleasure to photograph the celebrities while the dance marathon continued. The acts were so funny. John and I had a good chuckle together and he had a terrific, infectious laugh.

A buffet table came out so the couples could take a short break and eat.

John said, "Time for us to eat."

I couldn't help noticing that he was a bit overweight and slightly bald when he took off his hat and jacket.

"The Waldorf has the best food. Are you done here? Can I help you pack up now?"

Feeling the leftover laughter from the comedy act, I giggled at all of his questions. "I'd love help putting the equipment in my car."

We drove to the hotel and I found out all about John without even asking. What a talker he was. He was there on business and was selling a game he had just patented.

The Waldorf Astoria Hotel was the most elegant place I had ever seen. For over a year I had immersed myself among the poverty-stricken residents of New York, so this was a treat for me. The stunning lobby was gilded with gold from floor to ceiling. The lobby's centerpiece had a charming old clock that was over eight feet tall and must have weighed tons. A sign below it read "Created for the 1893 Chicago World's Fair" and around the base of the clock were the likenesses of several presidents and Queen Victoria. At the quarter hour, it played the Westminster chimes.

The famous Cole Porter was playing, "Night and Day" on the piano while we looked at the menu. It was such an emotional, moving, and romantic song. John tapped his spoon on the tablecloth to the rhythm.

"Have anything you want, my dear."

I whispered, "I'm not a fussy eater. Please order for me."

This way, I avoided having to worry about the price, as I was out of touch with eating out. I glanced up at the magnificent gold ceiling high above us.

After John ordered the veal for both of us, I said, "Tell me about the game you invented." I rearranged my blouse under my suit jacket, trying to look presentable after working all day.

He answered with enthusiasm. "I designed and just patented a parlor game after I lost most of my savings and my job in the crash. I've spent all my spare time inventing it, between looking for work." He paused and gazed at me, just like Chip used to do.

"Tell me about it." I enjoyed the hotel's featured Waldorf salad and popped a grape into my mouth.

"Players move around the game board buying or trading properties, and develop them with tiny houses and hotels. Rent is collected from their opponents with the goal to drive them all into bankruptcy, leaving one person in control of the entire economy." John's face glowed as he spoke to me with zeal.

"What a fascinating concept, playing a fantasy get-rich-quick game during the Depression. You're quite a clever man." I told him I had been to the patent office with my dad as a young girl. Talking about my father now gave me a sweet happiness instead of a feeling of sadness, like it used to. Mother used to say, "Time heals all wounds." Funny how I always seemed to pull her anecdotes out of my memory on different occasions.

Our dinner arrived and we chatted between bites. The mashed potatoes were the creamiest I had ever tasted.

"I'm staying here at the hotel for a while, waiting for a famous game company to decide to take a chance on me," John chattered. "How is your veal?" He adjusted his fashionable bow tie.

"It's scrumptious. Thank you for inviting me. I don't think I've ever had veal."

After a dessert of vanilla ice cream, John walked me to my car.

"What are you doing tomorrow? Can I see you again?" He brushed his fingers through his thinning hair as his eyes locked on mine.

"Well, uh, I have a lot of film to develop..."

"The next day then? Can you meet me for lunch? The Waldorf has fabulous buffet lunches."

"I could maybe meet you on Tuesday. Thanks for the dinner, John, it was wonderful."

He opened my car door, but before I could slip inside he touched my shoulder and kissed my cheek. A tingle floated through me. It had been a while since I had been touched by a man.

"See you soon, Addie." He watched as I drove away.

I immersed myself in work, developing my photos and perfecting my writing. My assignment on earning money during the Depression was accepted and printed by the editor of *Time*. And, I was happy to land freelancing work with *The Saturday Evening Post* after showing the editor my work from *Time*.

Mr. Lortimer, the senior editor, glanced at my sorrowful photo of a newspaper boy. "This is a powerful photograph. It invites you into another person's world without actually going there. The photography from the dance marathon is sensational, especially with the celebrities. I see that *Time Magazine* only published one from the dance. Maybe we could print the rest. I like how you have the ability to evoke feelings instantly. The *Post* publishes more photographs than *Time* and I could really use these. We used to employ a full-time photographer when the economy was better."

I felt confident enough to discuss a few story ideas with Mr. Lortimer and he seemed quite pleased with them. My first idea was to write about tips on how to save money, which I had learned through my street observations and talking with people. I wrote about rolling your own cigarettes, and how shoes could be worn longer by using tape and cardboard for the souls. Tattered coats could be lined with blankets and socks could be used for gloves. Neighbors could swap different sizes of clothes for their growing children. I added that bicycles were the cheapest mode of transportation. One mother told me that by hiking into the country, free food could be found, such as blackberries and dandelions, and one could even shoot wild game. I took

131

photographs of bicycle riders and a man waiting to shine shoes who was rolling a cigarette.

I was pleased to write an upbeat article for a change. It cheered me up and helped others during this bad economy. The more photos I got accepted with my articles, the more money I received. I was pleased that I was surviving these hard times, and hopefully helping others through them at the same time.

John and I enjoyed a scrumptious lunch. "I love your hat, by the way. Tell me all about your week." He was wearing a dandy new suit.

I smiled. His many compliments warmed my heart. I told him about the two assignments I was working on and he listened intently to every word.

"Tell me, how's the progress on selling your game?" I took a sip of coffee.

"I got an advance and I'll be staying a few more weeks to oversee the design."

After eating a ham sandwich, he asked if I wanted to see the prototype of the game. I did, but that meant that I was also saying yes to going up to his hotel room. I thought about it, and after finishing my lunch, I said, "I'd love to see it."

A short time later, we were alone, going up in the elevator to his room. I looked down at my gloves and fidgeted.

"Did you like the lunch?" John smiled and moved closer to me.

"Very much. I forgot to thank you."

"My pleasure." John gazed into my eyes and I knew he could see that I wanted him. He pulled me in for an eager kiss.

The elevator bell dinged and we went into his fancy room. After seeing the grand bed as the centerpiece, I felt uncertain that I had made the right decision. It had been over a year now since I had been with Chip.

John rolled out a huge, round piece of oilcloth on the brocade bedspread. There were rectangular real estate properties around the entire circle, all cleverly hand-inked by him.

"I love the symbols drawn on the properties, the train, light bulb, and the cute faucet on the Water Works utility," I said as I took it all in. "You're a talented artist. I can only draw stick people." I touched each square.

"Ah, but you, my dear, can paint with your camera. I looked up some of the magazines you've been published in at the library. God gives everyone different gifts in life, doesn't He?" John packed the game away.

The current between us was strong. We stood and kissed for a long time. Before I knew it, we fell upon the bed and thoroughly enjoyed each other. John was a gentleman in every way.

Marathon dancers

Chapter 21
Speakeasies, 1931-1933

Prohibition makes you want to cry into your beer and denies you the beer to cry into.

— Don Marquis

I couldn't keep John off my mind. He was a clever, entertaining man, smart like Martin and fun like Chip. I felt a connection with him when we talked about his patent. He also continued to remind me of my dad.

After lunch the following week, I shared an article I had written for *Collier's Magazine*. He read part of it out loud, savoring every word.

WHAT CAN WE DO TO ESCAPE THE MISERY?
By Adeline Peterson

Picture shows are plentiful and popular. One of the biggest crowd-pleasers playing is Frankenstein.

For a nickel, a person can see a double feature with a newsreel. Theater owners have lowered their ticket prices as much as they can. Yes, it is an unnecessary luxury, but if you can spare it, this is a wonderful escape from hard times.

Come on out to dish night, Mondays at the Lyceum Theater, West 45th Street. For ten cents, you get a complimentary piece of dinnerware, and by going every week, you can collect an entire matching set. The set will include soup bowls, coffee cups, saucers, a gravy boat, and dinner plates.

On Wednesday nights there is bingo. It is played between features and after the newsreel. It is now called SCREENO. A number dial and a spinning needle are projected onto the movie screen. Patrons are provided with toothpicks to punch out the winning numbers on their cards. This is an inexpensive way to see a movie and try to win the cash prize — all on the same night!

John stopped reading, "Clever photographs you took." He pointed to the photograph of the giant spinning needle on the screen.

I told him that one had taken some setting up because it was dark in the theater.

"Your published articles and photographs are very original. Addie, you're a talented young lady." He stroked my hand across the table.

I gave him a proud smile. "*Collier's* editor told me that after printing my story, he got a call from the theater to place an ad." I leaned in closer and kissed his cheek.

John was only in town once a month now, overseeing the production of his game, which had been bought by a famous company. He always called and we'd meet for lunch or dinner at the hotel.

One day, during a fine lunch of roasted chicken, I got up the nerve to ask a burning question. "Tell me about your home in New Jersey."

He looked down at his plate for a moment, then whispered, "I want to be honest with you, Addie. I am a married man, but my wife is very ill and we do not have relations."

"I'm also married and won't be divorced for a few more years. I guess we have marriage in common."

John lifted his downturned face and gave me an enthusiastic grin. "It's Saturday night. Will you go with me to a speakeasy to have a drink? I know where one is."

I glanced at all the people around us. "Let's talk about it outside, after dessert," I whispered.

Outside the hotel, I explained to him that I did not drink because it was illegal. My mind shifted back to the orator, to Martin, and of course, my mother's voice was in my head again.

John, being the persuasive man that he was, talked me into going, just to look. He convinced me that it would enhance my knowledge as a reporter and I reluctantly agreed.

John said, "You know, Mr. Roosevelt's running against Hoover and is opposed to the Volstead Act. If he's elected, I think alcohol will be legalized."

"Oh..." was the only answer I could come up with. I needed time to process this idea.

"Do you know why they're called speakeasies? It's because of speaking quietly about such a place so as not to alert the police or neighbors."

"This makes me nervous, John. My mother called them 'dirty saloons.'"

"Like I said, this will be good for your writing, Addie." He looped his arm through mine.

"Hmmm," I mumbled.

After strolling down a few city blocks, we came upon an unmarked door front with a uniformed doorman standing beside it. He looked us over, then pulled open the door. Inside was a tiny, dark, wood-paneled room that was completely empty.

John went up to a large drawer in the wall, pulled the handle, and called inside, "Two Brandy Alexanders." He dropped in some change and pushed it back in. A few minutes later, the secret drawer opened containing two cocktails. John took them out and handed one to me. He drank his and watched me until I took a small sip.

"Oh my, it tastes so sweet." I finished it, feeling a tingle of guilt mixed with delight.

"On to the next one!" John led me outside. "That speakeasy is called a 'blind tiger' or 'pig' because the seller's identity is hidden."

"I have to admit, it's a clever design."

Next, we went to Chumley's Grocery Store. As we entered through Pamela Court, my eyes darted about in worry. John felt along the left frame of a plain brown door.

"What are you doing?" I whispered into his ear, then noticed a small peephole in the middle of the door.

He pointed to a brown circle the size of a penny and pushed it.

A man wearing an ordinary shirt opened the door, looked us over, and announced, "Come on in."

John explained that the police didn't know the door had a hidden buzzer.

Inside there were couples laughing and having a good time.

John ordered me a Bee's Knees, which I thoroughly enjoyed as it was sweet as well as tart. He said it was a combination of honey, lemon, orange juice, and gin. John had a straight gin. We left, then walked a few blocks. I giggled the whole way.

John laughed along with me. "Let's go to the 21. You'll love this one."

"How many speakeasies are there?" I asked a little too loud.

"Someone told me that in New York City alone there are thousands."

We came to a building that displayed a large number 21 with no other sign. It had multiple, colorful statues of horse jockeys adorning the front.

John opened the door for me. A few well-dressed people sat at tables sipping tea with a lovely tea service centered in the middle. John went up to a ten-foot-tall, narrow bookcase full of leather-bound law books. He seemed to count the shelves with his eyes, then reached to the far right and pushed one of the volumes aside, exposing a small lock hidden in the case. After he clicked it, he pulled on the bookcase and half of it became a door. John led me down a dark, narrow, musty-smelling staircase. If I hadn't heard laughing and chatting somewhere down below, I don't think I would have followed him. When we reached the bottom, there was a full-sized bar and a party going on. After ordering two drinks, John told me that the entire bar could be rotated and hidden behind the brick wall in case there was a raid. There were also invisible chutes into which liquor could be quickly sent to an underground cellar hidden in the building next door.

After one more round of drinks, my legs felt wobbly. John looked at my flushed face while I continued to giggle.

"We'd better get something to eat. You'll love the Cotton Club." He held my hand firmly, and with a smile, began walking me to the subway outside.

Once inside the club, I was dazzled. The elaborate elegance of the vast nightclub was arranged in two concentric tiers of tables laid out in the shape of a horseshoe. Murals trimmed the walls around the room.

John pulled out a chair for me at a table covered with a fancy lace tablecloth. A red tuxedoed Negro man came and greeted us with menus.

After looking it over, I said in a quiet voice, "John, the food is so expensive." I rubbed my temples and felt dizzy for some reason.

"A floor show is included with a meal and I've heard it's worth it."

"Order for me, please."

The top of the menu had Chinese food and the other half had American. Food from another country was not something I was familiar with.

John ordered Chinese chop suey and a venison steak. The waiter asked what we wanted to drink. John requested champagne for after our meal. We shared the plates and my wonderful date watched me as I enjoyed this new dining experience.

I excused myself and went to find the powder room. On the way, I noticed incredible paintings depicting scenes of the Western frontier of the 1800s. Upon inspecting one closer, I was astonished to see that it had been painted by the famous artist Frederic Remington. There was one outside the lounge of a cowboy killing an Indian. The painter's style was natural and I could feel the frightening action it evoked. Outside the powder room was a Remington sculpture on a marble pedestal. The ornate label on it read "The Bronco Buster." The bronze horse was reared up on its hind legs. I had read about this famous artist and was thrilled to see his work in person.

When I got back to the table, there were two glasses of champagne waiting. I looked around and saw bottles of liquor on all the tables and the upper-class society types drinking. I felt a bit out of place in my outdated dress.

John insisted I try the champagne. I took a sip and was pleasantly surprised. The bubbles were grand!

"John," I whispered, "why's there so much illegal alcohol openly being served here?"

"The Cotton Club not only has a lot of political connections, but plenty of bribery money," he said in a low voice.

The chandeliers dimmed as the velvet curtains opened on the stage. The bandstand was a replica of a Southern mansion with large, white columns and a backdrop painted with weeping willows and slave-like quarters. The band played on the veranda of the mansion. A few steps down was the dance floor.

The Duke Ellington Band played wild, jungle-type music. The young bandleader was perfectly turned out in a top hat and tails. Out came exotic Negro dancers. Like the sign outside advertised, they were all "Tan, Tall, and Terrific." One dancer wore a skimpy jungle bathing suit with feathers and bangles strategically placed. All of the dancers looked like flamboyant savages, moving fast and furious to the music. I noticed that the entire audience was White and all the performers were Negroes.

The next act featured the glamorous Lena Horne, a Blues singer. Fog surrounded her on stage. Her voice and swaying body captivated our emotions. John moved his chair next to mine and put his arm around my shoulder. He whispered, "The fog is produced by a dry ice machine."

After the show, we returned to the Waldorf at 3:00 a.m. and spent the night together in a blissful alcoholic haze.

The next morning over a late breakfast, we sat at a far corner table in the restaurant.

"So, Addie, tell me. What do you think of speakeasies now?"

"Oh, John, I can't thank you enough. I was thoroughly enchanted by the Cotton Club and you were right; it was a good education for me to learn about all the different types of speakeasies. I think I just got converted to the 'wet' side! I enjoyed drinking and I could see that many people do. I hope Roosevelt wins and does make alcohol legal."

"I'm voting for him, that's for sure. We need a change. It's hard to believe how many years the Volstead Act has remained in force. Legalizing alcohol and taxing it could really help our economy. Seems like it would end all the mob corruption from bootlegging," John added.

"Tell me something...I was wondering about the Negroes at the club. Do they have their own separate speakeasies?"

"Yes, they do, but there are a few integrated clubs. What do you think of that, honey?"

"I'm not prejudiced and I've witnessed Negroes struggling as much, if not more than Whites in this difficult economic time.

They deserve to escape just as much as all the other races in the city."

"I'd be happy to bring you to an integrated club where all colors mingle together and have a good time."

John beamed at me. His enthusiasm for life was contagious and I looked forward to every date.

With Franklin D. Roosevelt running against President Herbert Hoover, the editor of *Time* had me attach Hoover's name sarcastically to everything. Mr. Felsenthal was not a fan of the president. Besides using "Hooverville" to describe makeshift dwellings, like the old boats floating in the harbor, there was also Hoover Stew, Hoover Blankets (newspapers for covers), Hoover Hogs (jackrabbits caught for food), and Hoover Wagons (broken-down cars pulled by mules). The president advocated "rugged individualism"; the idea that every man should fend for himself and government handouts to the unemployed did great damage to people's self-esteem.

In a radio address, President Hoover insisted that it was not the government's job to address the growing economic crisis; it was up to local governments and private charities. Hoover's plan was not working and the Depression raged on. When election time came, Roosevelt won with overwhelming victory and there was cheering all over the city. The newly elected president wanted a "New Deal" for the American people, to establish programs for relief and reform as well as recovery. Unlike Hoover, he promised that the federal government would improve the failing economy. When FDR won the election, he announced, "I pledge you, I pledge myself, to a New Deal for the American people."

Toward the end of the year, the thirteen-year-old Volstead Act was repealed with the 21st amendment, which made for open, celebratory drinking in all the secret clubs. The excitement on the street was fun to photograph and I wished John could have been with me. I had enjoyed visiting the speakeasies with him. But he was coming to the city less and less now that his game was in production.

With the establishment of the Works Progress Administration, or WPA as everyone called it, I had plenty of freelance work. The news media was thrilled with my upbeat articles and photographs showing Americans being put back to work by the government. I provided stories and photos of new playgrounds, public buildings, roads — even a new airport was being built.

I wrote and photographed for as many newspapers as possible. I worked seven days a week, developing film all day on Sundays. It was difficult to survive because of the expense of paper, typewriter ribbon, photographic chemicals, and flashbulbs. Once in a while, I would acquire a new camera or new lenses so I could stay up to speed with the new technology and create the best shots possible.

I only saw John a few times a month and we treasured our time together. Martin had never once contacted me and soon became a faded memory.

One progressive newspaper hired me to write about how Negroes were surviving the Depression. It occurred to me that I had never seen any on the breadlines. Domestic Negro women in the city who were employed by rich White women were now working at starvation wages. I was sent on assignment to Harlem and was able to get information from a few Negro church pastors. The church was where relief was provided. I found out that the Depression was especially hard on urban Negroes because they had to be more resourceful than the Whites. In a way, they were used to poverty, having to care for each other's children and creatively manipulate their family's resources. Rent parties were typical where, for a small admission fee at someone's home, there would be a dance and the money raised would help pay the rent. It was fun for me to photograph one of These dances. My article and photographs were well received by the editor and it was always a relief to get paid.

Duke Ellington

Duke Ellington at the Hurricane Club

The 21 Club

The Cotton Club

Chapter 22
Mr. Roy Stryker and the Resettlement Administration
1934-1935

The guy who takes a chance, who walks the line between the known and unknown, who is unafraid of failure, will succeed.
— Gordon Parks

A surprise phone call from a Mr. Roy Stryker came. He asked if I would be interested in a salaried position as a photographer in the historical section of the Resettlement Administration. My interest piqued. I enjoyed my freelance jobs but the unpredictable income was always worrisome.

As I traveled to Washington, D.C. for the interview, it brought back memories of going there with Dad. I had learned a great deal from him on that trip to the patent office, and it had enhanced our relationship.

My mind drifted as I drove through several states. John, of course, was living with his wife, which didn't make for much of a relationship for us. Now that his board game was in full production, we saw each other less often.

I finally arrived at the Resettlement Administration, happy to stop obsessing over my personal relationship. Mr. Stryker's office had an amazing assortment of historical photographs that covered every wall, and also adorned several desks in his enormous, cluttered office.

"I'm very pleased to meet you, Miss Peterson. I've seen your fine work in *The Saturday Evening Post, Time,* and *Collier's.*" Mr. Stryker greeted me with warmth and ran his hand through his thinning, salt-and-pepper hair. He wore wire spectacles, almost like those Martin wore. Mr. Stryker lit his pipe, then asked me for my portfolio.

My hand twitched a little as I handed it to him across the desk, but I forced an optimistic smile.

He studied the photos of the hogs at the meatpacking plant as well as the bull in the Metropolitan Bank. "These are well designed, artful photographs. I'm happy to see that you have taken pictures of animals. I need a rural photographer." He turned the pages of my large portfolio. "Nice, candid photos of everyday people in New York City. Tell me, Miss Peterson, would you be interested in photographing agricultural hardships in No Man's Land?"

I swallowed hard. "No Man's Land?"

Mr. Stryker chuckled. "It's a place in the Dust Bowl."

"Dust Bowl?" My eyes blinked as I tried to regain my confidence.

He tapped the various photographs while he spoke. "Your photographs of common people in the soup lines, living in Hoovervilles, and selling apples on the street corners are perfect examples of the types of photographs the Resettlement Administration needs, except that it would be in the Panhandle instead of New York City."

"Thanks for your compliments, Mr. Stryker, but tell me...what's the Panhandle?'

The delicious cherry smell from his aromatic pipe drifted by me.

Mr. Stryker laughed again while adjusting his wire spectacles. "Sorry, I'm jumping ahead. I forget city people haven't heard of these places. I have a position available in the Panhandle of Oklahoma, which is the northwest region. I can lend you a few books so you can learn about the Dust Bowl and No Man's Land. I need a photographer to cover that area."

After I gave him a quizzical look, he added, "Miss Peterson, I know you're qualified to be a photographer with the RA, but perhaps you'd rather stay in the east and work here in Washington?" He studied my face as he waited for my answer.

"What would the job entail?"

"I have a position that requires an assistant." Mr. Stryker watched my reaction closely.

I was full of hesitation but said nothing. I wasn't sure I wanted to be anyone's assistant.

"Miss Peterson, my intuition tells me you would be a perfect photographer for our historical department in this agency, or in the Dustbowl, whichever assignment you choose. I have very few women on this project. Dorothea Lange covers the California migration. I need photographs of the people who have remained in the Dust Bowl. This would be a good opportunity for you to advance your career. I can see you have the talent for it, but do you think you could move out there and live among the farmers?"

"To be truthful, I have never been out west. I need time to think this over."

Mr. Stryker walked over to his well-stocked library and pulled out several books. "Here, you can borrow these. My heart goes out to the needy people in the west. I grew up on a farm in Colorado and ended up here after getting an economics degree at Columbia University. I co-authored a book on economics, which included photographs I selected. It was well received and helped me get this job. Photographs complement and enhance text to a great degree, don't you think?"

"They sure do." I looked at the titles of all the books piled high on his desk.

"I'm authorized to hire over forty photographers to visually show how the government's New Deal programs are helping people rise out of this depression. In the west, the Resettlement Administration has requested photographic documentation of what hardships the farmers are going through and how its programs will benefit them."

He added a folder of photographs of the poor people of Washington, D.C. to the pile. "I'm sure that after you look over all these materials, the right decision will come to you."

I nodded in agreement. "I've been immersed in informing the public about the difficulties of living in New York City during the Depression. I think I'm ready to expand my career in a different direction." My self-assurance was coming back to me now.

"I know by your work that you are a very capable young lady." He handed me my portfolio, then put his business card on top of the books. "Are you staying over in Washington?"

"No, I drove in from New York." I leaned over to pick up the stack of books.

Mr. Stryker swept them up into his arms. "I'm glad you have a car. It will be needed for this job. Here, let me help you out with these."

I directed him to my station wagon and he put the materials inside. "Call me soon with your answer. I'm looking forward to hearing from you."

"Thank you for this opportunity. I'll let you know."

These were my mother's words. She always told me to take my time when making big decisions.

The long drive home gave me time to reflect on the choice between the two jobs. There was something holding me back from taking the position out west, and that something was John. If I worked in Washington, it would be easier to see him. But if I did that, I would only be an assistant. I was anxious to get back to talk it over with him and wished I had his phone number. I did miss him. John had all the characteristics I wanted in a man. When I reflected on my husband and then Chip, I found John to be smarter, self-confident, and more adventurous. He was a self-starter, like me. I looked forward to seeing him on Friday so he could hopefully help me with this big decision.

Back in New York, after a night of sound sleep in my apartment, I went through the thick folder. I was so absorbed in the images that the ringing of the phone startled me.

It was John and he sounded distraught. "I miss you, Addie, but I can't see you on Friday. I haven't been able to go anywhere. My wife is getting worse. It has something to do with her stomach. I must stay in New Jersey and take care of her. I'll call you when I can..."

In the background, I heard a frail feminine voice calling to him. He hung up without saying good-bye.

Chapter 23
1935-1936 — No Man's Land

Let's begin to cover the main street of America... just to see what the heck occurs on it.

— Roy Stryker

I pushed John out of my thoughts as best I could, even though I kept hearing him say, *I miss you.* A move out west was starting to feel like the solution to my dead-end relationship. I tackled the books Mr. Stryker had given me. I looked over the map of Oklahoma and found what was called the Panhandle, or No Man's Land. It was made up of three counties: Cimarron, Texas, and Beaver. It was shaped like the handle of a cooking pan and bordered the states of Kansas, Colorado, New Mexico, and Texas. These states were very large compared to the smaller states on the East Coast. Just the Panhandle of Oklahoma was bigger than the entire state of Connecticut.

I learned about the Homestead Act of 1862, which encouraged western migration by providing settlers with 160 acres of public land. In exchange, homesteaders paid a small filing fee and were required to complete five years of continuous residence before receiving ownership of the land. The history of No Man's Land was fascinating. The Cherokee Indians had been the first to occupy the Panhandle, but in 1885, sadly, they were chased off into reservations when White settlers began to immigrate to this section of the Oklahoma territory. It was called No Man's Land because settlers could not claim the land there. The United States Interior Department ruled that in this 170-mile, neutral strip of public land, squatter homesteads were invalid because it had not been surveyed and Oklahoma was still not a state. One official stated, "No man can own this land!" Thus the catchy name was born.

The settlers surveyed their own land, but Congress would still not accept the new territory. It took more than four years for the tenacious people to get the government to survey it and secure their homesteads. Then they were able to borrow against their land for seed and farming equipment.

The more I studied, the more I wanted to go there. I was intrigued by the thought of traveling across the United States and photographing farmers, families, and the problems they were having because of the horrific dust storms.

Two weeks later, and with no word from John, I called Mr. Stryker and accepted the position in Oklahoma. On the phone, he told me he was overjoyed to have me join his staff. I gave away almost everything I owned except for my photography equipment, some books, and my trusty Royal typewriter. With my Ford station wagon packed, I headed to the RA office.

"Nice to see you again, Miss Peterson. I studied your portfolio more thoroughly and I'm even more impressed with your photography. I know that you have the sensitivity and compassion for this work," said Mr. Stryker as he puffed on his pipe.

"I've read all the books you sent home with me," I responded, enjoying the aroma of his pipe. "I think I'd like to photograph the Dust Bowl and its people."

"The Oklahoma Panhandle is the hardest hit area of the country. Do you think you can handle living there for over a year?"

"I will do my best," flew out of my mouth. There was one of my mother's sayings again, and I almost laughed out loud.

"Good. The RA will pay a ranch family rent and food for you while you work."

Mr. Stryker boxed up flashbulbs, developing equipment, and extra cameras. It felt like Christmas to receive all these gifts from him without having to worry about money.

We carried the boxes out to my car. "Good luck in Oklahoma,

Miss Peterson. Mail me your work every week. I look forward to seeing what you come up with."

The drive to Oklahoma would take me about a week, depending on how many hours I drove each day. Most of the states were a delight for my eyes, full of mountains, rivers, valleys, forests, and lakes...until I got to Texas. That's when I had to roll up my windows because the dust kept billowing in from the expanses of empty farmland that was parched and bare, even though it was springtime. It was so hot; the hottest weather I had ever experienced. I kept a hanky in my lap to mop my face.

Oklahoma was supposed to be as flat as Texas. Sometimes I worried about where I was because the scenery never changed. There were very few cities or houses on this route. My mind wandered. No trees! On Long Island, there was an abundance of trees, and there was the Sound to swim in to relieve oneself from the heat. At Cornell, every view had been breathtaking for me, with luscious green hills and abundant waterfalls. Even in New York City, there were trees. I fretted over whether I could really live here for a long time.

When I reached Boise City, Oklahoma, I had only thirty miles to go, heading east. I decided to spend the night in a room above a tavern so that I would be well rested before meeting the family I would be living with for a year.

The next morning, over a simple breakfast, I read *The Boise City Times.*

The dust storms continue to get worse. There were fourteen powerful dusters in '32, and in '33 we had thirty-eight of them. Can anyone remember 1931, when we had bumper crops and abundant rain?

Before I got into my car, I looked up at the sky and thought how much bigger everything looked out west. I drove down the newly paved Highway 64 until I saw the name "Douglas" hand-painted on a weather-beaten mailbox. I turned down the dirt road.

A quaint, plain farmhouse came into view. I got out, stretched my arms, and retrieved a few bags. I saw several hogs rooting around for food, which reminded me of my early photographs. There was a herd of cattle off in the distance. I tried to imagine what a dust storm would be like as I glanced up at the blue sky and watched a few cotton-ball clouds drifting high above.

As I carefully walked up the worn, squeaky steps to the front porch, the nail heads popped up. The farmhouse appeared to have originally been blue but now was a faded gray with a few blue spots. I wonder what the Douglas's would look like and felt a bit unsettled at the idea of living with complete strangers.

I knocked on the weathered door. Mrs. Douglas greeted me with a warm Boston accent. Her lovely, small-print, red-flowered apron covered most of her blouse and skirt. She wiped her hands on it and tucked in a few loose strands of light hair into her bun. "Praise the Lord you've landed here on a quiet day."

I followed her inside, my suitcases in tow, to a small, unfinished room.

"After you settle in, please come into the kitchen for some tea."

I looked around the room and was glad to see a closet large enough to be used as a darkroom.

Over tea and plain wheat biscuits, I learned that Mrs. Douglas had graduated with an English degree from a private women's college in Boston before moving out west. Her daughter, Nell, came in the kitchen with a basket of eggs while we spoke.

"Nell, this is Miss Peterson, who is going to stay with us for a while."

The little girl shyly smiled at me, her bright-blue eyes sparkling. Nell's thin, white-blond hair was cut bluntly right below the ears and her bangs went straight across her forehead in a crooked manner. Although her haircut was odd, she was an adorable child. Little Nell went to the sink to carefully wash the eggs while Mrs. Douglas and I got to know each other.

"Do you have other children?" I took a bite of the homemade biscuit.

"No, our twin boys died at birth. I guess we were lucky to

151

have Nell." She gave me a sad smile, then poured more tea. "I came here in 1927 with my inheritance money. I got 160 acres in No Man's Land for free, thanks to the Homestead Act. I found a ranch hand in Boise City to enlarge the 14 x 16 shack already on the land. Then I bought animals and farm equipment. I ended up marrying my Tex. He's such a strong, hardworking man." She glanced out through the kitchen window toward the dusty fields. A tractor plowed up dirt in the distance. "In '29, when you had the stock market crash in New York, we had an abundant garden, and a new tractor and combine. We were one proud family with a bumper crop of wheat, and two years later obtained the title to our property. Then the Depression hit and the rain stopped."

Nell dried her hands and sat in her mother's lap. Mrs. Douglas smoothed down her daughter's fine hair and gave her a biscuit.

"How brave of you to move out here alone." I took a sip of tea from the fine china cup, wondering if it was from Boston.

"Tell me about yourself, Miss Peterson. Mr. Stryker only wrote a little about you. He did send one of your photographs and I can see why you were hired." She pointed to one of my photos, which was on a small table in the corner. It was the one showing the curvaceous row of hogs waiting to be slaughtered.

"Thank you. Please, call me Addie." I told her all about photographing the Depression in New York City.

"Sounds like you have had a pretty interesting career. I hope you find Oklahoma just as rewarding. By the way, call me Lorene. You'll practically be family living here all year. Nell, help me do the wash while we chat. We cannot waste this clear day."

They took their clothes outside and I followed. Lorene and Nell scrubbed the clothes on washboards while we exchanged stories about our lives. I could tell by little Nell's wide eyes how much she enjoyed the conversation. Lorene told me how they raised broomcorn, millet, turkeys, chickens, and cattle. When the weather changed, they raised only wheat. Many of the animals had died.

I helped hang the wash on the clothesline. As I put wooden clips on numerous sacks printed with rectangular patterns, Nell hung up her dress, which I noticed had the same plaid pattern as one of the sacks. I asked Lorene where the bags were from. She answered in a surprised voice that they used to have flour and sugar in them.

Lorene pointed to one of Nell's dresses, which had a design of tiny blue flowers sprinkled on a white background. "I made that dress from the chicken feed bags. I only had to purchase a zipper, a few inches of lace, and a ten-cent pattern, which I use over and over. Use it up, wear it out, make it do or do without." She giggled.

I laughed with her. "My mother used to say that same catchy phrase."

Lorene added, "So did mine!"

I noticed Tex's underwear on the line. It had beautiful mallard ducks printed on it.

After all the wash was hung, Lorene thanked me and said that I should take photographs while it was still good weather.

"Yes, I must be off to capture pictures of the people and their land here. I'm happy to be in this beautiful state instead of the crowded city. Thanks again, Lorene, for your kind hospitality."

After I gathered my photographic equipment and put it in my car, I drove down the only highway around for miles. The sky was full of white, billowing clouds and there was no rain in sight. I rolled all the windows halfway down. It was hot out already, even though it was early spring.

I decided to spend the day photographing the general area before I spoke with any of the Douglas's neighbors. I hummed a song by Lena Horne, which reminded me of being with John at the Cotton Club. It brought up sad feelings that our relationship had ended. I was glad to have a new start to take my mind off of it.

The fields all around me were being plowed. I spied a crooked, hand-painted wooden sign fastened to a post on a barbed-wire fence. The sign practically yelled out: YOU GAVE US BEER, NOW GIVE US WATER! I reached over for my Leica. As my fingers touched it, I suddenly felt Dad's presence. It was a comfort as I began this new assignment in unfamiliar territory.

I took a few close-ups, then set up my tripod for some distance shots.

I hope Mr. Stryker will like these, I worried.

That sign told an instant story about the previous year, when President Roosevelt had been on his whistle-stop tour to see the Dust Bowl crisis in all the western states. He came out after the storms blew dust all the way to the East Coast, and supposedly, onto his desk in the White House.

As I traveled on, I took photos of emaciated cattle contrasted by fairly new farm equipment. I took a long-distance photo of a farmer wearing frayed overalls and an old straw hat, who was planting a row of small trees near his farmhouse.

After driving back to develop the film in the closet of my tiny room, I saw Tex, still plowing up the fields. Lorene and Nell were preparing dinner. I asked if they needed help, but Lorene smiled and shook her head. "I'll call you in when it's ready."

That night, on my night table, I saw several folded magazines. I picked one up and was pleasantly surprised to see articles written by Lorene. I thoroughly enjoyed her story in *Atlantic Monthly* about farm life in Oklahoma.

After a breakfast of tea, homegrown wheat cereal, and eggs, I mentioned, "Your articles have wonderful, descriptive prose and I like how you paint a picture about life on the plains for the people Back East. They're truthful and present some sad facts, but I noticed you always end them in a positive way."

"Why, thanks! I do try to bring hope to my people. I've been fortunate to receive many assignments from the magazines. Last year, my articles about our crops made more money than the crops themselves! Too much wheat is being produced, which is devaluing it. Now we have the dust storms, which makes it difficult to produce anything."

I thought about what Mr. Stryker had said about paying rent to the Douglas family during my stay. I was happy that I could at least help in that small way.

Chapter 24
The Dustbowl

It was like a shovelful of fine sand being thrown into your face...
— Alvin D. Carlson, homesteader

Alone sheet still hung on the line, flapping in the gentle breeze. *Maybe it will be cooler today,* I hoped. I left early to avoid the intense heat, which made it difficult to be in the hot car. After a productive shoot the day before, I felt comfortable with my decision to come out to the Panhandle instead of staying in Washington as an assistant.

In a neighboring field, cute rabbits hopped in and out of the newly cultivated furrows. I stopped the car and got out with my camera to catch them scampering about. I spent quite a while focusing on the groups of rabbits, then put on my close-up lens to take a photo of a single bunny.

As I focused on a distant shot of seeds being cultivated by a tractor, I looked toward the west and saw a hazy rim of dust on the horizon. Flocks of birds flew by and the earth-colored, rolling cloud appeared to be coming closer. It was fascinating; even spectacular. It began to rise in the sky, forming a shape like a mountain. I took a series of photographs as it came nearer.

Maybe this means it will rain... I thought hopefully.

More and more rabbits began hopping across the fields, away from the cloud. The expansive brown cloud drew even closer. It churned across the farmland, picking up pulverized dirt along the way. I began to hear a whooshing noise and now the cloud looked like a black, sideways tornado. When the fierce winds reached me, the howling sound snapped me out of my trance. The storm roiled higher and higher with a fury. My skirt flew up and dirt and sand peppered my bare legs like tiny knives. I choked on the dust as I gathered up my equipment and ran back to my car, which was

155

now barely visible. I blinked my eyes to get the dirt out as I felt for the car door handle, then yanked it open. As I gripped the handle, an electric shock convulsed through my body and knocked me to the ground. Stunned, I sat there, numb and in the dark, as the dust storm swirled around me and blotted out the midday sun.

Tears mixed with dirt flowed down my face. I managed to crawl into the car and close the door, my body tingling and shaking from the static electricity. My scalp felt prickly and my hair stood out on end in wiry wisps. I found a hanky in my skirt pocket, wiped my face, then blew my nose. After I composed myself, I started the car and drove slowly down the highway. Dirt pinged against the headlights, which barely cut through the midnight in the middle of the day.

As I drove along the fence lines, blue flames leaped from the barbed wire. I tightened my hands on the steering wheel to keep them from shaking. Was I getting closer to the ranch now? I hadn't been that far away when I started taking photographs...or had I? I hadn't really paid attention. At last, with squinted eyes, I thought I saw a mailbox. It said Williams on it, which I thought was the Douglas's neighbor. I crept slowly down the highway, looking for the next mailbox as the wind slammed against my car and made it weave. Finally, I pulled over and saw the name Douglas, and turned down the road to their farmhouse.

When I got out of the car, the storm pelted my entire body with dirt and sand as I blindly felt for the front steps. I crawled up to the porch, tugged open the front door, and tumbled inside.

There, sitting at the kitchen table saying the Lord's Prayer, were three shapes with flour sacks over their heads. A kerosene lamp flickered in the midday darkness. Lorene greeted me, got up to get another flour sack, poured some water on it, and told me to put it on. I noticed it had small eyeholes cut in it. I did as I was told. My face stung from the sand coming through the cracks of the house. I sat down and had to force myself not to shout, "When will it stop and will it take the house?" But I couldn't interrupt the calming prayers. Even little Nell kept up the pace of the chanting, leaning against her mother for comfort.

Lorene said, "It'll be OK, Addie. It'll be gone before you know it."

Tex added, "These dusters always have a beginning and an end. When it's over, it will be beautiful again, reminding us of why we settled here."

I noticed him holding his daughter's hand and was glad they couldn't see my tear-stained face.

The next day, the storm was over and a major clean-up was in progress. Lorene and Nell were wiping up all the dirt and dust that had seeped in through the windows and doors. Tex was out re-sowing because the storm had piled large drifts on some of the furrows.

"You did good, coming back right away. Tex put a chain on the back of your car." Lorene dusted all the furniture a second time around while Nell cleaned the windows.

"A chain?"

"It's to ground the car so your engine won't short out. Static electricity builds up in the dusters and the metal on your car will cause sparks to form. It can shock you."

I was glad Lorene didn't ask if I had gotten shocked. It was something I wanted to forget. The haunting image of the blue flames on the barbed wire was still etched into my mind.

With caution, I opened the front door and glanced toward the western horizon, looking for a duster. I would *not* be caught outside in one again. The sky was a beautiful, solid blue and there was no wind. Birds chirped happily all around me. I walked around a few piles of dirt to get to my car and checked the back to see where Tex had attached the chain.

I gathered my equipment and drove down the highway once again. I passed children who were walking to school. They looked like space creatures with black goggles over their eyes and strips of sack cloth wrapped around their noses and mouths. The boys wore oversized bib overalls with the cuffs rolled up. The girls wore dresses similar to Nell's. They each carried a lunch pail in one hand and a book in the other. I pulled over and snapped a few photographs of them until they scurried away. As I continued up the highway, I noticed a few dead rabbits and birds along the roadside that had died of dirt suffocation.

I spent the rest of the day photographing the aftermath of the horrific dust storm. In Boise City, shop owners had to shovel dirt away from their doors just to be able to get inside.

I sat at a table in a shop that had goods for sale and ordered a cold bottle of Dr. Pepper to wash down the dirt that had accumulated in my mouth, then read *The Boise City Times*.

BLACK BLIZZARD ARRIVES

Yesterday's dust storm was the biggest ever, rising 10,000 feet, and it was 200 miles wide. Winds were up to 65 miles per hour.

Folks are hoping we don't have 38 of these storms like there were in '33. There do seem to be fewer but they are larger. Temperatures continue to climb to 110 degrees this month.

Horses and cattle are missing from running away from the storm. Please let your neighbors know if you see any stray animals about.

Respiratory illnesses are on the rise, with over 31 people dead from pneumonia. The Red Cross is distributing free World War I gas masks. Come to their headquarters in town to get one.

When I got back to the ranch, I found Lorene cleaning up the garden. I helped her shovel, then she got a broom and swept off part of the garden that had turned to hardpan soil. While we worked, I asked her about interviewing families. Most of the people I had approached seemed unsociable. Lorene explained to me that I probably acted like a city person and was much too direct.

"My people are private but proud. Tex calls us the 'next-year people,' full of hope and not wishing to talk about their troubles all the time. When you talk to our neighbors, try to say something positive before you begin to talk about problems. Also, when you take as many photographs as you do, your camera is always in front of your face and it creates a distance—a barrier—between you and your subjects."

"Thanks for being honest with me. I feel fortunate to share your home to learn about your life here." Deep in thought, I continued to help her straighten out the garden.

After the dinner dishes were washed, Lorene handed me a flier and asked if I would like to go to a rabbit drive.

MAKE WAR ON RABBITS
Come to the Johnson family farm for a rabbit drive.
1:00 PM Saturday, July 20
Bring bats or clubs.
Bring the whole family to help.
No guns.

"What does this mean?" I asked as my eyebrows rose.

"We have a problem here with rabbits. They are ravaging our land. People think it's because the farmers have killed too many coyotes, which has caused the rabbit population to explode. Haven't you noticed them?"

"I have, but I thought it was part of being in the west. They sure are cute little animals."

"Nobody looks at them that way anymore. Nine rabbits can eat as much as one steer and we cannot afford to feed them. They eat everything, even the bark off the fences and anything green. They even gnawed on the handle of Tex's shovel." Lorene shook her finger while she ranted about the rabbits.

"But why did the farmers kill the coyotes?"

"You are smart, Addie, but you don't know much about the country." Lorene smiled, then explained that the coyotes were attacking the farm animals. I wanted to ask further questions about the rabbit drive, but held my tongue and decided to just experience it for myself.

Dust storm

Farmer and children walking in a dust storm

Dust storm

Chapter 25
The Rabbit Drive and the Grasshoppers

We need to work out a plan of cooperation with nature instead of continuing what we have been doing in the past — trying to buck nature.

— President Franklin D. Roosevelt

On a steaming-hot day of over a hundred degrees, we all packed ourselves into my car, including the family dog, and headed off to the rabbit drive. Lorene and Nell wore matching new skirts with bright-yellow daisies on them. I complimented the outfits and Lorene told me the flour company had recently added a new design on their sacks. She placed a big basket of food next to my film, tripod, and two cameras. Tex threw in a few baseball bats. While he drove, he whistled a lovely tune called "Home on the Range." I had read that this was the president's favorite song.

There must have been over fifty families there and it was quite a party atmosphere. Nell laughed and played a clapping game with the other girls. The dogs barked and chased rabbits while the women visited with each other. One youngster did a cartwheel and I saw a rooster and the word "Nutrena" on the back of her bloomers. Another girl flipped in the air and I saw a lion's head on her underwear.

All the talk was about rabbits. I overheard one woman say, "I had my entire garden eaten up in one day by those nasty critters."

Another lady added, "We planted a few small trees around our house to break the wind from the dusters and hordes of rabbits came. Now there are only sticks in the ground."

I stayed in the background to get some good shots, then moved up close when Mr. Johnson began to speak. I decided I would only use the Rolleiflex Mr. Stryker had sent with me. What a terrific camera this was! I had grown too accustomed to using my Leica. The Rolleiflex was compact, lightweight, and had a long strap that hung down to my waist. Just a quick glance in the viewfinder and I could take a photo discreetly and still talk to people without a camera in my face. Most people were too busy getting on with the business of trying to survive and didn't want to be photographed.

Small clouds of dust billowed up due to all the activity and I was glad I had worn my tailored boys' trousers, unlike the other women, who wore their best long skirts.

"Thank y'all for comin'!" Mr. Johnson had to shout above the dogs yipping. "We'll have some watermelon at the farm after we're done. Now, everyone spread out. When I whistle, circle in toward the gate."

He brought his fingers to his lips and whistled, and the circle of farm folks tightened. Thick swarms of jackrabbits hopped furiously into the air. Everyone began to hoot and holler, which drove the rabbits toward the center, where there was a pen past the open gate.

I remained in the foreground to photograph the event and tried to get a picture of the rabbits jumping high into the air. The noise of the dogs and people shouting made it hard for me to concentrate.

Mr. Johnson gave off a long, sharp whistle as he shut the gate. The women and girls wandered away and the men and boys climbed into the pen. Before I knew what was happening, bats and clubs swung up and down in the air.

I was completely unprepared for this experience. The rabbits began to scream as they were being clubbed to death. I had no idea that rabbits made such a horrific noise. My hands shook on the shutter release as I tried to keep the camera steady. The continuous, high-pitched, *"BBBB"* of the rabbits completely unnerved me, as did the wild scene around me. Boys who looked to be only five years old were swinging their bats while their fathers egged them on. My stomach churned as I tried to shut out the screeching and kept clicking away. The dogs on the outside of the fence went crazy, wanting to get in on the action.

I finally moved away to settle my nerves. I went to the car and got my tripod so I could take a long-distance shot of the mothers socializing juxtaposed with the swinging bats in the distance.

After it was all over, the farm women gathered food from their vehicles and set out a feast on the Johnsons' porch.

I packed all my camera equipment into the station wagon and rested in the front seat. I didn't have an appetite after what I'd just witnessed, and when I closed my eyes, I kept hearing the screams of the rabbits even though it was all over.

Because nothing was wasted, people brought home rabbits to be skinned and boiled for food or to be used for feed for the farm animals.

On the way home, Lorene glanced over at her husband, who was enjoying driving my station wagon. "I heard the Johnsons say it was a successful drive and there were so many rabbits killed that the leftovers would be shipped to feed people Back East."

"I reckon there were over 6,000 jackrabbits slaughtered today. I'm going to a rabbit drive next month where rifles are used, and there's an ammo truck for anyone who runs out of bullets."

Lorene gave him a worried look.

Tex added, "Only the men are going."

I remained quiet the rest of the trip back to the house, the rabbits' screams still racing through my mind.

It took about a month to mail all of my developed photos to Mr. Stryker, along with articles about what it was like to be in a real duster and at a rabbit drive.

Two weeks later, Lorene handed me a letter.

Anxious to read what Mr. Stryker had to say, I eagerly opened the envelope.

> *Dear Miss Peterson,*
>
> *I am pleased with your work. The photographs of the beer sign, dust storm, rabbit roundup, etc. are all constructed in a professional way as well as with an artistic flair. I like how your photos convey a feeling of hope and show the simple pleasures of life on the plains (like hanging up the wash).*

I sent a few of your photographs to a national weekly magazine (see enclosed).

Now that you have settled in, it is important to record the many government programs that are aiding the people there. For all further assignments, I want you to photograph the New Deal federal relief programs.

Keep sending me your best photos, or if you don't have the time to develop them just mail me your rolls of film. I'll send you copies of what I like.

Let me know if you need anything,

Regards,

Roy Stryker, RA

In the large envelope was *The Saturday Evening Post.* It had my spectacular photograph of a duster right on the front cover. I felt so proud. This magazine was large format. I flipped through it and saw that it contained the most photographs I had ever seen in a publication. Inside was another one of my pictures with the headline: THESE ARE THE PEOPLE OF OKLAHOMA, WHO SURVIVE ANY DISASTER THROWN THEIR WAY.

Under it was my picture of the children walking to school wearing gas masks. The pride I felt upon seeing this made me feel like I was making a difference in the world.

I looked over the magazine with a critical eye before sharing it with Lorene, and was pleased to see that my photographs had elements of honesty, compassion, and realism.

Lorene was enthusiastic about my pictures and articles in *The Saturday Evening Post* and suggested further ideas for me to explore. What I liked the most about living out west was the endless photographic possibilities awaiting me.

Six months went by faster than I could have imagined. Lorene and I were becoming fast friends. She confided in me, telling me that no one ever really got used to the dust storms, and she hated how they rolled in without warning. I found it comforting to join in with the family prayers during the storms. I appreciated Tex saying that the dusters did always end. The love in this family was strong and spilled over on me. I began to feel secure in this harsh environment.

The following week there was yet another dust storm and hordes of grasshoppers descended on the Panhandle. Inside the farmhouse, Lorene, Nell, and I peered outside through the grasshopper-covered window. They were so thick, they blocked out the light and darkened the room.

"Damn locusts!" Tex yelled from the table.

"What are locusts? I thought they were grasshoppers," I whispered to Lorene.

She explained to me that they were, but when there were swarms of them, they were called locusts.

I grabbed my camera to sneak outside only for a minute, even though Tex shouted at me not to. The buzzing noise was deafening. I photographed the chickens pecking heartily at the instant feast that had appeared before them. Then more and more of the voracious insects began to arrive, scaring the chickens back into their coops for an early roost. The locusts didn't seem to hop; they just crawled on the ground in a solid mass. I bolted back into the farmhouse after they hit my camera lens and clung to my clothes. When I opened the front door, a mass of them followed me in. The whole family got up and starting swatting them with rolled up newspapers.

"I told you not to go out there!" Tex growled, his eyes ablaze.

I apologized, embarrassed by my boldness, and helped smash the insects.

Early the next morning, the storm was gone. Lorene went outside, then came back crying. "My cucumbers, tomatoes, and watermelon...they're all gone. They cleaned us out. Could anything more go wrong living in this godforsaken place?"

Nell was frightened by her mother's tears and began to whimper.

Tex put his big strong arms around them both. "We'll get through this. We have each other and the Good Lord to keep us together." He glanced over and gave me a heartwarming smile.

Rolleiflex camera

Jackrabbit drive

A locust swarm

Chapter 26
Civilian Conservation Corps

The Corps has changed my life around and made me a better person mentally and physically. I have learned social skills, communication skills, training for natural disasters.

— CCC worker

It was consoling to hear the preacher's reassuring words and to be part of Lorene and Tex's close-knit family as we attended church services in Boise. I felt the same serenity I once felt as a child when our family went to our "church" in the woods.

Before we left, I bought a newspaper to keep up to date on the latest news, and read it in the car on the ride back to the farm.

BOISE CITY TIMES
PLAGUES OF GRASSHOPPERS

In an eight-hour period over 23,000 locusts per acre descended on the Panhandle. The insects arrived like a huge, dark cloud and the sun was momentarily hidden, turning day into night. They were a solid, moving, powerful mass, able to travel great distances, cleaning out most of the green vegetation in range with their insatiable appetites. Cornstalks were eaten to the ground and many fields were left completely barren. Mr. Howard H. Finnell, Department of Soil Conservation, said the drought causes them to populate.

The Corps will be coming to help us clean up the tremendous mess of grasshoppers and eradicate the live ones.

The CCC will save the day!

"What's the CCC?" I pointed to the article in the paper.

Tex shook his head. "We don't need them. I can set out vats of kerosene and poison the critters myself."

169

Lorene knew only what the letters stood for, which was Civilian Conservation Corps. I assumed that this was one of the government programs Mr. Stryker wanted me to report on.

That Monday, I went in search of scenes to photograph and found the highway thick with dead bugs.

Just ahead, I saw a sign: YOUR CCC AT WORK!

I pulled over to take a photo of it, then noticed young men wearing uniforms shoveling up the locusts and putting them in boxes. They were also pouring a thick liquid along the sides of the roads. My nose caught the scent of molasses. I took a few shots, then walked up to the men and asked what the substance was.

One young boy spoke out while the others stared at me. "Poison for all the bugs."

An older man yelled at him to keep working, then asked, "Who are ya, lady, and what's it to ya, anyway?"

I showed him my camera and said I worked for the Resettlement Administration. He told me they were too busy to answer my questions and gave me directions to their headquarters. I knew he just wanted to get me out of the way.

This was exactly what Mr. Stryker wanted me to photograph and I assumed that the CCC was probably one of the New Deal programs. After putting all my equipment into my car, I carefully drove away, weaving in and out of the grasshoppers. The sound of my tires crunching on the dreadful dead bodies was disgusting.

Several miles ahead I found a group of buildings with a sign similar to the one on the road, but larger. The first building had a hand-carved sign that read: CCC OFFICE.

I parked the car, got out, smoothed down my wrinkled skirt, and gave my cheeks a pinch for some color. After meeting the workers on the road, I was a bit intimidated, but I put the camera strap around my neck and hid my Rolleiflex inside my blouse, then knocked on the door.

A deep voice boomed out, "Don't knock! Come in!"

I stepped in with caution.

A large, rugged man with a close-cut beard, wearing a khaki uniform with the insignia "CCC" on his shirt, sat behind a desk. "Oh, pardon my abruptness, ma'am. I thought you were one of the workers. Have a seat. May I help you?"

A blush reddened my face. I hadn't seen such a handsome man in a long time. "I'm Adeline Peterson, a photographer for the Resettlement Administration. I was interested in obtaining information about your organization."

"Where're you from?" His dimples flashed when he spoke.

"New York."

"Must've been a shock to land here."

My face flushed. "Yes, but I feel useful being here. There never seems to be a dull moment between the dusters and the locusts."

"What would you like to know about the Civilian Conservation Corps?"

"There's very little I know about it except that I thought maybe it was one of the president's New Deal programs, like the RA."

"Right ya are. Here's a brochure about the Corps."

I reached across the desk for it. "Thank you, Mr....uh..."

"Name's Smokey. Really, it's Stanley, but I got the name from fightin' forest fires." A grin spread across his face.

"My boss wants me to write about government programs that are helping the Panhandle." I gave him my best smile.

A group of boys interrupted our conversation as they came in to report on the work they had done cleaning up the locusts and asking what to do next. They looked me over in a sly way. After Smokey told them to keep poisoning the locusts and cleaning them up throughout the three counties, they left looking disappointed. I imagined they were probably sick of doing that job.

"Come back tomorrow at 1:00, Miss Peterson. I'll have more time to show you around and you can use your camera." He nodded at the huge bulge inside my blouse.

I thanked him and left to shoot more photographs.

That night, after developing my film, I read the booklet about the CCC. I learned that the Civilian Conservation Corps had been established within the first hundred days of President Roosevelt taking office. It provided men and boys with training and gave them jobs as part of the Emergency Work Act. They were paid $30 a month, but were required to send $25 of it to their families back home. In the brochure was an oath to be read and signed in order to volunteer. What an innovative new program. I looked forward to interviewing Smokey and thought about what camera equipment I would need.

The next afternoon, I arrived at the CCC headquarters at one o'clock on the dot. Smokey greeted me, eager to share his knowledge, and gave me a tour of the facility. It was set up like an army post, with commanders who taught the men discipline and a work ethic. The barracks at the Beaver County facility held 200-300 men. I looked out at the sea of neatly kept cots and saw a wood stove for heat.

The next building was a recreational hall with card and pool tables.

"This is the education building—the one I'm the proudest of." He swung an arm out toward rows of desks, walls of books, and open cabinets full of paper, envelopes, and other supplies. "The CCC helps the illiterate learn how to read and write. Many of our men have had very little schooling because of having to support their families. Here they learn how to write letters home, and some even learn how to read blueprints."

After jotting down a few notes, I asked, "What age do you accept into the program?"

"As young as sixteen. Our boys are sworn in and leave as men with constructive skills. We teach them how to drive and repair farm vehicles, as well as how to cook. Everyone gets plenty to eat and free work clothes to wear." Smokey spoke with great pride.

I photographed the signs on the buildings as the workers went in and out.

Smokey said, "Nice camera. I've never used one."

"Would you like to learn?" I asked, looking into his lively green eyes.

"Sure. Come back tomorrow and I'll take you to another project we're doing, then you can show me."

I met Smokey the following day at a state park, where his crew was constructing a building. I snapped a few photos with my Leica.

"Let me try," Smokey said.

He touched my fingers and looked into my eyes, then gave me a quick kiss. It felt natural and I enjoyed it. My entire body flushed with passion, wanting more.

Smokey pulled back. "Now, where did you say the lens was?"

I laughed and batted my eyelashes, then handed him the camera. I explained all the components and what they did while Smokey held it and tried it out. Our attraction for each other seemed mutual and I found myself consumed with desire.

Workers with the Civilian Conservation Corps

Chapter 27
Operation Dust Bowl, 1937

Even the government said, unless something is done, the western plains will become as arid as the Arabian Desert.

— Homesteader

The following morning, Lorene told me about a new high school that was being built by the Work Progress Administration and would be worth photographing. Excited, I gathered my equipment and headed out.

After a successful shoot at the school, I drove by an abandoned field and saw a man in the middle of it in a full dress suit carrying a large leather briefcase. He stuck out like a wart on a pretty face as he inspected the area and bent down to sample the soil. He was absorbed in his work and didn't notice me. I took a few candid shots of him, then called out as he stood up in the middle of the barren field, which had been stripped of all vegetation.

After I introduced myself, he nodded and said, "Mr. Stryker wrote you'd be in these parts. I'm a soil scientist. Howard Finnell. Glad to meet you."

"Yes! I read about you in *The Boise City Times*."

Mr. Finnell spouted a wealth of information while I followed him around like a dog seeking food, frantically scribbling notes in my notebook. Finally, we walked over to a row of newly planted trees for a bit of shade. He mopped his face with a kerchief. He was quite an enthusiastic talker and I had to ask him to slow down so I could keep up with all the information.

Mr. Finnell told me that if the farmers would follow his plan, much of the land could be as productive as it had been in the past. "Miss Peterson, I've recorded all my methods. Would you like to read about them?"

"That would be helpful. Mr. Stryker has wanted me to

photograph and write articles about successful New Deal programs. Could I take a shot of you by these trees?"

"Of course. My job depends on good publicity." He brushed the dirt off his nice dress pants.

I took a few close-ups, then a couple of distance shots of Mr. Finnell among the young trees.

He reached into his suitcase and handed me the typed paper he had written. "Here, read this and let's get together next Friday. I'll meet you at the tree planting in Cimarron County. You'll see it as soon as you cross the county line."

When I got back to the ranch, I told Lorene about Finnell's project, which was called "Operation Dust Bowl."

She caught my enthusiasm. "At last, the government is concerned about us forgotten people here in No Man's Land! Now there might be hope. I wonder what Tex will say about Mr. Finnell's methods of solving our problems?"

"After I digest Finnell's theories, I'll be curious as to what Tex's opinion is as well. He's such a practical man."

In my little room, I read the dissertation. Howard H. Finnell was a soil scientist with a degree in agriculture from Oklahoma A&M and the head of the newly created Soil Conservation Service. Mr. Finnell had over thirteen demonstration projects in the states making up the Dust Bowl, with the CCC and the WPA implementing them. When I read he that was involved with the CCC, my heart raced. *Smokey must know Mr. Finnell*, I thought. I smiled. Maybe I would see Smokey again.

On Friday, I photographed the CCC workers, in their denim outfits, planting tree seedlings on the farms where the owners had agreed to participate. Mr. Finnell supervised an eleven-man team working near a farmhouse. As I clicked away, I felt someone touch the back of my neck. It was Smokey.

"Hi beautiful, I missed you," he whispered, then went off to chat with Mr. Finnell.

I followed behind as my heart fluttered with excitement.

Mr. Finnell told him that just one team of men could plant 6,000 rows of trees, which were essential for windbreaks to protect the land and farmhouses.

"I've got the crew for you," Smokey answered.

"The landowners are responsible for the care of the trees after they're planted. This will stop their fields from blowing."

"Sounds like a good plan."

Before Smokey left to round up more men, he said to me in a low voice, "Wait for me until I get back."

I gave him a smile and continued to photograph the tree planting.

Smokey came back with more workers. He talked me into going back to camp with him, where we watched lunch preparations in the mess hall and I took pictures of the men being trained as cooks. I enjoyed watching him as he pointed out new cooking equipment and explained how the CCC could certify the men to get jobs as cooks when they got out.

As we walked toward his office, I asked Smokey about the Negro population and the CCC. He told me there were over 143 separate CCC camps for Negroes, and they received equal pay and housing. His eyes lit up as he chatted. Smokey's dimples gave me the irresistible urge to kiss him. He put his arm around my waist and flashed me an "I want you" smile, then led me to his bedroom, which was attached to his office.

Smokey played with my hair and I stroked his soft beard. We were mesmerized by each other's faces. Then we fell onto his bed in a passionate embrace and began to undress each other. When Smokey nibbled my earlobe, his soft breath aroused me. He was a tender lover, exploring and kissing every part of my body. He rose above me and we became one in a soothing, rocking rhythm, which culminated in delightful, miniature explosions tingling throughout my body.

After we made love, Smokey felt my bare shoulder with his rough fingers. "I'm fallin' for you, Addie, and I can tell you feel the same. Our affair is having a sweet beginning. How long are you plannin' on bein' in the Panhandle?"

"It's all up to my boss and whether my work meets his expectations."

"Well, babe, your work drive is the best I've ever seen, especially for a lady. You'll probably be here a long time. I, on the other hand, never know where I'll be sent or when."

"But you're the head commander here for the Oklahoma CCC. Why would you be sent anywhere else?"

"The Conservation Corps is just like the US Army. They can uproot me and replace me at a moment's notice. As much as I regret saying this, our relationship will likely have an end."

"Oh..." I turned away from him, dressed quickly, then made up a reason to leave. "There's a church social tonight. I have to get back early to clean up."

"You look pretty clean to me."

"Thanks," I mumbled, and left.

During dinner, Tex and Lorene asked me about my day. I told them all about the CCC and explained about Mr. Finnell and the tree project.

Tex shrugged his shoulders. "Planting more trees means spending money we don't have. Droughts come and go and its all nature's doing. The rains will come and we'll soon be back in business with a boom once more."

I began to say something about free trees, but he got up and went outside.

Before I left the next day, Lorene said, "Addie, please tell me all you find out from Mr. Finnell. Even if Tex acts like he knows everything, I think it's important for us to stay informed."

"Don't worry, I'll share all I learn from Finnell. I've read his credentials and he's quite an intelligent man. He's not just a book-smart scientist. I've seen him sharing information with all the farmers. Mr. Finnell's set up over twelve agricultural demonstration projects manned by the CCC and WPA. His heart is with the people of the Dust Bowl, but he wants them all to know that they cannot keep mismanaging the soil."

When I found Mr. Finnell, he was talking with a farmer at the McCoy ranch. I photographed a few of the plows and heard him explaining plowing methods. We visited many farms and ranches together.

That night at dinner, I told Lorene what Mr. Finnell said about how the new plows the farmers had bought were ruining the land. It was not helping the production of crops and they needed to go back to using the Lister plows.

Tex interrupted me, shaking his finger. "No way am I going to use that back-breaking Lister again when I have a brand-new, faster plow. Who does this highfalutin man think he is, going around givin' everyone advice?"

I answered in a subdued voice, "I can see how you would feel that way, but Mr. Finnell says the Lister makes deeper furrows, which in turn holds the water better, so the crops can grow more. Do you think this is true, Tex?"

Tex thought for a minute. "Maybe." He went outside to finish his work before nightfall.

Lorene touched my hand. "He means well and does have a tender side to his gruffness."

I smiled. "Yes, I've seen that soft side of your husband, especially with Nell."

During the week, I learned all about cover crops and shared the information with Lorene that night at dinner. The only way to control the terrible erosion from the dust storms was by planting grass for ground cover, like the buffalo grass that was once native to that area. Mr. Finnell explained to me that the farmers had to stop harvesting crops and leaving the fields completely barren.

After Tex finished his stewed rabbit and dumplings, Lorene asked him in a kind, soft voice what he thought about planting cover crops.

Tex snapped, "No way am I going to plant useless buffalo grass. I don't have time for that." He moved his plate aside and went outside to sharpen tools.

I continued to accompany Mr. Finnell and shot some terrific photographs while learning all about the area. Mr. Finnell petitioned the Secretary of Agriculture for $2 million in emergency funds to offer incentives of 20 cents an acre for those who used the contour listing method on their land. Most of the farmers signed up. I asked Lorene if she thought Tex might. She replied she wasn't certain, as he was a stubborn man and might not take government handouts, but said they sure could use the money. We planned a day to invite Mr. Finnell over for dinner, to see if perhaps Tex would sign up for the incentive program after meeting him in person.

When that day came, during a special meal of roasted pork and corn, Mr. Finnell talked nonstop about all the government programs. I was worried that he might seem too boisterous and would make Tex clam up. Tex said very little, yet before Mr. Finnell left, he signed up to receive the money and even agreed to allow a crew from the CCC to plant more trees around the farmhouse. Now, the Douglas family would receive a check from the government by reducing their wheat plantings by 39 acres and planting buffalo grass instead.

Smokey and I got together occasionally. He showed me various projects the men were working on and I documented them with photographs for Mr. Stryker. But most days I spent with Mr. Finnell. I tried to resist Smokey's magnetic charm, but seemed to always give in. It took me months to understand why I tried to refrain from his amorous ways. I guess I wanted a man who would make a long-term commitment, and I knew that man was not Smokey.

At long last, seven years had passed since Martin and I had been in contact, and I sent away for papers and filed for divorce. When it wasn't contested, I was free! I made a vow to myself to never marry again, though I thought it would be nice to have a marriage like Tex and Lorene had. Smokey and I seemed to have an equal connection. Chip had been a fun companion but was a bit immature for me. My thoughts moved on to John. *He's married,* I reminded myself. *You were a fool to want to continue that relationship.*

I did appreciate Smokey's honesty when he said early on that our affair would eventually end because of his job. Several times I almost told Lorene about Smokey, but was too embarrassed to mention our loose arrangement. I learned to take things day by day and enjoyed the time we had together, though not having a solid relationship like my parents once had sometimes nagged at me.

The WPA

Chapter 28
1937, Mr. Finnell

All that is needed is to make a better use of the rain that is received. Moisture conservation is the answer.
— H. Howard Finnell

"Miss Peterson, have you ever been up in an airplane?" Mr. Finnell asked.

"Yes, I have. It was quite a few years ago. I took a few aerial shots of a skyscraper for *Architectural Digest.*"

"What type of plane were you in?"

"A Travel Air 4000."

"Perfect! I need you to go up in an open-cockpit plane to shoot specific pieces of farmland. I will use the photographs, along with my soil samples, to decide which parcels have the best chance to grow crops again and which should be restored to grassland. This way the farmers will see proof that the Soil Conservation Service methods work."

Mr. Finnell introduced me to "Boots" Carpenter, a crusty old barnstormer who earned his money by stunt flying at all the county fairs. His plane was a battered Curtiss Jenny biplane. It was frightening to look at as I compared it to the Travel Air, which had been in pristine condition.

On Mr. Finnell's map, he showed us the specific areas he needed to have photographed. Since I would not be able to sit side-by-side with the pilot in this plane, Boots had the map and was to hover over specific areas, which would be my signal to photograph the land below.

Mr. Finnell left to continue taking his soil samples. I looked at Boots as he put his helmet on over his salt-and-pepper hair.

"Ready for a ride in this baby?" Boots patted the fuselage but kept his eyes on me, a silly grin pasted on his leathery face.

I walked around the long-winged plane to avoid his

obnoxious ogling.

"How old is this airplane?" I touched the propeller and remembered that the pristine Travel Air 4000 was a 1929 model and had a top speed of 130 mph. This airplane was filthy and dull gray with dents all over it.

"It's over forty years old. It's surplus back from when I was in the Great War." He threw a helmet at me. "Let's go."

"What's the airspeed?" I persisted, determined to get my questions answered.

"Seventy-five mph. Come on. Time's a-wastin'."

Boots had to lift me by my waist to help me up onto the wing so I could climb into the plane. When I settled into my seat, he handed me all my camera supplies, then swung the big propeller to start the plane. I wondered whether this crappy old plane would get off the ground and stay in the air. This was going to be much slower than my previous flight in the Travel Air. My fingers fidgeted as I tried to organize my equipment in the tiny cockpit.

It was a slow climb, even though Boots had it at full throttle. Once I got used to the loud clattering noise of the Curtiss Jenny, I enjoyed the marvelous view of Oklahoma from the air. I kept my film holders loaded and ready.

Far below the plane, I saw a few green patchwork areas and a lot of dull-brown, barren areas full of half-buried wheat and corn, and rivers of sand instead of water. Sometimes the sand rose up into the air like curtains, causing me to choke. We passed by endless fields that should have been green with crops but instead showed only wind-driven ripples in the sand that covered them. I photographed various animals dying in the drifting soil. It was disturbing to see the devastation.

I kept up the pace of unloading and reloading the film, which was done hidden from the light inside the big black changing bag on my lap. The sun was at the perfect angle and the photographic light was optimal. I got some terrific shots.

Boots hovered over productive pastures marked on the map that had been plowed according to Mr. Finnell's method. Then we appeared to be returning to the airstrip. The sun was still high. Confused, I wondered why we were heading back so soon.

Suddenly, the airplane flipped upside down, rolled over a few times, then arched up and around in a complete circle. I clutched the edges of the cockpit. I started gulping air and screaming, then threw up all over my equipment. The plane leveled off and we made an abrupt landing that was so rough, I vomited again.

Boots helped me out as I wiped my mouth on my sleeve. I was shaken and furious.

"Why the hell did we go upside down? Did something go wrong with the engine?" I snapped as I tried to settle my churning stomach.

Boots had a sheepish look on his face. "I was practicing my barrel rolls. I have a fair coming up next month."

"Why did we head back so early?"

"The fuel supply only lasts two hours in the Jenny. We'll go up again tomorrow."

I felt miserable and didn't say anything more as I dragged my equipment to my car on shaky legs.

The next day, Boots met me at the plane. "Good morning, Miss Peterson, how are you feeling today?" he chuckled.

"I'll tell you right now, I'm not going up in that plane if you plan to do any of your fancy tricks again. Aren't you being paid for this job?"

"Yeah." He kept his glance on the ground.

"Well, without me as a passenger you'll lose this work."

"I apologize, Miss Peterson. It won't happen again." Boots had an embarrassed, stupid grin on his face.

"I'm counting on that. Now, let's go up. And no more monkeying around."

It took many months to get all of the Dust Bowl states and specific land areas photographed for Mr. Finnell. Mr. Stryker's letters were encouraging. Many of my photos were published by *The Saturday Evening Post* and *Collier's Magazine*.

One evening, Mr. Finnell joined us for dinner to discuss reducing the number of Tex and Lorene's cattle. Farmers were paid up to $16 a head for any healthy cow, and $1 to slaughter any malnourished cattle. Mr. Finnell asked Tex if he was interested.

Tex hesitated. "I hate to admit it, but we're having trouble affording the feed for our cattle and we don't have the pastureland for them to graze on."

Lorene glanced at her husband's worry-lined face, then squeezed his hand as she rose to clear the table.

When I witnessed the affection Tex and Lorene had for each other, it made me wish I had the same. I hadn't seen Smokey in quite a while, so decided to go by his office the next day. I longed for his touch as well as being able to talk with someone besides Lorene.

He greeted me with enthusiasm. "I missed you, Addie. You never told me where you're staying or I would've come by to see you. What have you been up to?"

I blushed, not wishing to have Smokey meet Lorene and Tex because of our casual arrangement. I told him all about my aerial photographs. I mentioned that Boots was the pilot and Smokey laughed heartily.

"I know that character. It must have been difficult to work with that old codger. Did he show off at all?"

"He did. I had to put a stop to his shenanigans from the get-go because Mr. Finnell had a deadline for the photos."

"Good for you. I'd love to see some of your shots from the plane."

"What about you? How's everything going here at camp?"

He eagerly told me about his work and shared a few anecdotes about some of the new recruits. Then he got up from his desk, bent down, and kissed me passionately. I reached up and put my arms around his broad shoulders.

A knock came at the door, interrupting our embrace. A fight had broken out in the cafeteria and Smokey had to leave to break it up. Disappointed, I left him to his work and headed back to the ranch.

A few weeks later, a CCC bulldozer was due to come out to the Douglas ranch to assist with the cattle project. I hoped Smokey would show up, thinking it would be the perfect opportunity to introduce him to Lorene and Tex. I went out with my camera equipment, looking for him, but he wasn't among the crew.

The neighboring farmers arrived to help with the slaughter. Lorene and Nell watched as a huge ditch was dug and the unhealthy, skeletal stock was herded into it. The farmers raised their rifles and began to shoot the unfit cattle. I forced myself to remain to photograph the horrific massacre. Nell sobbed into her mother's apron as a starving little calf was pushed into the ditch. Lorene picked up her daughter and ran inside. The noise of the crowded cattle, bellowing and snorting, paired with the piercing sound of the shotguns, made it hard for me to concentrate and keep the camera steady. After the emaciated cattle were killed, the bulldozer buried them all in a massive grave. It was a difficult day for us all. We had a light dinner that night and retired early.

The next day, Lorene shared with me an article she had published in the *Atlantic Monthly*.

Here in the Oklahoma region called No Man's Land, we have been struggling to maintain our precious farms and ranches. As we get deeper and deeper in dust, a soil scientist, Mr. Finnell, was sent by the government to educate the farmers on how to effectively deal with the drought. With great reluctance we have had to cull our emaciated cattle. Some were shipped to a packinghouse to be slaughtered for distribution to families on relief.

In Cimarron County alone, two tons of smoked pork, sixteen tons of beef, seventeen tons of flour, and thirty-three tons of coal were received in the surplus commodities program.

Thanks to Mr. Finnell, the federal government will pay farmers to sell some of their land back to be taken out of production. It is then reseeded as grasslands to reduce the dangerously eroded land. This smart, enthusiastic man has been a gift to those of us trying to survive in the Dust Bowl. Mr. Finnell instituted free trees for our farmers with crews from the Civilian Conservation Corps to plant them. He teaches better farming methods for these difficult drought times. I have a great respect for this soil scientist, who proselytizes his hope for our

Oklahoma prairies.

While we cannot control Mother Nature, we need to use new methods to be able to cope with whatever comes our way.

We continue to live and enjoy our non-storm days, when the sunset in Oklahoma changes from bright blue to multiple shades of orange. The American finch flies by, showing off its yellow feathers. The glory of the sunsets with the brilliance of a starlit sky at night...this is what keeps us in Oklahoma.

I enjoyed reading Lorene's writing as she exposed the naked truth, laced with delightful, positive prose. I was glad the people in the east would receive a little view of life out here in the Dust Bowl.

Curtiss Jenny

Curtiss Jenny

Chapter 29
Homestead in Reverse

Our efforts to manipulate the forces of nature to fit our own convenience are wrong. Instead we should attempt to harmonize our farming operations to fit conditions as they are rather than as we hope they will be.

— H. Howard Finnell

Government officials wanted to end all forms of relief. In the *Boise Times*, it said they wanted the people to move, then "re-wild" the entire drought-ridden plains area.

Tex was one of several hundred men who had signed up with "The Last Man Club." Every farmer got a special membership card if they pledged to stay and persevere on their own land.

The Resettlement Administration was already buying up farms and offering displaced farmers loans to get them to move. Tex called it homesteading in reverse, or he'd say those farmers were just "plain ol' quitters."

Rumors of the perfect climate in California, with an abundance of work in the agricultural industry, enticed hundreds of families to give up and migrate away from the Dust Bowl in search of a better life.

I received a letter from Mr. Stryker along with five startling photographs. They were of a young mother who looked gaunt and haunted with worry. Her children clung to her, frightened and helpless. I looked at the photos with a sharp eye before reading his letter. The mother was sitting under a tattered tent that was held up by a single piece of wood. On a bench sat a rusty lantern and an empty tin plate. In another photo, the mother was nursing a babe in her arms in her ragged sweater and checkered dress. Her hand held up her weary, worried face and the other arm cradled her hungry baby to her breast. In the next photo, her eyes were closed in exhaustion. The last photo showed her two other children in worn, oversized clothes, their faces buried deep in her frail shoulders, melding the melancholy family into one image.

In Mr. Stryker's letter, he explained how these photographs raised awareness of the plight of the destitute migrant worker. The family lived in a camp of field workers in Nipomo, California. Their livelihood was devastated by the failure of the pea crops that had frozen. The mother and her children had been living on the frozen vegetables and wild birds caught from the field. She was a widow, her husband having died recently from tuberculosis. The family could not move on because she had just sold the tires on her car to buy food. Mr. Stryker wrote that the photographer was Dorothea Lange, who was employed by the RA to document the migration to the California. She sent the photo of the destitute migrant mother to the editor of a San Francisco newspaper. After publishing it, the editor informed federal authorities and the government rushed a shipment of 20,000 pounds of food to the camp. This single photograph caused tremendous impact and effected change to help people.

In the rest of the letter, he explained Lange's photography techniques. She shot exposures of the woman by working closer and closer from the same direction with a Graflex camera. Lange climbed on top of her car and shot from above, which gave the subject more stature and esteem.

Mr. Stryker requested that I shoot photographs of people migrating out of Oklahoma. He suggested that I should not only focus on faces, but objects that tell stories, such as the lantern, the empty metal food plate, and the battered truck with no tires. He added, *Your job will be to raise awareness of the plight of the impoverished farmers and their families who were forced to leave their land and move.*

I put the letter down, dispirited. Instead of photographing the rehabilitation of the Dust Bowl, I was now assigned to photograph the migration out of it. I would need to gather strength from deep within to document the people who had given up their land and were moving on. After focusing for months on just aerial land photographs for Mr. Finnell, I had been unaware of the mass migration that was now underway.

I had been in Oklahoma for two years now and had gotten to know some of the families intimately. I asked Lorene if she knew anyone who was moving to California. She asked why I wanted to know, and looked depressed after I asked for a list of who was leaving.

I headed out with my Rolleiflex camera so I wouldn't intimidate anyone while photographing them. As I drove down Highway 64 out of town, sure enough, there were streams of vehicles with makeshift homes attached to them. Trucks and cars had been made bigger in order to haul an entire family and their belongings. One 1934 station wagon had a wooden crate built on the side with a goat in it. All kinds of people were blowing out of Oklahoma, just like the dust storms.

I shot photos of piles of household goods roped to the tops of slatted truck beds and on wooden platforms affixed to the backs of station wagons. I captured a whole family in a tent on a flatbed truck, along with a small stove and rusty metal garbage cans containing precious items. The ribbed canvas tops were like modern-day covered wagons. People were leaving in their houses on wheels to become fruit tramps picking in orchards in the west.

The first families to leave were the sharecroppers and tenant farmers, who were headed out to greener pastures to try their luck. Besides, it wasn't their land anyway and they weren't producing enough crops to pay the rent.

I took a photograph of a farmer I picked up hitchhiking. He wore worn, dirty, blue-and-white striped bib coveralls and had only one suitcase in his hand. Filled with hope, he told me there was plenty of work in California picking grapes or tomatoes. The farmer said he was tired of living on relief, which made him feel worthless. When I asked about his family, his face fell. He said they'd had to move in with his parents, who had a small savings. He would send for them after he made enough money.

What astonishes the eye? This is what Mr. Stryker wanted me to photograph. The farther I drove out of the state, the more people I saw living in tents on the side of the road. Those not lucky enough to have tents were in ramshackle shelters made of cardboard, rags, sticks, or scrap metal, or they simply slept in their vehicles. Some people were completely out of funds and food. The children were dirty and shabby, their anxious parents clinging to each other in the squalor of the roadside encampments. Remembering Mr. Stryker's request to not just show people's faces, I also photographed their clothes and belongings.

When appropriate, I asked a lot of simple questions. "How long have you been on the road?" or "Where are you from?" I would ask respectfully, "Would you mind if I photographed you?" The answer was usually, "Sure, why not?"

I learned to be polite as well as friendly, which encouraged natural conversation as well as better, more natural photographs. Some families seemed happy, looking forward to a new life, while others appeared to be worn down with worry. I interviewed owners of farms who couldn't pay their taxes, had their land foreclosed on, and had packed up.

In front of one farm, I shot a large, hand-lettered sign on a wood post: FOR SALE: CROPS, STOCK, TOOLS.

Many of the farms had been mechanized, with machinery replacing workers. One farmer told me that when the rains came back, people wouldn't be needed anymore. He said that after buying his tractor, he'd let go of his help. Everywhere I saw deserted homestead shacks on treeless landscapes.

Day after day, I'd walk around and take pictures of story-telling objects, such as a flat tire off of a truck or abandoned, skinny chickens pecking at useless dirt.

I got back late one evening and apologized to Lorene for missing dinner. I went straight to my room, trying to process what I had seen—the faces of despair, hunger, and misery from the defeat of losing a home and purposeful work. The children were the hardest for me to photograph, with their grimy faces, and babies that were nursed until the malnourished mother's milk dried up. Their future looked dim to me as I gazed into squinted eyes full of fear and anguish. These hardworking people were tragically defenseless. The suffering I witnessed was too much to bear and I went to sleep quietly crying to myself.

The next day, instead of facing it all over again, I stayed home to develop film. Before my eyes appeared portrait after portrait of the sad, weather-beaten families.

A few weeks later, Mr. Stryker sent me a copy of *The Saturday Evening Post.* There, on page seven, were several of my photographs. Pride of my work filled my soul, easing the pain a bit and making it all worthwhile.

One afternoon, I stopped by a farmhouse where a family sat out in front, apparently packed up and ready to leave. Much to my surprise, I learned that they were just returning from Bakersfield, California, after working the season, rather than leaving.

The worn-out farmer told me, "They just aren't friendly out there and only care about cheap labor. We slept a lot, ate very little, worked when we could, and saved our money and came back. There're too many people in the camps, no running water. Most of us felt like we were in a den of dogs or pigs. One day, I had to sleep in a row of carrots to hold a place in the field to earn sixty cents a day pulling them up. We got tired of living on wheels, so here we are again, back in our real home in Oklahoma."

I glanced at their shack and sadly understood how they felt.

As I drove down the highway, I pulled over and sat for a while, deep in thought. My heart went out to these folks as I listened to them and tried to understand their plight. If I could produce photographs that showed at a simple glance the conditions people had to endure, maybe I would make a difference, just like Dorothea Lange had.

Photographer Dorothea Lange

Oklahoma Dust Bowl refugees

Squatters alongside the highway

Migrant workers

Migrant couple

Migrant mother

Poor mother and children

Old photos of sand drifts

Chapter 30
An Old-Fashioned Gully Washer,
1938

Choose a job you love, and you will never have to work a day in your life.

— Confucius

Lorene handed me a letter from *Life Magazine*. After thanking her, I retreated to my room to read it.

Dear Miss Peterson,

Our publication needs a war correspondent to cover the possible invasion of Czechoslovakia by Germany. You have been chosen to represent Life Magazine *because of your outstanding photography and reporting.*

As you are probably aware, the Germans have just occupied Austria and our government is concerned that Czechoslovakia will be next. We are interested in covering the common people of this country and their reaction to this impending possibility. Please let us know as soon as possible if you are interested in the job.

Wilson Hicks, Editor
Henry Luce, Owner
Life Magazine
New York, New York

I was honored, as well as surprised, to receive this invitation. I headed off to see Smokey to seek his advice. I had never been to Europe and was so involved with my own country I hadn't been following politics.

Smokey was in a classroom preparing to teach about firefighting. He was writing on the chalkboard as I opened the door. He immediately came to me and gave me a delightful kiss.

"What a wonderful surprise to see your adorable face first thing in the morning."

"Oh, Smokey, you must read a letter I just got from *Life Magazine.*"

"Okay," he said, turning serious as I handed him the letter.

After reading it, he exclaimed, "What an opportunity! I bet you'll be famous someday."

My face reddened. "Do you think I should take the job?" I felt overwhelmed after reading the words "war correspondent."

"Of course, sweetheart. You've been selected. Why would you want to turn down the job of being a war correspondent?"

A group of men came into the classroom. I took the letter, gave Smokey a wave, and left.

When I got back to the ranch, I found Lorene in the kitchen canning with Nell.

"I'm surprised to see you back so early, Addie," she greeted me.

"Can I show you a letter I got? I'd really like your opinion."

After reading it, Lorene expressed an opinion similar to Smokey's. "Why are you hesitating about such a terrific opportunity, Addie?"

"I guess I don't have that much confidence in myself. And besides, the thought of covering a war in a foreign country sounds frightening."

Lorene looked surprised and listed all of my accomplishments since arriving in Oklahoma. "Oklahoma was like a foreign country to you when you first arrived. I'm sure they wouldn't send a woman into an active war zone."

I touched her shoulder. "Thanks, Lorene. You've been a true friend to me."

When I went to see Smokey the next day, he was in the classroom reading some notes. "Hi, beautiful. Been thinking about you. You're going to take that job, aren't you?"

"Maybe," I answered, looking out the window.

"I'm headed outta here for California next week, also," Smokey said with a grand smile.

"California? Aren't you needed here?" My voice rose and my

lips pressed together tightly.

"Nope, I'm being transferred. There's more population there and I'm needed to set up another Corps program."

"How long have you known about this?" My face fell.

"About a month, I guess. I'm itching to move on, anyway."

He came closer to me. I stepped back.

"I've got an appointment with Mr. Finnell. I have to go now," I murmured before he could convince me to stay.

Smokey had a hold on me and I didn't want to believe that our relationship had to end. I had even been fantasizing about maybe settling down here with him.

On my last day in Oklahoma, I woke with a start. What was that noise on my window? I sat up in bed and held my breath as I listened. It was rain! It woke up the entire family, and Nell was allowed to go outside in her nightgown. We all watched as she danced barefoot in the showers, twirling about in her nightie. When Nell stuck out her tongue to drink the rain, we all burst out laughing.

I was packed up and ready to go. Two years of living and working with this wonderful family made it hard for me to leave. Tex gave me a bright, broad smile and a light handshake. Lorene gave me a handmade blouse from the latest flour sack design and kissed my cheek. Sweet Nell hugged me tightly. I turned away to hide my streaming tears.

Somehow, I had run out of time to say farewell to Smokey, but he was probably already in California anyway. And so, I left for New York during what the farmers called an "old-fashioned gully washer."

Chapter 31
A New Adventure, a New Assignment

Be passionate and be involved in what you believe in, and do it as thoroughly and honestly and fearlessly as you can.

— Marie Colvin, war correspondent

I stopped in Washington to return all the RA equipment I had borrowed. It was wonderful to see Mr. Stryker again. He gave me a warm hug. I felt like a precious daughter of his, returning home for a visit.

"Addie, it's good to see you. Congratulations on obtaining a position with *Life Magazine*. It's becoming the most influential photojournalism magazine in the world since *Time* acquired it."

"Thanks, Mr. Stryker. I can't believe I'm going to Czechoslo...Czechoslovakia." I laughed. "See? I can barely pronounce it."

"Well, I believe it. You've been one of my finest photographers. I'm very proud of you and I'm pleased that I got to see your career blossom and grow."

"I couldn't have done it without you." I wiped a tear from my eye, feeling emotional after leaving Oklahoma and moving on to an unknown adventure. It was time for me to let go and broaden my horizons.

My confidence soared after chatting with Mr. Stryker. I drove on, and soon reached New York City and got a room in a hotel.

The next day, I met with Mr. Luce, who quite pleased to meet me.

"Miss Peterson, you are the first female photojournalist for *Life* and will be perfect for the job in Europe."

He explained that Americans were eager for information and photographs about Czechoslovakia. He gave me various pieces of equipment and told me to buy whatever else I needed.

I drove to Brooklyn to my favorite camera shop. My heart raced as I noticed all that had changed since I'd been gone, but I nostalgically enjoyed the buildings, which remained the same. I passed the familiar gargoyle building I had photographed many years ago, and stopped to look at the statues.

At the camera shop, I inquired about Mr. Smith, but was told he had sold the business. After I handed the new owner a long list of items I needed, he cheerfully introduced himself and asked why I needed all the equipment. When I told him where I was going, he showed me how to make a few basic camera repairs.

"If you have a camera break down, I'm sure you will have trouble getting it fixed in that country."

I thanked him for his help and purchased a few extra parts and tools.

I sent 600 pounds of equipment to the Hotel Ambassade in Prague, Czechoslovakia. This included 93,000 peanut flashbulbs, film packs, five cameras, twenty-two lenses, developing tanks, developer, plus my ten-pound Royal typewriter with extra ribbons and paper.

The rest of the week I practically lived at the New York City Public Library. I had spent years isolating myself in my own country and was now being called upon to report on Czechoslovakia, a country I knew nothing about.

I hadn't been to a library in a long time and it was like savoring my favorite candy once again. I absorbed what I could about important events in Europe. First, I studied the unarmed, friendly country of Austria. In 1933, Austria's chancellor, Engelbert Dollfuss, had banned the Austrian Nazi party and a year later he was assassinated. The German Nazi party had infiltrated Austria over several years and the annexation drew very little opposition. This country had six million Germans, and the Chancellor of Germany, Adolf Hitler, was from Austria. My insatiable curiosity had me looking over Hitler's 1924 autobiography, *Mein Kampf*, which meant "my struggle." It had recently been translated into English. There was one sentence that caught my eye, which read: "People of the same blood should be in the same Reich."

I learned that just that past February Hitler had summoned the chancellor of Austria, Kurt Schuschnigg, to a meeting in Berchtesgaden, Germany, to accept the appointment of the Nazi leader as minister of the interior. Chancellor Schuschnigg would not agree unless Austria could remain independent. That March, Hitler ordered German forces to invade Austria. In Vienna, Nazi mobs rushed through the streets, crying "Heil Hitler" and "Down with the Jews." The Austrian chancellor was arrested and put in solitary confinement as Germany took over the small country.

Most of the sources I read agreed that Germany wanted centrally located Austria as part of their strategy for taking over Central Europe. Why else would it want a poor country with problems? After studying Czechoslovakia, I could see why this country could be next. The Germans resided in a part of Czechoslovakia called Sudetenland, which was very rich in raw materials. After studying the map, I saw that Czechoslovakia was practically attached to Germany, just like Austria.

After days of research in the library, my interest was piqued and I was full of energy, anxious to see for myself whether Germany would take this country. Whether they would or wouldn't remained to be seen, but one thing was certain: I would be there to document it all.

I had two more items on my to-do list: I had to sell my precious car and call my brother Jimmy to tell him about my new job in another part of the world. After I filled him in, and after hearing all about his growing family, I had an idea.

"I would love to give you my car," I said with enthusiasm.

"You would do that?" he asked in a melodious voice.

"You deserve it and it would bring me good fortune to give it to you."

"Thanks, Addie! My wife and kids will love it!"

I drove up to the country the next day. When I saw Jimmy's beautiful wife with her big, bright smile, and the children jumping up and down begging for a ride, I felt like I had just delivered a Christmas tree. I was thrilled with my decision.

After Jimmy drove me home, I asked him to wait while I went into my well-packed apartment and brought down several boxes. They contained all my past and present photographs.

"Take care of these for me, will you?" I said. "And take care of your precious family."

We hugged. As I watched my brother drive away, my emotions stirred with sadness and my stomach fluttered in anticipation of my upcoming adventure.

Chapter 32
A Trip Abroad

War reporting is still essentially the same — someone has to go there and see what is happening.

— Marie Colvin, war correspondent

The preparations for getting ready to leave the US were time-consuming. The editor of *Life* had arranged for me to meet an interpreter in the Soviet Union. After that, we would take a train to Czechoslovakia.

I would sail to my new job abroad on the *SS Normandie*. Upon seeing the ship, it left me awestruck. It was tall, like a skyscraper, but on its side.

Crowds of families were seeing people off. Before boarding up the ramp, I stopped, put down my two bags, and took in the joyous ambiance. All the kissing, hugging, and cheering was contagious.

Once on deck, I leaned over the railing, waved, and blew kisses, pretending that *my people* were wishing me a wonderful journey. A deep, loud horn blew twice, signaling the departure of the grand ship.

One young couple, dressed in what I thought must have been honeymoon attire, asked me why I was going to Le Havre, France. When I told them I was on my way to Czechoslovakia, they were stunned and asked me why in the world I would go there.

"I'm going to report on an impending war," I explained.

The young man said, "A war? That's not possible." His face turned from happiness to a frown.

Not wanting to ruin their obvious blissful state, I changed the subject and asked them if they were on their honeymoon. This pleased the couple and the lovely girl asked how I could tell.

"By your clothes. Your two-piece lace suit is perfect for wearing after a wedding. Besides, both of you seem to be very much in love."

They looked into each other's eyes once more and held hands, their faces aglow. I knew they wanted to be alone and left, saying that I had to go find my cabin.

After checking in at the busy counter, a classy uniformed steward grabbed my suitcases and led me up two sweeping staircases, each with elegant chandeliers hanging from the ceilings high overhead. Beautiful oil paintings of France covered every wall on the way to my cabin.

Most of the passengers I passed wore the latest style in clothing. Men wore two-button, wide-notched lapel worsted suits and women modeled gowns in various shades of pastels with matching hats. It made me feel self-conscious; I wished I had taken the time to buy a few new dresses.

I overheard a few French conversations as we walked, and was pleased to be able to decipher a few familiar words like *bon*, *avoir*, and *mon ami* from the one-year class I had taken at Cornell.

The steward unlocked my cabin door, handed me the key, and left after I tipped him. The cabin was a bit of a shock after being in the spacious rooms below. It was the size of a large closet. The fine wood paneling was nice but the bed was quite small. At least the fancy bed coverings felt comfy.

I unpacked my bags and put away my clothes in the tiny wardrobe. I tried to sit on my bed to read one of my mystery novels, but had to lie down to be comfortable.

It was hard to stay in that tiny space for very long and I finally decided to venture out to eat lunch in the dining room. I sat at a small table in the corner and looked over the menu. The view leaving the harbor left me feeling eager about my new adventure. After a while, the city skyline disappeared and the gorgeous blue ocean was all that could be seen.

I couldn't feel that the ship was moving and was pleasantly pleased because getting seasick was not something I cared to experience.

A handsome naval officer came by and introduced himself. He asked if I was dining alone. After I replied yes, he said he would be glad to dine with me. Captain Laurent suggested that I try the fresh fish for lunch. "How is your trip so far, Mademoiselle

Peterson?"

"Lovely. But I can't even feel that we're moving."

The captain explained, "The SS *Normandie* is only six years old and is well balanced. Why, it is the fastest ship in the world! We are carrying 3,000 people to Le Havre, a prime vacation spot."

"Oh, my! This is like a small floating city."

His French accent had a mesmerizing, silky, slightly nasal sound.

After our scrumptious meal of fish, freshly baked rolls, and vegetables in a savory sauce, the captain leaned in and told me, "Keep your eyes on the lookout, there are many celebrities on board."

"Like who?"

"I am not allowed to say. But I'll tell you one, Cary Grant, who is with another famous actress." He winked. "I will not tell who she is."

After Captain Laurent left to assist the admiral, I went back to my cabin and retrieved my book. It was too claustrophobic for me to read there, so I went up to the deck and stretched out on a canvas lounge chair. I became thoroughly entertained watching people stroll by as I looked for celebrities.

After several weeks, the trip was coming to an end. I occasionally thought about Smokey. I had become quite smitten with him when I was in Oklahoma. The influence of living with the Douglas family had spurred the dream of settling down with him. But it was not to be. He was in California and I was on my way to a faraway country.

While we were docking in Le Havre in Northern France's Normandy region, I stayed on the top deck and enjoyed the view of where the Seine River met the English Channel. No wonder so many honeymooners came to this place! I was glad I had kept my small Leica with me and took a few minutes to photograph the picturesque town with its abbey towers and chapels among quaint cottages, all surrounded by sparkling blue water.

While departing with the cheerful crowd, I asked a couple for directions to the train station. I had to take a train to Paris, then continue on to the Soviet Union.

I arrived in Paris in the early twilight and found the *Nord*

Express train station that would take me to Saint Petersburg. After looking over the timetable, I was thrilled to find that I had two hours before it left. I strolled around the magnificent city, enchanted by the unusual architectural designs of the Eiffel Tower and the Arc de Triomphe. No wonder it was called the city of lights—all the buildings were enchantingly illuminated. I would have loved to have spent a few days there but I knew my interpreter was expecting me.

It was getting late and I had to walk briskly to catch my train; not an easy task dragging two heavy bags. I giggled, then stopped as an old woman puffing on a long cigarette walked past me with a huge, fluffy cat on a leash. I couldn't resist taking a photograph. My watch said I had only a few minutes. Out of breath, I asked the first person I saw if the train to Saint Petersburg had left yet. He spoke to me in rapid French so I had no idea what the answer was. I stood there sweating with nervousness. A train pulled up and I asked the conductor if it was the train I wanted. He confirmed it was the correct train and helped me on with my bags.

I walked through the rows of tattered old seats and sat down just as the train left the station. I tried to rest my head on the window but decided to find the dining car to order a drink to settle my nerves. The waiter did not speak English so I pointed to the beer bottles lined up behind the bar. The beer was dark and strong and made me sleepy.

When the helpful conductor walked by, I asked where the sleeping car was. As he brought me through to the next car, I asked him how old the train was. He said it was built in 1896 and added, "As you can see, it needs repair."

The conductor showed me an empty berth on the lowest level of four curtained beds. I thanked him and settled in. The bed wasn't very comfortable but the rocking motion of the train lulled me to sleep.

The next morning, I washed my face in a small sink in the corner of the berth area. Then I found some comfortable clothes to change into in the next car, at the end of the corridor where the toilet was.

Famished, I went to the dining car for breakfast, sat down, and was immediately served tea without even asking. A young mother and her son came by, pointed at the seat across from me, and asked in what I thought was Russian if she could sit down.

I answered, *"Oui,"* in French, the only foreign language I knew.

The mother chatted with her son in a strong and aggressive-sounding language while smoothing down his hair.

The breakfast menu was written in three languages. A smartly dressed waiter came by and I pointed to the English language version. The Russian mother ordered next. While I waited, I glanced out the window and watched the ordinary, flat terrain go by.

The waiter brought all three of us the same meal. It was served in a bowl and was what the menu said was *kasha*, which I discovered was a porridge. I spooned some around the bowl. It tasted plain and I lost interest in it. I tried one of my fried eggs, which was oily, then put the second one on a piece of buttered toast, which tasted better. *Tvorog* was listed on the menu, which turned out to be cottage cheese. I ate only a little bit, but I did enjoy the strong Russian tea.

It was a bit lonely on the train after discovering that the only person who spoke English was the conductor. My mind wandered during the two-week journey as I thought about destiny. There had been many twists and turns in my life. I never knew what was going to happen. How much control did a person have over their path in life? Was God leading me? I never dreamed I would be going to a country with a name I had to practice pronouncing. Maybe it was my relentless wonder and curiosity that caused all the unpredictability in my life.

At last, the train arrived at the Vitebsk rail station in Saint Petersburg, Soviet Union. I wondered where my interpreter would be and how I would find him. I got off the train, put my bags down, and photographed the clean, magnificent station. There were tall columns of marble and antique chandeliers high above. I marveled at the sight of it all. It was cleaner than New York City, that was for sure.

Chapter 33
Prague, Czechoslovakia, 1938

What we must fight for is to safeguard the existence and reproduction of our race and our people, the sustenance of our children and the purity of our blood.

— Adolf Hitler

My interpreter, Mr. Ivanov, picked me out of the crowd right away because of the camera strapped around my neck. He introduced himself in a thick Russian accent and hailed a cab. He was a large man with a nose that matched his size, and looked more like a bodyguard than an interpreter.

Mr. Ivanov was a quiet man and I remained silent for the most part, but then I was tired from being on the rocking train for so long. We arrived at a modest hotel after crossing over a great stone bridge. I noticed many gold-domed buildings in the distance. My interpreter took my bags, not allowing the doorman to touch them. He pointed to where I should sit down and went to get the keys to our rooms.

A few minutes later on the elevator, Mr. Ivanov said in a stilted voice, "Go to bed early. We are taking a train at 7:00 to Prague. I will meet you in the hotel café at 6:00." He opened the door to my room, put my bags inside, handed me the key, and left before I could say thank you.

The next morning, we had a plain breakfast of *kasha*, which I hadn't like on the train, a boiled egg, and weak coffee. I hoped the food would be better in Czechoslovakia. We headed out on a two-hour train ride. We crossed the Tatras Mountains on the *Kosice-Zilina* express train as it rolled through fields of ripening wheat and young green oats.

Mr. Ivanov remained quiet, leaving my mind to drift back to Oklahoma. I looked out the train window at the abundant wheat and hoped the Oklahoma farmers were seeing as much wheat where they were. I had left the state after a rainstorm, and the people were filled with hope once more. A smile spread across my face as I remembered little Nell dancing in the rain.

At the first stop, a German Nazi in full uniform came into our compartment and sat down. I looked over at Mr. Ivanov, who stared out of the window. He then reached into his coat, pulled out a metal flask, and took a sip of something from it.

In a polite voice, Lieutenant Schmitz introduced himself and ordered several cans of beer from a waiter who came by. After he had downed his fifth beer, his tongue began to loosen. I watched in strained silence as the officer got out a German map. In English, he asked me if I was American. He looked at my stylish black rain boots from New York, which had exposed my identity, and I answered, yes. I felt uneasy about meeting a Nazi for the first time.

He flattened the map against the wall of the train carriage, wet his pencil on his tongue, and proceeded to circle what he called the "true boundaries of the German people." The officer became engrossed with circling various countries, then said with a red face, the veins in his neck bulging, "These are German territories."

As he continued to mark certain areas, his voice rose. "If German is spoken here then it is German territory. The Czechs belong to the Fatherland and we must claim it."

I boldly asked, "Why do the Czechs have no right to their own country?" I noticed all the countries he marked had German names instead of their real names, and were *not* part of Germany.

The Nazi's eyebrows arched. "The Czechs are stupid people. They have no culture. They need us."

I glanced at Ivanov, who said nothing and continued to stare out the window.

I took a deep breath. "I've read that the Czechs have built a good nation that compares well to other countries the same size."

The Nazi's face grew a darker shade of red and he said in a loud voice, "They have allowed Jews into their country from Austria. It is now contaminated with them. Jews are swine and the German people will stop them for the good of the world."

My Rolleiflex camera hung around my neck. My fingers itched to take a photograph of the Nazi officer. When he looked out the window, I glanced down into the viewfinder and discreetly turned the focusing knob. As I pressed the shutter release, I coughed to mask the noise, hoping to get just one shot of the German's crisp uniform and glistening medals.

Mr. Ivanov poked my side, which I took as a signal to not risk taking another photograph.

I kept my thoughts to myself as the train slowed, and watched the fields of wheat outside my window, heavy with thick heads of grain. The German officer folded up his map and got his baggage. As he stormed off, I took a few more photos without looking down at my camera.

Mr. Ivanov's huge brown eyes widened when he heard the sound of the shutter release, then he turned away and sipped his alcohol.

After we reached Prague, Mr. Ivanov hailed a cab to the Hotel Ambassade. There were hordes of international journalists in the lobby. Were they all there waiting for a war to begin? I sat on an elegant chair as my interpreter checked us in. I heard two attractive ladies speaking English, and wandered toward them like a magnet. They were talking nonstop about Czechoslovakia, England, and France. I caught on that they must be reporters and introduced myself.

The tall, leggy blond gal in trousers looked me over. "Who are you attached to?"

"*Life Magazine.* Who are you with?"

"*Collier's.* Martha Gellhorn. Glad to meet you." She shook my hand jovially.

The petite brunette introduced herself. "Virginia Cowles, *Sunday Times,* London. Looks like we've all landed here at the right time, before the war breaks out." She straightened her brown tweed suit and walked to a table in her matching, fashionable high heels to get an ashtray.

Martha put a hand in the pocket of her gray flannel trousers. "Tons of press have been descending upon this hapless country. I hope they survive the Nazis."

"I do too," I replied, glad I had spent time studying this country in the library.

"I intend to get a good story before a war occurs, but I will not be cut off in those mountains with people who speak such a difficult language. It's more than I'll risk." Martha inhaled a cigarette.

"How's your Czech?" Virginia asked me.

"I don't speak any but I'm here with an interpreter."

"Lucky you. The language here is insane. Consonant crazy. I know three languages but this one I'll never fathom."

I thought Virginia's accent was from London, but in fact, it was a refined Boston accent.

Martha Gellhorn added, "I know German but most of these people don't speak German and many of the Sudeten Germans speak only Czech. The Austrian refugees that fled speak German."

Virginia whispered to me, her huge gold bracelets jangling on her dainty wrists. "We got a tip from a Nazi official that the German army is preparing to cross the frontier."

Martha added, "I told him that this would mean war and that France has a treaty to protect Czechoslovakia, just as England looks over France. He answered that no one will fight for this backward country, just like Austria didn't." She adjusted the sweater tied around her neck.

Mr. Ivanov came with my bags and a key. I introduced him to the reporters. He nodded politely and motioned toward the stairs.

The following morning, we had a bland breakfast of dark bread, butter, boiled eggs, and weak coffee at the hotel café. Mr. Ivanov told me he had been to Prague a number of times and suggested that we take a guided tour.

Flabbergasted, I replied, "There's a tour of Prague at a time when a war could occur?"

He responded in his matter-of-fact way. "There are plenty of foreign correspondents here, like yourself, who would like to learn about Prague."

Before I could comment, he reached for my camera equipment and headed out of the hotel. I scrambled after him.

On the way down the cobblestone street to where the tour would start, I took a few shots of Prague's architecture. It was a photographer's paradise; an ancient, well-preserved city. The tall buildings were adorned with fine gargoyles, which reminded me of the photos I had taken so long ago in New York City. I felt like I had been dropped into the 13th century in this magical, medieval place.

We had a young, well-versed guide who spoke English as well as Czech. He said, "Prague is the jewel in the Crown of Central Europe. This city is nestled in a picturesque valley with high hills topped by castles. The Vltava River is spanned by seventeen bridges. First, we will walk to Old Town to see the famous *Orloj*."

Our small group of travelers, speaking in many languages, walked down the uneven cobblestone street. May was cherry blossom time, and the pink blooms were lovely to behold against the historic backdrop of the city.

We stopped beside what the guide said was a medieval astronomical clock called *Orloj*. As we waited for it to begin its hourly show, our guide explained what we were about to see.

"In 1410, a clockmaker and a mathematics-astronomy professor created a clock to replace an old one in this stone tower here in Old Town Square."

I stared up at the complicated system of colorful dials, rings, hands, and pointers. I felt like an ant at the bottom of a skyscraper. Mr. Ivanov helped me set up the tripod. It took me a while to get what I hoped would be the perfect shot of this marvelous invention.

The guide continued in English with his heavy Czech accent. "When looking at the clock, you'll see the astronomical dial, which shows the position of the sun and moon. The zodiacal ring indicates the time of sunset, and the calendar with medallions represents the months. It displays the stars as opposed to the sun, so astronomers know exactly where to point their telescopes to find specific stars at any given moment. The calendar dial tells the date, each saint's feast day, a pictorial depiction of the seasons for each month, and the zodiac signs. This is marked by a human hand pointing to the Gothic Arabic numbers on the outermost ring of the clock. Because sunset changes throughout the year, the outer ring moves ever so slowly to adjust."

People from all over the square began to gather, stretching their necks so they could see the clock tower. I photographed the bright, sparkling gold amid the shades of vivid blue on the clock's face. The multiple hands and rings of the clock, as well as the small statues, exhibited an assortment of bright colors. I took many pictures while listening intently to the guide as he explained the intricate masterpiece.

"Ladies and gentlemen, get ready for the show. The clock's time is almost on the hour. Be sure to watch the four evil statues of greed, lust, vanity, and death as they tremble in fear of the apostles."

The spectacle began as the dishonorable statues on the sides of the clock became animated: a skeleton ringing a bell, a Turk shaking his head, a miser with a purse full of money, and a vanity figure looking in a mirror. Then two small windows opened up to reveal the twelve apostles emerging, two at a time, to greet the city. The whole performance ended with the crowing of a golden rooster that popped out of a window, then the ringing of a huge bell at the top of the tower. The crowd clapped and I photographed the fascinated reactions of everyone around me.

The tour guide adamantly proclaimed, "This clock was built in the 1400s. We were a free nation then and we will remain a free nation now!"

The crowd cheered in agreement. All the movements of the astronomical clock were extremely elaborate to photograph. I made a note to come back at different times of the day to get the right light. I was glad the clock tower was within walking distance of the hotel.

The tour proceeded to cross the famous Charles Bridge over the swan-filled Vltava River. The bridge was built in 1357 and was lined with lovely detailed sculptures, linking the east and west banks of the capital. I focused my camera on the distant golden spirals of the gothic churches, the colorful baroque buildings, and the stone towers of castles. I could see why Prague was nicknamed "the City of a Hundred Spires."

It was hard for me to fathom the age of this country. Hearing about the 12th century from the tour guide was a new concept for me. America didn't even exist back then.

As we walked back to the hotel, I thanked Mr. Ivanov. He had been correct—the tour of Prague was indeed worthwhile. I marveled at the engineering skills that allowed people hundreds of years ago to construct a clock that would be difficult to replicate today. The guide had said it had to be continuously renovated and repaired. I couldn't help worrying what would happen to that incredible masterpiece if Germany bombed the capital.

Elaborate statues on the Prague Astronomical Clock

Astronomical Clock in Prague

Chapter 34
Sudetenland

Sudetenland is the last territorial claim which I will make.
—Adolf Hitler

Ivanov and I hired a car so that we could venture out into the countryside. I wanted to use my well-tested method of wandering around and talking to whoever I ran across in order to meet the people of Czechoslovakia, just as I had done in Oklahoma. I was very lucky, and pleased, to have an interpreter.

In the fields, men were cutting wheat with scythes. Women wearing scarves and large skirts were tying it into bundles. I got out and took some beautiful shots with my Leica when the sun was in the perfect position in the sky. In the next province, Moravia, I shot a few photos of a farmer who had stopped to sharpen the blade of his scythe with a file. There was very little modern machinery used.

Mr. Ivanov spoke to a few people for me. The farmer asked why so many Americans were coming to their country, and wondered if they were not happy where they lived. I asked Ivanov what his reply was. He explained that we were visiting Czechoslovakia to report on how the people were doing and in case a war broke out. One farmer told him that Hitler may have taken their neighbor, Austria, but that the Czechs would die for their country and keep their independence, as they did after the Great War. Another man told him, "Freedom will never belong to those who will not die for it and I will join the army if necessary."

I photographed his face, which was filled with conviction as well as courage, as he stood there firmly with a scythe in his hand.

His wife added, "We're a happy people because of the land reform act. Twenty years ago, we used to be slaves of the landowner without pay. Now we are a prosperous people and are proud to live in a country that has made us free."

As we got closer to the border of Germany, we came upon an airbase. I shot frame after frame of Czech troops who showed a splendid display of courage and readiness to fight for their country. Their airplanes gleamed in the sun, ready for combat.

We could see across the northern border to Germany that there were routine movements of German troops. Photographing the Nazi military armament gave me a chill. I stayed close to Ivanov, who I knew had a pistol beneath his jacket.

As I took one more photograph of the Czech troops on one side and the Nazis on the other, Ivanov said, "It is getting late. We must return to Prague."

I reluctantly packed up, hoping these shots would be sufficient to send to *Life Magazine* so that the American people could better visualize an impending war.

During the ride back, I felt confident that I could complete my assignment, even if a war did break out and I had to leave. Not only did I have a good interpreter, but Ivanov was indeed a perfect bodyguard. I felt safe for the time being.

The *Istanbul-Berlin Express* was a fast, ninety-mile ride from Prague to Aussig in Czechoslovakia, where the Sudeten Germans held their yearly election. *Life* had sent a telegram telling me to cover this important annual event. During the trip, I was able to question Ivanov about it, and he explained that this part of Czechoslovakia was called Sudetenland, named after the Sudeten Mountains on the northern Czechoslovakian border to Germany. He told me that this area of Czechoslovakia was very valuable because most of the natural resources of the country were here. Every year, a rally was held in Sudetenland. Ivanov mentioned that the Nazi party was bound to win the election because of having just taken over Austria.

The view outside the window was full of wheat fields again. I enjoyed the sound of the speedy locomotive, but soon got tired of seeing only fields with no trees, houses, or buildings. I had read in an American newspaper that the drought in the Midwest was over. I sure hoped so. I missed my Oklahoma family and said a silent prayer for them as the train whizzed along.

At each stop, the train became more and more crowded with peasants holding bundles and baskets, and headed for the third-class carriages. A well-dressed lady with a suitcase got on and sat across from us. She chatted to me in German. I could only smile. Mr. Ivanov reluctantly translated what she was saying.

At the next stop, a Nazi officer came on board with a suitcase and could not find a seat. He glared at the lady across from us, who held her Star of David necklace tightly in her fist. The officer tried to yank her baggage from the rack over her seat. She jumped up and stood in his way. He slapped her on the face so hard she fell against the door of the compartment. I glanced at Ivanov, who looked away.

"Jewish swine!" the officer yelled in German, then looked me over and repeated it in English.

The lady put her hands over her face so she wouldn't be slapped again.

"You Jewish swine, you'll be taught your place!" the German officer shouted at her.

A Czech guard, hearing the commotion, came to our compartment and helped the woman with her baggage, then took her to a distant carriage.

The Nazi grinned and put his bag on the rack over the seat. Ivanov turned his head and looked down as I glared at the officer.

After I heard the Nazi officer say "Jewish swine," it jarred something inside me. The Nazi with the map, on the train to Prague we had taken a few weeks ago, had used the same phrase.

I'm a quarter Jewish on my mother's side. What makes people hate innocent people they don't even know? I wondered.

The German officer smiled at me. "You must be an American."

"Yes, I'm an American photographer and journalist."

"I can tell you are American because Americans always have a recognizable expression on their faces. They always look like they are worried about something."

He was right about me being worried. I certainly did not want to be slapped.

After the officer drank the many beers he had ordered, his voice grew shrill. He banged his fist on the table. "It is the destiny of the German race to claim Czechoslovakia. I am a link with history and Hitler will lead us, making the Czechs tremble in their boots! The Sudeten Germans of Czechoslovakia must be part of Germany! The German race must be all one for the New Order of Europe. Did you know that Czech soldiers have constructed granite barriers on our borders wide enough to let only one car pass at a time? Our Germans on the other side drove two tanks down the road and smashed their barriers to pieces." His voice grew louder, and when he said the word "smashed," he stomped his big black boot. "That showed those Czechs who is really in charge! You know, the German Army may cross the entire frontier any day now."

I looked over at Ivanov but couldn't tell what he was thinking. His face was always blank.

"That would mean a world war," I blurted out, causing Ivanov to push his elbow against mine.

The Nazi continued, "Not at all. When Germany takes over Czechoslovakia, it will only take a few days."

"What about France's treaty with Czechoslovakia? And the fact that England supports France?"

The officer made an obnoxious guttural noise. "No one will fight for the Czechs."

I was shaking, worrying about what I would find at the end of the train ride to Aussig on the border of the German frontier.

When the train came to a stop, the Nazi officer got off with a swagger. I started to get up but Ivanov pulled at my skirt, indicating that I should wait until the Nazi was gone.

I had an uneasy feeling as we got off the train and headed to the election meeting. Would I see German tanks coming toward us? Did I have the guts to follow through with photographing this event?

As Ivanov and I went to the town hall, I stayed close to him for protection.

It was a nightmarish experience as I looked around and shot photographs of the heavily decorated hall filled with German flags, and swastikas fluttering and filling every corner as well as the ceiling. On the walls were posters and large photographs of all the Nazi leaders. All around us could be heard the halting dialect of over 6,000 German men. I wanted to hide in Ivanov's heavy Russian coat, but knew I had a job to do.

As Ivanov helped set up the tripod for my Speed Graflex and a string of flashbulbs, I let the photography equipment take me away from my fear as I concentrated through the viewfinder on my camera. Being the only woman, I stood out like a sore thumb but bravely shot photo after photo of uniformed Sudeten guards and the Waffen-SS soldiers. To top off the ear-splitting *heils* of everyone greeting each other, there was a German band playing marching songs. Beer flowed throughout, which Ivanov freely partook in.

Silence fell as Konrad Henlein stepped up to the podium. He was the leader of the Sudeten Germans in Czechoslovakia. I recognized his face from the newspapers.

Not understanding one word, all I could do was observe and shoot photographs. Each candidate that followed used furious gestures and shouted. After every speech, the crowd would burst into a frenzy of chanting, "Sieg Heil" over and over until the next candidate appeared.

When the performances were over, Ivanov told me what had been said. The Czechs were an inferior race and the Czechoslovakian Sudeten Germans were tired of being ruled by a race of peasants. I reflected on my trip into the country. The so-called peasants I had met were a proud and intelligent people, not an inferior race.

Later that night, back at the hotel, I woke to the sound of airplanes. It had been a restless night for me, full of images of swastikas and the shouts of "Heil Hitler." I put my clothes on in a rush, grabbed my Leica, and went outside to see six German reconnaissance planes passing overhead in formation. Prague was still asleep and the streets were deserted. I walked to the railroad station a few blocks away and saw that several hundred Czech soldiers had gathered on the platform. Was this beautiful, charming old city about to be turned into a battlefield?

I walked back into the Hotel Ambassade, where everything was completely normal. The floors were being washed, mail was being sorted, and newspapers delivered. Mr. Ivanov was waiting for me and started yelling that I should not be alone, that he could lose his job. He calmed down after I told him I wouldn't wander off without him again. We sat down in the empty hotel restaurant, drank watery coffee, and had a slice of tasteless, dark rye bread. I was getting tired of this plain food.

A man from the United Press rushed in and sat with us. In a breathless voice, he reported, "The Czech army has called up a hundred thousand reservists and has ordered mobilization to wait for the Germans to come over the frontier into Prague."

I started choking on a piece of bread as I thought about being there if a war broke out. I couldn't stop coughing and had to spit it all into my napkin. Ivanov merely glanced at me, then out into the lobby. It was maddening how he expressed no emotion whatsoever about the possibility of an impending war.

I tried to drink my coffee to clear my throat but had to put it down when my hand kept shaking the cup. I went out to the lobby, where I heard one press reporter say to another that he was not interested in waiting around for a war and was leaving.

Virginia Cowles was sitting there reading her *London Times*. I didn't interrupt her but saw her eyes get wider and wider, and she kept mumbling surprised exclamations to herself. After she folded up the paper, I walked over and asked her if she thought there would be a war.

Virginia answered in an agitated voice, "In my opinion, Adolf Hitler is a dictator and a maniac. People are fooled by him with all the clever words he uses. There are still guns, tanks, and planes furiously being manufactured in Germany. All the newspapers from England treat the Sudeten-Czech crisis like it's a simple problem. To answer your question about war...I think it is a real possibility."

Within the hour, the lobby was swarming with journalists from all over Europe. Telephones rang constantly on the front desk and messenger boys ran around waving telegrams.

That night, Prague was full of crowds gathered on the boulevards shouting, "Long live Czechoslovakia!" and "Down with Heinlein!" Police kept the crowds moving, concerned over clashes between the Czechs and Germans.

The crisis blew over a few days later after the British and French governments reprimanded the Czech president, Beneš, and asked him to demobilize the Czech army. I breathed a sigh of relief as I huddled around a radio with a group of reporters, listening to the broadcast from Britain.

The *United Press* reporter said to me, "Don't get too relaxed. It's only a matter of *when*, not *if*. The only way Czechoslovakia will remain independent will be with a battle."

To my surprise, the usually stoic Ivanov spoke. "We shouldn't worry. Czechoslovakia has a deep alliance with France and the Soviet Union. They fought with them in the Great War, and with their help, Czechoslovakia will triumph."

It was the first time I had heard him speak with such emotion.

The reporter replied, "France has her own frontiers to preserve and has no desire to fight after the last war without Great Britain's help."

Ivanov answered flatly, "Great Britain will help because of its strong alliance with France."

The reporter retorted, "We shall see."

"Yes," said Ivanov. "We shall see."

The Rally

Chapter 35
Nuremberg, Germany, 1938

The wolf is always hungry.

— Unknown

For the reporters, the summer months were filled with anxiety approaching alarm. The same question was on all our lips: Was Czechoslovakia waiting to be plucked by Germany or would they defend themselves?

It was early September. Time was flying by for me, being in a foreign country with endless photographic opportunities. I picked up a telegram from the front desk with a new assignment from *Life*. I was to go to Nuremberg, Germany, to report on Hitler's annual speech to the German people.

My trusty interpreter Ivanov and I took the short train ride to the event. Once there, I began snapping photos right away. There were millions of red, white, and black swastikas fluttering from window ledges. Long red pennants flew from the turreted walls of Nuremberg Castle in the distance. It was a cold, windy, unpleasant fall day, punctuated by somber gray buildings every-where — a stark contrast to Prague's magnificent architecture. The foreign diplomats and journalists from our hotel acted strained and anxious, clustering together and speaking in low voices. I felt like we were all being watched.

We joined several reporters at the local *taverna*. It was the place to be, where all the foreign press gathered to exchange information. They were mostly drinking the German, robust beer over the tasteless coffee. One reporter told me to be careful using the phones at the hotel because the lines were being tapped.

A lively discussion ensued. Everyone wondered whether Czechoslovakia would cede just its Sudetenland border to Germany, and whether that would prevent Hitler from taking over the rest of the country. Some reporters said it would be a wise move to give Germany Sudetenland; that, after all, this was where most of the three million ethnic German people of Czechoslovakia lived. One journalist said the Czechs did not want to lose Sudetenland; it would put the Reich too close to Prague.

A diplomat joined in. "I've been at every Nuremberg annual Nazi rally since Hitler became chancellor in 1933, and mark my words, he will want it all. One piece will not satisfy that dictator."

A press reporter added, "Hitler doesn't really need all of Czechoslovakia, just the German-speaking areas. Besides, he has openly stated that he is opposed to war and is recovering from losing during World War One. Germany is a fine country now with no unemployment."

The diplomat argued, "There is no unemployment because the armament factories are working triple shifts. I have been to the airplane factories. Germany is churning out the latest, fastest bombers. It's obvious to me that Hitler is *not* opposed to war."

I found the conversation both fascinating and enlightening. I silently absorbed it all, wondering what would happen next.

Ivanov and I roamed all over the ancient streets of Nuremberg. He carried my equipment while I photographed the shoppers and storekeepers, as well as many soldiers. The soldiers wore heavy black boots and khaki uniforms with a swastika pinned on the sleeve. Most of them were tall and blond.

I pointed at signs I saw in various shops and beer gardens, and asked Ivanov what they said.

He answered, "Don't point. They say *Jews not wanted.*"

I took a photograph of one of the signs. I knew Ivanov would disapprove, but felt it was an important element to capture.

The market newsstands displayed an abundance of anti-Semitic literature. I bought a few charts, brochures, and books to read later. There were charts about hair, eye color, and instruments to measure noses and heads. These were made to assign physical characteristics to Jews.

I asked Ivanov, "Being Jewish is a religion. How can the Nazis identify that you are Jewish, just by your looks?"

Ivanov replied, "Not having blond hair and blue eyes is not the primary way to identify Jews. Back in the 1400s, Jews were expelled from Germany; then, in the 1800s, Jews were permitted in this city as free citizens. Now they are being expelled once more."

That night, in a corner of the hotel lobby, I asked Ivanov to translate the literature I had bought. He explained the pictorial chart of the 1935 Nuremberg Laws. He showed me that the Nazi Ministry of the Interior classified people as either Aryan, Jewish, or *Mischling,* meaning mixed blood. It was based on the number of Jewish grandparents a person had.

The top portion of the chart displayed the Aryans as white figures. Aryans had no Jewish blood in either their paternal or maternal grandparents' lines. The next category, *Mischling,* was displayed as gray figures. The *Mischling* First Degree had grandparents that were both Jewish and Aryan. The *Mischling* Second Degree had only one Jewish grandparent. The chart's main purpose was to show which groups were forbidden to marry. Jews and Aryans could not marry each other. *Mischling* Second Degree could not marry a Jew or another *Mischling* of Second Degree.

"This is very confusing...and downright bigoted. Why are they perpetuating such hate?" I demanded to know.

Ivanov looked around and whispered, "Keep your voice down. The Nazi premise is to prevent any situation in which the Jewish bloodline might be strengthened. Their main goal is to create a pure Aryan race of people."

Next, Ivanov translated the seven articles of *The Reich Citizenship Laws* I had purchased. It stated that marriages between German citizens and Jews were forbidden or invalid. Extramarital intercourse between Jews and Germans was forbidden. Jews were forbidden to fly the national flag. A Jew could not be a citizen of the Reich, vote, or hold public office. All Jewish officials had to retire as of Dec. 31, 1935. If they had served in the World War for Germany or her allies, they would receive a pension. I learned that the Nazis divided all Europeans into a hierarchy of desirables, undesirables, and disposables.

Ivanov pointed to the bottom of the paper. "This is a list of prison sentences and fines for anyone violating the laws."

As Ivanov pushed all the literature aside, I saw that he had tears in his eyes.

"This is outrageous! It's hard for me to believe that an entire nation is behind such hate!" I exclaimed with passion. "I have Jewish relatives and I'm ashamed that I didn't stand up to the German officer that slapped the woman on the train. I—"

"Adeline..."

I stopped talking. This was the first time Ivanov had spoken my name.

"I must confide in you. My wife and I are Jewish. Please keep this information private." Ivanov's face flushed as he looked down and fiddled with his hands.

I patted his hand and looked into his eyes with sympathy. "I have Jewish grandparents, and even in my country, it is hidden. This Nazi regime is a frightening experience for both of us."

"Yes, I am very worried for my motherland, that Germany might take it next," Ivanov said under his breath, then added, "We must never discuss this in public."

We said good night. I was happy to finally feel a close connection with Ivanov in this faraway country.

The annual Nazi rally wasn't until the next day. Ivanov and I presented our papers at the Foreign Office and the Ministry of Propaganda so we could visit nearby Nazi schools and camps. I knew this would be a great photographic excursion. In a hired car with a black-uniformed chauffeur, we went to Junkerlager, a Nazi youth camp a few miles outside of Nuremberg. I photographed hundreds of young, lean, brawny, blond-haired Germans devoted to several hours of physical exercise each day. The rest of the day they studied racial science, eugenics, and heredity. It was a three-year training program where they lived and ate together in tents while training to be future Aryan Nazi leaders.

I had Ivanov ask one of the lads if they had other classes, such as literature or history. The boy shook his head and went back to studying.

Next, the chauffeur drove us to a school where the children were being drilled in the same subjects as the youth camp. The principal of the school told us that Hitler wanted to expand superiority of the German race, and spoke of the Führer like he was endowed with superhuman qualities, like a God. I photographed a few classrooms, which were all filled with obedient children.

The next day, we went to the Nuremberg rally. It was held at night, which presented a photographic challenge for me. Tanks, guns, armored cars, and goose-stepping troops overflowed the streets on their way to the rally. Ivanov and I followed the dense crowd to the stadium. Nazi political leaders had gathered from all over Germany, waiting for Hitler. I found out later that there were over 200,000 spectators in attendance.

Everything in Nuremberg was displayed on a gigantic scale. I shot photos of the hundreds of gilt eagles and thousands of flags. I focused on the huge, burning urns at the top of a stadium, with their orange flames streaming high into the black sky. Hundreds of soldiers from the Nazi army assembled in mass formation, each carrying a Nazi flag. Searchlights beamed into the black of night. A full band played music that had a religious solemnity to it paired with the steady beat of drums. I tried my best to capture it all.

Hitler arrived ahead of three motorcycles and was followed by a fleet of black cars that rolled into the arena. There, in the lens of my Graflex, stood Adolf Hitler, the Chancellor of Germany, with his hand outstretched in the Nazi salute. He climbed onto a box in the grandstands amid a deafening ovation. I was thrilled to have the opportunity to photograph this famous man, but felt conflicted about it since he was such an evil person. I made sure Ivanov remained by my side.

Political leaders followed Hitler, including Konrad Henlein, head of the Nazi party in Czechoslovakia, each one carrying a flag.

When Hitler spoke, the crowd fell silent but the drums

continued beating. Whenever he paused, the multitudes broke into a roar of cheers, swaying back and forth, chanting, "Sieg Heil!" I photographed tears streaming down people's cheeks as I heard the chant of the Nazi military-like hymns.

As the Führer spoke, I got as close as I could. The man was of modest height. He had sharp, magnetic blue eyes and brown hair. I focused on his toothbrush mustache. His eyes were hypnotic, ablaze, and bulging as his strong voice blared. Since I didn't know German, it was terrifying to hear the sound of his whiny, bullying voice. He was indeed a powerful showman. My whole body tingled with nervous electricity when he spoke and I had to steady my hands to keep my camera from shaking. The constant drumbeats added an almost spooky feel to the rally.

When his dramatic speech ended, he left his box, breaking the spell, and the magic vanished as the crowd chanted, "Heil Hitler!" over and over again. The Chancellor of Germany left, now just a small figure lost in the crowd. I followed his movements using my telephoto lens. Nothing on his face or in his gait seemed significant or powerful as he got into his car.

That night, Ivanov and I sat in the café of the Nuremberg Hotel and had a few beers while he told me what Hitler had said. "He said that the Sudeten Germans are tortured, oppressed creatures and need more rights, which only can be obtained with Germany's help. They are suffering among the Czechs as a minority. If democracies intend to protect Czechoslovakia, then this will have grave magnitude. The last sentence Hitler said was, 'Germany will capitulate to no one.'"

I could see that his face was full of anxiety. "Will there be a war? Will they take all of Czechoslovakia?" I asked as I motioned to the waiter for another beer.

"Hitler never mentioned war." Ivanov ordered a drink.

"How horrible for the Jewish people. Many of them recently fled persecution in Germany and went to Austria, then Hitler took over Austria and they went to Czechoslovakia. Where will they go now?"

Ivanov's eyes remained fixed on the foam of his beer.

When we got back to Prague the next day, a press reporter told us that martial law had been declared and President Beneš had called up reservists to restore order at the Sudetenland border. Hitler's speech had inflamed the Czechoslovakian Germans and they were rallying to secede from the non-German Czechs while Jews fled the area.

We sat in the lobby and listened to a broadcast from Germany. Ivanov translated as Dr. Dietrich, the German press chief, announced: *"Our Führer does not want a war. He can get what he wants without a war. We are a superior country with no unemployment. When we get Sudetenland, we will stop building guns and build stadiums, parks, and houses in Czechoslovakia. War or peace, let President Beneš of Czechoslovakia choose now."*

Ivanov shook his head in a dejected manner.

The next morning, I had to beg Ivanov to let me go outside to see how Prague was fairing after the rally. He carried my equipment with reluctance, telling me it might be too dangerous to venture far.

We saw workmen feverishly digging shelters in the park. Trucks with loudspeakers drove through the streets, telling people where to go to be fitted with gas masks. Women were lined up to buy food in shops that had windows with brown paper taped on them to keep the glass from shattering in case of a bombing. Children carried gas masks in their hands. People kept looking at the sky, waiting for German bombers. I shot photo after photo of the anxious Czech people.

Ivanov and I wandered around Old Town, trying to find a place to eat. I took a shot of a crew painting the streetlamps black. This way the city would be hidden from the sky, which would prevent enemy air attacks. We walked to a nearby neighborhood where most of the houses had paper taped on the windows, just like in the city. I photographed school children cycling down a dirt road with long, gray cylindrical gas masks hanging over their handlebars.

Thousands of civilian recruits carrying suitcases and bundles streamed in and out of the station to go the Sudetenland border to fight.

After I shot an endless number of photographs, Ivanov said in a stern voice, "We need to go back to the hotel. It is not safe here."

The hotel was full of European press correspondents and all the telephones were ringing at the front desk. I listened closely to the reporters with apprehensive speculation.

"Do you think the bombing will start tonight?"

"Will the British Prime Minister Chamberlain come to an agreement with Hitler?"

I sighed, thinking about the hopes and fears of Prague, which seemed to be swinging back and forth like a ship pitching in a storm.

That Saturday, we wandered around and I took more pictures of the chaos in Prague, but now the activity was mixed with the daily tasks of ordinary life. Men were getting their haircuts and children were going to the cinema amid shelters being dug.

After returning to the hotel, Ivanov said, "I suppose you would like to go to the border to see if there is a war going on?"

"Yes, I must." I was surprised that he had suggested it, and was glad to avoid an argument with my trusty interpreter.

"I will have to bring protection then." He patted his hidden weapon.

The thought of needing a gun was worrisome but I kept my thoughts silent. I definitely wanted to go to the border.

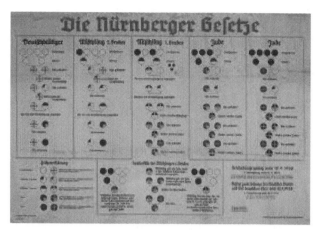

Pictorial chart of the 1935 Nuremberg Laws

Adolf Hitler

Chapter 36
Prime Minister Chamberlain and President Beneš, 1938

How horrible, fantastic, incredible it is that we should be digging trenches and trying on gasmasks here because of a quarrel in a faraway country between people of whom we know nothing.
— Prime Minister of England, Neville Chamberlain

We traveled along all the borders and on the line of defense and saw the barricades and guards. Soldiers were in high spirits, ready to defend their country. There was no panic, just waiting. I spoke to one Czech army officer and he confirmed that they were mobilizing with the consent of Britain and France. Czech soldiers had constructed granite barriers to allow single cars to pass through from Germany to Czechoslovakia for inspection.

I tried to steady my shaking hands to photograph German troops marching toward the Czech frontier in unusual concentrations. The troops stopped right before the border and remained in line. I was grateful that Ivanov stayed by my side, ready to protect me. I captured the contrast of the Czech soldiers, with their fixed bayonets and steel helmets, standing among peasants working in the fields of the peaceful countryside.

As we reached the Sudeten district, I shot the white posts along the road with swastikas marked on them in red chalk, and telephone poles with "Heil Hitler" written on them. All the Czech signboards had been torn down and lay scattered along the side of the road. There were very few vehicles around. The declaration of martial law had established order.

When we reached Harbersbirk we saw the remains of a violent riot that had taken place there. A policeman who stopped us for our papers told us that the Sudeten Germans had broken into the

Czech police headquarters and had killed four policemen. In front of the headquarters, we saw smashed furniture and glass from broken windows. I asked if I could photograph the destruction and he said, "Yes, order has been restored."

In Edger, a town not far from the frontier, the main square was deserted. Czech policemen and soldiers were the only visible people. As we drove through, it seemed like a ghost town, but we discovered that the people were still there. Everyone was hiding inside.

Ivanov and I went into a café to try to get a cup of coffee and some lunch. The owner was startled when we walked into the empty store.

Ivanov asked, "Are you open?"

The sad, tired man answered, "No, business is suspended."

"When do you think you will open again?" I asked.

He glanced outside and slowly replied, "When the German army marches in."

"Do you know when that will be?" I said.

"Probably any hour now."

We drove back to Prague in silence, both wondering whether Germany would really take over the Czechoslovakian Sudetenland.

Back at the Hotel Ambassade, the desk clerk asked us, "Why did you return? I was certain you had gone back to your country. It is dangerous here now. All the frontiers are closed, there are no trains running, and most of the telephone wires have been cut."

Ivanov requested two rooms on the ground floor, which he later explained was safer than an upper room, in case of aerial bombing.

A press agent from France said to us, "There is no way out of Czechoslovakia now. The only communication with the outside world is by telegraph, which takes about eighteen hours to receive. We're trapped here, probably for the duration. You know, the cession of Sudetenland would bring the Germans only ninety miles within the city of Prague. I don't know about you, but I didn't bring enough film, equipment, or clothes."

I remained silent, allowing my mind to absorb what he had said.

Over breakfast the next day, I saw Virginia Cowles, one of the few reporters who had remained. I noticed that she was not dressed in her usual high-fashioned outfit and heels, but instead looked very plain as well as tired.

"Tell me, Virginia, do you know what's going on? Any word from the British prime minister?"

"I've read as many Paris and London newspapers as I could get a hold of. They seem to say that the Czechoslovakian government should consider cession of the Sudetenland. The German newspapers say the Sudeten Germans belong with Germany. I personally think that it's all been provoked by German agents because of the Nazi rallies held there. All of the American reporters in Europe know that Henlein and Hitler's propaganda continues to get the Germans to believe this. The German press is merely Hitler's mouthpiece."

Virginia lit a cigarette and I noticed that her hand shook.

She continued, "I've heard some reporters argue that the Czechs might be better off freed from a disloyal population. But I'm not the only one who thinks the pro-German Sudeten revolt has been engineered by the Nazis. In my opinion, there are plenty of Czechs that get along with the Sudeten Germans. After all, they are an optimistic, democratic people with a well-equipped army."

"Thanks, Virginia. You're a wealth of information. I was just at the border and there are German troops ready to cross. Tell me, do you think if Czechoslovakia cedes just Sudetenland that Hitler will be satisfied and won't want the entire country?"

Cowles crossed her legs, took a drag from her cigarette, and leaned in closer to me. "I feel that no matter what concessions might be made to Hitler, he will not be satisfied. I know for a fact that Czech president Beneš expects England and France to aid their troops in the event of a German invasion."

"But certainly they will. After all, France has a treaty with Czechoslovakia and Britain always backs up France. Our President Roosevelt has sent an urgent message asking all nations directly involved to have a conference and to establish peace."

Virginia's voice dropped to a whisper and she looked around the lobby. "I'll tell you in confidence that if Prime Minister Chamberlain doesn't come to an agreement soon, the German army will take the Sudeten territory by force. I think Hitler wants to take all of Czechoslovakia to gain access to the grain fields of Hungary and the oil and mines of Rumania."

"America is hoping Britain and France will stand up to Germany. As you know, America does not want another war. One press reporter told me that Germany wouldn't want a world war after losing the last one. What do you think is going to happen?" I bit the inside of my cheek.

"Your guess is as good as mine. All I know is that the German domination of Europe would be the first step to the disintegration of the British Empire." Virginia punched out her cigarette, stood, and left without another word.

It was a waiting game. The few press reporters that were left milled around the lobby, gathering information from each other and reading the newspapers to find out what was happening.

I could hardly stand it. I unconsciously yelled out, "In the *London Times,* it says British Prime Minister Chamberlain is having a second meeting with Hitler at Berchtesgaden, Germany, to discuss the annexing of Sudetenland. That is in the same city where Hitler met the Austrian chancellor just this past February. That meeting was obviously worthless because Hitler invaded Austria and annexed it within a very short time after that. History is repeating itself."

"You must lower your voice. One never knows when there could be a German nearby," Ivanov scolded.

A few days later, while in the hotel lobby, I listened to a BBC broadcast. Chamberlain and Hitler had a second meeting. The British prime minister, after pressuring Czech President Beneš to consent, offered Hitler the parts of Sudetenland that had German-speaking people if he would demobilize all German troops on the border. Hitler demanded all of Sudetenland and told the British prime minister that he would march all his troops into Czechoslovakia until he got it. Chamberlain refused but was not convinced that Germany wanted to dominate all of Czechoslovakia.

In an American newspaper, Roosevelt stated that the United States would not line up with all the democracies in a "stop-Hitler" movement, but he did believe that Chamberlain had the ability to avert a European war. He sent an appeal to Chancellor Hitler and President Beneš, urging peaceful settlement of the problem.

The tension of the remaining reporters in the hotel was like a live wire swinging and spewing sparks into the air. France, Great Britain, and America believed in peace with arbitration, but did Germany believe the same?

A final meeting was held in Munich, Germany. Chamberlain invited French Prime Minister Édouard Daladier and Hitler invited Italian Prime Minister Benito Mussolini. Czech President Beneš did not attend and relied on Chamberlain as an intermediary to transmit all of Hitler's proposals.

The next day, September 30, 1938, at precisely 2:00 p.m., all the press reporters gathered around the radio to hear the results of the meeting. The same question lingered on everyone's mind: Would there be a war?

British Prime Minister Neville Chamberlain spoke: *"We have signed the Munich Pact giving Czechoslovakia Sudetenland to Germany to bring peace and honor in our time. Chancellor Hitler has promised that Sudetenland would be his last territorial demand in Europe. We have successfully averted war."*

A few of the reporters cheered while others remained stone silent and motionless. I overheard a French correspondent talking to a Brit. "We've had just about enough of this man Hitler. He's gone too far this time."

The British reporter responded, "We do sympathize with this small nation, but we cannot involve the whole British Empire in war."

The next day, I reluctantly photographed people weeping hysterically in the streets. The headline of the Prague newspaper translated: *"Absolutely Forsaken."*

That afternoon, the President of Czechoslovakia, Edvard Beneš, stood in the huge square in front of our hotel. The square was strung with loudspeakers and crowds of people assembled. Ivanov had to translate for me as I took notes to send to *Life*.

"Our country has partitioned Sudetenland to Germany and has averted war. Our country will not be the smallest. There are smaller countries than ours. We will continue to have peace in Czechoslovakia."

It was a short speech. The Czech National Anthem played over the loudspeakers.

I took a photo of a Czech reporter who dropped his pencil and buried his head in his hands. Thousands of people shook their fists, screaming, "NO!" "Down with Beneš!" "Let Czechoslovakia live as one country!"

Hundreds of Czech policemen surged into the square to prevent a riot. A heavy cord was placed across the streets that led to the palace of President Beneš. The cries of the people were excruciating to hear; they sounded like wounded animals. The question on everyone's lips was: Would this president be able to prevent a total takeover of this fragile country?

Chapter 37
Refugees, 1938

The crown of our tree is pruned somewhat, however, if we descend to the roots, the tree will spring afresh with new twigs in time.
— President Edvard Beneš of Czechoslovakia

Czech, Jewish, and anti-Nazi German refugees arrived on trains at the station. I intuitively felt that this did *not* look like peace. I photographed shot after shot of dejected homeless people. I'd heard that over 3,000 people had to leave their homes. Where would they go? I pushed that worry out of my mind so I could concentrate on photographing the crowds. I focused on mothers carrying babies and holding the hands of young children. I followed the masses of displaced people and found them going to hastily equipped shelters in Prague. Inside, I took pictures of dazed, unhappy families.

"Please, Ivanov, see if you can requisition a car. I have to see what is happening in Sudetenland," I said to my guide.

Ivanov shot me a cold look—one I had seen before—and shook his head, then went to get a car. When he came back, he reported, "Just as I thought. There are no cars to hire."

I walked into the hotel and bribed the concierge to borrow his car, much to Ivanov's disappointment. After packing my equipment, we were on our way.

We stopped for dinner in Budweiser, the last big town before the frontier. It was filled with people eating, whispering, and staring into space.

I had to talk Ivanov into going to the Czech police station to find out the exact route of the German army. The police inspector, who spoke English, pulled out a map and studied it, then asked if I was from America.

After I said yes, he replied, "A wonderful, wonderful country. Now, first go to Oberplan; it is seven miles from the Austrian frontier. You'll never find it at night. I'll send you with one of our officers and a map."

"How very kind of you," I replied.

The police officer had blond hair and babyish pink cheeks. He looked young, maybe only twenty years old. The inspector gave him his orders. Ivanov told the officer he had to cover up his uniform, so he left for a moment, then came back wearing a long black coat.

Outside of Budweiser, we came upon a troop of Czech soldiers standing by the side of the road who had just withdrawn from the Sudetenland territory. As we crossed the new boundaries of the Third Reich, we came upon Sudeten peasants heavily armed with rifles, who inspected our papers.

We drove on to Oberplan. A dozen, tough-looking male peasants sprang out of the bushes, surrounded our car, and thrust their rifles through the open windows. One fired in the air as a signal of danger, causing fifty more men to appear. Most wore large swastika armbands and homemade Nazi badges pinned on their coats. I tried to control my fearful shivering.

A Nazi officer commanded in German, "Produce your papers at once." He snatched them from us, then looked them over, as well as the car. "What are you doing here?"

Ivanov and our Czech police officer remained silent.

I spoke up. "I'm an American reporter. I wanted to watch the German army cross the frontier."

With a nasty scowl on his face, the Nazi officer commanded, "Get out. Come with me to the courthouse."

Several of his men pointed their rifles to direct us to the village courthouse so we could be searched. The local führer searched us for firearms. He told Ivanov to empty his pockets and confiscated his pistol.

"What nationality are you?" he asked Ivanov in English.

"Russian."

"A Bolshevik?"

"No, I'm a White Russian."

Quite suddenly, the führer grabbed a rubber truncheon, swung it, and cracked it down on the desk. "You are now in the Third Reich."

He turned to our Czech policeman and ordered him, in German, to take off his coat. Our policeman stood there in full Czech regalia with fear in his eyes, exposed as if he were naked.

The führer shouted, "A Czech! We've caught a Czech!" He approached him and again hit the desk with truncheon. "You are in the Third Reich, don't you know that? Why are you prowling around in our village?" Not waiting for an answer, he plunged his hand into the policeman's coat pocket and threw a pair of gloves, keys, and a wallet on the desk. Out of the other pocket, he pulled a revolver. His voice trembled with rage and he kept cracking the truncheon on the desk. He turned to the audience of Nazi soldiers and shouted, "Take him outside and show him how we deal with Czechs!"

The Czech policeman's pink baby face turned white. Two Nazis grabbed his arms and dragged him out of the room.

I felt bile rise in my throat and held my hands tightly together to prevent them from shaking.

The führer shouted to one of the men holding a submachine gun to keep us under guard. "Shoot them if they move," he ordered.

After a terrifying hour, we were allowed to sit on a hard wooden bench, a gun never leaving our faces. I glanced down at my watch and saw that it was two o'clock in the morning. I was glad I had my Graflex camera and knew I could throw it at anyone's face as a weapon. I whispered to Ivanov, "Will that Nazi come back soon?"

He replied, "Don't worry. Germans are afraid of Americans."

"Why? They aren't afraid of Britain or France."

An S.S. German in a black uniform arrived at 3:30 in the morning. If I hadn't been so worried about our fate, I would have fallen asleep. He bowed, clicked his heels, and with a severe, unsmiling face, examined our papers. "Hmmm, a foreign journalist." He grabbed my camera from my lap, smiled with glee, and ordered our release.

With as much respect as I could muster, I asked about our Czech policeman. I didn't have the nerve to ask for my camera.

The Gestapo agent's mouth tightened. "That is a different case and it will be dealt with separately."

Ivanov and I were finally released.

Once outside, we heard wild cries in German: "*Sie kommen gleich!*" ("They're coming!") In the village square, the people were in their best clothes, shouting, waving swastikas, drinking beer, laughing, and even dancing. I felt frantic without a camera and started formulating words in my mind to convey my experience in writing instead.

The German troops were arriving and taking over. I felt sickened by what I saw. We went to a small inn across the square to get some needed sleep. I tossed and turned, fretting about the loss of all the photographs on my camera as well as the fate of our young Czech policeman.

The next morning, as we drove to the barrier posts near Hohenfurt, we saw the village people holding flowers and wreaths, waiting to welcome the German troops. We didn't dare cross into Germany, fearing we might not be allowed back in again.

In contrast, in the next town, we watched terrified Czechs and Germans alike seeking to salvage the few possessions they could carry as they fled to Prague. I missed my camera and wanted to capture images of their disillusioned, bitter faces to send home to America, so our people could see what was happening in this faraway land. It was clear to me that not every German in Sudetenland wanted to be annexed by Germany. Many of the German people who lived there had never been to Germany and the only thing they had in common was the language.

It was difficult getting back, as many of the bridges had been bombed and the roads were blocked with farm wagons and machinery. All along the roads, the Czech army came toward us in retreat. Their faces showed a range of emotions; bewilderment, sadness, hurt, and shame. Horses were brought back by cavalrymen to return to the farmers.

On the way to Prague, I had Ivanov stop by Budweiser to tell the inspector about our borrowed policeman. After we told him what had happened, I asked him if he was going to send help. The inspector was greatly distressed. "The Germans will kill him. He will never return."

I wanted to tell him how deeply sorry we were, but the words wouldn't come. Instead, I had a complete breakdown and began weeping. Stoic Ivanov gently put his arm around my shoulders and led me back to the car. The drive back to Prague was long and quiet. The rain made the roads, and my mood, worse.

Czechoslovakian refugees

Chapter 38
Hitler's Arrival, 1939

Czechoslovakia has ceased to exist.

— Adolf Hitler

In Prague, the people were resigned. They pulled the strips of paper off their windows, lit the streetlamps, and threw away their gas masks.

I spent the following day typing furiously on my typewriter to make up for the confiscation of my camera and the loss of my photographs. The headline of the article I sent to *Life Magazine* read, "HAS EVIL WON?"

A week later, we drove to Karlovy Vary in Sudetenland to hear Hitler's speech about getting his new territory after the Munich Pact. Looking out the window of our hired car, the gray, rainy clouds made my mind wander. I longed to know whether Oklahoma was getting any relief from the drought. I'd had no contact from Lorene and felt an empty longing for a female confidant.

The town was overflowing with German troops and S.S. men. Armored cars poured in with banners, propaganda leaflets, and swastikas. With my Rolleiflex, I took pictures of the huge erected wreaths with flowers that spelled the words: *Wir danken unseren Führer.* Ivanov told me it meant: "We thank our leader."

When Adolf Hitler arrived on that dim, rainy day, the crowd cheered with a frenzy of "Sieg Heil!" as he appeared on a balcony. The same tense feeling washed over me, just like when we were in Nuremberg. Hitler's face had a sinister look. Was it just my imagination because of the disdain I felt for this man? I would know once I developed my photographs. The people around me acted as though he were sacred. The air was filled with joyful noises.

Führer Hitler's speech was in his loud, forceful voice. *"I knew I would be standing here one day..."* Ivanov translated in my ear.

All I could think about were all the Sudeten Czechs, who had left their homes to live in shelters in Prague.

Back at the hotel café in Prague, an old man heard us speaking English. He was a German writer who had spent two years in a concentration camp after writing defamation pieces about Hitler. He had moved to Prague only a few years ago.

The worried man pleaded with us, "The Germans will be here soon. Please...help me get away."

"But you'll be all right. You're in Prague, not Sudetenland," I tried to reassure him.

"I know the Germans will come soon and take over the entire country. Hitler is never satisfied. I'm Jewish! Perhaps in America I can practice my religion. Please, I cannot go back to the horrible camp. I am too old to do the work the Nazis make you do there." He grabbed my shoulder in desperation, until Ivanov stared him down and he released his grip.

"I wish I could help you, but I am not going back yet. I'm a reporter and I must finish my assignment." I patted his shoulder sympathetically.

Ivanov interrupted, "We must leave now."

I followed Ivanov to the lobby and sat down with a heavy heart. I asked him, "What is a concentration camp?"

"It's a work camp the Germans devised for political prisoners. I think the first one was in Dachau in 1933."

I was one of the few reporters remaining in this upheaval. Most of the foreign reporters had left shortly after the Munich Treaty. *Life Magazine* let me stay to catch the scoop first, should Germany take the entire country.

I read the *New York Times* in the lobby. Prime Minister Chamberlain said in his speech to the House of Commons that he had not betrayed Czechoslovakia; that Great Britain has saved the country from annihilation and could now develop a national existence in neutrality. I bit a fingernail, thinking, *I'll find out soon enough.*

Each month, the number of Nazi soldiers increased, disrupting the railway and supply systems. They incited riots and disturbances, then announced on German radio that the Prague government was unable to maintain order and sent in more troops.

I reported back to *Life* that Sudetenland was where most of Czechoslovakia's resources were, and now it was part of Germany. How could the rest of the country possibly survive?

Ivanov and I witnessed the German Wehrmacht and Luftwaffe descending en masse on the Czech borders. I took photographs as best I could but I was extremely careful. I didn't want to be arrested or have my equipment confiscated again.

October, 1938 was a somber time and the weather continued to mirror the dismal mood. President Edvard Beneš resigned under German pressure and fled to London. He apparently did not want to be murdered as Chancellor Dollfuss had been when Germany took over Austria. Britain began permitting refugees to enter their country.

I sent some photos to *Life Magazine* and typed an article on my Royal. The signing of the Munich Pact was called peace, but there was none to be found here. The Germans had now dismembered Czechoslovakia. It was a country that had tried to hold up its umbrella against the storm of the Nazis, but it was blown inside out and became useless.

It was freezing cold in November. Ivanov donned his handsome fur hat, or *ushanka* as he called it, and let the ear-flaps down as he fastened straps under his chin. I saw him feel for his pistol in his heavy coat and wondered if he had bought another one. We walked around in the city and I took several pictures of the many troops of Germans, until the cold penetrated my gloves and my hands could take no more.

Ivanov and I shared a copy of the *New York Times* in which Virginia Cowles was reporting from Berlin. She wrote about the *Kristallnacht pogrom* — the Night of Broken glass — where mobs of Nazis roamed Germany's streets destroying synagogues, businesses, and assaulting Jews. Germans who murdered Jews were not jailed. Rape was punished only because it was a violation of the law for the Protection of German Blood. There were over 400 anti-Semitic laws now. Ivanov felt that Germany hated Jews and blamed them for losing World War One.

Every day we read bad news about the Jewish people in Germany. Ivanov was becoming more and more agitated. Thousands of Jews were being shipped in train boxcars over the border into Poland.

Over our usual dinner of potatoes, pig knuckles, and purple sauerkraut, Ivanov said, "The Jewish believe and live by the Ten Commandments. We are scientists, educators, and scholars, not criminals. The Germans are taking over just like in Austria. Adeline, I must inform you that I have to return to my country to protect my family." His gaze fell to the floor and he dropped his fork.

"I hate to see you go, Ivanov, but I understand. Your family must take priority." I touched his hand across the table.

He searched my face as he picked up his fork. "Will you be all right here?"

"Please, don't worry about me. I have learned how to get around and will find people who speak English." I tried to use a strong voice, but it cracked as I squeezed his hand in reassurance.

Ivanov left the next day with fear in his eyes. I stood in the hotel lobby, tears flowed freely down my face as I watched him go. I remembered Ivanov angrily reading the Nuremberg laws to me in Berlin. What was happening to the world and why were innocent people being persecuted? I ran up to my room and threw myself on the bed, sobbing with an overwhelming feeling of helplessness.

The new year of 1939 blew in with fierce wind and snow. The Gestapo remained everywhere. It was a cold like I had never experienced. I stopped wearing skirts and dresses and wore two pairs of trousers I had brought, one on top of the other, when I went outside to photograph the slow, sneaky takeover of Czechoslovakia. I couldn't have cared less about the stares from the people in the lobby, who rarely saw women in pants.

The Nazis began to agitate in Slovakia, the eastern portion of the country. Rumors continued to circulate about the incorporation of the entire country into the Reich. The succeeding president, Dr. Emil Hácha, proclaimed martial law to try to restore order. Then he gave Hitler free passage for German troops through all the Czech borders.

By March, despite all concessions, Dr. Hácha was summoned to a meeting in Berlin. I avidly followed Virginia Cowles's reports from Germany. Hitler threatened a bombing raid against Prague unless Dr. Hácha signed an agreement to allow Germany to take over. The frail president collapsed onto the floor. Upon being treated by a German doctor, he finally signed, allowing Hitler to take over the entire country of Czechoslovakia.

On March 15, during a raging snowstorm, the Nazis were flowing through Prague like a river that had broken through a dam. Hundreds of red, white, and black swastikas fluttered from the window ledges of buildings. The beautiful town had swelled to three times its size. The sound of leather boots crunched in the snow and there were rows of S.S. uniforms. I captured photographs of the heart-wrenching event with extreme caution, still terrified of being arrested again.

The faces of politicians, diplomats, and journalists were full of strain and anxiety. Czech women wept as terrified Jews covered their faces in fear when the German troops swept down the streets. Many of the Czech citizens jeered, shook their fists, and bravely hurled snowballs at German tanks.

The Gestapo ordered silence with their weapons, to allow Hitler's speech. I photographed every part of the intimidating event.

Later that day, I found one of the few English speaking reporters who summed up Hitler's speech for me. He translated: "We are here to protect the German people's life and liberty. Germany will end the aggressive terrorist Czechoslovakian regime."

What aggressive Czech terrorists was Hitler fabricating? I spent the rest of the day developing film and typed a report to send to *Life*. *The Reich has taken over without opposition,* I wrote. *Will the Czechoslovakian Republic become one big concentration camp now?*

I sent photos of the Nazi invasion that showed the look of devastation on the faces of the people of Prague.

In the weeks that followed, the Gestapo was everywhere and a curfew had been set. Great numbers of Germans were brought into the country and they took over the school system. The official language was now German. The Czech language was forbidden, even though most of the people of Prague didn't know German.

The German Nazis began the persecution of the Jews immediately after their accession to power. Ivanov told me before he left that the Jews had been in Czechoslovakia since the 11th century. The Nazis now required all Jews to register and their property was impounded. Jewish children were excluded from schools and the adults had their jobs taken away. They were prohibited from going to theaters, restaurants, using public transportation, and even going to parks. Jews could only shop in specified places and at certain times. I was thoroughly sickened as I photographed the intense, nervous, and bitter city of Prague as it suffered because of a battle unfought. There were whisperings of rage and grief about the betrayal of Britain among the Czechs. Bus after bus brought the ex-citizens of Czechoslovakia to the Terezín ghetto right outside the city of Prague. The Jewish people were humiliated, impoverished, and now isolated.

At night, alone in my room, I thought of my own country, the United States. It was the most powerful democracy in the world, yet had been of very little help. Britain's strategy of appeasement with the Munich Pact did not satisfy Germany and had simply delayed the inevitable. It took Hitler only six months after getting Sudetenland to take the rest of Czechoslovakia. I felt that pacifism was not working, and that only war could fight fascism.

Life telegraphed me to come back to New York. My work was done and they had further assignments for me. I left with a heavy heart. What would become of all these poor souls?

Mourning the annexation of Sudetenland, a woman, unable to conceal her misery, dutifully salutes the triumphant Hitler.

Chapter 39
April 1939, The Downfall

This is a sad day for all of us, and to none is it sadder than to me. Everything that I have worked for, everything that I have believed in during my public life, has crashed into ruins. There is only one thing left for me to do: That is, to devote what strength and powers I have to forwarding the victory of the cause for which we have to sacrifice so much. I trust I may live to see the day when Hitlerism has been destroyed and a liberated Europe has been re-established.
— Prime Minister of England, Neville Chamberlain

I left Czechoslovakia with a deep sadness for a people I had grown to care about. It was strange to be back in my own country without a home to go to or friends to see. I found a room in a boarding house and was given a few humdrum jobs by Mr. Luce. The once exciting city of New York now seemed dull. My first assignment was to cover a high-society fashion show, and it felt trivial to me. Wasn't it was my destiny to travel and report on the war in foreign countries? Hitler had taken over Austria, Czechoslovakia, and now was advancing into Poland. How could I stay in New York and photograph fashion shows when the world was being gobbled up by Hitler? The United States seemed to remain in an oblivious bubble. I didn't want to do the same.

Toward the end of August, I followed all the newspaper stories about Poland. It was frustrating to read articles by my colleague, Virginia Cowles, who reported about Poland from Berlin for the *London Times*. Cowles wrote that planes, tanks, and guns were in position, ready to invade Poland with stormtroopers that lined the main avenue in Berlin. I read that Hitler had annulled his 1934 nonaggression treaty with Poland, then listed the atrocities the Poles had committed. Cowles reported that Hitler was once again telling lies, just as he had about the Czechs before Germany invaded Czechoslovakia.

On my way to the subway, after covering the latest fashion show, I read the screaming headlines from the *New York Times.*

GREAT BRITAIN AND FRANCE
DECLARE WAR ON GERMANY
POLAND INVADED

I hailed a cab to the office and I begged Mr. Luce to send me to Poland. He praised my work in Czechoslovakia but told me there were no interpreters available in Poland, and, unlike Czechoslovakia, no English was spoken there. My boss handed me an address and told me he needed me to cover a cat show.

It was humiliating to report on cats and clothes when there was a war about to happen. After the event, I picked up a copy of the *New York Herald Tribune* and avidly read war correspondent Sonia Tomara's report on Poland. Sonia Tomara was the only female reporter in the capital of Warsaw.

Jealousy got the best of me until I researched her qualifications. Sonia was from Russia, and with her family, had fled to Paris during the 1917 Russian Revolution. She became a secretary for the foreign editor of a French newspaper since she was fluent in many languages, including Polish. Now, she was a reporter for the *New York Herald Tribune* and had been sent to Poland.

Between Virginia's reports from Berlin and Tomara's eyewitness reports from Warsaw, the war in Poland began to unfold. Britain and France signed a series of agreements with Poland. Poland did not have a chance against Germany without their help. Poland fought for fifteen days alone. In May, France did not send enough troops and was in the wrong areas of Poland to fight. Sixty French bombers were promised to Poland and never arrived. Cowles reported from Berlin that the German Luftwaffe had over 3,000 planes; Poland had only 397, most of which were from World War One. Poland did have a fully mobilized army of a million; Germany had 1.5 million.

In August, a nonaggression pact was signed by the USSR and Germany. This gave Stalin the right to also invade Poland, with more than 1,000 planes and 4,000 tanks.

Every time I read about the Soviet Union, I worried about my friend Ivanov, and wondered how he was faring in his country with his family.

In the living room of the boardinghouse, I heard Sonia Tomara broadcast from Warsaw to America. The German army had surrounded Warsaw on all three sides with ceaseless aerial and artillery bombing. Tomara reported that the narrow Polish Corridor was militarily indefensible because its long frontier was easy to penetrate. The Polish government was now fleeing while its people were being massacred.

By the end of September, Warsaw had capitulated. France and Britain were pressured to rescind their troops so as not to provoke the Germans. Germany and the USSR divided Poland. The Soviet Union would wind up with about three-fifths of Poland and 13 million of its people as a result of the invasion.

Time reported the Polish *blitzkrieg*. I discovered that the new word meant "lightning war." Yes, it sure was a lightning war. It began on the first of September and ended on the twenty-eighth of the same month. It only took one month for Germany and the USSR to take the country over and for Poland to cease to exist. Britain and France did declare war on Germany, but did not do enough to prevent the takeover.

This was all very alarming to me. Why didn't our great, powerful country stop the Nazi invasion? They obviously were hoping that the French and British could stop it without them.

In October, Sonia Tomara reported that 70,000 Poles had died and 133,000 were wounded. The Germans rounded up many of them for labor. The Polish Jews were put in ghettos and had to wear armbands, just like the Jews in Germany. Over 1.7 million Poles were shipped to Siberia and put into concentration camps. The remaining Poles had their language declared illegal. There was also the organized kidnapping of an estimated 50,000 blond, blue-eyed Polish children to be shipped to the Reich to be raised as Germans.

Every piece of news I read reminded me of the takeover of Czechoslovakia. Hitler's plan was dismally familiar to me.

Execution of Polish priests and civilians in Poland

Germans march through Warsaw

Chapter 40
Finland, 1939-1940

Bravery is not being afraid to be afraid.
— Marie Colvin, War Correspondent

It was the end of November, approaching the new year of 1940. Mr. Wilson Hicks, the executive editor of *Life,* called me into his office and told me his various resources had disclosed the possible threat of a Soviet invasion of Finland. He asked if I was ready to cover a possible war in a country that spoke English as well as their national language.

I eagerly agreed. Mr. Hicks told me that the winter months in that country were ungodly cold and questioned whether I still wanted the assignment. I assured him that Czechoslovakia was a cold country as well, and I knew how to survive freezing climates. I smirked, remembering when Ivanov had told me to rub my nose frequently to warm it up so it wouldn't freeze off.

I was eager for the adventure. I'd had trouble settling in New York City, anyway. I had gotten used to the constant photographic opportunities in Czechoslovakia and was looking forward to work that was important and had a purpose. With only two weeks to prepare, I spent time in the library, studying the history and maps of Finland.

Finland was a highly literate, democratic country. I wondered whether they could win a war against a bigger military force, such as the USSR. My thoughts again turned to my friend Ivanov. I found his address and wrote him a letter to find out how he was doing.

Life Magazine obtained a letter from President Roosevelt, introducing me to American Foreign Service officials in Finland and asking them to assist me with my reporting. What a privilege to receive such a valuable letter! It felt like gold in my hands.

I finally boarded the *Westenland*, a Dutch ship carrying wheat to Belgium. As I walked up the gangplank, I saw many departing foreigners speaking different languages. Open emotions of sadness were displayed, with tearful eyes and lingering embraces. There were only forty-five passengers filing up into the ship as the departing bell clanged. It had a capacity of 544, but probably not that many people were interested in leaving in November to go to the frozen north, especially with an impending war.

The lights of New York City were mesmerizing as the ship pulled out. I spent most of my time in my chilly little cabin, as I did not hear my language being spoken. The food was scarce and atrocious. I escaped by reading my mystery novels, then cleaned and organized my camera equipment.

On the tenth day, I ventured up to the windy deck and spoke to the attractive bi-lingual Belgium captain. We were the only ones outside in the blustery weather. He told me we would reach the coast of Britain the next day, and that we had to avoid crossing the heavily mined English Channel. The captain was a talkative man and told me about a new German weapon called the "magnetic mine." It was a giant globe studded with spikes, dropped from German airplanes into shipping lanes, which was attracted to the metal hulls of ships, at which time it detonated. He said that just yesterday a Dutch ship had struck a mine and had gone down with 150 lives lost. We stood together at the railing in silence, feeling the swelling rhythm of the waves.

Suddenly, the captain yelled, "Oh my God!" He grabbed me and spun me around. "Turn away!"

Confused, I said, "What's going on?"

"There are bodies floating in the ocean."

Shocked, and being the curious reporter that I was, I craned my neck to look over the railing at the churning ocean below. Acting on instinct, I snapped a few photographs from the camera that was tucked inside my coat.

There were over a hundred bodies floating all around our ship, all bloated, their exposed skin a blistered greenish-black color. Most were floating face down with their arms and legs dangling under the water's surface. I gagged and stopped shooting when I saw a seabird land on one body that was face up, and start picking at its eyes. The captain ordered me to go inside.

Back in my cabin, I hugged my freezing body as I thought about the lifeless, bloated bodies bobbing in the vast ocean. Where had they come from? Who were they? Had they hit a mine? That night, my dreams haunted me as my mind replayed the surreal scene over and over. I woke soaked in sweat, thinking, *It's all part of living in a time of war...*

As I dressed for breakfast the next morning, my shaky fingers could barely button my blouse. Would the *Westenland* hit a mine? I began to question myself. Did I have the fortitude to endure another war?

I left my camera in the cabin and headed for the dining room. I sat at the captain's table for breakfast.

He leaned over and whispered to me, "Do not mention what you saw to anyone. I do not need any hysteria on my ship."

I agreed and sipped watery coffee from my cup. As I put it down on the saucer, it clattered.

After eating a meager meal, the captain left. I made myself go back up onto the deck, and was relieved to see wavy blue water for miles and miles and nothing else...no other ships and no bodies.

I was frustrated by how shaken I was after seeing the dead people floating in the ocean. I had been chosen by one of the largest magazines in the United States to cover the war. I knew I had to suspend my feelings and become like a machine in order to record with my camera to inform the world.

I got off the ship in Belgium and flew to Stockholm, then went on to Helsinki. At the hotel, I was happy to discover that most of the Finns spoke English as well as their native language. After unpacking in my room, I went down to the hotel café and enjoyed a wholesome, delicious dinner—a welcome comfort after being on the ship. My hotel room was spacious and the bed was cozy, and I fell asleep with the vision of the floating bodies once more.

The next morning, at 8:00 a.m., I was jolted awake by the sound of a bomb being dropped on the city of Helsinki. I leaped out of bed and stumbled to throw on my clothes. I retrieved the new Graflex camera I had purchased to replace the one that was confiscated in Czechoslovakia, and ran out into the street amid the ear-splitting shrieking of the air-raid sirens. As a second bomb dropped, I shot photo after photo of the people, moving in a trance, headed for shelter. Other citizens remained in their doorways, silently watching. No one cried. No one ran. There was an eerie calmness about the whole event.

My camera captured stunned eyes and rigid postures. I couldn't believe a war had just begun. I felt the spooky silence and the tension of waiting for another bomb to fall from the low, slate-gray clouds in the sky. After staring at the sky for a few moments, I went back into the hotel and attempted to eat some breakfast to calm myself down, then hid in my room. It was uncanny that I had arrived the day before the Soviets invaded Finland.

At 2:00 p.m. the piercing wail of the sirens began again. I forced myself to go outside and heard the roar of bombs once more. I steadied my trembling hands and photographed Soviet Ilyushin DB-3 bombers as they dove close to the ground, dumping their heavy bombs. The explosions made a tremendous, terrifying sound and the earth shook with each impact. Four blocks of flats erupted in flames. A grayish cloud of smoke drifted up from a school directly across from the hotel as it burst into flames, turning the sky into a pinkish hue.

I shot a few frames, then ran out of film packs and switched to my Leica. I tried to put aside my worry. Were there still children in there? Fire trucks roared by. Firemen put out the fire as the building crumbled to the ground.

I heard the air-raid sirens again. My lungs were choked with smoke and I ran back into the hotel café to take cover. In the lobby, a few windows had shattered and the concierge was sweeping up the mess. Two firemen came in, the pungent smell of smoke on their uniforms, and sat near me in the café. They hurriedly ate a light meal for energy to carry on with their work. Hoping they spoke English, I asked about the children in the school.

The tall one looked down at his plate, paused with his fork in the air, and said with a stilted British accent, "We will dig the bodies out later."

I could only mumble, "Oh..." I pushed my meal aside and went up to my room to get some sleep, knowing that the next day could bring even more horror.

In the morning, I was surprised that I had slept at all. I sat up in bed and listened for bombs to fall or for the sound of the warning sirens. I forced myself to dress, grabbed my camera, and ventured outside. This time, I wore a leather coat under the fur coat I had splurged on in New York after reading about the extremely low temperatures in Finland. It was a dark, frozen morning. It had been cold in Czechoslovakia, but nothing like this climate. I rubbed my nose until it was warm and thought about my friend Ivanov.

I took heart-wrenching photographs of a mother in a long wool skirt, headscarf, and a bulky winter coat, waving down a bus to put her children on. She tearfully kissed each child, each with a suitcase, then slowly walked back to her home without them. I peered at them over the rim of my camera. Where were the children going? I knew there was no school.

Would Helsinki be bombed again? I turned my fur collar up on my neck for warmth. As it began to snow, I was glad I had bought boys' rubber boots. For the rest of the day, I shot the migration of children leaving on buses as they continued to be evacuated from the city. I saw children in hearses, trucks, and even cattle cars, all headed to the train station. I found out that they were being moved to safety in the country farther up north.

Two days went by without further bombing, and I cautiously ventured down a road outside of the city with my camera. I wore more clothes this time; woolen pants, underwear and socks, my two coats, fur-lined gloves, and a wool scarf to protect my nose.

I came upon a filling station where a school bus had turned over onto its side. I stood, unable to move, staring at it as my imagination flooded my head with images of dead children. I walked gingerly around it and screamed when I saw a dead man pinned beneath it. His arms were crushed but his boots looked brand-new. Snow fell on the poor man's disfigured face. As I took a photograph of his body, bile rose in my throat. I turned and vomited in the snow. I trudged back toward town as my mind kept picturing the poor bus driver. My watch indicated that it was only 4:00, but nighttime descended early upon Finland in the winter.

I went straight up to my room, skipped dinner, and put my camera away. I took off my coat and boots, then buried myself under the blankets and drifted into a fitful sleep. The dead bodies I had seen from the ship were upsetting but surreal, and somehow were not as frightening to me as looking at the body of the bus driver. My first, close-up image of a dead man was etched into my dreams.

A flurry of clean-up began in the city of Helsinki the next day. I shot pictures of the workmen getting out of trucks to clear glass and debris off the snow with shovels. I wondered...how did they know the bombing was over?

I wandered around the capital. Most of the buildings were blown through, exposing large holes. A fireman let me go with him into an apartment house after I told him I was a reporter from America. I knew without asking that he was looking for remaining bodies, but I tried to push that thought out of my mind in order to do my job.

We climbed two flights of stairs and went into an apartment with no door. I looked at the soaked family photographs hanging on the wall amid blown-up bits of personal possessions scattered all over the floor. Flower-printed curtains, soaked by the fire hoses, were now stiff with icicles after being exposed to the outside air.

This photograph will tell a sad story of the aftermath of a bombing, I thought, clicking away.

Firemen continued to dig out burned and crushed bodies from the building all day long, carrying them outside and dropping them in trucks. I pushed my emotions aside and numbly photographed the dead, then a procession of Finns following coffins being carried to the cemetery.

A week later, the firemen were still finding people. Lost children were announced daily on the radio. I shot images of silent, homeless people carrying possessions in knapsacks and suitcases while others just clustered together in doorways, whispering to each other. I thought that the Finns were a remarkably steady, stoic people.

I photographed a mother with red cheeks and two scarves wrapped around her head, pushing her baby in a buggy, which had a fur rug in it to keep the baby warm. I asked where she was going. She said there were tents in the forest.

"Won't you freeze?" I asked.

She replied in a neat, stilted English, like a governess, "No, ten people can fit in one tent. That will keep us warm."

"Aren't you afraid?"

The young mother answered, "Why should we be afraid? We have done nothing wrong." She pushed her buggy away in the deep snow.

I shot streams of villagers taking refuge in the forest, thick on the roads, and traveling with horses to haul their belongings. I was proud to photograph the amazing resilience of ordinary people during a time of war. Though it was distressing to watch, I knew that this was where I was supposed to be. This certainly was more important than photographing a fashion show.

The month of December was one of the coldest. Just when I thought the bombing was over for good, at 1:00 in the afternoon I spotted Soviet planes flying overhead in the cloudy winter sky. The noise of bombs being dropped shook my body and made me shiver. I quickly photographed the Finnish machine guns on the roofs of office buildings, shooting up at the bombers. I made it inside just as the sirens began to wail and another bomb dropped outside the hotel.

A few days went by draped with a worrisome quiet. I soon became stir crazy and carefully crept out of the hotel to go the hospital to photograph the victims. In the first bed was a handsome young man with thick blond hair, his face flushed with fever. He looked my way and greeted me in Finnish. Not getting a response, he switched to English. He asked me to hold his hand and told me he had been shot in the back and couldn't move. His breathing was quite shallow as I patted his hand. The hospital was where I learned the real tragedy of war. I stayed all day, visiting and comforting the patients while taking the occasional photograph. I left full of grief for all the patients. I searched the sky for planes and, seeing none, headed back to the hotel.

Two weeks passed and there had been no bombs. Then, once again, I heard the roar of Soviet planes flying above just as I opened the heavy lobby door. I looked up and instead of bombs, saw something fluttering through the gray, snowy sky. Thousands of papers drifted down and littered the snow-laden streets.

A blond-haired, plump young boy stood outside near me, his hands placed firmly on his hips, his feet set apart in an angry stance, and with a stubborn, serious look on his face. When it became quiet, he said to me, "Little by little I am getting angry."

I said sadly, "I am so sorry this is happening to your country," and picked up one of the papers, stuffed it in my pocket, and went back inside the hotel.

The clerk read it for me: "It says 'You know we have bread, why do you starve?'"

I had a perplexed look on my face. He crumpled it up, threw it away, and told me they were propaganda leaflets to get Finland to surrender.

I sighed. War was complicated.

Chapter 41
Alonzo and the War

To foreign correspondents: the Finnish government will not refuse to take part in negotiations for the restoration of peace. Nevertheless, anyone who believes that the Finnish people can be brought by the threat of force, and the terror already launched, to make concessions that would denote in reality the loss of their independence, is mistaken.
— Finnish Foreign Minister Vaino Tanner

In the hotel lobby, there were seats set up around a grand radio. I heard a broadcast from Moscow.

"The war in Finland was started by Finnish revolutionaries and we will end it."

People began to chatter among themselves in Finnish. I asked a man sitting next to me what everyone was saying. Finnish was not a language that could be picked up in a short time, and I was always begging people to please speak English.

He answered me in an unfamiliar, accented, angry voice. "The Soviets are telling lies to their people. Finland is a peaceful, self-sufficient country. They don't need the Soviets or want them here. Finns are not a panicky population and they will do what it takes to defend their fine country."

I looked closely at the strikingly handsome man's jet-black, wavy hair and matching mustache. "Your English accent is very unusual. You're not from here, are you?"

"No, I'm from Italy, sent by the government to report on the war." He took my hand and kissed it, then introduced himself. "My name's Alonzo Rossi. Are you American?"

"Yes, I'm here to do the same. Name's Adeline Peterson." I still felt the kiss on my hand.

Alonzo continued to tell me his opinion of Finland in his

charming, passion-filled accent. "The Finns are tough, smart people who can survive anything. Did you know the illiteracy rate here is only one percent?"

I shook my head.

"My main worry in this war is that the Finnish are a nation of three million fighting against 180 million Soviets." He paused and looked into my eyes. "Can I buy you a drink? You would love Koskenkorva Viina."

"What does it taste like?"

"It's a Finnish vodka, but it's a marvelous, sweet drink."

Before I could answer, he took off for the café and brought back two drinks.

I sipped the delicious liquid. "You're right, it has the perfect sweetness."

We enjoyed each other's company, but after two drinks I became too drowsy to finish my sentences and got up to leave.

"I must get some sleep. Thank you for your company, Alonzo," I said, hoping I wasn't slurring my words.

Alonzo stood up and kissed my hand. "Join me for breakfast in the morning. I know the best meal to order."

"I would like that."

As I climbed the stairs that led to my room, I touched the hand that had been kissed by the charming Italian. I had never had my hand kissed before and was surprised by the passion it stirred in me. The sweet alcohol helped me slide into a deep sleep. I dreamed about Smokey in Oklahoma.

The next morning, I went down to the café for breakfast and found Alonzo, as promised, waiting for me. His neatly combed hair was so dark that it had an almost blue sheen when the light hit it just right. I admired his Italian-style clothes.

The steamy hot, baked rye porridge with molasses Alonzo ordered was delicious and filling. He ordered so much food that I just sampled bites of most of it, while he told me what everything was. There was a sweet, donut-like pastry filled with stewed apples and sprinkled with sugar. I told him I loved the cardamom buns with cinnamon on top as we sipped hot apple cider.

Alonzo was quite a chatty man. He reminded me of John from so long ago. He was full of enthusiasm, which filled the void for my need for meaningful companionship. I loved the intonation of his Italian accent and hung on his every word. It sounded so seductive.

As we finished breakfast, he gingerly touched my shoulder and asked if I wanted to share a car with him to go to the Karelian front.

Surprised, I asked, "Are we allowed?"

"We can go to the military office to try to get papers."

"I could show my letter from my president, introducing me."

At the military office in Helsinki, Alonzo tried to persuade the commanding general to allow us to go the front. He explained that we represented two countries that wanted to help Finland win the war with words and photographs.

The perplexed general looked us over. "Impossible. I cannot allow a woman to go to the front."

I reached inside my coat for the precious letter from President Roosevelt and handed it to him. After reading it, the general displayed a slight smile and asked, "Do you think you can walk eight miles through forests that are thick with trees and granite boulders, and snow drifts as high as your necks—or in both of your cases, over your heads?"

We both foolishly nodded.

He looked the letter over again and called in a young lieutenant, who towered over us. "Drive these reporters to the front after they pack."

The lieutenant grinned at us, turned to the general, and answered, "Yes, sir."

The commanding general handed me the letter, then wrote and stamped one for Alonzo.

We went back to the hotel to pack up. I stuffed a bag with camera equipment and wore most of my clothes for warmth. I met a smiling Alonzo in the lobby, who eagerly helped me with my heavy bag, then leaned in and gave me a surprise peck on my cheek.

Outside, our guide was waiting by the car, which was painted white to camouflage it in the snow. He kept slapping his gloves together to warm them up. As he and Alonzo chatted, their breath formed puffy clouds in the cold air. I observed our guide's coat, which had a high collar and large, over-the-knee boots. A gray Finnish astrakhan cap covered his head. Alonzo asked him how old he was. Our lieutenant was only nineteen and his nickname was Viskey.

Once out of the city, the lieutenant drove down narrow, unmarked, glassy roads, sometimes skidding on the ice. It reminded me of skating on the frozen ponds in the woods behind our house with my brother. There was no heat in this borrowed army vehicle and I hugged myself for warmth. Alonzo pulled me close and put his arm around me. We produced a comforting, cozy warmth in the bitter-cold car.

Viskey took us to a farm just as total blackness descended upon us. The lieutenant told us former President Svinhufvud of Finland resided there and was housing soldiers on their way to the front. We would stop there for the night.

The president greeted us and introduced his wife. They were quite a tall couple, but then Alonzo and I were on the opposite spectrum of height—almost *everyone* was taller than we were.

We all sat in front of a finely built, large stone fireplace that crackled with an inviting fire. The president's wife handed us steaming-hot cups of fermented apple cider. The elderly couple complemented each other in appearance. The president wore a warm lumberjack shirt with high brown boots. His wife wore a high-neck, thick gray-and-white-striped sweater with a long wool skirt and boots that peeked out from underneath. When I complimented her on the sweater, she said with pride that she had knitted it herself.

After a second mug of cider, the president told us the story of his life. "I have dealt with the Russians before, when Finland was part of the Russian empire. I was exiled in a Russian Siberian prison camp for three years because of my anti-Russian position as the prime minister of Finland. Years later, as president, I helped suppress Finland's Communist Party and we became an independent state. Our people despise war and this war is a disaster, but we will not give up easily. We have no choice. Finland is an exceptional country with no unemployment or hunger. We take care of our old people and school is available for the young. Finland has cheap land and a fair division of wealth.

Finns are a free people and we can talk freely and read anything we want. You know, Finland has a brave army of a half million, with a population of 2.5 million. The USSR wants to use part of our country as a naval base but when we refused, this is when the war began. We will defend our country." The former president spoke in an animated voice with strong conviction.

The night wore on and we became drowsy from the effects of the hard cider. Mrs. Svinhufvud brought us all upstairs to our beds. The lieutenant was given the first room. She opened the next room, which had only one double bed, and said good night. I hesitated as we went in, and thought she must have mistakenly thought Alonzo and I were married. Alonzo was delighted and kissed me all around my neck, then on my lips as he twirled me onto the edge of the bed. It was easy for me to succumb to Alonzo's advances as the alcohol had me flushed with desire.

He was a slow, attentive lover, twirling my hair with one finger, then softly stroking my cheek. He kissed my hardened nipples through my blouse, then helped me slip off my many layers of clothes. He was filled with a sparkling energy that flowed over me as his body surrounded me. We fell back on the bed, laughing and playing with each other. It had been quite a long time since I had been with a man, and my desires were aflame once again. Afterward, a satisfying sleep descended upon both of us.

In the morning, we had a proper Finnish breakfast of *villi*, which was creamy, fermented milk with blueberries. Mrs. Svinhufvud offered us bread that was filled with cheese and had a long Finnish name.

We wanted to get to the Karelian front early, and thanked the former president and his wife profusely for their warm hospitality. For our journey, they gave us apples that had been stored from their orchard.

The president's wife invited, "Come back in the summer and stay. The war will be over then and it is very beautiful in Finland at that time of the year."

Viskey, our young lieutenant, drove for three hours as best he could on the extremely narrow roads and slippery bridges. He stayed in first gear the whole time.

At one point, we were stopped by a Finnish guard, who looked over our papers. "Where are you going?"

The lieutenant answered, "We are going to the front to report on the progress of the war."

The guard looked at me curiously, then declared, "Don't go over any bridges. They're all mined. We lost one soldier already today."

Viskey nodded as we slowly pulled away.

Alonzo held my hand in reassurance as I gazed into his deep, caring brown eyes.

We went through a thick forest of pine trees and passed a few white camouflaged trucks that blended into the snow. Four hours later, through snow-covered fields, we saw gun flashes from the Finnish batteries a mile away. We were now at the Karelian front.

Viskey pulled over and we watched bursts of lightning followed by the loud noise of the shells exploding when they landed. The noise was deafening. I held my ears.

Viskey informed us that the Soviets were only a few miles away and the Finnish soldiers were going to attack from the rear.

I rolled my window down to take pictures, feeling falsely secure inside the vehicle. Soldiers passed us, tramping through the snow with white overalls covering their uniforms as camouflage. They pulled small, lightweight sledges piled with bicycles, supplies, and skis.

We got out of our vehicle. I snapped photographs of the Red Cross going by, using sledges as ambulances.

An officer stopped his truck beside us. "What are you doing here? Let me see your papers." He looked them over, then shouted, "Go back! You are in the way. Go to Viipuri. The Soviets are done with us there. Go to the largest church for refuge. Quickly, you must leave! This is sheer stupidity! You are blocking us!"

We drove into a ditch to allow a caravan of supply trucks to pass. I began to shiver and felt half frozen. Alonzo hugged me tightly.

Upon reaching the bombed city of Viipuri, we were invited to eat supper in a church. Our eyes filled with delight as we looked at the "help-yourself" table that was piled with an abundance of food. There was meat with gravy on large platters and a variety of fresh loaves of bread on others.

We sat with a general, who kept the conversation light at first. "We feed our soldiers well in our country, but do not allow alcohol in order to maintain a disciplined army at all times." He poured himself a large glass of milk from a ceramic pitcher.

"The food is wonderful." I savored a bite of hot, creamy macaroni and cheese.

The general asked us what we were doing there. Alonzo explained that we were reporters and wanted to tell our countries about the progress of the Soviet invasion.

The informative general said, "We've had two battalions of Finnish soldiers that moved and circled the Soviet lines last night. I am proud to say we have cornered an entire Soviet division into a sector."

After our meal, the general showed us positions on his scale map, saying, "We fight like Indians because we know our dense woods. Skis give us tremendous speed and we can move faster than the Soviets can run. Our guns use three- or six-inch shells, while the Soviets use ten, but their firing is very inaccurate and many shells don't explode. Even with their low-flying planes, their bombs don't always work. I am proud to say that we are doing well on the southern front."

We were shown a room in which to sleep. I wondered whether, like the president's wife, the general assumed we were married. Or maybe it didn't matter in this country.

Alonzo and I stripped off each other's clothes in the chilly air and slid into a bed piled high with blankets. Our lovemaking was slow, with touching and kissing over every inch of our bodies. The second time we were on fire and exploded into bliss, ending in a satisfying sleep.

A knock came on our door at 8:00 a.m. with the announcement that breakfast was ready. With only a few hours of sleep, we knew we had better eat when we could.

After breakfast, the general asked us if we would like to visit the Viipuri prison to see how the captured Soviets were being treated. We both agreed, being the curious reporters that we were.

A driver took us about a half-hour away as a beautiful light sprinkling of snow fell from the sky.

The chief warden of the prison was a slim man who wore a pince-nez—glasses without earpieces held in place across the bridge of the nose. As he spoke to us with a stammer, I studied his glasses and observed that they had two tiny nose pads that helped the glasses stay on his face. A cord was attached that fell down the front of his uniform.

The warden brought us to where the clean but tiny cells were located. Alonzo knew Russian and interviewed a Soviet pilot in the first cell. As tears rolled down the pilot's face, I tried to unobtrusively photograph him. I asked Alonzo what he had said. The prisoner had told him that he missed his pregnant wife and children. Alonzo gave him a cigarette from a pack he always carried around to give as gifts. The warden vehemently disapproved, but Alonzo argued with him and the warden finally agreed to allow Alonzo to give one to all the prisoners. They ranged in age from the late thirties to the youngest being only eighteen. Alonzo told me that most of the captured pilots had only ten hours of combat flight training, and were told that the Finns had no Pursuits or anti-aircraft planes, which was a lie. As we left the cells, the prisoners cheered and waved. I felt sad for them and their families.

It took us three hours to drive only twenty-five miles to get back to Helsinki. Now it was snowing relentlessly, and the car skidded and spun on the ice, sending us precariously in and out of ditches.

We finally came upon a large, round tent and our driver suggested that we stay there until the weather cleared. We went in the opening and met a group of pilots who were there waiting for the snow to stop. On the airfield, there were no planes to be seen; they were all hidden in fields in dugouts. The pilots told us that the fast Pursuits had been imported from Holland, as there were very few Finnish airplane factories.

One of the men got out a guitar and sang a lively Finnish folk tune. Some of the other young pilots joined in. We were offered a simple lunch, and I took the opportunity to question the pilots about their progress in what they called the "Winter War." The squadron commander told us about bringing two planes down in one day. He added that yesterday they had fought alone against twelve Soviet bombers. The pilot explained that Soviet bombers were good, but slow, and that their Pursuits had greater speed and could fly at much lower altitudes than the Soviet planes.

The following day, the weather cleared and we bade the jolly group of pilots good luck, then were driven back to the hotel.

Upon arriving, the concierge handed me a telegram from *Life Magazine* telling me to send all my film and reports from Finland and to get to France to cover a possible German invasion. I had learned by now that the staff of *Life Magazine* had an uncanny sense of politics about predicting the events of war.

Alonzo's face fell after I showed him my telegram.

I had an idea. "Come with me! We'll cover the war together. We make a great team." I stroked his arm and gazed into his large, chocolate eyes.

"I cannot, my darling. I am assigned to stay here until the Finns win this war. Let's keep in touch and meet up later."

"I hope so. I have enjoyed working with you." I winked and leaned in closer to him. "And playing with you," I whispered in his ear.

"I as well," he said with sadness in his voice.

We linked arms and walked to the café.

Later that day, I went back to the military office and showed the general my telegram.

He gave me the once-over and sneered, "Why are you wandering around Europe at a time like this? Where is your handsome Italian?" After he saw my face fall, he patiently told me, "I can get you on a wheat ship but you will be risking your life. There will be plenty of German Navy ships in the same ocean."

I didn't say anything, but thought, *This won't be anything different than what I have already experienced.*

I went back to my room to pack up, then looked all over the hotel for Alonzo, but he was nowhere to be found. I sighed with disappointment. I was beginning to feel like a seasoned war correspondent.

Finnish ski troops

Chapter 42
1940, Paris

France has lost the battle but she has not lost the war.
— Charles de Gaulle, President of France

In just three months, from March to June of 1940, Germany had conquered Czechoslovakia, Austria, Poland, Denmark, Norway, Belgium, Luxembourg, the Netherlands, and it looked like France was next.

There were three other female war correspondents and many male reporters in my hotel in Paris. I wandered the streets with my camera and met a refugee, a mother from Belgium. She had left with her nine children and made it to Paris with only two; the others were killed by a soldier with a machine gun on the train. When she told me her story, she didn't cry or show any anger. I saw only defeat on her face while photographing her. I focused in on her vacant, expressionless eyes while her remaining children clung to her. My mind drifted to the migrant mother I had photographed a few years ago, who'd had the same look.

I shot many displaced people flowing in from Belgium as well as Holland. There were twenty Belgian boys who had walked together from Liège to Paris without their parents. I read in a newspaper that the American Red Cross had reported that over five million refugees, mostly women and children, had flowed southward from Belgium and Luxembourg into France.

Within two weeks of being in Paris, I heard that the Germans were only seventeen miles away. The Royal Air Force was losing many of its bombers. I was desperate to find a French government censor to approve my dispatch to *Life* so that the wire operator could cable it.

Then total chaos broke out in the hotel. All the reporters milled around the lobby, speaking many languages in frantic voices.

I found a British reporter and asked what was going on. He said to me, "The Germans are coming closer. I think we'd all better get out of this country."

I ran up to my room and packed fast. It took two trips to bring all my belongings down to the front desk. I desperately asked the concierge if he could store some of my camera equipment.

He answered in a meek, shaky voice, "I can if the hotel doesn't get bombed."

I had no choice. That would have to do. I put on my hat, fit what I could into two suitcases, and gave the concierge the rest. Outside the hotel there was more confusion. The streets were filled with people carrying their luggage and assorted belongings, all trying to hail a cab, just as I wanted to do. Taxi after taxi was stuffed with people trying to leave before the Germans completely took over.

I had to walk along the Champs-Élysées with my hefty suitcases bumping against my legs and weighing me down as I headed toward the railway station. On the boulevard, I found myself stranded with hordes of fleeing people.

A deafening noise of confusion permeated the air; the sounds of scraping automobile gears, shouting, and cursing. I couldn't stop coughing from the thick smell of petrol. The air-raid alarm wailed amid the unmistakable sound of bombs exploding. On the way to the station, I saw signs in windows that read "No Rooms Available." I finally got there, completely out of breath and exhausted. There were so many people crammed into the station that some even sprawled out on the floor, waiting for a train to come.

A steady stream of desperate refugees kept coming and coming. I took a few shots of people as they hurried by. They all seemed to have the question, "Where will we go?" plastered on their faces. I regretted leaving most of my equipment behind. But how could I have dragged a few hundred pounds on foot?

After an hour of this mass chaos, it started to rain. I was almost overcome with worry. People yelled to each other in shock, "Will we be defeated?"

I waited for a train but didn't even know where I was going to go, or where I would sleep that night. Worry and helplessness spread over my weary body, as it did with the thousands of refugees around me.

The trains never showed up. After waiting for hours, I pushed my way out of the station. As I walked down the crowded boulevard, it was clogged with sad, disillusioned Parisians, many walking, many pushing bicycles. Thankfully, the rain had stopped.

I couldn't help but shoot a picture of a hearse, loaded with children, taking them to safety, just as I had seen in Finland.

An hour later, after dragging myself down the road, I was startled when a small black car pulled up beside me. A man rolled down his window and yelled, "Hurry! Get inside! Let's get out of here!"

The man looked familiar. It was Bill, one of the war correspondents I had met in the hotel lobby just the other day. I piled my heavy suitcases on top of Bill's belongings in the back seat, scrambled into the front, then locked the car door as people surrounded the vehicle and began to pound on it, trying to get inside.

"Thanks, Bill. What a relief to be getting out of here. How did you know it was me?"

"By your American hat."

"How did you get a car?"

He smirked. "Pure bribery."

I breathed a sigh of relief and took off one of the many coats I was wearing. Bill watched me out of the corner of his eye and smiled when he saw me notice.

"Your name's Adeline with *Life Magazine,* isn't that right?"

"Yes, and you're with *Time?*"

"I am and time is something we don't have right now. My plan is to drive to the South of France, to Le Verdon, a port near Bordeaux."

"And then what? We must get out of France altogether. The bombing has started."

"I found out from a reliable source that a British cargo boat is picking up refugees there." He brushed his subdued, carrot-colored hair back and raked it with his fingers.

"I certainly hope it was a reliable source." I gave him a grateful smile.

"Well, Adeline, I'm counting on that also but I guess we'll have to find out."

Whenever we had to stop, people would bang on the car, asking for a ride, but there was no room in the two-door Citroën. Streams and streams of refugees with pots, pans, and even dogs, moved as far away as possible from the advancing German army.

It began to rain again.

When I shivered, Bill asked, "Are you cold? Put your other coat back on."

"No, I think I'm fatigued. It's depressing to pass all these sad, homeless families and we can't do anything for them." I put the coat around my shoulders and wiped the tears from my eyes. "That hearse transporting the children to safety reminded me of being in Helsinki after it was bombed."

"Were you there alone?"

"Yes, *Life* sent me to cover the war there." I had a longing for Alonzo but didn't mention him.

"Gotta admire a gal who's that brave. Tell me, what was it like in Finland?"

I described my experience there and asked Bill where he had been sent by *Time Magazine*. He told me Norway.

We passed the time swapping stories about our adventures. The thousands of French refugees fleeing to the South of France, just like we were, created a lot of traffic. Along the way, we passed ditched vehicles on the side of the road that had run out of petrol.

Bill worried, "It usually takes five hours to get to Bordeaux, but with all the people we'll be lucky to get there by daybreak."

After a long drive, we were finally able to board the *SS Madura*, a small British cargo ship. There were over sixty journalists aboard. If there hadn't been a war going on, it would have made for a nice party. Everyone was very tired. We were served a breakfast of only tea and bread, but it was welcomed.

That night, during a dinner of meat, rice, and a potato, everyone at our table discussed where the safest place to sleep would be. Several people said it was better to sleep below deck in case we were bombed. The ship was crammed with about 1,600 hundred passengers, with a capacity of only 180. When it was time to bed down, I stayed as far away as I could from Bill, but we had only one blanket between us and he was quite a large man. Nonetheless, I fell asleep easily from exhaustion.

An explosion woke me up in the middle of the night. Terrified, I rolled into Bill's arms.

Bill hugged me with reassurance. "Don't worry," he whispered. "I'm sure they missed the ship."

Hitler takes over France

Chapter 43
The Blitz
England, May 1940

I have nothing to offer but blood, toil, tears and sweat.
— British Prime Minister Winston Churchill

In Dover, England, we were greeted by a group of women who passed out lemonade and sandwiches. They were a welcome sight as they reassured all the tired travelers. Bill and I checked into one of the only rooms available.

After opening the door to our room, he said, "Don't worry, I'll sleep on the couch."

I grinned but kept my thoughts to myself. *I'm not worried, but I'm a little disappointed to have a double bed all to myself.*

The next morning, we both cabled our jobs and told them where we were.

In the days that followed, we read everything we could get our hands on. Churchill had tried to persuade French Premier Paul Reynaud to continue to fight. Roosevelt agreed to furnish war materials but refused to declare war. Shortly thereafter, the French prime minister retreated and the Germans captured Paris.

I shared with Bill a few of the photographs I had taken in Paris. While he looked at them, I worried that I had left the bathroom there in disarray after developing them. But, of course, I'd had to make a hasty, unexpected departure.

"This one of the sad Belgian mother with the clinging children shows heart-wrenching emotion," he said. "You sure can paint with that camera of yours." Bill gazed into my eyes for a moment, then showed me an article he was working on.

"And you can paint with words in a marvelous way." I went up on my tip-toes and kissed him after reading it.

Bill gave me a magnificent grin as we went over catchy,

278

original phrases together to enhance his journalistic style. After typing for a while, he went down to the lobby and wired a story to *Time* with the headline: FRANCE SOLD OUT!

I went to the café in the hotel and sat at a table with a reporter from the *Chicago Daily News*, Helen Kirkpatrick. She asked me how *Life Magazine* was treating me as a war correspondent, then told me about her employment. Helen said when she first tried to get a job at the *Daily News*, the publisher told her he liked her credentials but the newspaper didn't hire women. I asked Helen how she replied to that. She told me she said, "I can't change my sex, but you can change your policy." The publisher hired her on the spot. We enjoyed exchanging our experiences as female correspondents and met for coffee whenever we could.

One afternoon, Bill and I went roller-skating at a nearby pavilion to take a break from work. It was a thrill for me. I hadn't been on an actual date since John, and that was at the Cotton Club over eight years ago. We skated next to each other at first, then Bill held my small hand in his. I could feel his joy at being with me. He seemed twice my size, guiding me around the rink with ease as I gazed up into his twinkling eyes.

Our fun was short-lived. Suddenly, the music was interrupted by the drone of planes flying overhead. We decided to climb to the top of Shakespeare Cliff to get a better view, and quickly removed our skates and dashed back to our room to get one of my cameras.

The water of the English Channel was a beautiful, bright blue. We climbed the cliffs and looked toward the outline of France. Below us was a quaint village with neat rows of houses with bright, colorful gardens. Small boats were anchored in the harbor. I set up my tripod while we waited for more planes to fly by. But all was peaceful and quiet now; there were no planes to photograph. Bill put his big, strong arms around me gently and softly kissed my lips in the warm summer air. After our kisses turned into "I want you" passion, we lay in the grass high above the shore as butterflies danced around us, the sounds of seagulls squawking in the distance. We made love for the first time as a soft breeze tickled our naked bodies. Afterward, Bill's light snoring made me fall into a little nap as we curled up together, basking in the sun, forgetting the war for a brief moment.

The sound of anti-aircraft guns cut through the air, startling us both back to reality. We jumped up and threw our clothes on. I took a few pictures, then we hastily climbed down the cliffs. When we got back to the hotel, we looked up and saw hundreds of Luftwaffe Messerschmitts, Junkers, Henkels, and Dorniers in the sky. I photographed them quickly, and Bill identified each one as we hurried into the hotel.

Once inside our room, Bill sat at his typewriter and tapped out his observations. When he finished, he bent over and kissed me as I sat on the bed.

"Addie, I think you got some perfect shots and scooped the other reporters. I've been watching you and your mind is set like a camera, always ready and waiting. You don't miss a beat."

His observations and compliments about my photographic skills nourished me. I kissed him, throwing my arms around his neck, and we fell onto the bed in an embrace. We made love once again with an intense desire and couldn't get enough of each other.

Bill awoke early in the morning. I was disappointed when he immediately got dressed.

"Get up, Addie, we must go down to the lobby to hear the latest news." He stroked my arm, tickling it to get me up.

Down in the lobby, reporters buzzed all over and phones were madly ringing. Helen came up to us and told us that the Germans had bombed the seaport.

Bill whispered to me, "I must get to London. Come with me, Addie. That's where the action will be."

On our way to the Dover station, enemy planes flew above us. One was hit by a tracer bullet, and as it went down in flames, it exploded in the air. The train arrived with all its windows blacked out. I caught it all with my camera before boarding.

When we got off the train in London, we saw searchlights in the early evening sky. Bill paid for the last hotel room available...and this one did not have a couch.

Nothing occurred in London for an entire month; only the seaports were being hit by the Germans. *Life* sent money to replace the equipment that I'd left behind in occupied Paris. I passed the time by developing my film in the closet while Bill tapped away at his typewriter. On some days, we explored London. It was a joy to see the Big Ben clock with its massive thirteen-ton bell. Bill hung on every word as I told him about photographing the astronomical clock in Czechoslovakia.

In September, London was blasted from 4:00-6:00 p.m. It was surreal. This couldn't be happening to lovely London! Then it was quiet and a second group of German raiders commenced attacking. I rapidly photographed the stages of the attack with a few cameras set up on the balcony of our room. St. Paul's Cathedral was directly in front of our hotel and was hit. If I hadn't been caught up in its beauty as it went up in flames, I would have been more frightened. The fire whipped hundreds of feet into the air and ballooned into a great cloud.

I took as many photos as I could stand, then began to shake so badly that I had to stop. I packed it all up, went inside, and threw myself on the bed, weeping.

Bill typed one last paragraph, then nestled beside me, stroking my hair, whispering, "Shhhh, shhhhh..."

The next morning, after a sleepless night, Bill got up and began pounding out a story on his typewriter. I left with my camera to wander around London to see the results of the intense bombing.

The beautiful cathedral was still intact, but almost everything around it had been bombed. I asked a patrolling Bobby why it had not been obliterated by bombs and fires the night before. The Bobby was told by the fireman that Prime Minister Churchill had sent word that St. Paul's Cathedral needed to be protected at all costs. Water was in short supply as the mains had been bombed, and even the nearby Thames River was low. An incendiary device had hit the dome, which began to melt, but it dislodged and fell into a nearby gallery and was smothered by a sandbag. Firemen patrolled the cathedral with sandbags and water pumps to douse the flames and saved it. I took a photograph of St. Paul's, surrounded by the rubble of all the other buildings, with the policeman in the background.

There were sirens positioned in different parts of the city. An "alert" was when the siren's pitch rose and fell. The "all-clear" was a continuous sound. Not every alert brought a raid and sometimes raids happened when no siren sounded.

After the second night of listening to the siren, Bill and I decided to take shelter and followed everyone into the underground, or the tube, which was London's subway system. We packed up some bedding, and for a halfpenny, bought a platform ticket and camped on the platform. There was a shelter marshal to keep order. We overheard him waking up an older man and telling him he was disturbing the peace. The old man argued that he was snoring and couldn't help it. The marshal told him that any further disturbances would mean prison time. I made sure I woke up Bill when he began to snore, even though the melodic sound often helped me get to sleep.

One lady told us that originally, people were not allowed to sleep in the tube because they got in the way of the troops who had to use the trains. Now it had become an ordinary means of protection from the bombing. During the night, arguments broke out. There was also a great deal of laughter, and people were even having sex right out in the open, as though they were still at home. The tube station soon became dirty, with people throwing their food garbage everywhere. Toilet facilities were limited. I photographed an iron bucket with a seat on it, meant to be used for a toilet. A marshal told me there were probably over 60,000 people down there and not enough station marshals to keep order.

We left early in the morning, an hour after no further bombs were heard, and went back to the hotel, vowing never to "sleep" there again. Between the noise of too many people, the smell of urine, and the squeaking of rats, one night was enough for us.

Bill discovered through contacts in the hotel that tube stations were not as safe as people thought. Bombs dropped by the Luftwaffe could penetrate through solid ground. The following month, in two different subway stations, this happened and over

600 people were killed.

He reported on alternative shelters the Londoners stayed in during the air raids while I photographed them. We became a wonderful team. Bill had quite a detective's mind and knew how and when to ask questions.

We saw deep trenches being dug in parks, which were lined and covered with concrete or steel and could hold over fifty people, but discovered they weren't very popular when it rained. There were special trains that ran from London, to take people out of the city to stay in Chislehurst in Kent, where people slept in caves. I took a photo of a family that set up their home in one cave and in another set up a shop to sell goods to people. Caves held church services and even music concerts. The practical British did what they could to lead a normal life during wartime. We visited a massive vault beneath the Fruit and Wool Exchange on Brushfield Street. Over 5,000 people used this filthy shelter, awash with urine and rubbish, with very dim lighting. Eventually, a shelter committee was elected and it became cleaner.

Night after night, the Germans bombed London. The government built Anderson Shelters, which were made from steel and could accommodate a family of six. People could put them in their back yards, half-buried in the ground. Poor people received the shelters for free; others paid what they could.

The word *blitz* was being used to describe the continuous bombing, just like it had been used in Poland. Every night the sirens wailed and giant searchlights swept the sky. We drew the black curtains across the windows. When we felt the shaking of bombs or heard a crash, we dove under our bed for cover.

From the balcony, the horror of it all was an awesome sight from a photographic standpoint—something I was ashamed to admit. The entire city was dotted with hundreds of fires. I could hear the flames crackling and firemen yelling in the distance. I was mesmerized by the color of it all. Whole batches of what Bill said were incendiary bombs fell, flashing a dazzling white, followed by a yellow flame that would leap up from the white center as an entire building caught on fire. Bill and I became immune to the possibility of being bombed and immersed ourselves in our work with a strong conviction to inform the

American public about the reality of the war in Europe. We wanted to shake our *Time* and *Life* readers, who sat in their comfortable living rooms in the US in their passiveness and isolation. When we weren't working, we entwined ourselves among the blankets on our bed to comfort each other and escape our fears of the war, if only for brief moments in time.

We heard on the BBC that night in the lobby that Prime Minister Winston Churchill had ordered British pilots to bomb Berlin. Reporter Virginia Cowles had sent a broadcast to the United States, saying, "Current reports in America that England will be forced to negotiate a compromise, or surrender, are unfounded and untrue."

While Bill sent over five cablegrams a day to *Time,* I bicycled around London with a camera. I photographed the chaos of rescue parties hauling the wounded and dead out of the rubble of smoldering buildings. I thought Finland had been a frightening place to be, but London was much worse. There were monstrous fires all over the city. Sometimes I caught rides on ambulances and fire trucks to better cover the disaster. I followed a fire brigade with my camera, taking pictures of the aftermath of the bombs and the resulting giant, raging fires. Each day, rescuers continued to search for further victims as the bombing continued every single night.

It was eerie to walk around and photograph the damage. Tenements were left standing, blown in half. An iron bed dangled from a crumbling wall. There was a church in ruins with only two of the walls remaining. I looked through my lens at one house and all that remained was a family photograph hanging on one ragged wall. I took pictures of rescue squads pulling out bodies while people tried to salvage their remaining belongings. It was grim watching the dead being put into vans and the workers sliding canvas-wrapped bodies onto trucks. Many people pushed wagons and perambulators top-heavy with possessions salvaged from their homes. I asked one mother where she was going, and she sadly answered to the ferry, to get to the other side of the Thames.

I saw a car that had been blown onto the roof of a house. The house had shattered windows and its shutters were blown off. I stood in the background and used my telephoto lens to take pictures of a mass burial of people in one common grave, pine coffins piled high. The Bishop of Coventry was in a long purple robe with mud caked on the bottom, performing the services. Families threw flowers on the pine boxes in anguish as a steam shovel filled in the dirt. The shabbily dressed mourners stood in the rain with forlorn, pale, tear-covered faces.

Many of the reporters said that it was Hitler's intention to break the morale of the British people; to pressure Churchill into negotiating. The Royal Air Force Spitfires and Hurricanes flew over the English Channel, but the RAF fighter pilots were outnumbered. Germany had air superiority while Britain was simply trying to survive. However, the bombing seemed to have the opposite effect, and brought the English people together to face a common enemy. Encouraged by Churchill's frequent public appearances and radio speeches, the Brits became determined to hold out indefinitely against the Nazi onslaught. Signs written on chalkboards stating "business as usual" could be seen everywhere in shop windows. The British were a stoic people and downplayed the atrocity. Instead of saying "bombing," people used the word "incident." This country continued to attempt a normal life. Everywhere I went, I was offered a cup of tea and a chat as England continued to be pounded by Germany.

St. Paul's Cathedral, 1940, the Blitz

Walking through the rubble of the Blitz

The Blitz, London

Taking shelter in the Tube

The Blitz, London

Chapter 44
Greece, 1940-1941

Until now we used to say that the Greeks fight like heroes. Now we shall say: The heroes fight like Greeks.
— Winston Churchill, British Prime Minister

When the naval cruiser *Elli* was torpedoed by a submarine of unknown nationality off the Aegean island of Tinos, Bill and I were sent to Greece. So, off we went to Athens.

Several weeks passed with no action. Both of us felt guilty leaving the never-ending Blitz in London. The Greeks were a relaxed people, moving slowly in this delicious climate, which made us feel like we were in an isolated bubble removed from the war.

Bill and I touched and kissed each other constantly, feeling a false sense of peace; a respite from the constant noise of the bombing in London. We swam every day at Phaleron Beach and ate dinner every night at an open-air *taverna*, taking delight in our newfound relationship. Afterward, we wandered the city in the sparkling brilliance of the Mediterranean moon.

Bill interviewed a few Greek soldiers in town, and one man said, "Let those Italians attack us. We'll fight them back!" Bill was told about the Italian soldiers on the Albanian frontier, but the censored Greek press was not permitted to report the small number of casualties. Of course, Greece had been preparing for an attack, like all the countries in Europe. I photographed men in their poorly fitted khaki uniforms, showing a presence everywhere under the burning sun. Women and children harvested crops, replacing the men who were now serving their army.

Just when we were both summoned to go back to London, we heard the rise and fall of the air-raid alarm. The warning noise was very familiar to us. The Italian troops were getting closer to the borders of Greece. Young men and boys filled the streets in an ordinary parade fashion, singing and waving British flags and flags bearing the white cross of Greece. The scene made for wonderful pictures. We looked up at the golden sunlight and bluer-than-blue skies as a single enemy reconnaissance plane flew over Athens. We found out there were enemy bombers dropping bombs over the city of Patras, 131 miles away from Athens. A hundred dead were announced.

In October, Bill and I obtained papers to go to the Albanian frontier. We traversed roads of slimy mud that ran along the edges of giant precipices. Our hired car crawled past long columns of men in their shoddy, ill-cut Greek uniforms, their boots gaping at the soles. I rolled my window down and heard the soldiers singing. Their pathetically equipped army consisted mostly of mules and a few ancient trucks that rattled over the rutted roads.

Once on the Albanian front, there was word about attacks by the army of Mussolini with planes, artillery, tanks, and mortars. The Italians were well equipped in comparison to the defenseless army of Greece. The Greek soldiers had only rifles and grenades but continued their cheerful spirit. I heard about an old man, whose only possession was a horse and cart, who offered them to the army.

It was a complete accident that we arrived at an artillery post just as the Greek forces began to attack, and we found ourselves within mere yards of a cannon. Bill helped me set up my camera. As I snapped photographs, I had to pause and hold my ears when the cannon fired. Above us, on a hill, we heard a machine-gun duel. The noise was deafening and I had to force myself to concentrate to get at least a few shots of the battle. After it was over, the Greek soldiers marched their Italian captives down through a ravine.

I had to push back my feeling of powerlessness as I crouched under a big rock overhanging a ledge, while missiles screamed overhead and struck around me. The barren, rocky hillside had no bushes to hide in. We were told by an officer to drop down flat when we heard the whistles of the bombs. The earth would shake as I clutched my camera, hoping that a bomb would not land on my prostrate body. As the aerial bombardments at the front began, we drove into the woods for some needed rest. Unable to sleep surrounded by the noise of artillery fire, Bill and I cuddled, holding each other for comfort.

The next day, we watched the futile attempt of a Greek infantry officer who ran out to shoot the Italian bombers with his small repeater rifle. A feeling of helplessness came over me in the fighting zone and gave me a grim sense of war's reality. Every time I heard the words "dirty macaronis" I reflected on my relationship with Alonzo, who had been a delightful, caring partner in Finland. I wondered...why is there war and what is it about human beings that we all can't appreciate our differences? Bill was quite wrapped up in his part of being in the war, and we seemed to have little time for serious reflection on the subject.

One morning, I looked up at the sky and saw over forty-five planes from the Hellenic Air Force. They resembled packing crates strung with wings as they struck fiercely at Italian airfields. The ill-equipped Greek soldiers successfully shattered the Italian Alpine division.

We drove back to Athens, overjoyed to see the city filled with British officers in their trim RAF uniforms. There were crowds of spectators on the city rooftops as enemy planes approached the Piraeus area. The first month was victorious and swept Greece with a fervor.

One afternoon, Bill remained at his typewriter in our hotel room while I set out to visit the Athens hospital. Hospitals were always a great source of information.

This hospital was crowded with the wounded and bursting with men in the hallways. I was amazed to hear the contagious, positive enthusiasm of the injured patients lying on their cots. Several soldiers told me they were anxious to return to the front as soon as possible to drive the "macaronis" back to the sea.

I treated one nice nurse to a shared meal in a nearby restaurant. She confided that she dreaded going back to work in the hospital. Ariadne was the daughter of a wealthy ship owner and had reluctantly volunteered to be a nurse without any training. She had tears in her eyes as she told me about the horrors of caring for the soldiers. Her days off were worse because she worried too much, not knowing what she was doing. I cheered her up the best I could. She left to return to the hospital and I sadly finished my meal.

It was the new year of 1941. Bill and I decided to take another trip to the Albanian front to witness the battle of Klisura. We wanted to see the advance and could only get there by a five-hour mule trip to a mountaintop overlooking the Klisura gorge. It was my first time on a mule and I was exhilarated at first. Bill had been brought up riding horses in Montana and coached me as we plodded along. After four hours, my body, loaded with camera gear, became quite sore. I managed to photograph a flash of artillery in the valley where the Greek forces were headed. I was glad I had brought my telephoto lens as I watched the Greek soldiers moving on. We were assured that we were safe from the danger of the Italian planes dropping bombs on us deep in the thick brush. The soldier who led us sang Greek ballads as our mules picked their way down the steep, rocky paths.

That night, as the crescent moon lit the crags of the mountains, we rode into a small, isolated village that had been taken over for use as Greek headquarters. Inside the Albanian home used by the general was a bright, scarlet carpet on the floor and no furniture; just a scattering of beautiful hand-woven pillows. We sat beside a cheerful, triangular-shaped fire hearth of Turkish design. The general proudly informed us that Klisura had been taken, Italian soldiers were continuing to surrender in considerable numbers, and another Greek victory had been won.

The general brought us to a room filled with about sixty soldiers. I was the only woman there. He said, "You and your wife can sleep in the corner."

I flinched at the word "wife," feeling like a lie had been told. The floor was hard and my body felt beaten-up from riding, but I fell asleep from sheer exhaustion amid the loud snoring of all the men.

We returned to Athens to develop film and send reports back to our country. From the King George Hotel, we saw a sky that glowed red and orange from the flames in Piraeus. The drone of approaching planes grew louder and louder. Tracer bullets from rockets shot red, blue, and green lights into the sky. Anti-aircraft guns bellowed and the walls of buildings reverberated as searchlights moved across the sky. I thought it was beautiful in a horrific way as I shot the sight through my camera lens from the balcony.

Bill had to get his scripts approved by six different censors before he could broadcast his news to America. He broadcasted from the Ministry of Press radio station in Zappion at 1100 hours and again at 1800 hours. I went with him and listened to the absurd, happy Greek music coming from the phonograph as Bill waited for the precise time. It was 3:00 a.m. Greek time. Who knew whether the broadcast would even be heard in America?

Bill and I made successive visits to the Albanian front. The Greek army was constantly telling jokes. They maintained a cheerful humor in the appalling conditions of March's heavy snowfall. They were often without food and supplies for days, making us feel guilty that we were free to come and go, depending on our stamina.

We followed the Greeks as they advanced in the heavy winter weather and saw mules die off by the dozens. As we traveled the waterlogged roads, I photographed the poor dead beasts bobbing in swollen rivers and rotting against the banks. The British had brought in convoys from Egypt but there were only two motor highways crossing Albania, both of which ended completely in wild, desolate mountains. Traveling by mule was the only way to go. As we rode, we heard the occasional boom of artillery and the crash of a bomb, then the faint clatter of machine guns as we headed high up into the mountains. The fascist planes flew above us. When six British Wellington bombers went after them, cheers sounded from the soldiers. Bill and I spontaneously joined in with their celebration, hoping that the British would rescue this beautiful country.

Chapter 45
"Hymn to Liberty," Greece

War does not determine who is right — only who is left.
— Bertrand Russell

It was a lovely springtime in Athens. Sadly, the German planes began to pass overhead once again and the sirens shrieked for weeks. German bombs fell in the Piraeus area with a dull thud.

At our hotel room, Bill and I woke to the sound of glass breaking in the courtyard. We saw people running, then heard a distant crash. We threw on our clothes and raced to the harbor. A British munitions ship in the Piraeus harbor, several miles away, had exploded, shattering the windows of the hotel. All the British ships in the harbor had been destroyed by a single Nazi bomb. The nation's second-largest city, Salonica, fell in two days, with the British unable to hold it. Greece was now in total confusion. There were air raids in Athens every night. It seemed that as soon as the huge Mediterranean moon came up, the sirens began.

I stood on the terrace and photographed the dogfights and enemy planes shot down in flames. But for every plane that crashed over the hills of Piraeus, another ten flew over safely.

The nights were the perfect time for the British parachutists to descend. The Air Force was becoming depleted by the Luftwaffe, with thirty-four planes destroyed at Larissa and another twelve destroyed at Paramythia. We went to report on the RAF and found over fifty fully trained pilots sitting around with no planes to fly. The Luftwaffe still had over a thousand. Weary Greek soldiers were returning home on foot and busloads of wounded poured into Athens.

In the lobby that night, Bill and I spied a reporter who was listening to German radio. We watched as a horrified look came over his face and asked what had been said. He summarized, saying that Alexandros Koryzis, Prime Minister of Greece, had committed suicide. The premier had come home from a cabinet meeting, went into his bedroom, and shot himself. He was found lying on his bed with a pistol in hand. The reporter, as well as Bill and I, wanted to know how the Germans could know about this graphic tale. We heard the next day that there had been a leak from someone in a high government position and it was indeed true.

Bill wanted to report this event back home, but censorship did not allow him to use the term "suicide." I had heard that word used in past wars and thought this odd. But severe censorship prevailed and Bill could only use the term "heart failure." He added that the premier had been found with a cross in his hand, hoping our country would assume that it was suicide.

The next morning, we saw people running in the streets and a crowd forming. We saw an angry mob attempting, with bare hands, to kill a traitor they were calling a "fifth columnist." Bill and I saw someone stab him with a dagger. The police intervened and carried off the unconscious figure who had a battered head, was bleeding, and had his clothes torn half off. We heard that he was a German.

A Greek man yelled passionately, "There are hundreds more like that traitor! We must kill every one of them!"

The alarm sounded all day and we hurried to get a news cable out to our magazines. The police ordered everyone to go the shelters, but most everyone ignored them.

On Orthodox Easter, we got word that the Blitz in London had ended at last. It was horrible to think that it had started in the summer of 1940 and ended in the spring of 1941.

This was the most beautiful time of year in Greece, when flowers of every color and variety were abundant everywhere. It filled me with a false, joyous passion as I snapped photos and smelled the fragrance mingled with the warm spring air. The church bells rang and I heard the comforting sound of the chanting priests.

The air-raid siren sounded, interrupting the calm, sacred event. Then silence fell as the bells stopped ringing, only to be replaced by the sound of the anti-aircraft guns and the dull thud of bombs. All day long we heard the brittle echo of gunfire and bombs. It was a disaster on Greece's most sacred day.

Bill continued to make broadcasts night after night while I photographed Stukas flying above and diving like silver swallows. The attacks came regularly every morning at 5:30 a.m.

Evacuation ships to Egypt were loading people at the Piraeus harbor, and were sometimes hit by Stukas. But people crowded on anyway, gambling with their lives. Families gave their entire fortunes for passage. The British Navy transported as many people as they could while the German army advanced swiftly only a few miles away.

I got a shot of a mammoth column of smoke that rose over the Piraeus harbor. I learned the next day that over 700 people were aboard the ship that was hit as it left the harbor. Sadly, it was the last evacuation transport attempting to leave Piraeus.

It was the last week of April. Bill had to ask permission from the military governor to make a final broadcast home because the wartime censors had left and the civil government had been dissolved. I photographed the strange sight of non-critical patients, dismissed from the hospital, walking along the roads in their pajamas. All of Athens waited anxiously for the Nazis' imminent entry into the city. Over a week went by. The entire city was filled with an eerie silence and there was little movement. All Greeks stayed at home, in hiding.

On a Tuesday, the Greek "Hymn to Liberty" played over the radio. Bill and I went out on the balcony, and in the distance, we saw a scarlet flag flying over the Acropolis. We hurried outside, Bill with his notebook and I with my cameras. There were scarlet Nazi flags flying everywhere: on the old palace, on the chapel on Lycabettus Hill, but the final insult was the one desecrating the sacred temple of the Acropolis. My fingers shook on the shutter while taking the photograph of it. Signs, or *verbotens,* were posted, stating punishments for insulting the Nazi flag.

Masses of soldiers, dirty and tired, came through the streets with blank, expressionless faces. Big black Nazi trucks flooded the roads. Bill and I were devastated as we watched the takeover of Greece by the German army.

One week later, the Nazis held a triumphal parade. They announced to all Greeks that they were to remain in their houses from 9:00 a.m. until they were told they could come out. Shutters were to be closed and no one was permitted to stand on balconies to watch. I was given a special pass to photograph it all. German civilians were flown down from Berlin and stood on the street corners, watching. Columns of Nazi conquerors goose-stepped stiffly down the streets while Nazi planes flew in formation in the sky. Tanks rumbled through the streets of Athens.

After the elaborate parade was over, Bill and I went to our favorite restaurant, Zonar's. Almost everything was the same — the decorations, the waiters, the furniture — but it was filled with only the dirty-gray-uniformed men of the Luftwaffe. As Americans, we were treated by the Nazis with friendly smiles and found it difficult to smile back at the German officers. The Germans had ordered the Greeks to reopen their restaurants so that they could enjoy a good meal.

As we sat there, I reflected on how the restaurant used to be filled with RAF officers, laughing and telling jokes. I looked around at the Nazis, who were like alien creatures in the way they walked, talked, and held their shoulders, and with their heavy, guttural German speech. I observed their wooden-like faces as they sat at the tables, cold and robot-like, the opposite of the easy-going, warm Greeks. They treated the conquered Greeks like they had done them a favor by liberating them from the British occupation.

We stayed in Greece to report on what it was like to live in the German-occupied country. After the Nazi conquerors lifted the curfew in Athens, Bill and I went to a movie theater that was featuring an Andy Hardy movie. It was difficult to enjoy it, being surrounded by Nazi soldiers who were all laughing.

The Germans printed editorials on how they meant no ill will toward the Greeks. By all appearances, the amicable Nazis were trying to win over the Greeks and to become one big happy family.

In the hospital, the Greek nurses told me they had been ordered to care for the German wounded and had to abandon their own kind. Then more *verbotens* were posted: Greeks were not allowed to mention the British or wear the British flag pins as before. I noticed that the Greek soldiers continued to wear their uniforms until they were told they would be taken into custody as prisoners of war. The problem was, many were not from Athens, and that was the only clothing they owned. So, they had to borrow clothes from their neighbors if they wanted to avoid persecution.

One day, right in front of my eyes, a Nazi soldier drove recklessly through the streets, killing a Greek child. He didn't even stop. He just drove away. A restaurant owner told me that a man in the country was shot to death after refusing to turn his only cow over to the Nazis.

Now, every Athenian home was forced to take in men of the Nazi army. Bill and I watched as Nazi officers went from house to house, inquiring how many spare beds there were. How horrible for the Greeks, to have the enemy army in their own homes, sleeping under their own roofs, and in their own beds!

In the days that followed, the Nazis looted everything, including clothes from the dry cleaners, as well as moving out furniture to drive it northward to Germany. They "purchased" goods with worthless money, calling it *"occupation marks."*

It was time for us to depart. There was nothing more we could do except report back to our country what had become of Greece. Because we could not board boats without Greek papers, we went to the Stadtkommandantur's office to find out where to obtain legal papers to leave.

An interpreter there asked, "Are you English?"

"No, I wouldn't be here if I were!" Bill boldly answered and handed him our calling cards.

"Ah, a photographer!" he exclaimed, looking me over. "What kind of things have you been taking pictures of?"

"Mostly the Greeks," I mumbled.

"Come back next week," he answered.

The Nazis used ridiculous excuses for refusing our visas. We were beginning to feel like captives, and stayed in our hotel room as much as possible.

I sat on the balcony, staring at the extraordinary, delicate beauty of the Acropolis in the early morning. It was as surreal as an oil painting. I couldn't take enough photographs of it, despite the Nazi flag hanging from it. I passed the time waiting to get out of Athens by photographing the Acropolis over the weeks and at different time periods of light. In the moonlight, it appeared ghostlike, in contrast to at sunset, when the columns were vibrant, strong, and glowing as they reflected the beautiful sunlight.

Now it was the hot season of June and the nights were thick with humidity. We still couldn't get a visa. Furthermore, we were forbidden to travel beyond certain zones in Athens and now we had no communication for our work. I was beginning to feel quite agitated and was afraid to use my camera lest the Germans would take it. Bill tried to reassure me that we would get out of there. He would sit in our room and type away. I had no idea what he was writing because there was no way his reports would get to anyone. I had already finished developing rolls and rolls of film.

I began going out to eat alone, but couldn't stand watching the happy Germans amid the sad, subservient Greeks serving them. Bill and I were talking to each other very little now. One evening, I paced in the hotel room until Bill gave me an annoyed look, then I settled down to escape into one of my mysteries, amusing myself by trying to guess the ending.

At last, toward the end of the month, we were granted permission to leave. We had our last meal in a *taverna* as the rain came down in gusts in a tropical downpour. Nazi soldiers filled the room. As we passed by the kitchen, we saw meat, but when we sat down the waiter said there was no meat, only cheese, salad, and rolls. That's all that was served to us while the Nazi soldiers ate the meat. The Nazis sang boisterously and pounded their feet on the floor. I dared not photograph all the uniforms massed together like a plague of locusts swarming around the tables as the rain beat against the walls and roof.

It was time to leave this dangerous occupied country. We packed up and went to the Tatoi Airport late the next morning. We took a regular Lufthansa plane carrying mostly German passengers. The first stop was Belgrade, before heading to Vienna.

When we got off the plane, a Nazi commandant took our passports, handcuffed us, and told us we were charged with being spies, and that we would not be released until our identities could be verified. We were whisked away to separate jail cells.

I wept on and off as I sat on the hard cot in my otherwise empty cell. Where was my camera equipment? What was to happen to us? Would we ever be together again? I kept picturing the Nazi in Oberplan hammering the truncheon on his desk while our young Czech policeman was being taken away to his death. Would Bill and I meet the same fate at the hands of these vicious Nazis?

We were imprisoned for two days and given only watery soup and hard brown bread to eat. Finally, a guard holding Bill's arm opened my cell. He roughly grabbed me and towed us both outside and put us into a car.

"Oh, God, will this nightmare ever end?" I whispered to Bill.

"I promise you it will," he said with a weak voice, holding me closely.

We were put on a small Junker plane. It had no seats, two pilots, and no passengers. As we took off, lightning flashed and rain stormed down. Exhausted with worry, I rested my head against Bill's shoulder and softly cried. Bill stroked my hair to calm me down.

I whispered, "What are we going to do? We need our passports and luggage."

"Addie, try to hold tight, we will be protected by our country."

"But, no one knows where we are!" I whispered a little too loudly. After Bill didn't answer me, I pushed my face into his coat.

We arrived in Vienna and were taken to a small hotel. I let out a sigh of relief.

The guard forcibly placed us in separate rooms. Being in a hotel room gave me a glimmer of hope that perhaps we would be released. After a while, I opened the door in an attempt to find Bill, but shut it when I saw a guard standing there. I rolled around on the hotel bed, starving and in a state of intense anxiety.

Late that afternoon, we were allowed to speak with the American consul in Vienna. He reassured us that they would do everything they could to get us home. We were given our passports and luggage, and were transported to Berlin by third-class train with a Gestapo guard in our compartment. We were taken to a nice hotel this time, but put in separate rooms again, given menus, and told we could eat as much as we liked at the expense of the Berlin Foreign Office. There was no scarcity of food there, like in Athens. Finally, after a terrifying week, we were put on a ship headed for the good old USA.

German soldiers raising the Nazi flag over the Acropolis of Athens

Chapter 46
Union of Soviet Socialist Republics, Late Spring, 1941

My most brilliant achievement was my ability to be able to persuade my wife to marry me.

— Winston Churchill

Bill begged me to go with him to the Soviet Union. He had been invited to an international conference put on by the Union of Soviet Writers.

"But I'm waiting for another assignment from *Life*," I told him.

"Marry me!" Bill lifted me up and swung me around the hotel room in his big strong arms.

"Why?" I laughed as my eyes danced in delight. "Just so I can go with you?"

"You know I love you and I'm tired of sneaking around or pretending we're married just to share a hotel room."

"What do you mean, pretending that we're married?"

"Like when I registered us at the King George Hotel in Greece."

"You registered us as married?"

"Of course, but because of your passport, I told the concierge we were married but you kept your last name. Then, there was last month's fiasco when the Gestapo guards wouldn't let us share the same room."

I remained silent and stood there, frozen. I never told Bill I had been married once before and I wasn't certain I wanted to make such a commitment again.

"Maybe...you don't love me?"

His face displayed a rejected look I had never seen before, as he always seemed like such a confident man.

"You've never told me that you love me." I put my hand on my hip indignantly.

"Can't you feel the affection between us? Aren't actions louder than words? We've been through so much together, especially in that near-death experience with the Nazis." Bill grabbed me and held me tightly. "I don't want to lose you, Addie," he whispered.

I broke his embrace and sat down on the sofa. "Oh Bill, I was so afraid of being without you every time we were separated last month. I must be honest with you, I've been married before. I'm thirty-six years old and absorbed in my work. Also, at this time in my life, I don't want to have children. I treat my work like an attentive mother caring for her family."

Bill sat down and put his arm around me. "My brother and his wife are both war correspondents in the Philippines and have a terrific marriage. They don't have any children. Besides, we're too busy for that. Addie, honey, I thought you felt the same way. When we make love it's like a magic potion only you and I can produce." He searched my face in a pleading way. "Think about it for a while." He put on his coat and left.

I stared into space, deep in thought. Just because we were extremely compatible in the bedroom didn't mean a successful commitment for life, did it? My failed marriage to Martin had left an indelible mark on me. I wasn't sure I could make that commitment again. *I have worked very hard for my independence in this man's world and I don't know if I can give that up,* I thought. Neither of us had ever said "I love you"...until today. That phrase was always sacred to me, though I never heard my parents use it with each other or me. I couldn't remember whether Martin had ever said it. Bill was right—his actions did show his love for me. We'd had plenty of crises during our short time together and our relationship had survived.

Time ticked by and I wondered where he had gone. I looked at his books, which were scattered about the room. There was a manual on photographic techniques he was studying.

Bill came back as if nothing had been discussed. "I'm hungry, let's go to dinner."

"I'll go freshen up."

We locked eyes for a moment.

In the bedroom, I put on an attractive dress with a heart-shaped neckline, along with a deep-colored lipstick called *Red Sequin*, and fashioned a nice Cupid's bow on my lips. Bill put on his dark-blue suit jacket, the one he always looked dashing in.

"Addie, you look ravishing in that dress." His eyes ran all over me as he rushed in to give me an impassioned kiss.

At dinner, the tension eased as we discussed what was happening in Paris and Great Britain. Chatting about work was always a safe subject, and something we both liked to do.

The date of the conference was getting closer and I found myself not wanting Bill to leave without me. When we made love every night, he began to say, "I love you," each time. I couldn't bring myself to say those words back to him.

"I applied today for a visa for us to go to Moscow," Bill told me one afternoon.

"Already?"

"There can be delays for weeks to receive our Soviet visas."

I noticed he'd said "us" and "our" and knew I had to make this life-changing decision of marriage soon. I got up and poured a glass of French wine. Bill sat down and shuffled papers at the desk.

"Bill, I need more time to think about marriage."

He frowned.

I quickly added, "I do love you and I will give you an answer after our trip."

"I'd rather get married before we go, but if you need more time, I'll wait."

I studied Bill's face. It reflected an honesty that compared to none. I threw my arms around his neck and kissed him with consuming passion. Heat spread to my cheeks from the wine. Bill swooped me up and set me on the bed. "Baby, we'll have great adventures together, I promise you that!"

Bill's equipment weighed only seventeen pounds, including his typewriter. My suitcases weighed over six hundred pounds after putting in 3,000 peanut flashbulbs, film packs, five cameras, twenty-two lenses, four portable developing tanks, bottles of developer, dressmaker pins, screws, a jeweler's screwdriver, and pliers. Plus, I had to have a supply of author John Dickson Carr's detective stories. Reading them was the only way I could relax and get to sleep at night. My favorite at the time was *The Case of the Constant Suicides.*

Life Magazine allowed me to cover a story on what the USSR was doing for war preparation, since I would be there anyway. The nonaggression pact between Germany and the Soviet Union was in effect, so I wasn't worried about my safety.

We received our visas quickly and arrived in Moscow in May during a fitful snowfall. We stayed in a plain room on the top floor of the National Hotel.

While Bill was busy writing and attending conferences, I wandered around to photograph the city. The weather presented many obstacles for photography. I coughed and shivered in my double coats. My fingers fumbled in my thick gloves. I'd whip out a yellow filter just as the clouds let the sunlight in, then the sky turned overcast and gray again. I finally gave up and put my camera equipment away.

I had high hopes for the month of June and was able to get some great shots of the Kremlin. Then hailstones began to pound my equipment and I had to pack it all up and return to the hotel. This country sure had fickle weather. I spent the rest of the day developing film in the bathtub.

We went to hear the leader of the USSR, Joseph Stalin, who was making a speech to the June graduating class of the Military Academy. In the speech, one glaring sentence shocked all the foreign correspondents there.

Stalin said, "Germany is our real enemy."

As I composed a photograph of Stalin, I chuckled. I had seen many giant statues of him that made him appear almost superhuman in size. The best I could tell, he was just a few inches taller than my five-foot-two height, and he was wearing high-heeled boots. The Soviet leader had on a plain khaki tunic. His face had a rough, pitted surface, and he had thick, wavy, grayish-black hair and a gray-speckled mustache. He was a very interesting subject to photograph.

As soon as we got back to the hotel, Bill typed up his notes, then tried to cable his story out, but it did not pass the censors. The following day, news spread among the reporters that before daybreak, German planes had flown over the Soviet border and dropped bombs on three cities. Bill's conference was over, but *Time* cabled him to stay in the USSR because of the impending war.

I got a scoop from one reporter that the American ambassador was importing tents from the United States. He was setting them up under trees in case we got blasted out of our hotels if a war broke out. His wife was making blackout curtains. *Life* cabled the hotel, telling me to stay where I was and to report all that was going on.

Bill and I drove to a collective farm where farmers gathered in a clearing in a grove of trees. We heard Churchill's speech blaring from an amplifier. Bill frantically took notes as I clicked away, capturing everyone's facial reactions as they listened to the speech.

Churchill's booming voice projected, "Great Britain will stand with the Soviet Union to meet their common enemy!"

All the farmers began to cheer. I photographed one farmer who had tears streaming down his face.

On our way back to the hotel, we saw many men who were trying to get a ride to Moscow to sign up and enlist. We picked up as many as we could fit into our car.

One farmer said on the way, "With Great Britain and the Soviet Union together, the Germans will be squashed!"

In Moscow, we wanted to read Churchill's speech but all the newspapers had been sold out. Back at the hotel, those who had a paper read it aloud so that everyone could absorb all the latest news. War had begun. The Soviets had already brought down 300 enemy German planes.

We went to the nearby tavern, always the best place to get the people's reactions to a war. Groups of Soviets were raising their beer glasses.

"To the great allies of the United States! To the solidarity of Britain! We will submerge the fascists in their own blood!" they chanted.

Out on the street, I photographed trainloads of naval guns going by as many of the troops headed to the border.

The lobby was eerily empty. I received a telegram from *Life*

Magazine inquiring whether I was still there. Two reporters told me they had just missed the last crowded plane to Stockholm.

The concierge insisted we change rooms to a safer corner suite. For the same amount of money, we had an immense bed piled high with quilts of blue satin and mounds of pillows. There was also a connecting suite that had a grand piano on a brown bearskin rug. This hotel room was the honeymoon suite, complete with gorgeous chandeliers and marble statuettes throughout. Of course, what thrilled me the most was the enormous bathtub, which I filled with trays of developer instead of bubble bath. The ceilings were dripping with filmstrips that hung from a cord I had strung between the water pipes and pinned to towels and window curtains.

The hotel suite had the perfect balcony facing the Kremlin and the onion-shaped domes of St. Basil's, Lenin's tomb, and Red Square. It gave me a magnificent, panoramic view of Moscow to photograph any possible air raids.

Bill and I were ecstatic to be there by accident on the cusp of a war. We had a fabulous time making love on the huge, luxurious bed—the same bed the Lindenbergs and Trotskys had slept in. Then we playfully rolled under the piano and consumed each other on the bearskin rug. It tickled and made my skin tingle as we rocked as one toward a crescendo of total ecstasy.

Bill threw on a robe and played a song on the piano for me, Bing Crosby's "Only Forever." I adored his voice, even though he didn't sound like Bing, and threw my arms around his neck, breathing in his delicious smell and hugging him tightly. Then we sang "When You Wish Upon A Star" and laughed and laughed in total bliss.

I stepped out onto the balcony and told Bill, "This is a perfect set-up for my photography. Look at the views of Red Square and the Kremlin."

Bill called out to me, "This hotel is so ancient the streetcars make it shake every time they pass by. What's it going to be like if the Germans start hitting the Kremlin?"

There was a knock on our door. A maid came in to show us our blackout curtains. The next day, I awoke to find a paper slipped under the door. On it was a statement that the military authorities had issued an edict that anyone seen with a camera would be arrested.

Panic-stricken, I turned to Bill. "What will I do? This is going to be one of the biggest scoops of my entire career, just like when I was in Finland the day before it was bombed. This is what I live for! This is what I'm paid for and I'm the only photographer here!" I became hysterical. "I will throw my camera like a hand grenade at anyone who stops me from taking photographs of the war!"

Bill smirked. "Calm down, darling, I know you'll find a way."

The next day, we were called to the American Embassy.

On the walk there, Bill counseled me. "Don't say anything. The less we say, the better."

We met with a stern, worried Ambassador Steinhardt. He looked at us with tired, pale-green eyes, which he blinked constantly. "No one knows how soon Moscow will be bombed, but when it starts I want you to know that the death and destruction might be catastrophic. My job is to protect the lives of the American citizens here. I advise you both to leave immediately. I can get you seats on the train to Vladivostok. It is your last chance to get out of here. When the bombing starts, there is no way to get you out and you will be trapped." He stared directly at me. "You do know there is an anti-camera law, don't you?"

Bill answered for both of us before I could say a word. "Thank you, Ambassador, for your concern, but it's important for our country that we remain and work."

The ambassador softened. "I am only doing my job, warning you of what you may be vulnerable to, but if you both decide to stay, the embassy will help you in any way we can." He gave us USSR military helmets and told us to wear them when necessary.

I couldn't help myself. I hugged the ambassador's thin-framed body. "Thank you, sir," I said gratefully.

On our walk back to the suite, we saw masses of men volunteering to serve. I fished out my camera, which was hidden in my coat, and quickly snapped a shot of a huge poster that read: FIGHT FOR THE LIFE OF YOUR FATHERLAND. Bill turned and gave me a glare, fearful that we would get caught.

Chapter 47
War in the USSR

Work is something you can count on, a trusted, lifelong friend who never deserts you.

— Margaret Bourke-White

In the first dramatic weeks of the war, men began teaching women how to take over their jobs so that the men could enlist. I discovered what photographs I could get away with taking and was able to shoot the inside of a cinema that had been turned into a school for women to learn nursing skills. All my attention turned to how the Soviet women were helping the war effort. Housewives learned how to drive trucks and salesgirls learned how to clean machine guns. Many of the women took over men's factory jobs. Even the children had jobs to do, like warning people to draw their blackout curtains or enemy plane spotting. The Soviet citizens always worked diligently at whatever they did, and now their efforts were centered on winning the war.

As the Germans drew closer to Moscow, the railroad stations filled with thousands of mothers and their children, camped out with their belongings, waiting to get on a train away from the city and out to the country. I reflected on the war in Finland and London, where I had seen the same kind of mass exodus occur.

Bill was given the opportunity to broadcast live to America every night at 10:00 p.m. — late in the evening because of the time difference between the USSR and the States. He invited me to go with him and I proudly listened to his deep, serious, succinct voice as he informed our people about the details of the war.

One morning, after falling asleep wrapped up in the silky blue quilt, we awoke to the sound of marching troops. I threw on my robe, grabbed a camera, and went out to the balcony.

Bill cautioned, "Be careful!"

I photographed the soldiers going to war. Bill joined me on the balcony to hear Stalin on the loudspeaker over Red Square.

"Comrades, citizens, brothers and sisters, men of our army and navy. The enemy is cruel and implacable. He is out to seize our lands watered with our sweat, to seize our grain and soil secured by our labor." Stalin seemed to be preparing the people for bad news. "A grave danger hangs over our country. In case of forced retreat of Red Army units, not a single engine must be left to the enemy, not a single railway car, not a single pound of grain or gallon of fuel."

Large crowds gathered around the loudspeakers.

"Diversionist groups must be organized to blow up bridges, roads, telephone lines, set fire to forests and stores."

Bill and I dressed in a hurry. He put his favorite fountain pen and his moleskin reporter's notebook in his coat pocket. I packed my father's Vest Pocket camera, as it could be folded and hidden easily. We ran out of the hotel and joined the crowds in Red Square. Everyone listened in dead silence. I glanced over at Bill's notebook as he scribbled, *The enemy must be crushed.*

Pravda devoted their entire front page to Stalin's speech. Queues a block long moved steadily toward the newspaper kiosks. When newspapers ran out, reprints were pasted up on walls and billboards throughout the city.

That afternoon, the ambassador visited us for tea with an escort of secret police, who guarded the hotel entrance and our room.

After I poured the tea, Bill anxiously asked Ambassador Steinhardt, "When do you think the first bomb will fall on Moscow?"

"Very soon. I'm here to instruct you to obey the laws, or *ukase,* as they are called here. You must always go to the shelter when you hear the warning sirens and make sure your black window curtains are kept drawn at all times. Blackout is strictly enforced. Allowing even a crack of light to show from your windows at night makes you subject to fines and imprisonment."

The ambassador's eyes bore into ours in an attempt to convey how serious he was.

After the ambassador left, I told Bill I was grateful that he hadn't mentioned the anti-camera laws again. Bill agreed, then settled in at the desk and polished a radio script to deliver that night. I went to the bathroom to mix my chemicals to develop my photographs of the crowds in the Red Square. As luck would have it, just as I was in the middle of developing the film, the sirens began to blast.

Bill knocked furiously on the bathroom door. "We have to go, Addie, hurry!"

"I'm almost done. Please...let me finish up." My heart raced as I worked as fast as I could.

Bill let out an exasperated huff and I heard him pacing in front of the door.

I came out fifteen minutes later, ready to leave, when the all-clear siren sounded.

Bill looked at me with a mixture of annoyance and understanding.

I kissed his cheek. "Sorry, darling. I know it was risky but I couldn't lose those photographs. I could never get those shots again."

"It must've been a practice alarm. We're lucky we didn't get caught staying here. Addie, your life is more important to me than your photographs. Promise me you'll remember that." His intense eyes remained on mine, waiting for an answer.

"Yes, you're right. I'll heed all the warnings from now on."

He hugged me long and hard.

The following night, the siren blasted again. I snatched my camera and Bill grabbed his notebook, and we dashed across the street to the subway.

The Moscow subway was a clean, amazing place; the total opposite of New York City subways. The platforms in the station had marble pillars. We gazed up at the ceiling, which was decorated in gold and blue mosaic. *New York City should take note of this fine subway,* I thought. We went down a long set of stairs with the rest of the crowd. I was instructed to sit on the tracks among thousands of orderly Soviets. Bill remained on the platform, waiting for the all-clear siren and hoping to make it to his broadcast on time.

Hours went by. This was obviously *not* a practice drill.

311

The man next to me wore a tunic and a lovely embroidered Kazak cap. He was reading old Russian poetry aloud. Across from me, a young girl was doing crossword puzzles.

After several hours, we heard the loudspeaker blare: "The enemy has been beaten back, comrades. Go home to your rest." The organized crowd left the immense subway shelter to greet the rising sun.

Once out on the street, people began running toward the Kremlin. I followed, feeling for my camera inside my coat. Right beside the Kremlin wall, across from our hotel window, was an enormous bomb crater. It was the first bomb to fall on Moscow. I was glad to have my camera with me and discreetly snapped a few photos. Repairmen arrived immediately and set to work filling up the immense crater.

I recognized the reception clerk from our hotel standing beside me. "They can't hit our Kremlin!" he exclaimed. "I hope they haven't bombed our Red Square or Lenin's Tomb."

Another reporter from the hotel said, "I heard they bombed the Italian and Japanese embassies."

We continued to explore the devastation, saddened by the sights we were witnessing.

While Bill was off broadcasting late that night, I climbed onto the roof and put my cameras to work. I placed two cameras on the balcony, shooting in opposite directions, to cover as much of the sky as possible. Incendiary bombs began to fall, making the horizon bright enough to aid in focusing. Beams from the searchlights crossed and recrossed the sky. Probing searchlights stabbed through the darkness. The crossing of the beams turned the entire sky into a brilliant plaid design.

In the square below, fireflies dodged the shrapnel that hit the pavement. I heard the drone of planes overhead and the whistle of bombs falling all over the neighborhood. The siren wailed, alerting everyone to get to the shelter. Frightened by all the noise, I moved all my equipment through the window and rolled under the bed. When the hotel windows shattered, I crawled to the door over broken glass, then fled down the staircase, hoping to find better shelter. Each landing was filled with glass and my shoes crunched with each step. The hotel shook and felt like it might fall apart. I knew I would never make it safely to the shelter, so I beat it down to the cellar of the hotel instead. Much to my surprise, I found several *United Press* correspondents there as well, chatting away about the latest news of the war, seemingly unaffected by all that was going on around us. I tried to calm my nerves as I found a seat and brushed broken glass off my clothes.

The all-clear siren sounded a short time later and we all went outside to see what had happened. A bomb had fallen on the Vachtangov Theater a few yards away. It was completely destroyed. I crept in and around the rubble and gasped. The actors, the audience—they were all dead, buried among chunks of the fallen building. I stood there, numb at the sight, hardly able to comprehend what my eyes were seeing. Still in shock, I grabbed my camera with shaking hands and snapped a few photos of the carnage. Unable to stomach the sight any longer, I made my way back out to the street. The memory of the dead bus driver I had seen in Finland flooded my mind. I pushed it away, not wanting to upset my stomach any more than it already was.

The hotel staff immediately cleaned up the glass in our room and boarded up the shattered windows. I began to measure the acuteness of a bombing raid by whether it was a two- or four-camera night. One night, while Bill was off broadcasting, the air-raid siren sounded yet again. It caught me with film packs in the tub right in the middle of developing. I dove under the bed when I heard an inspector knocking on all the hotel room doors to make sure everyone had gone to the shelters. I stayed there and started to count, hoping I could get back to the tub before the film was overdeveloped.

The following day, we removed all the paintings, statues, and bronze lamps from our rooms, as we were told that everything in the room could become your enemy during a bombing.

When Bill left to broadcast the news, I went out on the balcony. I knew he thought I was in the shelter but I could not resist the golden opportunity to photograph any possible bombings. The sky was filled with twinkling stars, then with brightly colored streaks of light as the bombing began.

One night, I was working with four cameras at a time. As the air raids increased, I varied the exposures. I had brought all seven of my cameras with me on this trip but made sure I never had them all set up at the same time. One single bomb hitting the balcony could destroy them all.

I set up a camera on the marble windowsill overlooking the Kremlin and another pointing in the opposite direction on the balcony. It was amazing to hear the Kremlin clock chime on each quarter hour through all the air raids. When bombs began to explode, I took my usual shelter under the bed, then cautiously crept out and changed the film, hoping all the rattling would not blur the exposures.

One evening, a German plane was shot down nearby. It was the first I had ever experienced. The noise was deafening. At that point, I took only a few more photographs, then rounded up my equipment and shoved it under the bed. I wrapped myself up in the quilt and crawled into my hideout, then stayed there, listening, in the dark.

The morning light woke me. All was quiet. I got into bed and waited for Bill to return.

Bill was grumpy when he arrived. "I hope you spent the night in the shelter. I was looking for you." He got into bed next to me, cuddled up close, and snored into a deep sleep.

Every night now there was bombing activity. The Germans were after the Kremlin. They dropped parachute flares, which looked like blazing umbrellas floating to the ground that lit up the entire city.

On Wednesday night, we heard the whining of a bomb and a building across the street gave way. I stepped out onto the balcony. Behind the Kremlin wall, an immense plume of smoke rose into the air. I grabbed my camera and photographed the frightening sight of the entire Kremlin palace being blown to bits. Bill yelled at me to come inside. The air-raid siren sounded too late. Patrolmen shouted and ran across the square toward the Kremlin.

Bill pulled me inside, grabbed covers and pillows, and we slid under the bed. We clung to each other until a calm silence fell over the city. Then we made love, glad to have each other, both of us embraced by a false sense of security.

Dawn crept in and still we heard no noise. Bill and I dressed, put on our military helmets, and decided to venture out into the bombed city.

Soviet officers surrounded the Kremlin. Bill put his arm around me with his coat open as a cover so that I could use my Rolleiflex to discreetly photograph the scene.

He whispered in my ear, "Addie, make it quick, just take a few. I do not want to be arrested. We'll be of no use to our country if we are put in jail."

I unbuttoned my coat and looked down into the viewfinder of my camera and quickly shot as many photographs as I could without getting caught. Bill squeezed my shoulder, signaling me to stop when a guard looked our way. I buttoned up fast and we left to go back to the hotel.

That evening, before Bill left for the radio center, he barked, "Get ready to go to the shelter. This hotel could easily be bombed."

I didn't answer him. I was busy going through my camera equipment.

"Do you hear me, Addie? Your life is more valuable than your photographs."

As soon as Bill left, I set up my cameras on tripods in perfect locations on the balcony. I studied the points of the horizon, and, should the firing begin, determined whether the illumination would be correct for the exposure. Less than a minute later, bombs began to fall, producing a red glow in the sky. I focused on the cathedral towers as anti-aircraft guns sent up flames behind their onion-shaped domes. There was a sharp whistling noise from the bombs as shrapnel tinkled on the rooftops and the street below. I put on my oversized helmet, changed film, added a telephoto lens to the Leica, and checked my focus. After the bombing was over and the city fell silent, I spent the rest of the night developing all my film.

As the weeks went by, the raids occurred less and less. It was time to send all my photographs to the censors to be checked before publication. The censors sent back the photos of the bombed-out Kremlin and the dead bodies in the theater. I took those photographs and hid them in the lining of one of my suitcases.

It was the end of September and the beginning of the autumn rains. Bill and I were determined to get to the front.

When we asked the general for permission, he questioned me. "Aren't you afraid?"

Bill grinned with pride as I answered, "I'm only afraid of going home without finishing my job."

"You're quite determined, young lady. It will be very cold there. Wear all your clothes and don't forget your helmets."

I thought about the climate of Finland. Now *that* was cold! I thought of Ivanov and his huge, furry Russian hat. Where was he? I had tried to find him but there was a war going on and it was impossible.

Bill and I traveled to the front with a group of war correspondents; four Brits, five Americans, and one censor. All men, of course. We rode in several cars with an armed chauffeur and a Soviet military officer as a guide. On the way, we ate hot sausage and black bread with sliced cucumbers in the cold car.

It was a difficult journey. We had to drive through streams of mud, and the chauffeur had to put stones and logs in front of the wheels for traction when we became stuck. As nightfall came, we spent the night in a schoolhouse on cots.

Breakfast was served when groups of pilots came in from the front. I wrinkled my nose at the raw fish we were served, and hid it in the buttery mashed potatoes in order to swallow it down. The black bread with slabs of cheese on it was delicious.

Many of the pilots wore the medals of the dead Nazi enemies they had taken down. The most coveted was the Iron Cross. The reporters took notes about the adventures the pilots shared while I focused my camera on their faces and stolen medals. The pilots told of courageous villagers who threw burning trees across the railroad tracks to halt munitions trains. They saw villagers shoot at German soldiers with rifles and throw rocks at them. One of the pilots said that more villagers were killed than Germans, but at least the enemy had been deterred.

The rain had lessened when we finally got to the frontlines of the battlefields of Yelnya after a long day of driving. It was now well past midnight. Our guide led us to the edge of the woods and we were instructed to run single-file across a meadow to a grove of trees about a quarter mile away. When we reached the meadow, the entire horizon was lit up. The Germans sent up star shells to light up the frontlines, to see if the enemy might be slipping across. I was not allowed to use my flashbulbs because it would reveal our position. The battery crew loaded and operated their big guns and the roar of the artillery was deafening.

Our guide was able to bring us safely to a cottage near a fire-gutted town and we slept on the floor in a room crowded with soldiers. We slept feet against heads. Darling Bill decided to roll me up in my blanket against the farthest wall, and took his place beside me to give me maximum privacy and protection.

I crept outside at dawn to take photos of all the soldiers on the move. It was raining and their faces were wet under their dripping, hooded rain capes, which barely protected their heads. I used flashbulbs to augment the weak light. As I worked, my camera shutter began to stick. This was the worst thing that could happen—it meant that I couldn't use that camera until it was fixed. Frustrated, I returned to the cottage, rummaged through my equipment, and found a new shutter. After a quick repair, I hurried back outside. The rain had stopped and the delightful early morning light lent itself to taking pictures of soldiers performing their daily camp tasks. I skipped breakfast, afraid another downpour would break my series of photographs, and kept working to make the most of the weather.

Today we were going to walk to the village to view the end results of six weeks of fighting. The guide gathered our group and warned us to be extremely careful because the ground was full of unexploded mines and shells.

In the car, Bill put his arm around me, kissed my cheek, reached into his pocket, and pulled out a goose drumstick. I kissed him back, elated that I was with such a thoughtful man. I hungrily ate my breakfast as we drove.

The village looked like a man-made desert. The treads of the tanks had ruined the fields. Only a few houses remained from a town of over 5,000. We saw piles of ashes everywhere. The town had been reduced to chimneys and scraps of roofs. The townspeople wandered through the ruins of their houses. A few cats showed up, but the dogs had become wild and ran away from us. I took pictures of people trying to cook the food the soldiers had brought them over broken bits of brick-and-plaster ovens. I photographed an old woman carrying hot coals from a neighbor in a Nazi helmet. Cooking in the middle of the rubble with no pots or utensils was a difficult task. The villagers used pieces of wrecked German planes and metal sheeting from tanks to form makeshift, shallow pans. Endless, sad photographic scenes met my eyes through my camera lens.

Bill and I explored the area outside the village. We looked at the dugouts the Germans had made with sandbags braced with logs. Inside were metal cartons, wicker baskets holding hand grenades, and landmines packed with straw. Bill picked up one of the many German helmets, which was much thinner than the Soviet helmets we were wearing. Soviet helmets, pocked with bullet holes, were scattered around in piles. I photographed one that had a name written in it. The bullet hole over the ear made it clear how its owner had been killed.

We walked for miles in the rain, way behind the soldiers, to a wasteland littered with the remains of the war. There were common graves where the Soviet dead had been buried, marked with painted red stars on pieces of old fence posts. I shot photos of a boot, the sleeve of a uniform, and even a rain-soaked German newspaper.

As we continued to walk, I stepped on something soft and unlike the surrounding ground. I froze instantly, then screamed as a green cloud rose into my face. I looked down and saw that I had stepped on a mound of moldy bread. Bill gave a nervous laugh and hugged me. Tears filled my eyes as I realized with great relief that I had not stepped on a mine.

We caught up with a few Soviet soldiers who showed us several German tanks that were filled with Soviet women's underwear and peasants' embroidered scarves and blouses. They took a few items to bring back and offered me a gorgeous, rich handiwork embroidered blouse. We were all glad to rescue the clothing from the enemy.

On the way back to Moscow, I asked the driver to let me out at one point to photograph the half-destroyed domed cathedral being used as a Soviet barracks. Hours later, it was a joy to be back in our hotel suite in Moscow. Bill sprawled out on the bearskin rug, studying maps before going to the admiral to discuss how we were going to get home. Watching him on the rug brought back thoughts of my quivering body as we rolled on it naked. If he hadn't been so absorbed in his maps, I would have been tempted to throw off my clothes and reenact that delicious scene.

British Admiral Cripps told us we could travel with a convoy. He had to obtain special dispensation from the State Department because of an American law forbidding citizens to travel through waters on the ships of a nation at war. Messages were sent out in "gray code" so that the information could not be decoded by the enemy.

A week later, the American ambassador, Mr. Steinhardt, informed us that the State Department had granted us permission to go home. He instructed us to not tell anyone of how we were to travel. We were headed for the Arctic in a military convoy.

While we waited for our visas, I had a huge amount of film to develop before leaving the country. I was able to get help from a chauffeur while Bill furiously typed his final notes. As fast as I could develop the film in the bathtub, the chauffeur would hang the pictures from cords strung everywhere in the room. What a sight! There were cords between the legs of the grand piano and across the statue of Napoleon. All over the suite there were dripping squares of celluloid. I dried them, sorted them, made up neat packages to be put into special military pouches, and brought them to the censors at the embassy, who would send the approved photos to *Life Magazine*. It was hard for me to leave them. I wondered which ones would be discarded.

We were instructed to bring as little as possible on our trip. All my camera paraphernalia took precedence. I started giving things away to women in Moscow, even my only pair of precious silk stockings, knowing they would be of no use to me in the Arctic. I gave away all my hats except for my warmest one. The only items I kept were a brilliantly painted plaster doll in a Russian costume and the elaborately embroidered blouse from the German tank.

Bill and I boarded a train to the town of Archangel. There we bought a few warmer clothes, including reindeer fur hats to cover our ears, which could be tied under our chins. I set up a timed camera to take a photo of us in our absurd but practical reindeer hats.

When we reached the port, up the ladder we went to board the ship. We were immediately given wide, thick life belts and were ordered to wear them all the time, even when eating or sleeping. Our convoy of twenty-two vessels left early in the morning in a soupy fog. Our 11,000-ton troop ship was from North Africa and was not insulated for the Arctic temperatures. But it was well-armed with machine guns, depth charges, and had four-inch guns mounted on the stern.

Upon reaching the White Sea, we heard German planes overhead, hidden by the fog. We were ordered to stay in our cabin. Bill fell asleep with a deep snore as I read a book in the corner. When I was sure he wouldn't wake up, I crept out with my camera gear. On the top deck, in my reindeer hat with a helmet on top, and a blanket over my coat, I set up my camera and waited for the fog to lift. I heard mines or bombs being dropped, but tried to ignore them so I could focus on taking a good shot. As soon as the fog dissipated, I was able to capture a mine being dropped by a German bomber. Satisfied, I came to my senses about my safety, packed up, and scurried back down to the cabin. I undressed and cuddled up next to Bill as his sleep noises lulled me into a deep slumber.

Several days went by, then, finally, the planes were gone. The weather cleared. The North Sea was full of mines. Thank God it was daylight and we were able to steer around the prong-studded balls bobbing in the water.

It would take us fifteen days to travel through seven seas. As we crossed the Arctic Circle surrounding the North Pole, I was in photographer's heaven as I took photos of the aurora borealis. The Northern Lights danced across the sky, bouncing off the surfaces of clouds, water, and ice, creating illusions of being in a dreamlike state. The changing white-green ribbons stretched and danced across the magical sky.

When we passed through the Norwegian Sea, I shot photos of hundreds of shiny porpoises as they raced with our ship and flipped high into the air. It was a joy to photograph these delightful creatures instead of photographing dangerous bombs.

I was exhausted from the frightful images of war bouncing in about in my mind. I couldn't wait to get back to my own safe country.

Anti-aircraft guns, Leningrad

Moscow air raid

The Kremlin being bombed, 1941

Chapter 48
World War II
December 7, 1941&1942

Usually I object when someone makes over-much of men's work versus women's work, for I think it is the excellence of the results which counts.

— Margaret Bourke-White

In New York City, the headlines screamed on all the newspapers:

JAPAN DECLARES WAR ON U.S. AND BRITAIN
HAWAII BOMBED WITHOUT WARNING,
ROOSEVELT WILL ASK CONGRESS TO ACT TODAY
1,500 DEAD IN HAWAII
CONGRESS VOTES WAR

Bill and I were both deeply distressed over the bombing of Pearl Harbor in our territory of Hawaii. The United States' involvement in World War II was now a necessary reality.

In the new year of 1942, I was asked to go to Washington, D.C., to become the first official female World War II correspondent. Mr. Luce, the owner of *Life Magazine*, had arranged an appointment with the U.S. Army Air Forces. I was annoyed with myself that I felt nervous going to the new Pentagon building for an interview. I was certainly more than qualified after covering six countries at war.

The interview seemed to go on forever and I tried to patiently answer the general's endless questions. After the general gave me my official credentials, he asked me to go to the War Department to help design uniforms for female war correspondents. I tingled with excitement as I clutched my official papers in my hand and left to catch the bus to the War Department. In no time, I stood before a sign that read "Army War College." I adjusted my skirt, straightened my posture, and marched into the building.

I spent days going over types of material with personnel from Abercrombie & Fitch. We decided to use the same material used for the men's army uniforms, except that a skirt was added and slacks would be tailored for a woman's build. Metal cutout insignias bearing the words "War Correspondent" were to be put on the shoulder straps, caps, and lapels. All war correspondents were to wear a green armband with the white letter "C" on it. There was much discussion over buttons, whether they should have eagles on them or be plain. I was pleased to be a consultant but at the same time amused by the seriousness of the entire process. On the last day, with a big, brand-new lipstick smile, I modeled a sample that the design company had made. I could tell by the staff's applause that it was a success.

After my patriotism was approved, I suffered through inoculations, and was issued a helmet, ladies gloves that were treated for gas, insect powder, sunglasses, mosquito netting, a canteen, a gas mask, and anti-gas attack salve. All of the supplies were put in a musette bag. I was then handed the first official Basic Field Manual for war correspondents.

On the bus back to New York, I read the War Department's brown booklet titled *Basic Field Manual, Regulations for Correspondents Accompanying U.S. Army Forces in the Field.*

War correspondents could choose where they wanted to go, but it was subject to Army approval. Travel was free. All war correspondents had an assimilated rank, which meant we were entitled to the same pay as officers if we were captured. Correspondents started out as second lieutenants, then could go up in rank. The Geneva Convention forbade correspondents from carrying a weapon. I read through the rest of the booklet, then drifted off to sleep.

When I got back to our hotel room, I learned that Bill had gotten credentialed while I was gone and was checking out his uniform in the mirror.

"What ya think, Addie?"

"Wow, Bill, you knock my socks off!"

I opened my suitcase and displayed my uniform with a huge grin and my eyes all a-glitter.

He laughed, embraced me, then gave me a long, spirited kiss.

When we went out to dinner with our new uniforms on, I touched his armband with the "C" on it and bragged that I had one also.

Over dinner, we gazed into each other's eyes and stroked each other's hands between bites of our meal. We had missed each other terribly while I was away, even though it had only been a week.

"Let's skip dessert, Addie, I'd rather have you!" Bill said playfully.

Later, after relishing each other in bed and renewing our relationship, Bill stared with a deep seriousness into my eyes. "Addie, you know I love you, don't you?"

"Bill, we've been together through many wars in three different countries, and I can truly say I love you also." I stroked my fingers over his smooth-shaven cheek and leaned in, inhaling the smell of his shaving soap.

"I'm shipping out tomorrow. I received an assignment from *Time* to go to the Pacific Theater. I am asking you again, will you marry me? Please say yes. I don't want to leave until I'm a married man." He put his arms around me in a strong embrace and waited for my answer.

"You're leaving so soon?" I pouted. "I will marry you, Bill, as soon as you come back on leave so we can have a long honeymoon."

"Do you promise me, Addie?"

"I do!"

We sealed it with a kiss.

Several months went by. Bill was away and I had not yet received an assignment. I wandered around the city, feeling lonely. I went to one of my favorite haunts for lunch, the Horn and Hardart automat, and was disappointed. There wasn't much available due to food rationing.

At last, I received a censored letter from Bill and tore it open hungrily.

> *My Darling Addie,*
> *I am on a small, 70' wooden trawler ship, the* King John. *This vessel was assigned to the U.S. Army Services of Supply. We are transporting about a hundred US soldiers from the 32nd Infantry Division. Our ship has been designated to be one of the first U.S. units to attack the* ~~Japanese~~. *We are going to the north coast of* ~~New Guinea~~ *to support the* ~~Battle of Buna.~~ *We have just departed* ~~Wanigela~~ *and are headed for* ~~Pongani~~ *on the coast. We are going to be landing the infantrymen and supplies on* ~~Wanigela.~~
>
> *I am assigned to report on the operations in the war.* ~~Wanigela~~ *is vital to the Allies as a forward staging base for troops and equipment to support the campaign against the* ~~Japanese~~ *beachheads at* ~~Buna-Sanananda-Gona.~~ *From* ~~Wanigela,~~ *we will transport supplies and troops along the coast.*
>
> *I miss you dreadfully. Have you received an assignment yet? I hope we both have time off together to get married and have a grand honeymoon when I get back.*
> *Love always and forever,*
> *Bill*

I missed him terribly as well. I took a self-portrait of myself in my new uniform. After developing it, I sent it to Bill with a well-thought-out love letter.

At last, I received an assignment from *Life* to distract me from my loneliness. I was headed to an impending war in North Africa. Relieved to have something to focus on, I tried to put my personal worries behind me and threw myself into my first love — work.

FM 30–26

WAR DEPARTMENT

BASIC FIELD MANUAL

REGULATIONS
FOR CORRESPONDENTS
ACCOMPANYING
U. S. ARMY FORCES
IN THE FIELD
January 21, 1942

War correspondents' field manual

Female war correspondents

Chapter 49
1943 North Africa

The enemy must be annihilated before he reaches our main battlefield. We must stop him in the water, destroying all his equipment while it is still afloat.

— German General Erwin Rommel

Flying to North Africa was too dangerous, so I took a ship to England, where I would then board a British convoy to get there. There were over 400 nurses and 6,000 British and American troops below deck in the hold. The convoy was extremely large and consisted of an aircraft carrier, several troop ships, and destroyers.

I bunked in a cabin with Scottish nursing sisters who admired and were envious of my slacks. On this trip, I had to pack light and took a small Rolleiflex, a Graflex, a Linhof, plus my good-luck cameras from the past: my Leica and Vest Pocket camera. I took only six of my usual twenty-two lenses plus my two war correspondent uniforms.

The trip would take five days. We spent the entire time at sea in the midst of a horrendous storm. The aircraft carrier pitched in waves that rose over fifty feet high. On deck, I photographed the ships bobbing about like little toy boats.

Despite the raging storms, we had to participate in three lifeboat drills a day, even though most of us were seasick. And we were ordered to march, which was nearly impossible with the rocking of the ship. I held on to the ropes strung along the decks as I struggled to my boat station and waited the fifteen long minutes until we were all released from the drill, trying to keep my balance as the ship tipped and rocked.

Mess was served three times a day, but very few people participated. I went down for soup. Dishes flew by and broke on the floor, and my soup spilled as we lurched from side to side. I overheard a few officers saying that we would never be torpedoed by an enemy sub in this weather, as no submarine could hold its aim long enough to hit us.

We were instructed to keep our musette bags packed and ready in case we had to abandon ship. I surveyed the contents of mine and removed the gas mask and various other items, then repacked it with chocolate, rolls of film, and extra socks. I would have to leave my large-format camera and most of my lenses behind, but crammed in my trusty Leica and telephoto lens in. I smiled, remembering all of the famous people I had used it on: Chancellor Adolf Hitler, Prime Minister Neville Chamberlain, President Edvard Beneš, Premier Joseph Stalin, and the former Finnish president, Pehr Svinhufvud.

Once we got through the Gibraltar Straits, the Mediterranean was calm. We were due to land in North Africa the next day. I spoke to an officer in the mess hall, and he secretly told me that we had been followed for days by a group of enemy subs.

Later that night, I woke to a loud thump and was thrown out of my bunk onto the floor. Though we were told to sleep fully dressed, no one ever did. One of the nuns in our tiny cabin switched on a flashlight and told us all to dress fast and get up on deck to see what was going on. I scrambled to get into my clothes and put on my required helmet, my heart was racing. I threw my musette bag over my shoulder, knowing that I would have to retrieve the rest of my equipment later. On my way up the many steps to the deck, I heard the megaphone screaming, *Report to your stations! This is an emergency!*

Once on deck, instead of joining the marching troops headed to the boat stations, I had the sudden urge to take one quick photograph under the midnight sky, with the full moon overhead for perfect lighting.

A crewman caught me. "Get to your station!" he yelled at me. "We've been torpedoed! Abandon ship!"

My mouth dropped open as I put my camera back into my bag.

The crewman yelled into his megaphone: "Abandon ship! Abandon ship!"

I scrambled to station #7 and found that my lifeboat had already launched overboard. I climbed over the rail into tiny lifeboat #14. I unconsciously held my breath as I got into the boat, which dangled precariously over the side of the ship. The nurses surrounding me were quiet but were visibly shaking, just as I was.

It was announced that there were not enough lifeboats. I heard two US Army nurses offer to stay behind.

Our lifeboat was filled with water that had splashed in from the torpedo impact. We were sitting in water up to our waists, stuffed into the little boat. My teeth chattered. But, while waiting for the descent of our lifeboat, I pried a camera out of my bag and shot part of the convoy that was sinking. I had learned that the greatest pictures are the untaken ones. I had to will my cold fingers to work.

As our lifeboat was lowered, one of the two men on board had to push our boat away from the suction of the ship with an oar. As we landed in the Mediterranean, our boat flooded as a large wave hit us. I screamed when a nurse fell overboard. I held on tighter and put my musette bag inside my half drenched coat and buttoned up, hoping to keep my one precious camera dry. Another wave spilled into our boat.

"Bail or we'll sink!" someone yelled.

"Use your helmets!" another person called out.

The helmets came in handy as we all began to bail with frantic movements. There were only two men on our boat and they could hardly find room to row us away from the vortex of the sinking ship.

I took one last shot of over a hundred men climbing down rope nets over the side of the boat. There were people swimming in the Mediterranean all around us among lifeboats and floating debris. Where was the nurse who had fallen overboard? We saw two lifeboats capsize, dumping more nurses and crew into the sea. Some were rescued. Others drowned.

In the distance, we heard one of the sisters crying, "Help me! Save me! Help me...save me..." her voice fading until there was silence. The nurses began to pray. I joined in to prevent myself from crying. The last time I had prayed was during a dust storm with the Douglas family...so very long ago. I remembered how comforting it was.

Our rudder broke and the men struggled to steer the rudderless raft.

We heard a voice call out from the convoy through a megaphone.

"Everyone keep back! We're going to drop depth charges."

Oh, my God, I thought. *There must be enemy submarines right below our lifeboats!*

A charge went off and the sea shook.

I tried not to worry but I was in the middle of the Mediterranean in a tiny lifeboat without a rudder, and most of my precious photographic equipment was going down with the sinking ship. Would we stay afloat or end up on the coast, captured as enemies? I stopped the negative voice in my mind by listening to the sisters saying prayer after prayer. Somehow, their prayers uplifted my spirit.

After a miserable night, finally, it was dawn. Everyone was cold, wet, and shivering, but we were alive. I felt in my coat for my bag with my only camera and film in it, and by the light of the sunrise, I took photos of the boatloads of helpless people.

The humor that occurred during this time of tragedy was unbelievable. I witnessed incredible courage as one soldier swam past us. He raised his hand in a hitchhiking motion and said, "Give me a ride? Got any room?"

Then a nurse swam by in her lifejacket and jokingly asked us, "Is this the way to North Africa?"

Another nurse pointed and called back, "Take that wave to the right."

Then singing broke out among all the lifeboats. *"You are my sunshine, my only sunshine..."*

I instantly thought of my Bill and remembered singing that song together in the Soviet Union. We continued to sing and bail water the best we could with our helmets.

By midafternoon, an English flying boat went by. We furiously waved and called for help. It spotted us and by nightfall, a destroyer appeared and rescued us, along with hundreds of our people.

We landed in Algiers. I was among all the nurses who had

survived and we were put up in a maternity hospital. Everyone was exhausted and distraught.

I had just fallen asleep when I was jolted awake by the sound of a German plane bombing the harbor right near the hospital. I ground my teeth, thinking that war was truly a terrible thing.

The next day, I went down to the harbor because I was told that our convoy might be towed to the shore. Then, I could see what could be salvaged. With renewed hope, I thought I might get my camera equipment back, but when I viewed the ship through my one telephoto lens, I saw it sinking down to the bottom of the sea. I wept uncontrollably until it was no longer in sight.

"My 1918 Vest Pocket is gone!" I ranted out loud.

Trudging back to the hospital, I wiped my eyes with the back of my hand, wondering why I had cried over a camera when so many people had drowned. It must have been from sheer fatigue over escaping a torpedoed ship, almost drowning in the middle of the sea in a lifeboat, and seeing the dead floating by.

After *Life* received the information of my plight in North Africa, my boss sent me a telegram at the hospital to go on to England with the rest of the nurses. I would be transported by jeep to a secret American bomber base for a new assignment.

It would be a while before we could get transportation to England, so I sent a telegram to *Life* asking that my mail be forwarded to the hospital where I was. I missed Bill tremendously and was anxiously waiting for a letter.

A letter did not arrive; only a large manila envelope with "United States Army Air Forces, Washington, D.C." as the return address. I opened it and inside with a letter was the photograph of me in my uniform that I had sent to Bill. My name and date were on the back. Puzzled, I wondered why Bill was sending me back my photograph. Then, I opened the letter.

> *Dear Lieutenant Peterson,*
> *We regret to inform you that your boyfriend, Lieutenant William S. Miller, has been killed. We found your photograph in his wallet and thought you should be informed.*
> *While off the north coast of ~~New Guinea~~ near ~~Pongani~~ a vessel mistaken for an enemy ship was bombed and strafed by a*

friendly ~~B-25 Mitchell~~ *from the* ~~3rd Bombardment~~ *Group. The* ~~B-25~~ *mistook the ship for a* ~~Japanese~~ *vessel. During the attack, Lt. William Miller was fatally wounded by shrapnel in his head and died in a boat on the way to shore. Another lieutenant was also killed and several others were wounded. The boat suffered severe damage and had to be withdrawn. William S. Miller was the tenth American war correspondent killed in action in the war and has been buried with full military honors at an Australian-American cemetery outside Port Moresby.*

> *Sincerely,*
> *United States Army Adjunct General*

I was numb. I dropped the letter on the floor and sank down beside it. I opened the package again, hoping to find a letter from Bill. Inside was Bill's moleskin notebook. I ran my shaking fingers over it but couldn't bear to open it.

I went to the hospital kitchen and got cup of tea. I sipped and stared into space, my mind clogged with disbelief.

After a fitful sleep, I got up at dawn and read the letter out loud, hoping it would sink into my mind that my Bill was really gone. I had just lost my best friend and my "almost" husband. I was furious with myself for not marrying Bill the first time he had asked me, before we had gone to the Soviet Union. If I had, I would have been notified of his death sooner and could have gone to the funeral. When I attended my mother's funeral service, the importance of it made sense to me. I could grieve with other people and knew that she really had died. It gave me closure. I had missed going to Bill's burial with his full military honors. Now I was left with nothing but disbelief and a stormy anger. Bill had been shot by an American pilot. An *American* pilot! It was incomprehensible that such an accident could occur. After reading the letter for the third time, I became infuriated by the word "friendly" and at the concept that his ship be mistaken for an enemy vessel. How could that be? Did they look that similar?

In the days that followed, I found the courage to read Bill's notebook. Inside it was that silly photograph of us in our reindeer hats on the convoy leaving the Soviet Union. I touched Bill's face in the picture. Tears welled up in my eyes. His handwriting was like a familiar touch to me. I felt the loop on his fancy letter "A" and the long tails at the end of each letter of a word. In the USSR, I remember leaning over his shoulder in that lovely honeymoon suite we stayed in, watching him write his well-thought-out reports. To my surprise, his notebook contained only a few war reports. The rest of the pages were filled with poetry. There was poem after poem proclaiming his love for me, with the hope for marriage. He was a creative wordsmith and my tears flowed with each paragraph I read. I placed the notebook on my bed and threw myself onto the pillow, sobbing endlessly. I had lost my one true love.

North Africa

Torch Troops near Algiers, North Africa

Chapter 50
B-17 Bomber, 1943

Without the B-17, we might have lost the war.
— General Carl Spaatz, Commander, US Strategic Air Forces

She was a Stradivarius of an airplane.
— Colonel Robert K. Morgan pilot of the *Memphis Belle*

After arriving in England, I was taken by jeep to a secret American bomber base. Once there, I waited for a telegram about my next assignment, and for new camera equipment and uniforms to replace what had been lost in the convoy. I stayed in a bunk most of the time and read Bill's poems over and over, still in a confused state of depression.

A few weeks went by before I finally received a package with replacement photographic equipment minus a Vest Pocket camera, which was not a necessity. I had requested cameras in smaller sizes after being torpedoed during the North African invasion. I received a compact, featherweight Rolleiflex, three small Linhofs, which also fit on a tripod, and lenses that were fitted with synchronizers for flashbulb equipment. They also sent one large-format camera for my new assignment.

My mood lifted a little when I was assigned to take a short trip to London to compose a portrait of Winston Churchill on his 68th birthday. It was a relief to throw myself back into work mode to circumvent the cloud of continuous sadness that seemed to stay within me.

Winston Churchill was a challenging subject, nervous as well as tired, and understandably so because the British Navy was having a difficult time with enemy submarines. I was happy to use a new, large-format camera to take 4x5 size photographs of this important man. I was able to get a good portrait of him with a birthday carnation in his lapel.

King George VI was touring the base when I returned, allowing me to photograph him as well. I was delighted when he complimented my hairstyle. After wearing a combat helmet in several theaters of the war, and having to stuff my hair into it, I had treated myself to a beauty parlor appointment in England. My new "Bette Davis" style, with a pompadour in the front and finger waves in the back, gave my plain brown hair a lovely new look.

I had fun on the base taking photographs of all the new bombers and threw myself into my work, only thinking of Bill at night.

One of the pilots came back from a mission, bragging to everyone that they had shot down their first enemy fighter. He said the sky was swarming with Focke-Wulf 190s and the B-17 was so close that the ball-turret gunner could see the red borders of the swastikas on the enemy planes. They fired on the enemy until the plane went down tail over wing. He ended his story with, "We bagged our first Jerry!"

Though I had been accredited by the Army Air Forces, which gave me the opportunity to photograph briefings and go on practice flights, I was not allowed on combat missions. Being a woman in a man's world was always a challenge for me. I was told that women were a distraction for men in combat, so women did not share the same privileges as the men. At first, no one from the press was allowed to go on missions, but the ban was lifted and two male war correspondents were allowed to fly on two different bombers. Only one came back. This did *not* help my case. Time after time, the commanding officer refused my requests to go on bombing missions. Although I had learned to be a bulldog to get my way and to never let go of something I wanted, I decided to be patient. I stopped begging for a while and hung out with the bomber crew.

On one particular day, it was bad weather for flying. The crew, looking for something to do, decided to paint my name on one of the bombers, which I took as a great compliment. The boys asked me to christen the newly named B-17 with a bottle of Coca-Cola since, of course, we didn't have champagne. The crew had to get permission for this event due to the bureaucracy of the US Army. Coca-Cola was expendable but the bottles weren't! Finally, Group Armament issued a directive permitting me to crack the bottle over the front guns of the Flying Fortress bearing my name, *Adeline*.

The next day was perfect for the christening party, and there was quite a crowd. I climbed a ladder to the nose of the bomber and broke the bottle over the front of the machine gun. Everyone cheered. General Jimmy Doolittle then gave a short speech, ending with the dramatic message, "May the 97th Bomber unit bring devastation to the enemy!"

I had met Doolittle once, with his wife, at a party before he became a general. Still desperate to go on a combat mission, I hoped to use this to my advantage.

The next day was perfect flying weather. I was asked to sign a bomb before one of the crews left on a mission. They would drop it on an airframe factory in Germany. I felt nervous about this but the crew reassured me that it would bring them good luck. I was on my way to see General Doolittle when they returned, all of them laughing and joking. They stopped me and the pilot proudly told me that they had "delivered" my signed bomb to the German factory amid a sky crowded with Focke-Wulfs, and had succeeded in their mission. He gave me a hug. "You brought us good luck, Addie!"

Blushing, I continued to make my way to the general's office.

General Doolittle and I had a friendly chat. I asked how his wife was and he asked me what I had been reporting on recently. I told him about my frightful adventures on the convoy to North Africa.

The general sensed that I wanted to ask him something. "So, Adeline, how can I help you today?" he said. He combed back his thinning hair with his hand and looked at me expectantly.

I drew in a deep breath. "Sir, I would like permission to fly in a B-17 to report on combat missions. I have been continuously denied this request, while male correspondents have already gone." I sat up straight and leaned in, trying to look confident.

He hesitated and looked me straight in the eyes. "Well, you survived being torpedoed, you might as well experience a bombing mission."

General Doolittle called on the field phone and gave permission to the commanding officer of the 97th Bomb Group to allow me to fly with them. Thrilled, I jumped up from my seat, thanked him profusely, and shook his hand.

"Be careful, Adeline," he warned, a somber tone to his voice. "You might not come back."

"Yes, sir," I replied.

I left filled with joyous anticipation that I would fly in a B-17 at last! Unfortunately, my excitement was short-lived. I got a bad case of the flu and the flight surgeon grounded me for two weeks. I was quite distressed by this until I learned that it was standard protocol for all fliers. Among other reasons, a descent from the high altitude of a bomber could burst my eardrums.

While grounded, I learned as much as I could about how I might photograph the inside of a bomber. The Signal Corps loaned me a K-20 camera. This was an Army Air Force camera made of rigid metal meant to withstand the vibrations of a plane. The K-20 had a high-speed shutter mounted on a cone to protect the lens, even when the camera was nose down on a flat surface for loading. It was a heavy camera to work with—eleven-pounds—and it took some getting used to. I was warned that the film lever might stiffen and could freeze in 40-below-zero temperatures at high altitudes, but it operated nicely even at temperatures below plus-20 degrees Fahrenheit.

I was given high-altitude clothes consisting of fleece-lined leather overalls, a jacket, leggings, and boots that were quite weighty. A good photographer never wears gloves, but I was given electric mittens and was warned not to take them off once we rose above 15,000 feet or I could lose my fingers. All this talk about freezing when we were going to fly over the Sahara Desert was hard for me to comprehend.

At the end of two weeks and with no more flu symptoms, I was cleared to fly and attended a dress rehearsal with the crew. The shiny B-17 was massive on the outside, but inside it was cramped and small, and stuffed with equipment and men. We sweltered in our high-altitude, cumbersome flying outfits. I practiced dragging my cameras around the narrow confines of the plane. One of the crew members told me that my energy would be depleted in the rarefied atmosphere and my clothes and camera equipment would seem even heavier. *Damn*, I thought, and continued to lug my equipment through the honeycomb of compartments.

I searched for places I could effectively squeeze in and out of to take shots. My large press camera would work well to show crew members in action at their posts. I practiced holding the K-20 camera on its fixed handle, keeping my elbows close to my chest for support and to prevent any part of it from contacting the plane, lest the pictures would be blurred by the vibrations.

One of the crew members, Sgt. Jake, showed me how to plug into the permanent oxygen line and how to use a portable bottle of oxygen. This would give me a few minutes of "roving" time around the plane. It was critical to master the use of oxygen; if I made a mistake, I would only survive for about four minutes without it.

Sgt. Jake was quite a looker with his boyish cleft chin and muscular shoulders. He pointed out the best viewpoint for taking pictures, which was the large, left waist window. It would be the perfect space to work in during the crucial point of the mission, when we flew the bombing run over the target. Like everywhere else on board, it was filled with machine guns and other equipment, and I would have to photograph around it all to get the best shots. But I was up for the challenge and my excitement grew.

The next day, everyone attended a secret preflight briefing. Briefings took place within minutes of departure. The commanding officer removed coverings from maps and charts on the wall and traced our flight plan. Our target goal was to destroy the El Aouina airfield in Tunis, North Africa, which was used by the Germans to ferry troops from Sicily.

With clear skies promising good visibility, we boarded the B-17. As the engines roared and the plane ascended, I clutched the handle of the K-20 camera until my hand throbbed. As the plane leveled off, small, puffy cumulus clouds drifted by my window. I relaxed my grip and smiled. I had achieved my goal of being the first woman on a bombing run!

The bombardier disappeared into the bomb bay to remove safety pins that were installed to keep the bombs from exploding in case we were shot down or crash-landed. This intrigued me, so I followed him into the black, cave-like bay and wiggled between the rows of bombs. As my eyes became accustomed to the dim light, I could see the bomb racks stacked as neatly as bookshelves in a library. The bombardier pulled the safety devices out of the bombs and stuck a few of them in his cap for souvenirs.

As I steadied myself against a stack of bombs, the plane jolted unexpectedly. I dropped a flashbulb and it shattered with a loud pop.

On the interphone strapped to my ears, I heard the bombardier scream, "Jesus Christ! What was that?"

I shouted back, "Sorry! It was just a flashbulb."

The crew laughed. Our communications were all connected and they could hear every word.

I took many photographs of the crew at their posts before I had to don my clumsy electric gloves at 15,000 feet. Gloves are never a photographer's friend, no matter how cold it is, but I certainly did not want to lose my fingers.

Soon we were near the Tunis lagoon and the planes got into formation. Over the Sahara Desert, I saw enemy Junker planes flying over us so close that I could see the swastikas painted on the sides, just like the pilot back at base had said. I became absorbed in where to be, how to use the oxygen, and working my new cameras. Never once did it occur to me that I was on a possible deadly mission. As with all the theaters of war I had been in, there was always the possibility of death, but the only way to survive was to push my fears far back in my mind, keep to the task at hand, and not worry or look too far ahead.

I was aboard the lead bomber of 32 B-17 Flying Fortresses. Our formation swung into the bomb run and grouped into position to drop bombs in a pattern on the target. Sgt. Jake was quite close to me in the tight space. In an effort to capture the right photographs, I needed his help to balance myself. As I contorted my body to snap pictures, he held on to me. I instructed him, "Oh, that's just what I want. Oh! Oh! That's a beautiful angle! Roll me over, quick...nice! Hold me just like that. Hold me tighter.

Perfect!"

Raucous laughter erupted in my earphones and I gasped, realizing how this sounded—surely sexual and not photographic! I was glad my bright-red cheeks weren't visible to the crew.

Out the window, I saw fiery red flashes and white plumes of smoke rising from the ground a mile high into the sky. I took photographs of what looked like a giant black spider with its legs spread out. Then I heard explosions near our plane and jumped, realizing that it was anti-aircraft fire from the enemy, and the black trails were fragments from an exploding shell. Sweat beaded my forehead when I heard in the earphones that our wing had been hit twice, but thank God it was only slightly damaged and we made it back to base safely.

Once back on the ground, a crewmember told me they had placed bets on whether the waist gunner would knock me out to defend our plane, or I would knock him out to defend my window position. I laughed and felt my cheeks flush. I truly felt like part of the crew.

The next day, I read the reconnaissance report of our raid. Our timing had been perfect. The bomber group had partially obliterated the German airfield and our mission was a success. I also read that two of the airplanes in our formation had been shot down. My hands began to shake. I realized then that I could have been killed had I been in one of those planes. I pushed the thought aside, proud of the negatives I'd sent off to the Pentagon by Army courier pouch.

Life editors received my material and laid out a terrific story. A photo of me in my high-altitude bomber outfit, camera in hand, landed on the cover with the title: "*Life's* War Correspondent, Lieutenant Adeline Peterson, Goes Bombing." The subtitle on the cover was: "Addie the Indestructible." It was a dream come true! I found out later that some of the Army Air Force men were using the cover as a pin-up. But what thrilled me the most was being honored in a bomber outfit instead of a bathing suit.

K-20 airplane camera

B-17 Bombers formation in a bombing run

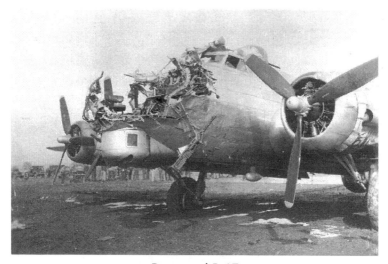

Damaged B-17

Damaged B-17

B-17 in flight

Chapter 51
Italy, June 1943

The soldiers have been wonderful, never a whimper. Always "Yes, Sir," even with their last breath. It is the amazing courage of these boys that spurs us on. We can't sell them short. They must always be our prime consideration.

— Alfred Hurwitz, MD

I put in a request to go to Italy to report on the war there. As a war correspondent, I could request a specific assignment but it was subject to Army approval from the office of the commanding general.

Transportation was free but sometimes I had to "hitchhike." This meant hanging around the military airport waiting to see if an aircraft had room and was going where I had orders to go. The other consideration was whether it had room for all of my equipment, which included cameras and supplies, a bedroll, two uniforms, and my handy Royal typewriter.

I heard there was significant rainfall in Italy and wanted to be prepared. The weight of the supplies was only 250 pounds — far better than the 600 pounds I had sent to Czechoslovakia. My clothes were the allotted fifty-five pounds for airplane travelers in war zones. I had to have both summer and winter uniforms, which included skirts, pants, heavy field clothes, boots, and wool underwear.

The editor of *Life* enclosed a note asking me to cover the Army Air Forces in the air as well as on the ground. It seemed that the airmen were always glamorized and not enough attention was given to the men on the ground, who were just as important to the war effort. He informed me that the ban had been lifted on photographing dead or wounded soldiers and that though unpleasant, these photographs were essential, as sometimes words were not enough to describe the devastation. I was glad about the ban having ended. I had photographed many dead and wounded in the past, only to have it all censored and discarded.

As I waited for transportation at the El Aouina airport in Tunis, North Africa for transport to Naples, Italy, I noticed that it was being restored by our allies, who had taken it over after the bombing. I reread the papers that I was to carry on me at all times.

Travel orders: Adeline Peterson, Lt., Army Air Forces, Photographer

1. *Take available military transport from North Africa to Italy, to such places within the Theater as may be necessary for the accomplishment of the mission.*
2. *Travel by military aircraft is authorized, rations in kind will be provided.*

By command of General D. Eisenhower

The second letter stated:

The bearer of this letter, Lieutenant Adeline Peterson, has been specially assigned by the War Department for the particular purpose of preparing a photographic record of military activities.

Lt. Peterson's reputation as a photographer more than justifies a request on my part that she be given every facility, opportunity for viewing and photographing activities without regard to censorship, which will be exercised by proper authorities at the completion of her mission.

Please provide Lieutenant Peterson with any necessary air or ground transportation in order that her mission may be accomplished as promptly as practicable.

Major General Johnson, USA
Deputy Theater Commander

I kept the precious documents in the pocket of my military blouse.

As I looked around the airport, I noticed massive amounts of debris from Nazi planes scattered about. I had photographed this airport being bombed from the Flying Fortress, and now our Air Forces had taken it over. I walked around where I could. I came upon a graveyard marked with black swastikas painted on scraps of wood. I looked closely and saw the date: January 22, 1943 — the same day as the bombing. It took my breath away. I couldn't help but feel a deep sadness. By now I had been involved in a great deal of the war, and I began to have a deep, personal worry about every country I had visited. My second concern was what America was doing to ensure peace in the future. I vowed to myself that while I was in Italy, I would carry around a small notebook and listen to people more before hiding behind my camera. I would keep my ears open and become more empathetic and compassionate. Maybe I could make a difference in Italy.

I hitched a flight to Italy. An officer of the army engineers was contacted that I was to arrive. A sergeant drove me in a jeep to a monastery in Naples where I would stay. It was a hidden gem behind a huge ancient stone wall. Apparently, the officer had convinced the Father Superior to put me up in this 14th-century Italian monastery. The frescoed, magnificent high ceilings gave me a lofty, spiritual feeling as a small black-robed monk carried my equipment to my room. We passed lovely, rose-patterned, elongated stained glass windows. My "room" was an empty, austere cell. It was one of 200 cells that housed this religious order of monks. It was so tiny the monk had to use a second cell to store my equipment.

At dinnertime, I met the KP monk, Fr. Marco. He was a short, fat man in a frock who worked in the old stone kitchen. He turned out to be a marvelous cook and I was fortunate to share meals with the monks living there — well over fifty of them. Dinner was big wooden bowls filled with pasta, spinach, and tomato sauce topped with garlic. Late that night, when we had all retired to our cells, I heard the monks visiting with each other, chatting and laughing loudly, just like schoolboys in a boarding school.

The next day, after a simple breakfast, I was picked up by a pilot and got to fly in a Piper Cub to some of the war-torn areas. The last time I had been on a plane was in the Jenny, when I had flown over the Dustbowl. This plane was half the Curtiss Jenny's size and felt like a birdcage, allowing easy viewing of the earth as well as the sky. It was a rich delight for my eyes as a photographer.

I rode in the observer's seat with Captain Bruce from the Grasshopper Squadron. He was from Idaho and was quite enjoyable to be with. His main job was to search for a "screaming meemie," which was a German mortar that had been harassing our troops. The Piper Cub was unarmed for superior lightness and maneuverability, but unfortunately, it was highly flammable because it was made of canvas. The Cubs were used to scout out enemy artillery from the sky, then radio back the gun positions to the ground crews so they could fire at the enemy.

While we flew over the destruction, Captain Bruce told me that all the Cub pilots were called "grasshopper pilots" and were the eyes of the artillery. The Piper Cubs arrived in Italy in packing crates from America and the pilots had to assemble them themselves and do their own test flights. The Cubs were also used to deliver rations to soldiers who were hard to reach in the summit area of a 4,000-foot-high mountain.

We flew over enemy lines into the hills surrounding the Cassino Valley. I photographed Italian people going through the rubble of their destroyed houses. I had seen this before, during the war in the Soviet Union, but it still made me sad. This area was called the "Purple Heart Valley" because so many soldiers had been wounded or killed there. I saw thousands of shell holes and many bridges that had been blown apart.

Captain Bruce explained that during the first day of the North African invasion, three Piper Cub observation planes had taken off from an aircraft carrier headed toward the mainland at an altitude of 600 feet, and were fired on by US Navy vessels who thought they were enemy planes. Then they flew over a nearby beach and were fired on by infantry troops. Two landed safely, but the third was shot down.

"How horrible!" I couldn't help it—I thought of Bill and tears streaked down my cheeks. Through sniffles, I explained that my fiancé had been killed off the north coast of New Guinea by "friendly fire."

The pilot took a while to react to what I said. "You are young as well as beautiful," he said sympathetically in a quiet voice. "Surely you will marry someone else."

I noticed he wore a wedding ring, and was about to protest, when he suddenly yelled, "Watch out! Now we're in Jerry territory."

He spotted the screaming meemie camouflaged in the bushes below and radioed the location back to the artillery gun crew. The pilot looked at his watch as I brushed my tears away and grabbed the right camera lens. Below us, on the valley floor, it looked like white popcorn bursting and scattering about. Instantly, a Long Tom shot at the enemy mortar and I saw bursts of black smoke from the destroyed screaming meemie.

Without warning, Captain Bruce went into the steepest dive I had ever experienced. I saw a group of four Focke-Wulf German fighters. Luckily, we were right below the treetops and our small Piper Cub was able to maneuver back to the airstrip and land safely.

Captain Bruce beamed with pride. "Mission accomplished," he said as he reached out to help me out of the plane.

I asked to be taken to the hospitals so I could cover the ground action of the war, as my editor had requested. The 21st Evacuation Hospital had over a hundred tents set up with over 700 cots, and was located behind Mignano near the hills bordering Cassino Valley. The hospital had a staff of over 300. I went to photograph the doctors and nurses, who were situated in tents with red crosses on them, only five miles from the front line. I had been in many hospitals through many wars and knew this was one of the best places for news coverage.

As soon as I arrived, a loud whooshing sound roared overhead and all the staff dropped to the ground. I followed suit. The sound came screaming toward us again and the mess tent next to us was hit. I gathered up my equipment and went outside to see the shell. Only a round crater remained. There were cans of food blown all over the place. The operating tent was fine, but there was no electricity because it had been wired with the mess tent. The surgeons now had to operate by the light of hand-held flashlights.

Every time a German shell rumbled over the makeshift hospital, we all fell to the ground. Changing surgical gloves, disinfecting surgical sites, and the sterilization of instruments had to be done over and over, each time it happened. The wounded were brought in frequently. The hospital was running short on blood and oxygen. I photographed members of the gun crew, who came in to donate blood whenever they could.

I watched as one of the surgeons placed a tube in the throat of a young soldier who lay on the operating table. I shot an image of his gentle, skillful movements as he worked to save the soldier from drowning in his own blood. It was getting harder and harder for me to take photographs in the midst of that much suffering.

The operating doctor must have sensed my nervousness. He glanced up at me. "Go right ahead and take pictures. It's not a pretty sight, but war is no pink tea party and I know it's important for the people back home to see what things over here are really like."

I gave a quick nod of appreciation. He calmed me right down and I continued photographing.

The attending nurse told me that the soldier had been brought in earlier that morning with a hole in his throat and wounds in his stomach. His injuries were caused by a shell that had destroyed one of the bridges where he and his companions were catching a little sleep. The surgeon siphoned blood from the patient's lungs through a metal tracheotomy tube and the soldier's own blood was being returned to him through an IV line. His windpipe had been broken and he was breathing through the hole in his throat.

I watched closely as the surgeon operated in his white cap and gown juxtaposed by his muddy boots. There was a card, like a baggage-check tag, pinned to the patient's arm, detailing when he was picked up by the medical corps, what they had done, and when they had brought him to the receiving tent of the evacuation hospital.

When the gentle surgeon was done, he said, "You can talk now, son. You'll be fine."

The soldier murmured, "I'm thirsty."

The doctor took a small sponge and put it on his lips to moisten them.

I was filled with worry. "Will he recover?"

The surgeon replied, "Oh, yes, he'll recover all right. He'll be as good as new."

Next, a soldier was brought in whose thighs were nearly severed by a shell blast. He had lost so much blood that he was getting a transfusion in both arms. He asked for a cigarette, then a piece of pie, and told the nurse, "Cover up my feet, I'm freezing."

She threw another blanket on him. As she did, he passed away in front of my eyes. As the nurse pulled the blanket over his face, she said to me, "They always seem to ask for their favorite food right before they die."

I felt honored to be with these amazing doctors and nurses, who had to push aside the sound of shells rocketing overhead while they tended to the injured. I felt good that I too had an important job to do — to portray the reality of war. Now that photographs of the wounded and dead were allowed by the censors, it would help the folks back home realize the important sacrifices being made for the war effort. I was capturing dramatic pictures to send off to *Life*, like one of a rifle on a boy's crushed leg being used as a splint.

As I observed the surgeon absorbed in his work, I became equally absorbed in mine, watching death occur at close range before my eyes over and over.

There was plenty of Italian mud everywhere, and mud was the nurses' enemy as it increased the chances of infection. The nurses had to build small dams and mud banks to keep the floor of the hospital tent from flooding in the rain. They made sure the tent pegs were tight to keep the tents from blowing away in the windstorms. I was lucky to be staying in the dry monastery, which was right near the hospital.

The next morning, I was surprised as I watched the nurses washing up using water in their helmets. One nurse noticed my interest and explained the proper way to bathe using a helmet.

"First you put the helmet on an empty ration can, put water in, get the water soapy, wash your body, but keep your boots on and do your feet last."

In the nurses' tent, I saw the items they had collected to make it more like a home, including an Arabian rug from Tunis and a full-length, gilded mirror from a bombed-out palace.

Lieutenant Sally Green was in charge of sixty nurses. I interviewed her as she carried several pairs of muddy boots through camp. She explained, "I think my girls might feel better if I washed their boots. Maybe they'll stop crying."

"Why are they crying?"

"I'm not sure. I've asked them and they won't say. I call it fatigue neurosis and I think they just can't help it. I've noticed that they only cry when the work is the lightest. When we get a bunch of wounded, they come out of it. They smile and tell jokes and get right to work."

I opened my mouth to reply, then shut it, deciding to keep my thoughts to myself as the lieutenant hurried to the nurses. This was exactly how I felt. I worked as much as possible to prevent myself from grieving over Bill. These brave young women had an incredible amount of stamina to get through this dreadful war. I had nothing but admiration for them all.

Italy

Chapter 52
The Purple Heart Valley, Italy

They seemed terribly pathetic to me. They weren't warriors. They were American boys who by mere chance of fate had wound up with guns in their hands, sneaking up a death-laden street in a strange and shattered city in a faraway country in a driving rain. They were afraid, but it was beyond their power to quit... And even though they weren't warriors born to the kill, they won their battles. That's the point.

— Ernie Pyle, War Correspondent

Colonel Avery, an engineering officer, took me back to Purple Heart Valley. He was as large as my Bill and just as handsome. Being with him made me feel heartsick. Bouncing in a US Army jeep, we wound our way through the rugged terrain of the peaks of the Colli Pass. We came to what the engineer said was "Hot Spot Bridge" — named as such because six of our engineers had been killed there.

When we got out of the jeep, he said, "Always place your feet in a jeep tract or in footprints; never step into the road or you could land on a German mine and be killed instantly."

I smiled at the memory of my panic after stepping on a "mine" of moldy bread when I was with Bill in the USSR.

After gingerly getting out of the jeep, I took a few photos of the Colli Pass and the valley below. As soon as I got back in, the colonel sped off down the road and around a curve. We passed by soldiers in ditches, crouching behind big rocks, and lying flat on the ground. There were deserted trucks everywhere abandoned alongside the road. A shell sailed by with a whizzing noise. I let out a gasp. The colonel kept driving.

When it was quiet, the colonel decided to stop. We hid behind a boulder and I took a rapid succession of photographs as an abandoned truck's gas tank burst into flames, then its ammunition exploded, sending orange-yellow smoke rising up over the valley.

When we heard another scream from an airburst, the colonel grabbed my arm and we jumped into a ditch. He held my arm for a moment as we crouched, heads tucked. He listened, then said, "You can stand up now for just a second, shoot only one photo, then duck down fast before the next one comes."

I did exactly as he said and was happy that Colonel Avery was helping me with my photography. He began to count, his eyes on his watch. "That was twenty rounds in seven minutes."

We heard another whooshing sound overhead. The shells were flying directly above us. After another few minutes, we saw a Piper Cub flying over our location.

"Now we can leave," the colonel said. "The Germans won't want the Cub to spot their gun positions. Those Jerries are after that Bailey bridge because it carries all of our supplies."

We climbed out of the ditch and dashed to our jeep, then sped toward the base of the mountain. The shelling started again. It sounded like the piercing, wailing sound of a baby crying as the shells sailed through the gorge. I looked back and broke into a sweat when I saw shells falling on the road right where we had been parked only moments before.

Colonel Avery remarked, "That Piper Cub saved our lives!"

We parked the jeep behind a hill and waited. *Are we going to make it back?* I worried as we again sat motionless and listened. *I must be crazy to be in the middle of a dangerous war like this.* I was determined not to let my nerves get the best of me.

After complete silence for over thirty minutes, I put on the bravest voice I could muster. "Is it safe to go now?"

The colonel nodded. "It's now or never." He drove over the Bailey bridge as fast as he could.

As we drove, I spotted two soldiers sleeping alongside the bridge. How could they sleep through all of the shelling? I steadied my lens as we drove, hoping to get a good shot of them. After focusing, I saw that one soldier had half of his head missing. I dropped my camera into my lap and felt my stomach pushing at my throat. They were *dead*, not sleeping! I hugged myself in an attempt to hide my sudden, uncontrollable shaking from Colonel

Avery.

It was totally dark when we reached the Engineers' Command Post. We found out that the Germans had managed to land only one shell on one corner of the bridge, and our engineers were able to patch it so that the crucial supply traffic could continue to flow to the troops.

I felt relieved when I was back in town and walking back to my safe cell in the monastery. There was a big difference between being bombed on the ground and being bombed in the large B-17 in the air. Being bombed on the ground felt far less safe. Even though Colonel Avery tried to reassure me that we were a very small target in the mountains and would be hard to hit, I was not entirely sure that I believed him.

A week passed before I got my courage back and went off on Highway Six with the colonel to a German-held mountain. We drove past tanks and mules hidden under olive trees. Soldiers hid in caves and ravines. I saw hand-lettered signs that read: *Warning: Mines not cleared beyond road shoulders.*

My Rolleiflex hung from my neck and a Speed Graphic with a telephoto lens rode on my knees, always ready for action. As we drove along, I would check the apertures and shutter settings to conform to the changing light values. My pockets bulged with extra film and film packs.

I snapped a shot of medical corpsmen, who wore helmets with red crosses on them. It was their job to bring the wounded back from the front. Soldiers filled every ravine, watching and waiting. Heavy machinery and artillery were tucked behind the olive groves, out of sight of the enemy.

Telephone wires were draped over rocks like cobwebs. The Signal Corps carried their communications lines forward while under shell fire. The telephone had become a major military weapon. It was fascinating photographing packs of mules with reels of telephone wire strapped to their backs. Other hardworking mules carried rifles and entrenching tools.

Colonel Avery pulled over so I could capture images of the working mules. I got out just as the rain began to come down in heavy torrents. I was still determined to take photographs, so I tugged the hood of my trench coat over my helmet and tried to use flashbulbs to hopefully brighten the pictures.

The colonel shouted, "Get in! We need to find somewhere to go until the rain lets up."

I got back into the jeep, glad he had put the canvas top up to protect us, as well as my equipment, from the sudden deluge.

As we rode along in the jeep, Colonel Avery told me, "The Germans are on the other side of this hill. This war is just like the Indian wars of concealment. The man who stays out of sight the most is the one who lives the longest. It's a game of hiding."

When we came upon a cave, we parked the jeep and ran inside to escape the bad weather. Much to my surprise, there were several soldiers already there, playing cards by the light of a lantern. I stood there in my GI boots, uniform trousers, and dripping trench coat with my helmet on.

"Gee whiz! It's a dame!" one of the soldiers exclaimed.

Apparently, they hadn't seen a woman in over three months.

I had fun taking photos in the cave of the boys playing poker.

"What are you writing on those shells?" I asked one of the infantrymen.

"Whenever the Jerries fire and we lose a man, we write the man's name on the next shell we fire at them," a soldier grinned.

Inside the large cave was a small oil stove, which was used to heat up a few cans of food. The soldiers shared their sparse supper with us. Colonel Avery had brought a little portable radio and we heard a German propaganda broadcast interspersed with swing music. The Germans had made recordings of *Pistol-Packin' Mama* and beamed it from Berlin.

The rain continued so we spent the night in the cave. The colonel insisted on giving me the only blanket he had and toughed it out without one. He woke me at dawn to have a cup of hot coffee with the soldiers.

Colonel Avery looked at me. "You're closer to the front than any girl has ever been. We're now ahead of most of the infantry. Do you still want to go farther?"

"Yes, I do, sir."

The soldiers said sad goodbyes to me as we left. As the colonel drove, I took a photo of the remnants of a jeep that had been blown off the road, along with the rain-soaked body of an Italian civilian beside it.

"In only a thousand yards we might see the Krauts," the colonel yelled over the sound of the drumming rain on the canvas top of the jeep.

I saw German uniforms in the distance and screwed on my telephoto lens. "Can I take a photograph here?"

"Yes, but you will have to take it after I turn the jeep around. We go in backwards, in case we need to get out of there fast."

The rain came down harder.

"Can I use a flashbulb?"

"Go ahead, but make it quick."

I was only able to get one shot of the Germans, who were crouched down in the grass. The flash drew attention to us and one of the Germans stood up, brandishing his weapon.

"God damn it," Colonel Avery cursed as he threw the jeep into gear.

The tires spun, splashing mud all over the road and making a terrible noise as the jeep swayed wildly from side to side. I looked back at the Germans. Now a group of them were standing and looking in our direction. My eyes got bigger and bigger as I sweated over whether we would get out of there before we were shot. Finally, we caught traction and sped away.

As we got farther away from enemy observation, I said meekly, "I'm sorry to have put us in danger, sir."

The usually friendly colonel grumbled something incoherent and stepped on the accelerator.

On our way back, the rain let up. Just ahead was a gun crew with a Long Tom, which I found out was a 155mm field cannon.

I was surprised when Colonel Avery stopped, parked, and said, "Aren't you going to get a picture of the Long Tom?"

I scrambled out of the jeep. One soldier looked me over and stared at my camera equipment; another greeted me and handed me cotton for my ears. Each time they fired the cannon, the whole crew turned away from the flash, shut their eyes tight, put their fingers in their ears, and opened their mouths wide to protect their eardrums. I copied this action, astonished at the tremendous blast I heard even with the cotton in my ears.

Now the whole valley was filled with our shells.

"Load! Ready! Fire!" the gun crew yelled before firing each round.

They moved forward toward the enemy. The cannon boomed again. I tried to catch a photo at the exact instant of firing. I ran to follow them forward and heard the colonel shout, "Watch for land mines!"

I looked down now for any mine stakes. When I got to the crew, I changed film and reset the camera for the next firing of the cannon.

It was difficult for me to work my camera and remember to keep my mouth open. I was a bit worried about my eardrums but the photograph of the Long Tom and the crew's faces was going to be sensational.

I returned to the jeep and Colonel Avery took off. The jeep pitched over the muddy, disintegrating roads on the long drive back to the monastery. It was difficult to write down the captions for my photographs, or remarks I remembered from the GIs in the cave, as the jeep ride was too rough. I gave up and shot photographs of the engineers rebuilding an entire Bailey bridge, which would take several hours, while still under fire from Germans hidden among the highest of peaks of the mountain.

We passed crowds of Italian families carrying mattresses, chairs, household goods, and babies, and being followed by children who were too large to carry. Colonel Avery stopped the jeep and handed out hard candies to as many children as he could. He gave a pack of lifesavers to a sad young mother with five children following her. The mother's face filled with joy when she received the candy. I beamed at the colonel and took a terrific photo of the event. I was happy to experience this gruff man showing his sweeter side.

In the mountains of the Cassino region, the rain came down in torrents once again and several of my lenses for the Rolleiflex camera stopped working because of dampness getting between the shutter leaves. My speed gun batteries were wearing out and my flashbulbs weren't working. I kept fiddling with my equipment as the colonel raced along. I would have to use only my Graflex now. I smiled to myself, feeling fortunate that Colonel Avery had a great respect for my job as a photographer.

Around the next bend was a group of Negro soldiers stacking ammo to be carried to the front.

"Please stop, sir," I said. "I must get a shot of these soldiers."

The colonel snarled at me and kept going. I wanted to take photographs of these brave young men, especially the Negro captain, and was disappointed that the colonel didn't stop.

As we sped further away, the colonel said, "It squeezes my heart in two to see a nigger wearing an officer's uniform."

I gaped at him. Was he serious? How could this be the same kind man who seemed distressed at seeing families leaving their homes and giving out candy to all the poor children? I had heard how hard it was for a Negro to enter Officers' Candidate School. I had seen Negro troops in North Africa, also transporting and handling munitions. There was very little opportunity for this race in the United States when we badly needed their help.

With courage, and in a quiet voice, I said, "The Negro race has been helping us win the war. Have you heard of the 99th Pursuit squadron here in Italy? Our White pilots in the bombers could not have succeeded without them leading the way in their Pursuits."

Colonel Avery gave me a cold glare as we continued on our way. I became lost in thought and prayed that my words might sway him from his prejudice.

We traveled over the winding roads of the mountains. I pointed at a cave. "I think there's a family living in there."

The colonel stopped this time. I photographed a woman with two babies, sitting in the cave and trying to make do with very little.

Colonel Avery asked her a question in Italian.

She replied that there were many families living in caves, and had been for over a year now, waiting for the end of the war so they could go back home. I told the colonel that I had seen British families living in caves in England during the Blitz. He looked quite surprised.

We got back to Naples late that night. I climbed onto my narrow cot in my cell. I was still wound-up after being at the front, but wanted to read. I read with a flashlight under my covers in observance of the blackout law. I tried to read *History of Firearms,* which Colonel Avery had given me, but ended up reading one of my mystery novels instead. Finally, I fell asleep amid the sound of intermittent artillery fire.

Naples was captured by the United States Fifth Army five months after I arrived in Italy. Germany had blown up everything in the harbor before they withdrew. They even bombed the city water system. I took photos of the sunken ships in the harbor. In the city, I captured pictures of demolished buildings, and hungry children climbing through the rubble and picking through everything. There was no electricity and it could not be turned on until the mines were cleared. The infantrymen were returning from the mountains in Cassino and I photographed them as well. Their tired, unshaven faces and blank, staring eyes made them look like the living dead.

In October, the air raids lessened as Naples became more crowded and the atmosphere was lighter. An officers' nightclub opened in the large wood-paneled board-of-directors room in the Bank of Naples. The president of the bank, a Mussolini supporter, was now in prison.

Though it seemed odd in the midst of the devastation of war, the thought of going to a social event lifted my spirits. At the bottom of my duffel bag, I found the only dress heels I had, along with a navy-blue crepe outfit with a cream sash and fitted shoulders. Silk stockings were nowhere to be found but I was able to buy a pair of gloves to match my wrinkled dress.

The nightclub was crowded with British soldiers, French officers, and GIs. The women were mostly Red Cross girls, WACs, and nurses. The walls of the club were decorated with VD posters. I had heard that there were prostitutes who were paid by enemy agents to infiltrate our soldiers.

Boys outnumbered the girls and I danced my heart out with joy, escaping the dreadful war, if only for a few precious hours. It was wonderful to see the nurses I had photographed in the hospital tents joyfully jitterbugging around the crowded dance floor.

Before I left for home, I went to the hospital to interview as many of our soldiers as I could. It was incredible hearing them speak of how much they appreciated America, and how they felt more patriotic after fighting. Many told me they had joined the US Army to get a free college education and looked forward to the fifty dollars a month for expenses and textbooks they would receive to help them better their lives.

One freckled-faced soldier told me, "I left my home and gave up a good-paying job to serve my country. I'm ready to go back now and buy a house, a car, and raise a family."

His buddy interrupted, "I'm going to the automat and eat as many desserts and as much meat as I can."

Another bandaged GI asked if I could take four dollars and buy a dozen roses for his girl when I returned to the States. "Can you call her and tell her I'm alive, then go and give her the roses?" He handed me the money and wrote down her phone number.

My list of soldiers was huge. They gave me messages with phone numbers and the addresses of their wives, mothers, and girlfriends.

The last soldier I interviewed and took photographs of told me, "I almost kicked the bucket but I'll make it. One of my arms is paralyzed but I can still eat! I'm goin' home to see my mom and girlfriend and I can't wait to kiss them both."

During my last week in Naples, I spent time getting all my film in order and wrote reports to send to the censors. I now had over three hundred action-packed photographs. I kept aside the small notebook of the soldier's addresses.

The next afternoon, after a savory lunch with the monks, I went to Colonel Avery's tent to give him my rolls of film. He would send them to the press censor in Rome in two official, big red Army pouches, then they would be delivered to the Naples airport to be flown to Washington.

As Colonel Avery took all my film, he said, "I bet you're ready to get back to the good ol' USA."

I answered, "Well, being a war correspondent has been my life. When I go home, I'm always afraid I'll miss something. I can't seem to stay there for very long."

The colonel stood up and touched my shoulder. "You were

very lucky, Adeline, to come back from the front lines without a mark. You must've had a lucky rabbit's foot in your camera case. Good luck to you, Lieutenant Peterson. Let's hope the war ends soon."

We shook hands and I left his tent thinking how proud I was of my accomplishments. I was still slightly distressed at having missed the opportunity to photograph the hardworking Negro troops, but there was nothing I could do about it.

Mr. Wilson Hicks called me to the Time & Life building a week after I returned home. He greeted me warmly. "Lieutenant Peterson, you are looking quite well after being on the front lines in Italy. I'm afraid I have some bad news."

Startled, I said, "Good God, have I done something wrong?" I sat up taller.

Mr. Hicks scratched his thinning hair, trying to find the right words. "A whole package of film has been lost from your Italy trip. You told me that you sent two, right?"

"Yes, the films were divided into two pouches. Which one was it?" I hoped it wasn't the aerial shots from the Piper Cub.

"I know one package of photographs arrived safely at the Pentagon in the military pouch. I don't know yet where the other one is. Maybe one disappeared from the censor's desk."

"I could never redo the photographs I shot there. You must authorize me to go to Washington to lead a search for the package." My voice rose in a high pitch.

After much pleading, Mr. Hicks loaned me his car and I took off for Washington.

The small, beady-eyed, censor handed me the single pouch. Under guard, I searched the censor's desk and even the darkroom. Nothing turned up.

Frantic, I yelled, "Where is my second pouch?"

The censor said with sarcasm, "Anything can happen here in the Pentagon."

I was furious. "You know, there's a war going on and I'm the one who brings the reality of it back to America."

I looked inside the one pouch. It contained all the aerial shots. The missing military pouch held the photographs I had taken of the ground war.

On the drive home, I gripped the steering wheel so hard my knuckles bulged. All my photographs of the Long Tom, the families and soldiers in the caves, and the close-up of the Nazis—gone!

Mr. Hicks let me contact the Army Press Headquarters in Rome. I was told that both military pouches had gone by courier jeep between Rome and the Naples airport.

"How could a big red pouch go missing between two large cities?" I screamed into the phone.

The office worker mumbled, "Sorry," and hung up on me.

Back in my hotel room, I paced the floor. *I can never go back and retake those missing photograph,* I thought, still enraged. I became lost in the memory of the families and soldiers in the caves, the Long Tom bombings, and pictures with the American soldiers and nurses at the dance. All were gone. Only the aerial photographs had been received.

My only consolation was that I still had my small notebook. Thank God, I had written the names and hometowns of the soldiers I had met at the hospital. Also, there were little cryptic notes I had jotted down about the bombings and caves. I could only hope that *Life* would print a story without photographs. It would have to do.

Wounded in Italy

Howitzer in Italy

Chapter 53
Normandy, France
D-Day Invasion
June 6, 1944

Your task will not be an easy one. Your enemy is well trained, well equipped and battle hardened. He will fight savagely.
— General Dwight Eisenhower, June 6, 1944

World War II now encompassed five continents, seven seas, and over a dozen fronts. After a short respite in the States, I was assigned to go to London, where there were over 500 accredited journalists and photographers waiting for orders to witness the Allied invasion of German-occupied Normandy, France. Our men had been preparing for the invasion for over two years now, and it was common knowledge for the Allies when the amphibious landing would occur. By June there were over 2.5 million troops in Britain waiting to cross the English Channel to Normandy.

The war correspondents, when not staying at various hotels, hung around the Ministry of Information headquarters at the University of London. This was a department responsible for publicity. The world's press was watching the clock and waiting with apprehension for the go-ahead to proceed to the English Channel to report on D-Day.

On June 5, General Eisenhower's planned invasion was delayed when a storm with high winds occurred. The sea invasion was postponed, causing further anxiety among the reporters.

Very early on the cold morning of June 6, I went outside my hotel room and saw that the sky was almost black with our bombers heading to the coast. The weather had cleared. I'd had enough of this waiting and was determined to scoop everyone and be the first reporter to go to Normandy. I hired a driver to take me to Portsmouth, which was right on the English Channel. During the three-hour drive, the driver was quiet, which gave me time to formulate a plan. I had him drop me off at a dock where there was an anchored ship.

As I walked down the dock in my uniform with my cumbersome duffle bag slung over my shoulder, I was stopped by a military policeman who asked me where I was going. I pointed to the white ship with a large red cross painted on its hull and thought fast, saying that I was on assignment to interview the nurses. I was able to show him my papers from the Deputy Theater Commander giving me the authority to photograph military activities, even though it had been issued a year ago for my trip to Italy.

When I got to the ship, I snuck on board and locked myself in one of the bathrooms. I waited until I felt the ship move, then peeked out cautiously. I knew I shouldn't be there and that I was going against all regulations. If I got caught, I would be imprisoned because of not having the proper paperwork from the Ministry of Information in London. Though I was in the wrong, it was exhilarating.

The hospital ship was the first to cross the English Channel and was filled with American doctors and nurses. On deck, I saw airplanes roaring above, barrage balloons, and gun flashes. The explosions jolted the ship. There were thousands upon thousands of bombers flying by and C-47 planes towing Waco gliders, which were to be dropped behind the beach of Normandy with soldiers inside, ready to fight.

This was an extraordinary sight in the sky. I set up my camera, took several shots, then focused on the ocean, which was filled with enormous ships. It was breathtaking to see so many ships all at once.

My uniform gave me the authority to move about and photograph the entire invasion with no one questioning my presence. Besides, there were more important things going on than who I was or why I was there. The medical personnel were busy preparing rooms for the wounded, as well as food.

Over the next few hours, I snapped photos of our dead

soldiers, body after body. They looked like swollen blobs, floating past the ship face down in the sea. This was the second time I had experienced this scene, and it reminded me of seeing my first dead bodies while on the Dutch ship heading to Finland.

I went inside to steady my nerves and drank a cup of hot coffee, then forced myself to go back on deck. Landing craft came by on the rough seas, bringing hundreds of wounded casualties. I tried not to get in the way of the streams of stretcher-bearers carrying the wounded while I shot pictures.

I followed them inside and heard a doctor bark, "Take the dead ones back. We only have room for the living."

I photographed the doctors performing surgery in the operating room. Nurses were busy cutting off boots and jackets. Amputations were performed almost every half-hour. It was a grisly experience and once again I tried to insulate myself behind the protective lens of my camera.

I admired the entire medical staff, who remained calm and worked with a dedicated efficiency.

The corridors in the hospital were now stuffed full with wounded and dying soldiers. I interviewed one disfigured, burned young man who was brought in on a stretcher. I focused my camera on his face. "How are you feeling, soldier?"

He raised his voice as best he could. "I'm not a soldier. I'm a fucking Marine!"

I was caught off guard by his language and quickly answered, "Okay, fucking Marine, how are you holding up in the war? Please tell me so I can inform the folks back home."

I had never used that nasty word in my life, but it worked. I was relating to him on his level. He managed a little smile for me as I shot a close-up.

I had learned to look deeply into my subjects' faces to connect with them without a camera in the way. It was hard to ignore their wounds. A chaplain administered last rites to a man with a severely exposed abdominal wound. I focused on the poor boy's face and wrote down his dog tag number.

In between moaning, he managed to say, "Who ya spyin' for?"

I put down my camera. "For everyone back home, so they will appreciate what you did for our country."

He passed away right before my eyes. The chaplain pulled a blanket over his body and began to pray. I joined in, my eyes filled with tears.

On D-Day plus four, I climbed into one of the water ambulances with the stretcher-bearers. We were headed for the Normandy shore to pick up the injured. Once on shore, we walked between white, taped-off areas that signified a mine-free path to a hospital tent. I saw several dozen medical corpsmen poking with spades, excavating bodies buried in the white sand marked with sticks. Each temporary grave had a canvas bag on it with the soldier's dog tag and personal possessions. The medics would dig up a body, slip it into a bag, then carry it up the hill to be buried in a proper grave. I shot frame after frame of trucks transporting the wounded down to the beach so the Red Cross crew could unload them onto stretchers, then take them to the water ambulances. I was quite taken aback to see that many of the wounded were German soldiers and were being taken to our hospital ship to be treated, then transported to England to be prisoners of war.

Back at the hospital ship, I interviewed the soldiers about the invasion. Thousands of infantrymen had jumped too soon from their transports to get onto the beach. Many had drowned from the weight of their equipment on their backs as they found themselves up to their necks in the water. The turbulent seas made them slip in the sand, and as the waves pushed them down, many never made it to shore. Our infantrymen experienced many surprise attacks from the Germans, who fired from the cliffs to the sands below. When our tanks landed, the drivers had to drive over the dead bodies that were scattered on the beach. One wounded tank driver told me privately that it was more than he could take and he threw up most of the way.

A battered soldier who lay on a cot waiting for a blood transfusion told me that the Germans hid in the woods above the high cliffs and could go through tunnels for miles without being seen.

The hospital ship went back to England with all the patients. When we reached port, I disembarked, set up my tripod, and photographed German prisoners being brought to a prisoner-of-war camp. One of the Germans spoke to me in English, but I kept silent because the Geneva Convention did not permit war correspondents to talk to prisoners of war.

Just as I was capturing my last shot, two army officers came toward me. "We need to see your papers," one of them said.

I showed them the letter from the Deputy Theater Commander, pretending that this gave me the authority to have boarded the ship, even though I was well aware that it didn't.

"Where are your papers from the Ministry? This doesn't give you permission to be here."

I remained silent so long that they finally handcuffed me.

"You are under arrest for disobeying military orders," one of the officers said sternly, and grabbed my arm.

I was outraged and yelled, "Let me get my equipment!"

The other officer picked up my large duffle bag.

I was taken by jeep to an American nurses' training camp outside of London. I was cited for going on the hospital ship and to the Normandy beachhead without having the proper credentials to go into the war zone. They took me to the nurses' barracks, removed my handcuffs, and walked out with my duffle bag as I shouted, "Hey, I need my clothes!"

I spent the next day pacing and worrying about my film. The excitement of my perfect scoop was becoming quite dim now. Late in the afternoon, an officer came by, dropped off my bag without a word, and left. I tore it apart and saw that all my film had been confiscated. My head began to pound. I needed to calm down and try to think clearly. I searched through my coat and found a notepad containing all my notes about the invasion of Normandy.

After two weeks of stir-crazy confinement, I was sent by freighter back to New York without my film. This was a distressing loss for me, but I had, in fact, disobeyed orders. I was just mad because I had gotten caught.

When I got back, I spent time typing up all my precious stories and sent them to the Army Press, feeling confident that they were original adventures that none of the other correspondents had sent in.

I did not receive another assignment until August 19, after war correspondent Sonia Tomara's article hit the newspaper. The headline read, "PARIS IS FREE. ITS FREEDOM IS HEADY AND INTOXICATING!" I received orders to cover the liberation of France.

After four years of German occupation, over 75,000 French had been killed. Paris, at last, was liberated. The Hotel Scribe was filled with war correspondents. On the first floor of the hotel, there were rooms with tables filled with army censors, busy at work. Couriers came and went with their bags containing the latest news. Another room was set up as a mess hall with only coffee, champagne, and K-rations.

Eager to check things out, I headed toward Notre Dame Cathedral. Suddenly, a machine gun fired, spraying the pavement near my feet. I darted inside the cathedral, where families were praying for their men who had died during the German occupation of Paris. I peeked outside and saw a man behind one of the church pillars. Then a machine gun shot from the church rooftop, up and down the Seine River.

When the gunfire ceased, I ventured out and saw two German soldiers lying dead on the side of the road, and more prisoners taken under guard by our Allies. I felt nervous that perhaps the war wasn't over here in France yet and decided to go back to the hotel to join the other correspondents.

The next day, back at the Hotel Scribe, Ernest Hemingway, a war correspondent, invited everyone to a liberation party at the Ritz Hotel. It was a jubilant event with reporters toasting with brandy and champagne all night long. After this fabulous celebration, I thought maybe the war was finally over in this city after all.

In Paris, it was a photographer's visual feast to capture the French singing, cheering, hugging, and the customary kisses on each cheek. I wore my uniform with pride. Parisians wanted to shake my hand or greet me with kisses, thanking me for being an American and helping their country.

With two other correspondents, I drove a jeep around the city. The French people threw flowers into the jeep and even insisted on giving us what little fruit they had. One elderly man, who stood in the doorway of a pub, gave us a bottle of wine while everyone in the pub cheered, *"Vive la France et Vive l'Amèrique."*

The French Forces of the Interior, also known as the French Resistance, asked if we were interested in viewing the torture chambers. They showed us where the Germans had tortured the French and told us that the Germans enjoyed slow torture as a grand game. We witnessed one room where prisoners were plunged for an hour into freezing water; another where they were electrocuted. Jets of hot steam were sprayed on prisoners. At a rifle range, we saw three wooden poles that had once had live human beings attached to them by the neck. The Germans shot at them with blunt bullets, tearing their flesh. There were mass graves, and the resistance informed us that many French victims had been buried alive at these sites.

I interviewed and photographed one woman who was part of the French underground resistance, and who had survived after being tortured. She walked with a limp and moved with difficulty because her shoulders had been broken and never reset. She held out her wrists, displaying that the handcuffs had been on for so long, they had left permanent, dark-brown stains on her skin. As I photographed her body, she took off her shoes to show me that the soles of her feet had been burned and were still healing.

I asked her, "How did you get away from the Nazis?"

Her face fell. "I was released because the Germans thought I had no more information to give them."

The last place the French Resistance brought us to was the tunnels, where the Germans stole French ammunition, then kept the French as prisoners. I brushed a tear from my eye after we were told of the atrocities of the Nazis. All the horrors were difficult for the correspondents to see and hear about. We were happy for the French that the war was over for them, and that healing could begin.

372

Frenchman weeps as Germans take over France

American soldiers keep watch

Crowds of French line the Champs Élysées during liberation

American troops march down the Champs Élysées during liberation

Liberation of France—An AFPU photographer kisses a child before cheering crowds

"Liberation of France" stamp

Chapter 54
Iwo Jima, February 1945

Simply there's no way to cover war properly without risk.
— Marie Colvin, War Correspondent

I received orders in February 1945 to go to our recently acquired island of Guam. Before leaving, I read the horrific dispatches about the bombing of Iwo Jima, a well-fortified Japanese island. The body count from the first five days was over a thousand, all from the Japanese sinking ships and bombing our Marines from their fighter planes. All the reporters read the daily reports about Marines being blown up while walking, sliding, or crawling on their stomachs over the slick sand of the volcanic island. The ruthless Japanese were killing our soldiers throughout the island and the United States was losing.

I was assigned to go on a C-47 filled with nurses who would go on to Iwo Jima to care for the many wounded. It took over twenty hours to get to Guam. I felt a camaraderie being with the nurses and our patriotism bonded us together during the long journey.

Upon arriving on Guam, I went to see Major Taylor, the Army's public relations officer, for permission to go to the front lines. I wore my rumpled uniform with a helmet firmly buckled under my chin and presented my papers to him in his large tent. I watched as he looked over my precious travel orders signed by General Eisenhower, even though those only allowed me to go to Italy. But I did have the recommendation letter from the Deputy Theater Commander stating my outstanding reputation.

The tired major stared me up and down while puffing on his cigar. "The front is no place for a woman," he said flatly.

I swallowed hard and decided to agree with him. "You are right, sir. But I have been to other fronts, and as long as our men are there I need to report back home what is happening to them. People need to know what a terrible but necessary war this is."

The major stood up, all six feet of him, and repeated, "The front is no place for a woman, accredited or not. Permission denied, Lieutenant Peterson. Case closed." He handed me my papers, turned his back, and shuffled papers on his makeshift desk. I worried that perhaps he had found out about my arrest during the Normandy invasion.

I left and went to rest in the nurses' tent. I thought about a strategy for what to do next. I needed to go about this from a different angle.

The following day, I was back in the major's tent and politely yet firmly pleaded, "Sir, no one can tell the wives and mothers of these men what is happening as effectively as another woman. This is my job; the only reason I am here."

Major Taylor's face seemed to soften. "My dear girl, we don't allow female correspondents on the front because men are very gallant and will always risk their lives for a woman, which distracts them from fighting the enemy...which, as you well know, is more important."

"I understand, sir, but this is my job. I have been to many fronts and I will keep asking to go to this one." I held my hands behind me so he wouldn't see them shaking.

This time he answered in a booming voice with menacing eyes, "And I will keep denying you!"

When I got back to the nurses' tent, I saw that the nurses were getting ready to board the hospital ship. I rushed back to Major Taylor and asked if I could go with them.

He seemed to be pretty sick of seeing me and let out an exasperated huff. "You may board the USS *Samaritan*. It's a hospital ship that is being dispatched to pick up the critically wounded in Iwo Jima. If nurses go there, I suppose I must allow you to go also, but stay away from any fighting and photograph only the wounded that are brought onto the ship. Do you understand?" His cigar smoke rose into the air.

My eyes widened and I beamed, "Yes! Thank you, sir." Then I saluted him.

He remained short-tempered and growled, "Remember,

Lieutenant Peterson, you may *not* leave the ship at any time. Do you understand my orders? You may *not* leave the ship."

I replied, "Yes, Major, thank you, sir," and quickly left before he could change his mind.

It took five days to go from Guam to Iwo Jima aboard the huge, four-deck hospital ship with large red crosses painted on its white sides. On the fifth day, we were anchored a few miles from the battle on the beaches. It had already been nine days since the Marines had landed on this island.

I woke to a megaphone announcing, "A Japanese bomber has been sited! Take cover!"

While everyone else scrambled to find safety, I climbed up to the top deck of the noncombatant *USS Samaritan* to set up my camera equipment. *Hospital ships are probably never subject to enemy attack,* I told myself as I worked, but apprehensively glanced at the sky.

Suddenly, a Japanese Zeke plane flew by and dropped a bomb into the ocean only a few miles from where I was standing. I ignored the announcement of "Take cover!" Instead of following orders, I focused on the enemy plane with my 50mm telephoto lens. My hands twitched as I took a few shots. After a Navy destroyer fired anti-aircraft guns at the plane, I folded up the tripod and ran back inside the ship, shaking but happy I had gotten the photos.

The battle continued to rage and over 700 casualties boarded our ship, which was far more than it was supposed to carry. I shot the small, newly designed Higgins boats as they bounced through the giant waves, transporting the injured. Some of the wounded Marines walked onto the deck, while others had to be carried by seamen. As I set up my tripod, I had to avoid slipping in the blood on the deck. I photographed the body bags, wrinkling my nose as the stench of decomposing flesh wafted by. Many of the men were naked except for their battle dressings. It got so bad at one point that I left my camera on the tripod and ran off to retch in the toilet. Every hallway was packed with stretchers, as there weren't enough beds to accommodate the masses.

Wounds on the badly burned and gangrene cases were packed with ice. Most of the wounded were in horrible pain, but at the same time, many were extraordinarily brave. One Marine, who was covered in volcanic ash, called out as he was carried in on a stretcher, "I'm still alive! I'm so lucky!"

I had photographed the wounded in Italy but found that I would never get used to looking at human bodies that were mangled and mashed and had missing limbs. My queasiness mixed with compassion. Sometimes, when I looked through my lens, I felt like I was watching a surreal horror film. I felt confident that *Life* would accept these shocking, graphic photographs now that they were permitted by the censors. I took breaks and ran up the stairs to gulp fresh air instead of throwing up. Then I went back below deck and took light readings while walking around the many bottles of blood going into the veins of the wounded.

After a few days on board, I was proud that I had managed to not vomit for a whole day, but that night my mouth felt sore as I looked through my camera gear, reloading it and placing it between pillows to prevent shattering in case the ship was hit. I decided to get some shut-eye and rubbed my jaw. I realized I had been grinding my teeth from anxiety and was wearing my enamel down on my back molars.

One afternoon, while on the bridge of the ship, I photographed American planes flying across the sky, bombing the island and leaving fire and smoke in their wake. The volcano brightened with a fantastic display of color from the firing. War could be terrible, while at the same time, a beautiful subject to photograph. I was glad to capture it all so it could be shared with everyone back home.

I traveled back to Guam with the wounded on the *USS Samaritan*, sorry I wasn't able to go to the front line, but proud of what I had recorded. I checked in with Major Taylor and begged him to let me go back. After a few days of persistence, he let me fly into Iwo Jima with strict orders that, once I had landed, I was to go straight to the field hospital where the wounded Marines were who were not yet well enough to be transported to the hospital ships.

I flew out of Agama, Guam, at 3:00 a.m. on a C-47 evac plane. My orders stated that I was to return the same day. This would prevent me from having to spend the night with the troops. It would be a brief trip, but perhaps somehow I could get to the front line to capture some needed photographs.

Upon first seeing the island from the plane, I saw that its inactive Suribachi volcano loomed 500 feet over its surface of white ash. It was a narrow, pear-shaped volcanic-rock island heavily fortified with Japanese troops less than 700 miles from Japan. This was the closest our American troops had come to Tokyo. The Japanese were using it as a radar warning station, and it had three airfields that provided bases for its fighter interceptors. Our B-29 bombers, along with P-51 Negro fighter escorts, needed the airfields for emergency landings for any of our disabled planes headed for Tokyo.

The C-47, which I learned was called a "goony bird," had to keep circling to wait for the sniper fire to die down. The pilot went in for a landing after waiting for ten minutes of quiet. I looked out over the towering, sandy hills of volcanic ash. It looked like another planet.

After we landed, the pilot yelled, "Run as fast as you can to that hospital tent over there." He pointed.

I grabbed my bulky, twenty-pound camera bag and got out of the plane as fast as I could. Once on the ground, my feet sank into the deep, ashy earth. It was no easy task to run to the three-tent hospital, but gunfire blasted in the distance and fueled my steps.

Inside the hospital tent, surgeons used upended crates for operating tables, and nurses held flashlights for them so they could see.

After introducing myself, I set up my equipment immediately, knowing that my time was short. I took a photograph of a Marine with a mutilated leg that was about to be amputated. Much to my surprise, he reached down to his side and pulled out a long, double-edged trench knife. I immediately backed away from my tripod and camera.

He asked in a weak voice, "Where are you going? I'm giving this to you. You'll need it out there to defend yourself. Take it!" His voice rose, then he mumbled, "I won't need it where I'm going..."

I stepped closer to him, looked into his tearful eyes, and reluctantly took the weapon. I patted his hand. "Thank you."

I gathered my gear and went outside to get a long-shot angle of the hospital tents. I attempted to climb up a sandy ridge, which was no easy task with a twelve-pound tripod and an eight-pound camera. I pawed my way up a slippery ridge over thirteen feet high. When I reached the top, I heard voices and dropped down flat, trying to ascertain whether it was the Japanese. Once it was quiet, I stood and set up my camera. All around me were Marines, lying flat on the volcanic ash, weapons in hand. I took a photo of them as I waved away invisible, whistling insects that flew past my ears in the hot, desolate wind. After a few more shots, I skidded down the steep hill as there was no action up there to film.

When I regained my composure at the bottom of the hill and dusted myself off, I looked up to see a lance corporal staring at me.

"What the hell were you doing up there, standing in full view of the Japs? Stupid dame! The Jap snipers had a full ten minutes to shoot at you while you were foolin' with your camera." He flicked his cigarette into the volcanic ash.

"There...there were no snipers," I stammered.

"Didn't you hear the sniper firing?"

"Oh..." The only noise I recalled was the whistling insects I had tried to swat away. My eyes widened. "Was...was that the whistling noise I heard? I thought it was insects."

"There ain't no insects on this dead volcanic island. If you had been killed, I would've had to spend the rest of the war filing papers to explain why."

"I'd better get back to the hospital." I ran as fast as I could in the ash to avoid any further conflict.

An hour later, outside the tent, I saw a lieutenant in a weapons carrier truck. Thinking quickly, I approached him and asked, "Are you going to the front?"

He looked at my uniform and my "C" armband. "Jump in," he said. "I'll take you there."

I knew I was disobeying orders but this was my one-time opportunity to get to the front. I'd risk the consequences.

It was a breathtaking ride on a narrow lane that wound toward Mount Suribachi. Twelve-foot waves crashed onto the beach below us with a deafening roar.

An hour later, high on a cliff, the lieutenant said, "Here ya are. This is the front." He got out and lit up a cigarette. "I'll wait to bring ya back."

I steadied my camera as I witnessed bodies being blown apart on the beach below by Japanese shells. The noise rose up to where we stood and it was deafening. I tried not to shake as I took photos in rapid succession of the frightening slaughter. I stopped and closed my eyes. It was too much to take in even though I was far away from it all.

"I'm ready to go back now," I said with tear-filled eyes.

"I thought you wouldn't want to stay long."

Numb, I got back into the jeep and the lieutenant zoomed out of there. As we raced back to the airstrip, I fidgeted. Would I make it in time to catch my flight to Guam?

When the jeep stopped beside the plane, the last wounded GI was being loaded on a stretcher. I jumped out with my belongings and raced to board with minutes to spare.

We flew over the sharp cliffs of Mount Suribachi, one of the wounded men lifted himself up from his board and pointed out the window. "I helped put that there."

Curious, I looked out the window. I saw a huge American flag flapping in the wind on the peak of the mountain.

Several weeks after returning to the States, I thumbed through *Life,* looking for my photographs. I spotted one I hadn't taken. It was of Marines putting up the flag I had seen from the airplane. This incredible photograph had Joe Rosenthal's name under it. Joe was an AP photographer I knew. He had scooped me with an incredible photograph. It showed over forty Marines climbing up the crater of Mount Suribachi, the highest point of the island, and planting the grand American flag.

My photographs in *Life Magazine* were memorable, like the one of the dying Marine receiving blood, which was also used on a poster by the American Red Cross to recruit blood donors. I had many momentous photographs that were duplicated in many publications, but Joe's photograph...now, that was dramatic! It captured the unyielding spirit of the Marines and made me feel proud to be his colleague.

Mt. Suribachi, Iwo Jima

Marines landing on the beach in Iwo Jima

Tracked landing vehicles (LVTs) approach Iwo Jima

A 37mm gun fires against cave positions at Iwo Jima

Marines burrow into the volcanic sand on the beach of Iwo Jima

First Iwo Jima flag raising

Iwo Jima

US War Memorial—Raising of the flag on Iwo Jima

Chapter 55
Okinawa, April, 1945

The Japanese fought to win. It was a savage, brutal, inhumane,
exhausting and dirty business.

— Eugene B. Sledge

I was the only nonmedical woman aboard the hospital ship *USS Relief,* which was anchored in the harbor near the island of Okinawa waiting for casualties to arrive. Sixty thousand of our troops were landing on Okinawa; a long, thin, lush tropical island over 900 miles from Tokyo. As I looked out toward the island from the dock through my telephoto lens, not one shot had been fired yet.

I hitched a ride on a small Higgins boat that was to deliver blood to the Army hospital on the island, and I was under strict orders to return that night. This recently designed boat made it easy to make an amphibious landing without sinking in the sand. We were dropped off at Orange Beach with the supplies and medics. When a fierce wind and rain hit, the boat driver shouted to us that he wouldn't be able to come back to pick us up that night due to the storm.

The supplies were gathered and we got a ride to the Marines First Division command post. When the commander saw me get out of the truck, he shouted, "Get that girl outta here, this is a war zone!"

Though he frightened me with his bark, I was getting tired of men's reactions to the presence of women, especially women with a very important job to do.

I was taken to the Marine Corps press camp, which was filled with only men. I joined them for a field-ration meal of ham and eggs. Everyone was tense as an attack was imminent. I had no choice but to stay the night in the tent. In the middle of the night, a kamikaze attack began. The sounds of the Japanese crashing themselves into the island was deafening.

Amid the exploding noise of our 155mm howitzers, a talkative AP reporter and I discussed the Japanese. We both agreed that it was hard to fathom killing oneself and blowing up a perfectly good plane filled with explosives by flying directly into the enemy. Another reporter added that the Japanese culture believed that being a kamikaze pilot brought honor to their family, with the promise that their souls would have eternal rest at the Yasukuni shrine in Tokyo.

An officer came in and told me it was still unsafe for me to return to the ship and had a medical battalion commander drive me to the hospital. I was under strict orders to remain in there, and to photograph the casualties and nothing else.

The commander was tight-lipped as I tried to engage him in small talk on the way. As we rounded a turn on the dirt road, a bullet whistled overhead. Without thinking, I screamed.

The commander yelled, "Keep yer head down and for God's sake, shut up!"

I did as I was told, pushing my face into my camera duffle bag on my lap until we got to the village of Nago. There, I photographed the shells of burned-out houses, the gaping holes still smoking. The commander gave me a sneer but allowed me to photograph the scene. There were no villagers in sight. I looked out toward the cliffs and saw people huddled in caves.

"Can we go over there? I want to see the caves," I asked timidly, knowing from my experiences in Italy that this was where all the villagers would likely be. It was also a fantastic photo opportunity.

He shouted, "Don't you know you're the only dame on this entire island? And you're under strict orders to stay in the hospital!"

Dejected, I put down my camera. I was glad when we got to the hospital, and even happier as I watched the disagreeable officer speed off.

The hospital was in an old frame-and-thatch schoolhouse on top of a rugged cliff encircled by rice paddies and terraced hills overlooking the sea. I entered the building and set down my duffle bag.

A doctor examining a patient looked up at me. "How in God's name did *you* get here?"

I explained my accidental situation of being stuck on the island due to the weather. After hearing that I had been on the hospital ship, we established a congenial relationship.

The operating room presented the opportunity for an interesting series of photographs. It had only a single electric light bulb that hung from the ceiling. The artillery fire had hit most of the windows, which were now taped together or totally missing.

While setting up my tripod, I heard the constant crack of artillery shots. Many jeeps came by, bringing in moaning, shot-up Marines with bleeding wounds. The doctor hung bottles of blood as his assistant, a Navy corpsman, held a flashlight for more light.

"I'm happy to help, Doctor," I offered.

The doctor said, "Look, I don't mind you being here but just stay out of my way and don't faint."

Determined to be of use, I proceeded to list all the hospital ships I had been on. He studied me for a moment, then reluctantly let me hold the flashlight while the corpsman attended to another patient. The physician sutured up the patient's gaping wound and the light began to flicker in my trembling hand.

"Keep it steady!"

"Yes, sir." I controlled my breathing, not being used to hands-on assisting away from the barrier of my camera.

On day four, I ventured out and photographed a tree that had burst into flames. Another male war correspondent who was photographing the bombing jumped into a foxhole for safety when the bombs fell a little too close. I followed. When all was quiet, we returned to the school hospital.

Another day went by and the terrible weather continued. I still couldn't return to the hospital ship. I was overjoyed to be in the middle of the action, stranded on the island with a legitimate excuse for being there.

Every night I was driven back to the press camp to sleep among all the men. But that particular night was worse. We could hear the boots of our soldiers and the sound of them putting cartridge clips into their rifles and firing. I knew it wasn't safe enough to photograph the fighting. It was too close. But I didn't like being useless hiding in a tent.

A report came in that there were thirty-three hits on seventeen American ships in the harbor, with the death toll being relatively even on both the Japanese and American sides of over 300 each.

It was now day six on Okinawa, and I still couldn't get back to the *SS Relief.* There was no Higgins boat in sight. From the hospital cliffs, I photographed a Japanese battleship as it was bombed by our planes for over two hours. It finally rolled over and exploded. I was thrilled to get that shot. I returned to the hospital, feeling useful and somehow invincible.

The next morning, it was a clear day, so I decided to pack up my camera equipment. A Marine MP, his .45 cocked, entered the schoolhouse hospital. "Lt. Peterson, you are under arrest for disobeying orders to not return to the hospital ship."

I almost protested until I saw his pistol pointed at me. I packed up all my equipment and was taken to a Higgins boat, which returned me to the ship. I was confined to my quarters for two days amid the constant kamikaze bombing on the island. When the hospital ship was filled to capacity with casualties, it returned to Guam.

When I got off the ship in Guam, I was met by two armed MPs, who confiscated my credentials. I was arrested and confined in a single tent with a guard posted outside. After a week of confinement, I was brought before the admiral, who read an official order to me.

"Lieutenant Peterson, you were authorized to go to Okinawa on the *SS Relief* with direct orders not to disembark. You were found on the frontlines on the island of Okinawa. Your war correspondent credentials are hereby revoked."

I was smart enough to not utter a word and was sent home.

As soon as I recovered from Okinawa at home in New York, I went to Mr. Hicks's office at *Life* and told him I'd had my credentials confiscated.

He shook his head in disgust. "And how did that happen?"

"I was the only nonmedical reporter on the hospital ship and was not allowed on Okinawa to report on the fighting like the male correspondents. I went on a Higgins boat delivering blood, and planned on returning to the ship before nighttime, but I couldn't get back because of storms. And then the battle began." I raised my voice. "I have been discriminated against for being a female war correspondent and I demand to have my credentials back!" Then I placed my sensational shots of the battle on his desk. "Will you help me?"

Mr. Hicks carefully looked over the photographs. "I've got a great headline for the magazine: FEMALE WAR CORRESPONDENT SURVIVES AND CAPTURES COMPELLING PHOTOGRAPHS OF THE BATTLE OF OKINAWA."

After the article came out, Mr. Hicks wrote a letter to Rear Admiral Miller.

> *The decision to discipline Miss Adeline Peterson for discreditable conduct is discriminatory because of her being a woman. A male war correspondent would never have been arrested and his credentials rescinded. I urge you to reconsider, as her excellent track record of seven years of war photography has been extremely valuable to the military.*

Mr. Hicks, along with my well-documented photographs, helped me get my credentials back just as the war was winding down.

Japanese gun caves, Okinawa

Marines land on Okinawa shores

Cave demolition by the Marines, Okinawa

Battleship *New Mexico* bombing Okinawa

The *USS Bunker Hill* hit by two kamikaze aircraft in Okinawa

Chapter 56
Buchenwald Concentration Camp, The Holocaust, Spring 1945

Get it all on record now — get the films — get the witnesses — because somewhere down the road of history some bastard will get up and say that this never happened.

— President Eisenhower

We knew. Most of the war correspondents had read reports about the concentration camps. The first was in 1941, in Majdanek, Poland. The Soviet forces found evidence that the Germans had demolished most of it to cover their tracks. The Auschwitz concentration camp complex, thirty-seven miles west of Krakow, was the largest slave-labor/death camp of its kind, built by the Nazi regime after annexing Poland in 1939. Soviet soldiers found over 6,000 emaciated prisoners alive when they entered it in January of 1945. Two of the main camps used prisoners for forced labor. The third camp was the killing center. Over a million Polish people were mass exterminated there in the gas chambers. The Nazis had killed almost all of the Jews in Poland.

Most Americans believed the camps were not as bad as the rumors stated they were. Our people thought the stories were just isolated instances of sadism by the Germans. After all, the Americans had used internment camps for the Japanese, Germans, and Italians, and the people in the camps were well fed and clothed. There were several war correspondents interned in a Manila POW camp. They weren't fed by the Japanese, but by the Red Cross and Filipino townspeople. Our civilians were not beaten, tortured, or made to work while interned there. I wasn't sure what I believed. I knew what I had read, but I had also seen the brutality of the Nazis. I feared the worst.

During the spring of 1945, I received travel orders to go to the collapsed country of Germany with General Patton and the 3rd Army. We were the first Americans to liberate a concentration camp in Buchenwald. The only facts I obtained before going were that it had existed for eight years in a wooded area on the northern slopes of the Ettersberg, near the town of Weimar in east-central Germany. Our troops were still fighting the SS on the northern perimeter of the camp, but the south side displayed white flags, indicating surrender. It was rumored that there were about 20,000 people in this large civilian prison camp. I had my doubts and was a bit skeptical. It was such an astronomical number. *Can it be true? Will I see evidence of torture or deprivation? Was the story of human beings put in ovens a fabrication?*

The country road to Buchenwald was lined with well-kept orchards and was lovely in the warm spring weather. I was assigned to Private Johnson, who had a German background and could interpret for me.

At the entrance to the concentration camp, General Patton ordered one of our men to open the locked, heavy metal gate with a hand grenade. The ten-foot, closely meshed barbed-wire electric fence with spiked coils had to be tested to see if it still had its 800-volt charge.

As I followed our soldiers into the camp compound, I smelled a strange, unidentifiable odor drifting through the air. All around me in the yard were human-like skeletons wearing loose, tattered, blue-and-white pajamas. They sat quietly in the sun searching themselves for lice. I instinctively gasped, then held my mouth shut as I stared at the creatures before me.

In contrast, in neat, clean military uniforms, SS Nazi men and women lined up near the fence line with blank stares, silent, holding surrender flags.

I clutched my Graflex camera, unable to bring it to my face. The overwhelming stench of death assaulted my nostrils. I tried to clear my throat by making short coughing noises. My entire body flushed with heat, even though there was a spring breeze in the air. A white surrender flag rippled in the air ten feet above me. I pressed my lips inward, biting them to control myself from vomiting. I forced myself to hold up the camera to look through the viewfinder as my eyes welled with tears. I managed a few shots even though everything looked blurry.

Suddenly, an extremely emaciated man walked by me and keeled over onto the dirt. Shocked, I remained as still as a statue. A nearby MP went to him, took his pulse, then sadly shook his head. I instinctively said a silent prayer as tears dripped down my face.

One poor soul touched my skirt and said something. Private Johnson interpreted, "Are you an angel here to rescue me? Am I dreaming? I've been here years waiting to die, just like that man. I was not expecting to live."

I felt ashamed that I didn't know what to do and was left speechless. My interpreter gently touched my shoulder and told me to say, "*Sie sind frei*" — "you are free" in German. I repeated it the best I could as the inmate gave me a small hug.

I dry swallowed and asked Private Johnson to ask a young, scraggly boy, "Why do you think you are here?"

The boy answered, "I'm Jewish."

"Where are your parents?"

"They got burned up."

My eyes widened. I held in my breath, shocked by the reality of being there.

I followed our soldiers farther into the compound. There were half-dead people dragging themselves about amid bodies rotting on the ground, their glazed, hopeless eyes full of despair. Most were naked, every bone outlined on their bodies. Others wore a ragged, striped prison-type outfit. All the survivors looked like shrunken scarecrows — the living dead.

The Nazis apparently did not have time to hide all the bodies as they had done in Poland. There were piles of dead, emaciated, naked bodies, with legs and arms twisted and tangled, stacked as high as cordwood. I froze in horror and tried to compose myself. I set up my large-format camera on a tripod. It was a relief to stand behind it. I was able to take shot after shot by putting an invisible veil over my brain to keep from getting hysterical over the appalling sights. Once again, my camera created a barrier between me and the horrific sights I saw through the lens.

The naked corpses had toothless mouths gaped open, some

with empty sockets where eyes used to be. It was surreal to photograph bodies that looked like limp, sick mannequins. I saw thousands of stiff bodies spilling out of carts and trucks, or piled unceremoniously in corners. The frosty night had frozen trickles of blood and yellow bubbles of mucus seeping from eyes and noses.

I swallowed repeatedly to prevent the bile from rising up in my throat as my stomach churned. My breathing was as irregular as my heartbeat. I closed my eyes, practiced my slow breathing technique from my childhood, then forced myself to do my job by peering through my lens into this hellish nightmare.

When I thought I saw a hand raise up and wave at me from the middle of a pile of decayed human beings, I screamed and knocked over the tripod. I ran behind a nearby building and heaved up everything in my stomach. It took a moment to gather my thoughts.

Get ahold of yourself, Addie! I admonished myself, trying desperately to control my breathing again. *You are the first war correspondent to witness the liberation of a prison camp and you'd better do your job! It's the only way to show America what really happened here so it will never happen again.*

I pulled myself together, retrieved my tripod and Graflex, put them in my duffle bag, and returned to where Private Johnson stood. With several of our soldiers, I entered one of the hundreds of barracks that were filled with two-and-a-half-foot-wide wooden shelves, with three to five men squeezed onto each of them, all waiting to die. The shelves stretched three tiers high to the ceiling of the barracks. All the men had serial numbers tattooed on their forearms or upper left chest. They had been branded like cattle.

The odor of excrement was hard to stomach. One inmate died right before my eyes and the others didn't seem to notice. Oh, the shame of it all. These poor human beings made my heart feel like it was breaking. I couldn't take out my camera; it would be like photographing animals in cages in a zoo. A feeling of awkwardness paired with an incomprehensible guilt for being invasive made it difficult for me to continue my work.

I snapped out of my worrisome thoughts when I heard the

inmates weakly calling out something in different languages. My interpreter told me they were asking if we were Americans, and if we had come to set them free.

Private Johnson told them, *"Ja, Amerikaner."*

I managed to utter, *"Sie sind frei,"* over and over as we walked past bunk after bunk. A few of the skeletal human creatures gave us a frail cheer. One ailing little boy began to weep and hugged my leg from his wooden "bed" as I passed by. Another prisoner told me they'd had to push their own brothers, sisters, mothers — their entire families — into the ovens, knowing they would be next.

I took very few photographs in the last barracks, feeling ashamed once again. After we talked to a few of the poor souls, they told us that Buchenwald was a slave-labor camp where they worked twelve to sixteen hours a day and were fed only watery soup and occasional scraps of bread. If they couldn't work they were beaten until they died, or they were executed. Hundreds perished each month from disease, malnutrition, exhaustion, beatings, and executions.

We heard General Patton commanding something and dashed outside. He was furious after he inspected the camp, where over 50,000 prisoners had died. He ordered his military police to round up over 2,000 residents from the nearby town of Weimar. These German townspeople were forced at gunpoint to walk around the camp to witness all the suffering prisoners and pile after pile of dead human bodies.

I photographed the townspeople as they were forced to go to the crematorium to view the charred remains of the dead. The oven rooms had thousands of bodies — stacks of bodies, jumbled heaps of bodies, bodies piled on carts waiting to be shoved into ovens and incinerated. The putrid smell of death surrounded us all. Some of the townspeople threw up and others tied handkerchiefs around their mouths. I got photographs of the citizens of Weimar covering their eyes after seeing half-burned human bodies in Buchenwald's cremation ovens.

The general, still fuming, shouted, "LOOK! Uncover your eyes! You allowed this! Look at what your leaders have done."

A few of the German citizens burst into tears. "We didn't know," they said over and over.

General Patton roared, "You knew! The odor of death is in your town; the smoke from the incinerated bodies can be seen from your houses!"

Next, the general ordered the townspeople, along with the remaining SS officers, to pull hundreds of dead bodies from the piles and put them in a pit the size of a football field that our soldiers had dug using the camp's bulldozers.

One SS Nazi protested, "This is not our job; it is the prisoners' job."

The general ordered, "If you Germans don't clean this up, you will be thrown into the pit to die!"

The American soldiers pointed their rifles at them as the SS and townspeople began to pull, drag, and carry the dead, naked, skeletal bodies into the pit. There were hundreds of piles. When they threw them in, the bodies tumbled down the sides like ragdolls.

A young American GI came up to me. "Come see this for your press report."

I followed him as they led me to a remote part of the woods where a few of our American soldiers were ruthlessly beating up a group of SS officers hiding in the woods.

A lieutenant came by, broke it up, and ordered the Nazis to get to work and clean up the dead bodies. He told our soldiers, "Senseless beating is not enough of a punishment for these people."

As I photographed the blank, unemotional faces of the SS Nazis, I could see that to them, this was nothing. Just another day at work burying the hopeless, nameless, subhuman beings they had starved and tortured to death.

Hours later, after the morbid process was almost over, a bulldozer filled in the first pit with dirt. I turned my attention to interviewing the town's citizens with the help of Private Johnson.

I had him ask, "Why didn't you do something? Tell someone?"

He had to press them to respond. They were all tight-lipped and silent.

One hausfrau said, "Our Füehrer could not have known about it. He would never have permitted this."

"It was none of our business," the town baker said.

A local physician agreed. "The business at the camp was not our affair."

The barber for the Buchenwald SS troops sneered, "Americans are too sentimental."

Private Johnson displayed emotion for the first time and punched his fist in the air. "This is what your Nazi leaders have been doing for years. Eight years here and twelve in Dachau. Don't tell me you didn't know!"

I reflected on when I had met the old Jewish man, the writer who had been imprisoned in Poland for the defamation pieces he had written about Hitler. He had recently fled to Prague and had begged me to take him back to America, insisting that Czechoslovakia would be taken over by the Germans just like in Poland. I did not believe him when he told Ivanov and me about the concentration camp he had been in Poland. At the time, we didn't think Germany would take over Prague. I wondered what had happened to him.

After many hours, when the burial job was done, I photographed a somber memorial service held at Buchenwald. Flowers from nearby fields were put on the grass-seeded pit and prayers were said in many different languages. Some of the prisoners attended.

Just when I thought I had seen and heard all the possible horrors, we went outside the Buchenwald camp to a nearby forest where all the trains had been left. There were more than thirty railroad cars filled with bodies in various states of decomposition. We saw over 3,000 dead that were to be shipped to another extermination camp.

It was too much to bear. My camera couldn't protect me from this. I ran behind a tree and let loose my pent-up feelings in a flood of tears. I sobbed into the rough tree trunk. After I could cry no more, I sat down to calm myself before returning to the group.

I overheard a few of the American soldiers talking about the atrocities and how no one back home would ever believe such a place existed. Their conversation gave me a jolt of determination. It inspired me to control my shaking hands and the nausea pushing at my throat. My work in Germany was valuable and proof of what the human race was capable of doing. My photographs would reveal the truth, no matter how terrifying. Mankind should never forget this dark time in history.

The fighting was still raging in the northern outskirts of Germany. When the hospital trucks arrived, the inmates were taken away for treatment. I photographed this scene with a prayer that some of them would somehow survive.

I left for the south end of Germany in a jeep with Sergeant Paul Smith, a correspondent for the military newspaper *Stars and Stripes,* to further explore the defeated parts of Germany. Paul was an American from German-Jewish parents who had changed his name from Schmidt to Smith. We drove through a village draped with white flags and some of the German soldiers cheered when they saw us coming. When we slowed down, a few piled their weapons into our jeep to show us they had surrendered. This lifted our spirits.

As we drove around the countryside, our noses alerted us to another extermination camp. The putrid smell of death hung in the air. There was a sign that read: "Erla Airplane Factory." Just outside the area of the factory, in the meadow, were the dead bodies of prisoners. When we got to the barbed-wire fence there was no building, but we saw many dead in frightful positions of escape. Sergeant Smith parked his jeep, pulled out his .45 pistol for protection, then unfastened the gate. Upon closer inspection, we saw piles of human bones, spoons, nails, and bowls in a huge, burned-out area where the factory should have been. Several skeletal survivors emerged with their hands up until Smith put his gun away. The sergeant asked why the factory had burned down. They told us that the guards had learned that American troops were coming. They lured most of the starving prison workers into a room with a vat of soup. The SS Germans then barred the doors, threw in hand grenades and an acetate solution, and set the building on fire. Only eighteen pale-yellow, extremely thin survivors managed to break out and run into the woods. The others were shot.

I had just taken a few horrific photographs of the charred bodies and the survivors when a jeep arrived.

A two-star general got out and shouted at us, looking suspiciously at the "C" band on our uniform. "What the hell are you two doing here? This place is raging with typhus."

I shouted right back, my voice full of leftover rage from the horrors I'd just seen at the concentration camp. "I've had my shots and I'm doing my job, that's what the hell I'm doing here! And you'd better send for a hospital truck."

The general didn't say one word as Paul and I got back into our jeep and continued to drive around Germany. We discussed why the SS had killed the inmates at the factory instead of setting them free since the war was over. We decided that they did not want anyone to know what evil beings they really were.

Margaret Bourke-White, war correspondent

Buchenwald

Human bones still in crematorium

German citizens forced to look at dead bodies at Buchenwald

Chapter 57
1945, Dachau

I pray you to believe what I have said about Buchenwald. I have reported what I saw and heard, but only part of it. For most of it I have no words.

— Ed Murrow, broadcaster for CBS

Dachau was the last concentration camp I visited. It was constructed in March of 1933, when I was covering the Dust Bowl in Oklahoma, oblivious to life in Europe, and only five weeks after Adolf Hitler took power. I felt a burning shame for my country that this prison camp had been here for eleven years without America being aware of it. This camp was the original model for over 40,000 concentration camps in the Third Reich. It had just been liberated a week earlier by the 42nd and 45th divisions of the U.S. Seventh Army.

I visited the 116th and 127th evacuation hospitals, which had recently been built to care for the survivors before they were sent home or homes were found for them. The nurses and doctors stayed in the luxurious houses where the SS officers and their families had resided. The SS families lived directly across the lawn from the crematorium. The mass murders could be smelled by the officers' children and their wives as they watched the chimneys spewing out unending human ashes.

Lieutenant Robinson was assigned to give me a tour of Dachau. On our way to the warehouses, he explained that the first year this was a forced-labor camp to construct and expand Dachau. Later, it was also used for German armaments produced by the prisoners. It was the main training center for the camp guards. As prisoners became too old or weak to work due to disease and starvation, they were disposed of by use of the ovens.

At the many warehouses, we saw all the prisoners' personal

belongings that had been taken from them. Innocent families were told they were going to be transported to new homes away from the war and to bring their most valued possessions. The lieutenant told me that during the first few years, the number of prisoners grew and other groups were interned at Dachau, including Jehovah's Witnesses, Catholic clergy, gypsies, homosexuals, and repeat criminals; anyone who opposed the Nazi regime and did not obey their laws. Jews comprised the major portion of the camp's population.

I photographed an entire warehouse full of hundreds of thousands of men's suits and women's outfits, each meticulously packaged, counted, and marked, probably by the prisoners themselves under the supervision of the Nazis.

There were stacks and stacks of rolled bundles with labeled weights on them. The lieutenant sliced one open with a knife and hair fell out of it. I choked in horror. This entire warehouse was filled with hair collected from the prisoners who had died. The lieutenant estimated that there had to be more than 14,000 pounds of human hair. Nothing was wasted; everything was used by the Nazis. Each successive warehouse was filled with other personal items; children's shoes, gold teeth, and spectacles. I reflected on the bizarre realization that all the packages were stacked and labeled neatly in piles, but human beings were dumped like garbage to rot in the sun.

Most shocking to me was the sight of the shrunken heads of inmates who had escaped and were recaptured, displayed to show the others what would happen if they tried to leave.

The last warehouse was filled with barrels labeled "Zyklon." The lieutenant explained that it was a deadly gas used to exterminate the prisoners. The Jews, after living in misery and filth for months, were told that they could shower and were ordered to undress. Then the SS guards pumped the blue gas Zyklon into the large, white-tiled shower rooms. The lieutenant discovered from German records that it took only a matter of minutes to kill over 1,200 people this way.

We went to the crematorium next. I took photos of the "meat hooks," which were the size and shape of horseshoes mounted in the execution room. The Gestapo forced prisoners to hang their own people on them to keep them straight before rigor mortis set in. Then they were put in the ovens to be burned.

Near the crematorium was a group of small white cells where inmates were kept in total isolation, away from all human beings, never allowed outside. This was an experiment to see if a person would go mad, or how long they could subsist on a diet of just watery soup and bread with no sun or human contact.

As more and more unaware families were shipped to Dachau by boxcar, it became less of a labor camp and more of an extermination center.

My mind began to race and my hands shook my camera. Did the SS guards hear the people scream in agony before they died? I stopped photographing and wept into my hands. The lieutenant paused, crossed himself, and said a prayer for all of the innocent people who had died there.

Lieutenant Robinson brought me to Dr. Nowalski, a former Polish physician. He had been an inmate for ten years at the camp and had made a full physical recovery, though he was still quite thin. He told me that Dachau was the first Nazi camp to use prisoners as human guinea pigs for medical experiments. Most of the cruel experiments were performed under the supervision of Dr. Josef Mengele, chief camp physician. Dr. Nowalski showed me Dr. Mengele's meticulous records on this outrageous research that spanned ten years and was conducted on children, women, and men. There were dates, times, names, and what tests were performed on each person. Many of the operations included castrations and sterilization. The medical records described in great detail how each experiment was done.

I shot photographs of huge, shiny metal vats still filled with seawater. The prisoners were made to stand in water up to their necks so the Nazis could learn how long a pilot could survive in salt water at low temperatures if shot down over the ocean. The doctor showed me records of the survival rates that proved it took 2 ½ hours at minus eight degrees centigrade for death to occur. Hundreds of inmates were infected with malaria, tuberculosis, and typhus, then treated with experimental drugs. Hundreds of human beings died or were crippled as a result.

Later, I toured the newly refurbished hospitals to meet the

refugees being treated. A man, about six feet tall wearing a striped camp uniform, was being examined by an American doctor. The patient weighed in at only 100 pounds.

The weak, debilitated man wept. "Everyone I know is dead. No one in my family is left. I am finished. I've been in this camp for five years. I won't make it."

The physician tried to reassure him. "You'll be fine. Keep eating. We'll take good care of you and you'll feel like a young man soon."

I could see in the refugee's eyes that he didn't believe him. He had probably seen too much death and knew that his time was near.

By my twelfth day at Dachau, the 120th evacuation hospital had helped thousands of refugees, but many died there from starvation, dehydration, and disease. Sadly, it was too late for some.

I photographed many former prisoners, now patients. They talked quietly with strange, tiny smiles. Their eyes were large and bulging, with visible jawbones cutting through their faces. They told of the abuse of systematically being tortured. If a prisoner was found with a cigarette butt in his pocket, he received between twenty-five to fifty lashes with a bullwhip. For not standing at attention when an SS officer passed by, prisoners' hands were tied behind their backs and they were hung by their bound hands from a hook on the wall for an hour. Another punishment was to be put in "the box" — a room the size of a telephone booth with only enough room to stand. One former inmate told me he stood for three days without food, water, or sanitation. Then it was back to sixteen hours of labor.

The last part of the camp I toured was the Angora rabbit farm. There were over 1,000 rabbits that were cared for by the inmates to supply fur for the linings of the jackets of Luftwaffe pilots. These animals lived in luxury in their own elegant hutches with specially prepared meals. The irony of it was disturbing; the rabbits were better cared for than the 800 people packed into barracks that could barely house 200.

Near the rabbits were the hothouses, where prisoners grew flowers for the SS officers' enjoyment. The inmates tended to vegetable gardens to help keep the SS strong. If a prisoner pulled up any of the vegetables and gorged himself, he would be beaten unconscious.

American reporters, senators, and congressmen, as well as members of the British parliament and their journalists, were beginning to arrive in Germany to publicize the atrocities of the concentration camps. A map was made, labeling all the camps and how close the German townspeople lived to them. Many of the German citizens lived completely normal lives within mere miles of the camps.

At Buchenwald, with war correspondents in attendance, a band played "Taps." There were fifteen flags representing all the countries the deceased inmates were from. Wreaths were placed on the grass-seeded pit to commemorate the dead with the inscription: *Buchenwald Concentration Camp – Fifty-One Thousand.* It was an extremely solemn occasion.

The war correspondents returned home to report to their countries. Martha Gellhorn from *Collier's Magazine* wrote, "We are not entirely guiltless, we the Allies, because it took us twelve years to open the gates of Dachau. We were blind, unbelieving and slow, and that we can never be again."

Lee Miller from *Vogue Magazine's* headline cried: "I IMPLORE YOU TO BELIEVE THIS IS TRUE."

I left Dachau with feelings of shame and revulsion. I arrived back in New York, my home state. It took me a while to have the nerve to write about all I had seen in Germany. I didn't have the courage to look at my notes or develop the photographs right away.

As time went by, I was ready to expose the atrocities that demanded to be recorded. I finally developed the rolls of photographs I had shot, and examined them as they dripped from the strung-up clothesline. For some reason, looking at the piles of tortured, dead human beings on my negatives was more startling than what I had seen in person. Nonetheless, I forced myself to develop them all, knowing that words could always be denied but photographs displayed the undeniable, stark reality.

Exhaustion set in as I lay on my bed and reflected on my own heritage. My mother's own people were Jewish; a well-kept family secret. I worried about my friend Ivanov. Had he and his young family survived this nightmare? *The entire human race has been affected by this atrocious tragedy,* I thought as I stared into the darkness. *It should never be forgotten or repeated, ever again.*

The atrocities of war

Glasses taken from victims of the Holocaust

Chapter 58
Nagasaki, Japan, 1945

The only use for an atomic bomb is to keep someone else from using one.

— George Wald

The war was over at last. Japan surrendered! After the atomic bomb was dropped on Nagasaki, it took Emperor Hirohito nine days to announce Japan's surrender by radio.

While waiting for the War Department's consent to report on the aftermath of the bombing of Nagasaki, I studied the events leading up to the atomic bombing.

President Roosevelt died in April while I was at the concentration camps. When I got back home in May, Adolf Hitler, Chancellor of Germany, committed suicide.

The United States had been dropping incendiary bombs, island by island, on six industrial centers in Japan. They were filled with jellified gasoline, causing everything to go up in flames. The Japanese soldiers were taught to strap bombs on their bodies and throw themselves under our military tanks to destroy them by suicide. Their pilots, the kamikazes, used their planes as suicide bombers as well. The German Luftwaffe had done the same. When I was in Germany, I had met and interviewed many of the hundreds of boys training at the Nazi youth camp for their army. The Japanese also trained young boys and girls to shoot with bamboo spears. There were many horrific parallels between Japan and Germany that made this war long as well as difficult to end.

By mid-June 1945, the Allies had killed over 260,000 Japanese but they would not surrender. It was an honor for their people to die for their country. There were over 140,000 Allied prisoners of war being held in over 130 Japanese military prison work camps.

None of the war correspondents knew about the successful July 18 atomic bomb test in New Mexico. It was a new, powerful secret weapon that took three years of research to perfect and cost two billion dollars to build. It was designed specifically to end the war.

A detonation sequence slammed the two halves of a uranium core together. This emitted a soundless flash, like a huge magnesium flare, and produced a fireball reaching about one million degrees Celsius—as hot as the sun. It had only been tested once in the New Mexico desert in a small capacity. There was no guarantee that the secret mission of bombing Hiroshima would make Japan surrender.

On July 27, our new President Truman issued the Potsdam Declaration to Japan, which was signed by our allies Great Britain and China. The Soviet Union was present but did not sign it because of a nonaggression pact with Japan. After reading the two-page document, I summarized the thirteen points to understand it better:

- The Allies of the United States, China, and Great Britain have met and agree that Japan shall be given an opportunity to end this war.
- The Allied Nations are poised to strike the final blows upon Japan and have resolved to completely devastate Japan, which has been embarking on a world conquest.
- We insist upon a new order of peace, security and justice.
- We have no intension of enslaving the Japanese but we will punish all war criminals.
- The occupying forces of the Allies shall be withdrawn from Japan as soon as there is surrender.
- The government of Japan must proclaim unconditional surrender of all Japanese armed forces or there will be prompt and utter destruction.

I understood by reading the declaration that Japan indeed was given fair warning of the atomic bombing. They responded to the declaration with intentional silence, which they called *mokusatsu*.

On August 6, no one knew about the two "secret" bombs

being assembled on the other side of Saipan from Guam. The atomic bomb dropped that day by the United States ruined ninety percent of the city of Hiroshima and killed over 80,000 people. The mayor of Hiroshima issued a proclamation to its people stating that the damage might be great but to keep up their spirits, don't lose heart, and that it was expected in war.

The atomic bombing of Nagasaki occurred three days later. The Japanese announced their intention to surrender and officially did so on August 14. His Imperial Majesty Hirohito of Japan said, "I do not desire any further destruction of cultures, nor any additional misfortune for the peoples of the world. On this occasion, we have to bear the unbearable." The next day, General Korechika Anami, Japanese Vice-Minister of War, committed suicide.

President Truman announced that the atomic bomb shortened the agony of war and saved the lives of thousands and thousands of young Americans.

I was one of the first war correspondents to go to Nagasaki a month and a half after the bomb exploded. There, I would see for myself the horrific and catastrophic damage the atomic bomb induced. Many of the correspondents were told there were no facilities to stay in and the ruins were infected. This possible rumor enabled me to be one of the few war correspondents there and I could provide an enormous scoop. I did have extreme anxiety over what I would see there, but I thought I was tough enough after what I'd seen in the concentration camps.

After a plane flight, I took a twenty-four-hour train ride into the remains of a city that no longer existed. The railroad station was gone except for the platform and the trains were miraculously running on time. There were scorched piers in the main harbor. I ventured out among the acres of devastation and ruins. I took my camera out of my suitcase and went into photography mode to ease the shock of it all.

A Japanese police officer came by and tried to take my camera, telling me, "Photographs are forbidden."

I held my precious camera tight. "Not for me, I have papers." I handed the officer my credentials and took my coat off to display my war-correspondent's uniform.

I continued to photograph the bombed city, in a state of shock as well as disbelief, and decided to focus on shadows. The frames of concrete buildings were still standing but had eerie shadows etched on them. The creepiest shadows were of people branded on the buildings, sidewalks, and stone steps. Concrete and metal were the only materials that had survived the bomb in the center of Nagasaki. There were shadows of birds on some remaining walls that looked like they had caught on fire while flying in midair. I wandered gingerly around the quiet, spooky city, shooting more and more outlined shadows—a handcart, a ladder, various trees, and telegraph poles. The shadows reminded me of photographic negatives. The flash of the bomb had produced negatives of items and people that no longer existed.

I got to inspect the ruins firsthand on this island of Nagasaki, which was the size of Manhattan with the ocean on three sides. It probably once was a beautiful sight. That thought saddened me as I looked around and took it all in. Exhaustion flooded my soul. I sat down among the rubble with my bags, hoping to find the strength to report to the Japanese lieutenant colonel I was supposed to find.

The smell of decay and fire still pervaded the air of the vacant city, four and a half weeks after the bomb had hit. I got out my hanky and blew my nose, which was filled with debris, and coughed a great deal of phlegm into it. With my camera in my suitcase, I sat for a while in the ungodly quiet, not a living creature around. I was surrounded by the shattered remains of a bustling city that once was. My mind wandered as I typed stories in my head. I was glad I had hauled my typewriter along with me. I felt a lingering loneliness, just as I had after Buchenwald and Dachau. I missed Bill and wished I had someone to share my feelings with about this nightmarish event.

Finally, I dusted myself off and began to walk. Somehow, I had to find the lieutenant colonel in this wasteland. Far in the distance, I saw a small group of people and trudged forward, my bags banging against my legs. I found several policemen who were sorting through the rubble. They told me it was forbidden to be there. I showed them my papers and one policeman kindly drove me out of the city to a hotel. He said he would send

Lieutenant Colonel Nakamura over later. On the way there, the Japanese policeman told me there were over 20,000 known dead and they were still looking for over 4,000 missing.

In my room, I washed off the smell from the bombing of Nagasaki, cleared my sinuses, put on a cleaner uniform, and went downstairs to eat a small meal of fish, rice, and tea.

Lieutenant Colonel Nakamura arrived. He gave a slight bow and asked for my papers. He was such a small man, just slightly taller than me, and wore an ill-fitted uniform. I presented him with my orders from General MacArthur.

I told him I would need a military policeman to take my rolls of film and reports to Tokyo for US censorship. I also requested a guide with a car.

The lieutenant colonel merely nodded. Then, after a moment of silence, he asked, "What kind of culture do you have in America to use such an abominable weapon on our people?"

I had a hard time replying, and answered in a quiet voice, "I would have to ask our people from Pearl Harbor, who were walking to church on that Sunday when your people bombed it without warning."

My honest answer seemed to touch the lieutenant's heart and after that, we got along better.

I interviewed Lieutenant Colonel Nakamura about the bombing. He had been walking high on a hill above the waterfront and told me about his experience.

"I saw one enemy plane fly over the city but that was nothing new. We frequently had American bombers flying over. At the beginning of the war, air raids were enforced with people going to the shelters. As the war progressed, they routinely carried on with their work and ignored the warnings. The air-raid shelters were totally inadequate and sometimes the air warning systems failed. I heard B-29s, and looked up with my field glasses and saw only two planes that were too high up for anti-aircraft firing. Then I saw three parachutes drop down, each with an oblong box. I thought they were dropping the usual pamphlet propaganda. Suddenly, a flame burst upwards; a yellow, hoop-like fire started followed by an immense cumulonimbus cloud of black dust rupturing upward. I immediately fell flat on the ground as I was trained to do. Forceful hurricane winds blew into the valleys and tore roofs off. It is said now that the bomb had the force of over thirty million sticks of dynamite. Every person caught within a half-mile of the hypocenter, which is the spot directly below its detonation, was immediately reduced to black char or completely vaporized by the bomb's 20,000-degree heat."

The lieutenant colonel paused, took out a cigarette, lit it, and smoked while continuing his observations.

"Firestorms blacked out the morning sun. It took until the next day for police and volunteers to come in. They established relief centers in tram stations and open areas, laying out mats for those who had survived. There were fires all over but the water mains had broken, so the fires continued to rage throughout the city."

The Japanese officer bowed his head and stopped talking. I held back my tears, wanting to comfort him, but was unsure how. I waited a few minutes, then quietly thanked him for talking to me.

Lieutenant Colonel Nakamura provided me with a car and a driver, who drove me around the edges of the city. I photographed twisted, pretzel-like pieces of bent steel where factories had once stood. I saw acre upon acre of charred beams, blackened walls, and tangles of burned debris. The driver pointed out where the American consulate was, two miles from the blast. It was the only building remaining. We came to the Catholic church, one mile from where the bomb hit. Just the face of it was left standing. An electrical plant three miles from the epicenter of the atomic bomb had not been damaged. Within two miles — that's where all the damage was.

I got out to walk around the city. My driver remained in the car. It was not an easy task, walking through all the debris. Walls had fallen across streets, roofs had collapsed, and doors were scattered everywhere. I stood there and imagined the blast squashing the roofs, the burning timber, and the collapsing ceilings. The closer I got to the hypocenter the more I smelled the odor of decaying flesh. It reminded me of Buchenwald and that familiar lump of nausea pushed at my throat once again. My heart pounded in my chest as I wondered what other horrors I might encounter.

I struggled through tangled iron girders and the twisted roofs of the factories to get back to my driver. I was concerned about the ground and possible dangerous radiation. On the way back to the hotel, the driver pointed out the remains of the unidentifiable Mitsubishi ship parts plant that had mostly Allied prisoners working there. All houses and factories had been hammered flat. A vast wasteland lay before my eyes, and I tried to capture it with my camera while processing the devastation of it all.

Farther away from the hypocenter of the bomb, we came to a so-called park. The freakish destruction had left singed leaves on the ground amid exploded tree trunks.

That evening, as I attempted to sleep in my hotel room, I rolled restlessly in tangled sheets. Frightening images floated in and out of my mind. I gave up trying to sleep, got out of bed, and typed all that I had seen that day. The rhythmic tapping of the typewriter expended my nervous energy, and afterward, I was able to catch a few hours of napping.

After breakfast the next morning, my driver dropped me off at the nearest working hospital where all the wards were filled with patients. As I walked through every corridor, Japanese citizens sat squatting and moaning on mats, waiting to be treated. A few fell over and died; it was too late for them to be helped. I put my camera inside my uniform out of respect and closed my eyes in mourning.

I interviewed two general physicians and an x-ray specialist. It had been over a month since the bombing and they still had 750 atomic patients, with over 360 having died in the first week. Most deaths were from burns, as many people had been caught in the debris and fires. One physician told me that anyone who was outside within a half a mile had been incinerated instantly. The doctor believed the ground was poisoned by the bomb and that the main effect was on the bloodstream. Blood platelets were destroyed, losing the capacity to coagulate and bleeding could not be stopped. Many patients died from a simple scratch.

One doctor stood beside a young, totally bald patient. "This man was exposed a quarter mile away from the center of the bomb. He was knocked down and not hurt but a few days later he began coughing up blood every day. Most of his platelets are dead and platelets are needed to enable the blood to clot in three to four minutes. His hair began to fall out in patches. There is nothing we can do for him, most patients with this disease die after a month of having the strange symptoms. We do not know how to treat this disorder and can only prescribe rest."

The patient said something in Japanese. I asked the physician what he said.

"He said 'my future is canceled.'"

The doctor's eyes fell in hopeless sorrow and I bowed my head also.

I walked away and stared out the window to gather the strength to continue my work. I remembered a patient in the Dachau hospital saying something similar.

The x-ray specialist told me the physicians were calling the affliction with late-developing symptoms "Disease X." The mysterious disease had symptoms of blackish mouths, limbs speckled with tiny, blotchy red spots, and noses that were clotted with blood with no signs of outward injury. Most of the patients had headaches, fever, diarrhea, bleeding gums, loose teeth, hair loss, throat and lip sores, and fevers rising to and remaining at 104 degrees.

One patient I interviewed said she was able to flee from the atomic area and was fine, but three weeks later she developed symptoms. I asked her what she saw after the atomic bomb hit.

She explained in a sad voice, "Day turned into pitch-black night, with fires breaking out all over. Windows burst and injured many people. It became a city of death. As I ran away, I saw large, black, oil-like raindrops falling and some people drank it from the air. They were thirsty from the heat of the bomb."

The doctor nearby added that the rain was radioactive and had poisoned thousands of Japanese citizens.

The tiny woman with speckled skin continued, "Many people were burned and bleeding and fled to the nearest water to quench their thirst and help their wounds. The reservoirs were filled with dead people who were boiled alive. The rivers were so congested with people escaping the heat of the bomb that many drowned. Swarms of people were on the roadway trying to get away from the center. As I was running, I heard shrieking and screams of, 'It hurts, it hurts, water, water!' On my way out of the city, I saw walking corpses with skin hanging off of them. They were frightening creatures without noses and only their teeth were recognizable..." Her voice trailed off and she rolled over and cried into her cot.

"Oh my God!" I exclaimed and paced back and forth on the hospital floor.

Now I was full of worry and asked the two physicians if it had been dangerous or poisonous for me to have walked through the hypocenter.

The older physician said, "The entire area should be closed off for an extended period of time. That ground is infected by lethal rays."

The younger physician disagreed. "I think people will be fine as long as they wear boots." He looked at my boots and whispered, "No one really knows yet."

A nervousness came over me. I regretted that I had tramped all over the hypocenter and hoped my thick boots had given me protection from getting the horrific Disease X.

The x-ray technician asked me in front of both doctors, "Tell me, miss, don't you think America did something inhuman by releasing this weapon against Japan?"

I hesitated and wondered to myself, *Would Japan never use unfair weapons?* I confidently replied, "The Japanese were warned once by the Potsdam Declaration and once again after Hiroshima. We were not warned when your army bombed Pearl Harbor. Over 2,400 of our people were killed and our military was destroyed."

After my response, I noticed that all the medical personnel turn away and got very busy doing their jobs.

That night in the hotel, as I lay there alone, I worried about myself. *Sure, I had my inoculations before I came here but there are no shots against Disease X...* For the first time in my life, I was glad I wasn't a daughter, wife, or mother. I rolled up my sleeves to check for red spots. I saw nothing. I knew if I were to die, I would only be leaving my brother Jimmy behind. He would be fine, having established a good career and a family of his own.

Though I was weary and my heart ached, I tapped out my

stories on my trusty Royal typewriter, which I had dragged all around the world, in and out of wars. I needed to expose the truth and was prepared to smuggle my stories out if I had to. In five days I would have to go to Tokyo for further censorship before returning home. I decided to skip it and hid the carbons in the lining of my suitcase.

In the morning, having only tea, I felt pity but no remorse. The war was over and this is what it took.

Nagasaki

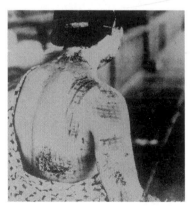

Patient's skin burned in a kimono pattern
after the atomic bombing of Nagasaki

Nuclear shadows left after the atomic bomb

V-Day

Chapter 59
Allies as Prisoners of War

Well, you know, it's nice to come back and see where you have been but the sad part about it is you don't like to remember.
— Ralph Griffith, POW Japan

There were 140,000 Japanese POW camps holding Allied prisoners and I knew I had to visit some of them to complete my job there. None had been liberated yet, and it had been over a month since Japan had surrendered. First, I walked over to the POW camp of the Mitsubishi Armament plant made up of British, Australian, and Dutch prisoners. The men were not sure that the war was over, even though the Japanese guards and officers had fled. They had nowhere to go and were waiting to be rescued. As I photographed this motley crew of over a hundred men, they looked just like the prisoners at Buchenwald. I asked if anyone had died at the camp from the atomic bomb.

A bony, underfed Brit spoke up. "The Japanese foremen allowed us to go into slit trenches when the air-raid siren sounded, because they needed us alive to continue our slave work. The day of the bomb we heard the siren, went to the trenches, and within a few minutes, the bomb blew into a mushroom climbing high up over the mountains. Eight of our men wanted to watch the bomb, got out of the trench, and were incinerated." He looked away from me, wiping away tears.

The men all pleaded with me and wanted to know when they would be rescued and taken home. I had no idea, but answered, "Soon, very soon," and left for another camp so they wouldn't see the lie in my eyes.

Hiroshima was swarming with war correspondents and I was glad to be one of the few reporters in Nagasaki. I had my driver bring me to visit Allied Prison Camp #17. This large camp had the

425

look of Buchenwald and was a chilling experience all over again. There were over 1,000 inmates there who had spent years enduring indiscriminate torture and deliberate starvation. Some had survived the Bataan and Cabanatuan death marches and had been transported there to be slaves.

As I approached the camp, the men were anxious to talk to a woman. Most hadn't seen or talked to one in years. I was a star in their eyes until they saw the horrified look on my face after seeing them close up. They were in their worn-out military uniforms, which hung on their starving bodies. Some had missing limbs and wore bandages made of rags or newspapers. I composed myself and described to them what I had seen at the German prison camp in Buchenwald. I wanted them to know that I understood torture.

First I asked them if anyone had seen the atomic bomb, since this camp was forty miles north of the hypocenter. The men said they'd just recently found out about the atomic bomb from messages that were dropped by our airplanes, along with food and supplies. Only those walking to the coal mine saw it in the distance and weren't sure what it was.

I wrote down all their observations: a flash, a mass of blackness, a cloud, a red ball floating in the air that became a mushroom-shaped ice cream cone. Some thought it was a thunderhead or a volcanic eruption.

This was a hard-labor camp in a dangerous Mitsui coal mine, 1,440 feet underground, run by the Japanese. Our Allied prisoners worked twelve to fourteen hours a day, seven days a week, in low-ceilinged mines ankle deep in a cold brook that ran through it. The prisoners drove hard rock and shoveled coal. Most of the men had been at the camp for over two years.

One man, a former dentist from What Cheer, Iowa, told me he deliberately had an inmate break his arm with a crowbar to get out of the nonstop work. He got thirty days' rest. Several men had purposely broken their bones just to get out of the forced labor.

The men told me about the Japanese overseers and their sadistic ways. The low roofs were difficult to stoop under in order to work and carry heavy timber through. Cave-ins occurred weekly. The overseers would hit them with shovels, dynamite fuse cords, pieces of coal, or they'd get fifty-two blows with a stick and were left bleeding when they didn't work fast enough.

An Australian told me about the bamboo torture, which was the worst. "I had to kneel on a piece of bamboo, toes stretched out behind me, with all my weight on my knees. The overseer balanced a full pail of water on my bent calves to increase the weight on my knees. I had to hold the pail with my hands behind me and not let it fall off, and was made to stay that way for hours."

Another prisoner added, "I was made to drink as much water as possible, then the boss jumped on my stomach, all because I was too weak to use a jackhammer."

One American showed me the scars on his head and face. They were from a "Jap" overseer who had taken a mallet and hammered on him until his eyes stayed completely closed and he couldn't open them.

Another American with one leg told me, "The roof in the mine was not braced and caved in on us. A Japanese amateur doctor amputated my leg and I got sixteen days off of work." He gave me a weak little smile. "Most of our injuries are operated on without anesthesia, putting legs or arms in casts without regard to where the bones or tendons should be placed."

A Brit asked me, "Do you want to know why I'm so skinny? I've only had soup and rice for three years except when the International Red Cross inspector came. Then the Japs brought out the Red Cross packages of canned salmon, pears, tangerines, raisins, and cookies. It was just a show because after the Red Cross left, they took it all for themselves. The neutral Swiss Red Cross inspected the hospital where medicines and morphine appeared just for that day. But no one ever inspected the inside of the dangerous coal mine tunnel."

An extremely thin American added, "I survived the seven-day Bataan death march in the hot sun with no food or water, only to be sent to this godforsaken place."

One man wearing shredded clothes barely covering his thin skin said, "We arrived in our uniforms and were never given anything else to wear." He held out his arm. His uniform sleeve hung in ripped pieces of cloth.

A hunched-over Dutchman with sparse hair exclaimed, "I was

taken outside in cold March because I was found with a pencil and paper. The overseers threw buckets of water over me and laughed as I shivered in the wind. Those Japs take great delight in all kinds of torture. I'm six foot three and can't straighten up anymore after working in a three-foot tunnel."

I looked around at all the prisoners. The whole group had mutilated bodies. Many had missing fingers, legs, feet, or arms, or teeth that had been knocked out by the guards. They had been beaten with hammers, saws, and even wrenches.

After getting to know the prisoners, I politely asked if I could photograph them. Most were happy to accommodate the request.

"Show the people back home how we have been starved and abused for them," one prisoner of war said.

One man wanted me to take a picture of him smiling with his missing, knocked-out teeth. Another prisoner displayed his missing fingers.

"I've had three years of mental and physical torture, disease, starvation, and death. Now I'll be home for Christmas thanks to the bomb!" one inmate said with joy.

"Show your photographs to the military and tell them to hurry up and get us the hell out of here," an Aussie cried.

I did my job the best I could and photographed them. Just as with the camps in Germany, the people had to know. Filled with guilt as well as shame, I could only manage to say, "I am so sorry." Then, hiding behind my camera, I lied and said, "You will be rescued any day now, I promise."

I packed up my gear and walked back to my driver, who waited in the car. Once inside, my sorrow came flooding out in convulsing tears. This long war was taking a big toll on me.

It took ten days after the surrender of Japan for the US military to barely begin to liberate over 140,000 POW camps in that country.

On my way back to the hotel, I saw Marines landing in the harbor with destroyers to transfer some of our Allied men home. I prayed that all of these brave men would stay alive to reunite with their families.

AUSTRALIAN WAR MEMORIAL   P00761.011

Dutch and Australian POWs in Japan

Chapter 60
Peace At Last
1945-1946

It isn't enough to talk about peace. One must believe in it. And it isn't enough to believe in it. One must work at it.
— Eleanor Roosevelt

After I arrived back at my Brooklyn apartment from overseas, I found myself weeping every day. It took me a while to sort out why. I had thrown myself heart and soul into various wars, abandoning a chance at being married and having a family. I felt displaced when I arrived in New York. Most people at home were now pretending that the war had never happened. My photographs were not published when I got back from Nagasaki. None of the reporters' photos were.

The United States was trying to erase the war, even though there were now over 50 million malnourished, displaced people moving across the war's bombed-out areas. Europe had been devastated by years of conflict during World War II, with millions of people killed or wounded. Industrial and residential areas in England, France, Germany, Italy, Poland, Belgium, and elsewhere were in ruins. Much of Europe was on the brink of famine as agricultural production had been disrupted by the war, and the country's transportation infrastructure was a shambles. At the Bergen-Belsen concentration camp in northern Germany, 20,000 people refused to leave. They did not want to go back to their countries of origin. The horrific memories of war there had been too great. Some of the displaced people eventually were persuaded to go to Palestine, Canada, or the USA. Britain was unable to help and was trying to rebuild their own country. There were now thousands of homeless, stateless people.

When I looked back at photographing seven long years of war,

I realized that I thought Nazi Germany was insane as well as evil, until I experienced stories of the cruel Japanese army. Now I didn't think any country involved in the Second World War had a monopoly on virtue or immorality.

Several months had passed and I was beginning to recover from my melancholy. It was the new year of 1946 and I was no longer a war correspondent. My parents, God bless them, had given me the tenacity to persevere. *Petersons always do their best,* rolled through my mind. I was now determined to be a "peace" correspondent. I put away my war correspondent uniforms — the only outfits I had worn for over two years — and went out to buy cheerful "peace" clothes.

I splurged in Macy's and bought cherry-colored platform shoes with open toes and 2 ½ inch heels. I bought a matching purse with a coin case and mirror. Three pairs of nylon seamed stockings in a red box wrapped in tissue paper were a joy to buy after years of scarcity. I had read that silk stockings would be available soon. In the intimate apparel department, I found nice, form-fitting briefs with attached garters to hold them up. For fancy occasions, I tried on a cute French rose-colored crepe dress that was soft and flattering for my now forty-two-year-old body. No more drab army olive gray for me! I also bought an everyday dress that was black-and-white checkered with big peg pockets and a matching belt.

For play, I chose denim dungarees with red stitching, copper-rivet pockets, and big red buttons that opened on the side. A red-and-black flannel, long-sleeved shirt went with it nicely. Loafers were back in style. I put a shiny new, 1946 penny in the slot in each one.

When I got back home I received a call from *Life Magazine* with an assignment. I was given the honor to interview and photograph Mrs. Eleanor Roosevelt. President Truman had recently appointed her to the newly formed United Nations. It was an international organization created to settle problems between nations with delegates from fifty countries. The president asked her, at the age of sixty-one, to be one of five Americans to go to the first meeting of United Nations General Assembly held

431

in London.

I flew to London to meet this inspirational, unique woman. She wore an ordinary dress with a belt, short pearls around her neck, and had wavy, gray-white hair. Mrs. Roosevelt confided in me that, being the only female delegate, she had to be better than all the male representatives, and had to read every single document written by the United Nations. I certainly could relate to being the only woman in a work environment. After chatting with her for over an hour in the hotel room, her enthusiasm filled me with inspiration.

Mrs. Roosevelt exclaimed positively, "I have a sincere desire to understand the problems of the rest of the world; a hope that I shall be able to build a sense of personal trust and friendship with my co-workers."

I enjoyed taking close-up pictures of her broad, wide smile and sparkling eyes, which enhanced her plain appearance as she spoke. I wrote down everything she said. Her sincere belief was that the United Nations was the only hope for peace in the world, with its goal of fostering cooperation between nations in areas of international law, security, and economic development. Mrs. Roosevelt was working on a committee that arranged informal meetings with delegates of different nationalities to resolve conflicts and bring people together.

I smiled in enthusiastic agreement as she said, "It isn't enough to talk about peace, one must believe in it. And it isn't enough to believe in it. One must work at it." Her voice had a contagious conviction.

When our interview was about to end, she kindly asked about my life and future goals now that the war was over. I surprised myself by saying that I wanted to be a peace correspondent, to help put this war-torn world back together.

Mrs. Eleanor Roosevelt gave me one of her pleasing smiles and said in her mighty voice, "I'm happy to hear that we share the same goals and wish you the best of luck, Miss Peterson."

I answered, "I wish you good luck in all your peace endeavors as well."

Back home, I developed the photographs of the late president's wife and furiously typed up my notes. The interview gave me the shot in the arm that I needed for a fresh career. Inspiration from this strong, powerful woman gave me a renewed sense of hope for the world. In the news, I followed her avidly as she worked with nations of different customs, religions, and governments to get them to agree that everyone was created equal. Mrs. Roosevelt became chair of the Human Rights Commission. That July, the constitution of the World Health Organization was signed by sixty-one countries.

Life Magazine was pleased with my new peace work and sent me to Harvard University to cover a speech by Secretary of State George C. Marshall. He presented the European Recovery Program (ERP) to rebuild the economies of Western Europe. Sixteen nations, including Germany, were invited to be part of the program and would assist the Economic Cooperation Administration (ECA) of the United States. With this new agency, European nations would receive nearly $13 billion in aid, including shipments of food, staples, fuel, and machinery from America. I captured quite a few good, serious photographs of General Marshall's presentation.

The next day, I had an appointment to take a photograph of General Marshall in his study. The general was in his full military uniform and was one of the most decorated military leaders in American history. He sat on a straight-backed chair with his legs crossed and hands folded together on his lap. Try as I might, I could not get him to smile. He wanted a serious pose and when I got back home and developed the picture, I captioned it: *We must restore political stability to ensure peace.*

Inspired by both peacemakers I had interviewed, I applied for a job with the Quaker's American Friends Service Committee. The agency needed a photographer to promote their work. This job was precisely what I needed in order to move in a positive direction to publicize peace.

Before I left for Europe with the American Friends Service Committee, I went to my home away from home, the library. I researched the Quaker organization, which had been established in 1917. The goal of this organization was to promote peace with justice with a practical expression of faith in action. The Quakers believed in active nonviolence and worked with people of many backgrounds. They opposed abuses of power and believed in resolving conflict without force or coercion. All governments and societal institutions were accountable in the world to have lasting peace. The Quakers believed there was a god in every human being. These were their main goals:

We work in partnership with people in communities around the world, respecting their wisdom about how to change their circumstances and offering our own insights with humility.

We trust the power of the Spirit to guide the individual and collective search for truth and practical action.

We accept our understandings of truth as incomplete and have faith that new perceptions of truth will continue to be revealed.

These goals and beliefs had a profound effect on me. It helped replace the cynicism and melancholy I had been experiencing upon returning to the States.

I went on a Danish freighter to Gdynia in Soviet-occupied Poland, where thousands of people from the war were suffering after the Nazi slaughter and starvation. I brought along two Rolleiflex cameras, flashbulbs, and hundreds of rolls of film.

At the Grand Hotel the next day, I met with the local Quaker team. We all drove in a truck to Warsaw, where over eighty percent of the city was in ruins.

Even though I was photographing bombed-out buildings, monuments, and suffering people, I felt I was serving an optimistic purpose being linked with an organization whose sole existence was to give aid to postwar survivors.

For six weeks I was to photograph the destruction from the war. I followed the Quaker organization to Czechoslovakia and Hungary to document the organization's goal of spreading perpetual peace.

I arrived in Prague late in the evening. I looked forward to visiting the fantastic astronomical clock in the morning, to see how it had fared during the war. It was hard to believe that it had been over eight years since I'd first come to this magical city.

After breakfast in the small hotel, I grabbed my trusty old

Leica. I couldn't wait to again witness the hourly show of the figures of the apostles and the other moving sculptures on the clock. Outside, in the early morning sun, I knew the light would be perfect.

As I walked down the cobblestone street, I couldn't keep the camera steady as I passed areas of flattened buildings and piles of rubble. I let the camera fall to my side and gasped. *Oh my God, this beautiful city did get bombed!* I was afraid to continue toward the clock tower and sat on the cobblestone curb, trying to take in the horrific view.

A few townspeople were going about their routines of shopping and work. They walked around various piles of debris and went into the buildings that were intact. I steadied my uneven breathing but the smell of the burned wreckage made that a difficult task. I closed my eyes and visualized the beautiful clock I had photographed so many years ago. I was terrified at the notion that it had succumbed to the war.

I dusted myself off and proceeded toward the clock. As I feared, it had been reduced to a charred tower. "No!" I screamed. It was barely recognizable! The clock's face was blackened and smashed. Only the Turk figure remained. I stumbled away, sobbing and shaking. "No!" I yelled again.

When I reached the hotel, I found the hotel clerk. I slapped my hand on the front desk and demanded, "What happened to the astronomical clock?"

The clerk could see my distressed face and calmly told me about the bombing of Prague. "It was an accident. Your American bombers arrived over Prague in May at the end of the war, and due to a navigational error, dropped 150 tons of bombs. They thought they were flying over Dresden."

"That's insane!" I choked. "My own country did this?" I slapped the counter again.

"Yes, miss, over ninety buildings were destroyed but what's worse is over 700 Czechs were killed." He looked down at his papers and tried to suppress his tears.

I was unable to console him or apologize for my anger. I left the desk and went up to my room. Lying on my bed with my sadness, I tried to sort out my feelings. I had spent a year in Prague and had visited the clock frequently. It had helped me get through the difficult times of the impending war. I also felt a deep shame that my own country had ruined the 13th-century icon of the city. The American bombing reminded me of when my Bill had died from "friendly fire." How horrific it is, that warfare can make such devastating mistakes.

I cried into my pillow, releasing my anger. After a brief nap, I went down to the café and brought some food back to my room, then spent the rest of the day in a depressed state.

The next morning, I went out into the damaged city and made myself photograph it, including the astronomical clock, hoping that somehow, if I showed the photos to my country, they would repair the city.

When I went on to Hungary, I resolved to continue my work to make a difference. All the war-torn countries had to be repaired and the refugees given homes.

I wrote personal letters to all my contacts, asking for donations of medicine, food, and clothing. My pictures were being used in the United States to raise funds for the Quakers to help refugees. There were many organizations using my photographs of destroyed buildings and of people with despair on their faces receiving aid. These included CARE, a relief agency; the Save the Children Federation; Christian Rural Overseas; and even the Girl Scouts.

I was given a 16mm spring-wind Bolex movie camera by the Quaker group and went with them to Italy. It was a new, powerful medium in photography for me to tackle. I filmed the postwar homeless trying to survive in the Magellini caves. It had been years since I had been in this same area and very little had changed for these poor people.

When I think back over my life and my career, I wouldn't do anything different. I have had many loves in my life. My one true love perished, and at my age, I don't feel that I can find another soul mate. I am happy with my memories and spend my extra money on my nieces and nephews.

My work carries on. The pain, the heartache, the losses, witnessing the horrors of war...it was all worth it. I feel like I made a difference. It brings me tremendous satisfaction now to help establish *peace*. I continue to surround myself with the peacemakers of the world, united in one cause: to recover from World War II. My greatest hope is that I leave this world with confidence that there will never be war again.

The End

Eleanor Roosevelt confers with John Foster Dulles and George Marshall at the UN, Sept. 9, 1947

About the Author

Jeane Slone is a board member of the California Redwood Writer's Club, a member of the Healdsburg Literary Guild, and a member of the Pacific Coast Air Museum and the SS *Jeremiah O'Brien*.

She is a partner in ESL Publishing, a dedicated company that prints quality books for second-language learners.
(www.eslpublishing.com)

She is also a volunteer tutor for the Library Literacy Program.

Ms. Slone has published four historical novels:
She Flew Bombers During WW II, winner of the national 2012 Indie Book Award (also available as an audio book through audible.com).
She Built Ships During WW II, which is also available in an ESL version with a workbook.
She Was An American Spy During WW II and *She Was a WW II Photographer Behind Enemy Lines*.
Jeane Slone's books have been optioned for a TV series titled "War Gals: Unsung American Heroines."

For more information, please visit the author's website:
www.jeaneslone.com

The author at the Grape Leaf Inn Speakeasy, Healdsburg, CA

The author in Prague

About the Front Cover

Constance Stuart Larrabee 8/7/1914 – 7/27/2000
Special permission to use the cover photo for this book has
been granted by the National Museum of Women in the Arts,
Washington, D.C.

Constance Stuart Larrabee was a renowned photographer who recorded the vanishing tribes of southern Africa and the World War II battlefields of Europe. Her African photographs are in the Smithsonian Institution's National Museum of African Art, and her World War II photographs appear in the Corcoran Gallery of Art in Washington, D.C. Yale University in New Haven, CT, has also staged a gallery of her work.

She photographed South African soldiers fighting their way up the Italian Boot, as well as the liberation of Paris with General Charles de Gaulle, in profile, addressing a crowd. In 1945-55 she served in Egypt, Italy, France, and England, attached to the American 7th Army and the South African 6th Division in the Italian Apennines. She also photographed numerous American, French, British, and Canadian troops.

Bibliography

BOOKS

Anderson, Christopher. *Margaret Bourke-White: Adventurous Photographer*. Scholastic Inc., Connecticut. 2005.

Atwood, Kathryn. *Women Heroes of World War II The Pacific Theater 15 Stories of Resistance, Rescue, Sabotage, and Survival*. Chicago Review Press 2013.

Bard, Mitchell, Ph.D. *The Complete Idiot's Guide to World War II*. Alpha Books, 2004.

Bernsohn, Al & Devera. *Developing, Printing, and Enlarging*. Ziff-Davis Publishing Co. Chicago 1939.

Bourke-White, Margaret. *North of the Danube*. Viking Press, 1939.

Bourke-White, Margaret. *Portrait of Myself*. Simon & Schuster, N.Y. 1963.

Bourke-White, Margaret. *Purple Heart Valley*. Simon and Schuster, 1944.

Bourke-White, Margaret, editor, Silverman, Jonathan. *The Taste of War*. Century Publishing, London 1985.

Bukey, Evan Burr. *Hitler's Austria*. The University of North Carolina Press, 2002.

Bourke-White, Margaret. *Dear Fatherland, Rest Quietly*. Simon and Schuster, 1946.

Caldwell, Erskine and Bourke-White, Margaret. *North of the Danube*, Viking Press, 1939.

441

Cohen, Stan. *The Tree Army, a pictorial history of the Civilian Conservation Corps, 1933-142.* Pictorial Histories Publishing Co., Missoula, Montana, 1980.

Collins, Jean E. *She Was There.* J. Messner Publishing, 1980.

Colman, Penny. *Where The Action Was.* Crown Publishers. N.Y. 2002.

Cowles Virginia. *Looking For Trouble.* Hamilton Publishing, 1946.

Davies, Norman. *No Simple Victory World War II in Europe, 1939-1945.* Penguin Books, 2006.

Duncan, Dayton, Burns, Ken. *The Dust Bowl, An Illustrated History.* Chronicle Books, San Francisco. 2012.

Feinberg, Barbara. *Hiroshima and Nagasaki.* Children's Press,1995.

Fisher, Andrea. *Let Us Now Praise Famous Women.* Pandora Press, London, 1987.

Fleischhauer, Carl and Beverly Brannan, editors. *Documenting America, 1935-1943.* University of California Press, Berkeley 1988.

Fleming, Candace. *Our Eleanor.* Atheneum Books, 2005.

Freedman, Russell. *Eleanor Roosevelt.* HMH Books for Young Readers, 1997.

Fleischhauer, Carl & Brannan W., Beverly, editors. *Documenting America 1935-1943.* University of California Press, CA 1988.

Fisher, Andrea. *Let us now Praise Famous Women, Women Photographers for the US Government 1935-1944.* Pandora Press, London & NY. 1987.

Gellhorn, Martha. *Point of No Return.* University of Nebraska Press, Nebraska 1995.

Gellhorn, Martha. *The View From the Ground.* Atlantic Monthly Press, NY 1988.

Gellhorn, Martha. *Face of War,* Atlantic Monthly Press, 1936.

Gellhorn, Martha. *A Stricken Field.* University Chicago Press, Chicago, 1942.

Golden, Reuel. *Photojournalism: 150 Years of Outstanding Press Photography.* Carlton Books, 2011.

Grimm, Tom. *The Basic Darkroom Book.* The New American Library, Inc. NY 1978.

Holliham, Kerrie Logan. *Reporting Under fire, 16 Daring Women War Correspondents and Photojournalists.* Chicago Review Press, 2014.

Hynes, Samuel. Matthews, Anne, Sorel, Nancy Caldwell, Spiller, Roger, Advisory Board. *Reporting World War II, Part One.* Library of America, publisher 2001.

Kennel, Sarah, Waggoner, Diane, Carver-Kubik. *Alice In the Darkroom.* National Gallery of Art, Washington, D.C. 2009.

Kirkpatrick Helen. *This terrible Peace.* Rich & Cowan Ltd, 1939.

Kodakery, A Magazine for Amateur Photographers. Eastman Kodak Co. NY 1919.

Lange, Dorothea & Paul Taylor. *An American Exodus.* Reynal & Hitchcock publishers 1939.

Litoff, Judy Barrett and Smith, David C. *American Women in a World at War.* SR Books, Delaware 2004.

May, Antoinette. *Witness to War a biography of Marguerite Higgins.* Beaufort Books, Inc. NY/Toronto, 1981.

Merrill, Perry H. *Roosevelt's Forest Army A History of the Civilian Conservation Corps.* Northlight Studio Press, Inc., Vermont, 1981.

Miller, Dorothy, *New York City in The Great Depression.* Arcadia Publishing, 2009.

Moeller, Susan D. *Shooting War Photography and the American Experience of Combat.* Basic Books, Inc. NY 1989.

Moorehead, Caroline. *Gellhorn A Twentieth-Century Life.* Henry Holt & Co. NY, 2004.

Mulvey, Deb, ed. *We Had Everything But Money.* Reiman Publications, 1992.

Newman, Amy. *The Nuremberg Laws Institutionalized Anti-Semitism.* Lucent Books, CA 1999.

Olian, Joanne. *Everyday Fashions of the Forties, As Pictured in Sears Catalogs.* Dover Publications, N.Y. 1992.

Ostroff, Roberta. *Fire in the Wind, The Life of Dickey Chapelle.* Ballantine Books N.Y. 1992.

Perritano, John. *America At War: World War II.* Scholastic, 2009.

Partridge, Elizabeth. *Restless Spirit, The Life and Work of Dorothea Lange.* Viking publishing, NY 1998.

Schwertfeger, Ruth. *Women of Theresienstadt.* Berg Publishers, 1988.

Signorielli, Nancy, editor. *Women in Communication, A Biographical Sourcebook.* Greenwood Publishing, CT 1996.

Smith, Jessie Carney. *The Handy African American History Answer Book*. Visible Ink Press, 2014.

Sorel, Nancy Caldwell. *The Women Who Wrote the War*. Arcade Publishing, N.Y. 2011.

Stryker, Roy Emmerson & Wood, Nancy. *In This Proud Land, America 1935-1943 As Seen in the FSA Photographs*, New York Graphic Society, MA 1973.

Thompson, Dorothy. *Let the Record Speak*. Houghton, Mifflin & CO., 1939.

Thomson, Harrison S. *Czechoslovakia in European History*. Princeton University Press, 1943.

Turner, Robyn. *Dorothea Lange*. Little, Brown & Co. Boston 1994.

Wason, Betty. *Miracle in Hellas*. The Macmillan Co. NY 1943.

Weller, George, Weller, Anthony. *First into Nagasaki*. Broadway Books. 2007.

Willsberger, Johann. *The History of Photography, Cameras, Pictures, Photographers*. Doubleday Co. NY 1977.

Wills, Camfield & Deirdre, ed. *History of Photography Techniques & Equipment*. Doubleday Co. NY 1977.

Wooten, Sara. *Margaret Bourke-White, Daring Photographer*. Enslow Pub Inc 2002.

FILMS

Burns, Ken. *The Dust Bowl* PBS 2012.
Burns, Ken & Novick, Lynn. *Prohibition*.PBS 2011.

Burns, Ken & Novick, Lynn. *The War:* PBS 2007.
Fest, Herrendoerfer, producers. *Hitler: A Career,* 1977,

Ratner, Angel, Kowarsky, Byrge, producers. *Night Will Fall.* Warner Archive 2014.

WEB SITES

http://www.aaa.si.edu/collections/interviews/oral-history-interview-Boots-emerson-stryker-12480#transcript

http://afe.easia.columbia.edu/ps/japan/potsdam.pd Primary Source Document of The Potsdam Declaration (July 26, 1945)
https://armyhistory.org/the-88th-infantry-division-in-italy/
http://www.authentichistory.com/1865-1897/5-technology/1-photography/

https://www.britannica.com/topic/Potsdam-Declaration

https://www.forces-war-records.co.uk/prisoners-of-war-of-the-japanese-1939-1945

http://www.history.com/topics/great-depression/pictures/soup-kitchens-and-breadlines/national-recovery-administration-sticker
http://marshallfoundation.org/marshall/the-marshall-plan/

https://www.ushmm.org/wlc/en/article.php?ModuleId=100061 31 UNITED STATES HOLOCAUST MEMORIAL MUSEUM WEB SITE.

97150153R10252

Made in the USA
Columbia, SC
10 June 2018